NINETEEN
LANDINGS

BOOK 1

Q Taylor

iUniverse LLC
Bloomington

NINETEEN LANDINGS
BOOK 1

iUniverse books may be ordered through booksellers or by contacting:

iUniverse LLC
1663 Liberty Drive
Bloomington, IN 47403
www.iuniverse.com
1-800-Authors (1-800-288-4677)

ISBN: 978-1-4917-3120-8 (sc)
ISBN: 978-1-4917-3122-2 (hc)
ISBN: 978-1-4917-3121-5 (e)

Library of Congress Control Number: 2014908171

Printed in the United States of America.

iUniverse rev. date: 05/08/2014

First,
to GOD
because without him
we are nothing.

Dedicated to Mary Hennigan, the best Creative
Writing teacher in the entire universe.

May the words within these books
fill you with the wonder of curiosity
and question.

*A writer's block can only be destroyed by the spark of your
idea and a pen.*

—Q Taylor

Some stories within these series of books are based on actual events, places or data. You decide what is fact and what is fiction.

CONTENTS

LANDING 1

THAT NOISE I HEARD

It is the end of a long and weary autumn day. Finally, with my hands sore to the bone, I escape under the moonlight and into my bed. Settling in, I rest comfortably, dreams of my previous hours of hard labor encircling inside my head.

Minutes became long and restless as I awoke on every two. Bags collect up under my eyes as I—for a small period—forget who I am or where I'm at. "Oh, how tiresome I have grown from the droplets dripping from the faucet, drumming on the sinks, dishes, and water pipes, brushing branches on windows, traffic, and the sounds of dogs and cats chasing rats!"

The mighty hour must have struck me again, taking me like a thief in the night into the land of dreams. I fall into a deep, dark, black abyss, worry free inside this empty place I seem to be. Suddenly, all was one and all was behind me as I slept in perfect peace and tranquility.

And then . . . a thud, a thump thumping startles me. "What could it be?" That odd noise I heard that rumbled through my floor. Both I and my graying, once-black cat sprung to explore. After another sound, a spine-tingling shiver followed, yet we continued following the pulsating sound to the front door.

Now with a sudden feeling of near death, I cover my chest from the dampness of the still midnight air. From maybe catching a whiff of a friend's sweet stench, my cat's twitching whiskers disappear into the shadows of downstairs as I call behind the floating fur of my pet that's no longer there.

"Whiskers?" I called out once, then twice, in return receiving no response or reassuring meow. As I step blindly onto something that squished between my toes disgustingly, the mere thought of the unforeseen poo or abandoned vermin sends me bowing to the mercy of a misplaced wet dish towel.

"How silly!" A faint and lonely smile from my face emits. Knocking, following the porch light being lit, triggers my "Hello, who is it?"

As the heart increases in flutters, wrinkled callused hands shake and quake around the custom-made golden knob that had served its purpose for many years. Bravely unlatching the top lock, I held my breath tiresomely and decided to face any fear.

Whoever, whatever it was, I was ready to face it, even if it meant the end of me. The door creaked and squeaked loudly as I opened it just enough to see.

But it was perhaps nothing but a sound that I heard. As Whiskers returned against my leg, rubbing, she purrs.

It must have been the wind and nothing more. It touched my robe and face; business papers blew off the old coffee table behind me, leaving me in a glance about my porch near the door. Quite nippy it was, so I batten down the hatches once more.

Climbing the obstacle called steps to my chamber, I crawl under the ghostly sheets like a tamed, bony, old lion. Into the midst of quietness, I return in the realm of the conscious stained.

Inside my cotton-linen cocoon, I float away in peacefulness. My undisturbed and unhampered eyes open disturbingly and close. Unwanted feet are heard stepping up the staircase; my warm blood ices cold.

Holding my position, I listen, counting. As the footsteps near my floor, I bury my head deeper into my bed. Breaking into a feverish sweat, I reassure myself that I'd previously checked the entire house. Still, thoughts of an unknown intruder dance about in my head.

Uncontrollably, my mind rambles on, thinking of all the friends I've lost and all the people whom I've mistreated, trying to willfully justify a reason or motive for my death. I fell flat, faint upon the mattress, sickened and with no energy left.

There's no reason at all for my murder. Nothing but hardship and hard work has occupied my life, I think as thoughts of unfortunate encounters churn my stomach. The low, stomping sounds sound even closer and send my nerves on edge. From under the covers, I ease and slide like a weasel around an unguarded nest of chicken eggs.

Not seeing a thing, I place my nervously quaking hands into a pair of old gardening gloves, then grab my cane. From over the railing, I peer down into the pitch-dark abyss. Slowly, the moonlight cascades into portions of my view, and the wind outside blows steady and brisk.

When the location of the easy-to-find matches and candles elude the frightened, sharpest of minds, the obvious light switches become misplaced and the flashlight hard to find.

Dropping to my hands and knees at the foot of the banister, I gaze with an eye-watering stare, not daring to blink and thus missing a sight. Glass breaking and shattering sounds motivate my legs, moving my soul in the afterlife.

Low to the ground, like a desperate spider, anxiety dragged me to the second floor of the house. The sight of the movement of shadows shook the core of my body, pushing me backward, jellifying my legs. My limp body loses its footing and tumbles inside its own robe. "Oh, what a horrible fate this is, this horror bestowed upon me quite untold!"

The fiend tightened its deadly grip around my neck, while inside bedclothes, my body dangled and twisted corpse-like for life and a swallow of breath. I unleash a licking with the strength of my cane with kicking and the last ounce of heroism left.

Yet . . . reality still somehow has its own way to reveal its ugly truth. My clothing remained caught and snagged on the banister, over my eyes and head, making the struggles for freedom, the efforts of no use.

I slip into slumber once more, a snap lays me on the floor unbroken and unharmed in my own time and place, as humanlike steps of Whiskers and another stray frolic down the stairs. My cat scampers over and licks me on the face.

The noise that had tormented me so had finally submerged to the light and come to its end. Exhausted, I lie relieved and relaxed under my mischievous feline friend. Rubbing her fur, I discover no signs of glass shards or meddling beneath the sensitive palm of my hand. Then . . . a familiar eerie noise I heard from upstairs startles me again.

LANDING 2

THE CABIN

The white-covered road curves and swerves behind bending trees of various sizes and shapes under the mass quantity of falling snow. Sarah, five years of age, rides with her mother to their getaway destination. "We're going to the cabin, to the cabin! We're going to a cabin, the cabin, la-la-da! Mommy, when are we getting to the cabin? It's taking a real long time!" Sarah, restlessly stuffed in a pink snowsuit and strapped snugly in her car seat, ended her fifteen-minute song.

"Soon, sweetie . . . soon," her mother replies, frowning and squinting through her constantly fogging window at the mild blizzard happening outside the car.

"I can't see anything, Mommy." Sarah's oval, thin-chinned face smiles brightly in the rearview as she seats her brown plush teddy bear beside her chair. "Don't be scared, Teddy." Licking her thin pink lips, she returns her attention to her mother and the road ahead. "I can't see, Mommy!"

"I can barely see myself, honey." The ends of her mother's short red hair protruded from under a red snow cap as her freckled face glow red from over her thin exposed neck. A large fitting coat warmed her from behind a seatbelt as her skinny, frail hands branch out from her sleeves like small tree limbs. "Now shhh! Mommy has to concentrate on the road. If I pull over, we'll be stuck for sure." Her mother calmly grips the steering wheel and continues onward.

Thick snow accumulated more on the slow traffic road the farther out the vehicle drove, covering everything in sight. Piling in large mounds wherever there was grass, the snow made the hilly landscape appear as a large bright mass at times. And as everything, including all signs of life, seem to have vanished, the lonely road becomes empty, bringing about fond memories of Sarah's father. "I should call your dad." Her mother searches her pockets and coat for the cell phone to call her husband, strategizing with both hands while keeping a close eye on the road.

"Daddy!" Sarah shouts out excitedly, placing both hands up in the air. "You should call Daddy! Call Daddy, Mommy! Mommy, call Daddy!"

"Okay, I am, I am. Hold on! You have to be very quiet, Sarah!" Her mother laughs. "Ah-ha, found it!" She raises a small black flip phone to the side of her face. Occasionally, she quickly peers downward and then back at the road, proceeding to dial her husband's office number. Continuing to drive in the blinding weather conditions, the car sped slightly off the road. The car fills with screams as gravel and muddy snow flew from between the treads of its tires that quickly found contact with the earth. Homes are spread out, and a man walking with small child through a snowy field in the distance becomes slightly visible. As the vehicle passes and leaves them miles behind, the street goes off road and into the snow-covered woods. "Whew, that was close!" Sarah's mother feels her racing heart. "Out of the office?" She presses the end call button on her trusty cell and thinks for a moment. *Okay . . . let's try his cell.* She raises the phone above the dashboard so she wouldn't have to take her eyes totally off the road. Dialing the first three digits, she accidently enters a wrong number. Her car slides; she cuts the wheel hard to the left, managing to maneuver out of it over Sarah's screams.

"It's okay, Teddy. Be careful, Mommy!" Sarah holds her teddy bear's right paw. "I can see between the front seats!" She speaks in a gruff voice before returning to her own sound. "Mommy?"

Still attempting to navigate and thumb the buttons on her phone, Sarah's mother dials the wrong number again. "Two, six, eight . . . I'm calling your dad. Well, trying to."

"Mom!" Sarah began to whine. "Mommy . . . Mommy!"

"Sarah, wait a second! Let me call your dad." She finally connects as the other end rings. "The cabin should be coming up soon."

"But, Mommy, what's that?" Sarah points to the windshield.

"Hello?" The deep soothing voice of Sarah's father greets and heats her mother's ear warmly as she looks up at a dark blur flying toward the vehicle. "What . . . John . . ." Making out the image of a very small person, the middle-aged woman, then screams in panic, dropping the phone. Slamming on the breaks, she tries not to collide with anything of the living. Missing the figure by mere feet, the small car takes flight downhill. Bushels and stems snap around them as the car uncontrollably flips and tumbles, exploding in glass. Into an old sturdy oak tree, the headlights burst and the remaining windows shatter in every direction. The impact knocks both mother and daughter into the tranquil realm of their own unconsciousness.

Smoke bellows into the sky, simmering under a cloud of settling snow and hidden debris. Thick black oil and antifreeze pour from under the twisted hood of the mangled automobile. Upside down, still inside their seatbelts, Sarah and her mother hung safely bruised yet intact a few feet from the ground. Dazed and terrified in the dreariness of passing time, eyes open to darkness and cold.

"Sarah . . . are you okay? Sarah . . . Sarah!" her mother calls out, beginning to cry frantically. Weakened with her slow-returning strength, she attempts to unlock her door and undo her seatbelt.

Sarah comes to and also begins to cry, making her mother more nervous and frantic. "Hold on, baby, I'm coming!" She pops the lock on the crinkled door, kicks it open, and crawls out of the severely damaged vehicle. The rear passenger door, having already been torn off by trees, allows her to gain access to her daughter, Sarah. Freeing her child, she pulls her away from the wreck and sits her in the snow. Checking Sarah for injuries the best she can, the troubled mother reaches for her cell to call for help. "Damn." She realizes that her phone is missing. As Sarah cries beside her, she looks back at the car. "Stay right here, baby. Mommy has to look for her phone so I can call someone to get us, okay? Now don't you move . . . Be a good girl for Mommy." She instructs, stepping off toward the car. Scared, shaken up, and desperate, she struts through the flurry and thick clumps of snow. A plump ball of light drips into a small puddle of flames around the car as it is totally engulfed by a blaze of fire right before her eyes.

One of the tires breaks loose of its axle and rolls away in a smoking spin past her leg. Disgusted and bruised to the core from the crash, slowly she turns to the view of her missing daughter. "Oh my gosh, Sarah? Sarah!" the now-worried mother calls out, frantically scanning the mysterious woods that now stood deep and dark around her. Receiving no response, the faithful and responsible parent nearly loses her mind in negative thoughts and concerns of what to do next. Having unconsciously snatched off her hat by its fluffy white puffball, she places it back on her head, eyeing the area that her daughter was last in. Spotting small footprints in the snow, she dashes off into the darkness after her child, disappearing under the shadows of strange trees and forest until only the faint echo of her calling the name Sarah can be heard somewhere under the stars.

Lost and alone, Sarah follows the sound of children laughing in the unknown. Coming to a sudden halt in the middle of a group of circling trees, she no longer hears the sounds of cheerful voices. The small child cries, realizing that she was now totally alone and definitely lost indeed. A deep growl belches out from the unknown darkness behind her, grabbing her full attention. Ceasing her sniffling, the loud sound of panting, bushes parting, and twigs breaking jumpstarts her heart and legs as she darts off without a second thought. Barely able to see through the snow, Sarah screams for her mother as the sound of a four-legged beast moving in her direction grew closer. "Mommy!" she cries out, running as fast as she can through the tough, cold terrain. Tears flung from her cold rosy cheeks as the brisk wind whipped across her face, frostbiting her fingertips. Catching her foot on what felt like a small stump, she loses her footing and tumbles face first into the snow. Opening her large swollen eyes, she clears her face and listens out for the frightening animal sounds that followed her. Hearing nothing but silence, she peers into the blackness of the woods and slowly rises from the ground. Glancing back at what she might have tripped over, her eyes adjust, and she follows her own skid marks to something black and clothed protruding from the snow. Hoping that it wasn't the remains of some type of buried dead animal, she stoops down and touches it.

Seemingly firm and hard, Sarah's curiosity forced her to lightly dust the snow from the uncovered portion of whatever it was. Another swipe of the hand revealed a small childlike skeleton and a clear view of an opening eyelid. Jumping backward, her screams are caught not far away by the ears of her mother as Sarah runs and stumbles into a tall pair of legs.

"Lose something?" A wild head of hair shadows the smiling wrinkled face and glassy eyes of a quite tall old woman. Calming the child with a crooked grin and the wink of one abnormally big yet sunken eye, she walks away and picks up the buried figure.

"No, it's not mine! Get it away! Stop . . . I don't want . . ." Sarah looks down at object inside the woman's hand.

"There isn't anything to be frightened of, sweetie. The night is full of wonderful surprises." The elderly woman holds up a beautiful doll wrapped in a damp, tattered baby blanket under the moonlight. "Awww . . . why, she looks scared, lonely, and far, far away from home. Why don't you give her some company and a nice home?" the wretched-looking woman holds the toy out to the little girl. "You could be the last face she'll ever see." She laughs a funny giggle and stands up straight and crooked.

"A doll baby?" Sarah looks at the woman with amazement. "She's not scary at all." She takes the doll into her arms.

"See? Nice, very nice. Oh, no, she's not scary at all. She's beautiful just like you. Why don't you give her a warm home?" The old woman dusted the snow from Sarah's light and dark, sandy hair and places her fallen skull cap back on her head. "Now how'd a sweet young lady like you end up way out here in the cold all by your lonesome? Are you lost, little one?"

"Yes! Our car crashed into a tree. I heard some kids, and now I can't find my mom. I think I'm lost."

"Well, that makes two of you. My pet is lost too. I just got him. He's a big fluffy, floppy-eared fella. Have you seen him?" the old woman asked as Sarah nods no.

"Sarah!" A familiar voice illuminates Sarah's face from beyond the trees.

"Mommy, Mommy!" Sarah returns, running off toward the sweet cackle of her mother's voice. And suddenly, when it seemed that she was lost again . . . her mother steps to her from out of the darkest of shrubbery.

"Sarah!" The five-foot-three woman catches her child like a large football in her arms. "Sarah, I love you. I love you so much. Don't you ever run off like that again! What were you thinking?" Tears pierce through the night, falling down upon Sarah's head and face.

"Mommy, these kids were calling me and calling for help, but I got lost! Then I tripped over this pretty doll, and she scared me. Then—"

"Sarah!" Her mother's interruption was more like a voice-over. As Sarah continues on talking, she tunes her daughter out, noticing a bizarre-looking silhouette creeping through the woods behind her.

"And then she found me!" Sarah abruptly ended, pointing in the direction of the silently approaching figure. "Well, umm . . . I think it's her."

Nervous and jittery, Sarah's mother pulls out the only source of light that she can think of—a lighter. Her trusty disposable orange butane lighter takes three flicks to ignite, gently illuminating the inside of her hand. Holding it up, she trembles at the slowly hiking shadow. "Hi, I'm sorry. I can barely see you. We're stranded. Can you help us?" She inches toward the figure with her daughter beside her as the person turns, beginning to walk in the opposite direction. "Wait . . . hey?" She looks down at her daughter. "Are you sure you know them? Did you really talk to them, Sarah?" They watch the mystery person recede quietly into the darkness. Following feet away, Sarah's mother quickly catches her breath and then decides to catch up to the woman. "Sarah . . . did you go this far? Excuse me, excuse me." She touches the back of the person's arm.

Bending down to pick up something, the large figure swings back around with an oil lamp secure inside an extremely aged hand. Revealing a round, pruned face and a head of wild graying hair, she stops the mother in her tracks, causing Sarah to bump into her mother's leg, making her scream.

The pug-nosed woman twists her face and speaks a cheery sound that shrilled past her tongue and false teeth. "Greetings."

"Ahh . . . so you do talk! Geesh, Sarah, you scared the crap outta me!" The frustrated mother harks at Sarah then returns her aggravation to the heavily dressed woman. "Didn't you hear me talking to you when we were way back there? Why didn't you respond? Didn't you hear me?" She gives the woman a tired, sweaty, and cold stare, curling the old woman's wrinkled mouth into a smile.

"Whatcha say? Oh, hold on for a moment while I put my hearing box back in. Gotta conserve my battery in this cold, you know?" She places an earpiece inside her ear that connects to a long wire that extends deep into her heavy old shaggy coat and tattered garments.

Looking up at the woman dumbfounded for a second, Sarah's mother is instantly befriended. "Look, I apologize for following you or being a burden, but we're lost. Can you please tell me where the nearest phone is, or could you take me to one?"

"Yes, I can, but unfortunately, I'm looking for someone highly dear to me right now. But the main road to town is just north of here, and the way that leads you back where you two probably come from is . . . that way, just over yonder there." The odd woman continues on her way. "You'll know where you are by the signs and litter."

"Wait, wait a minute. You said you were looking for someone. Who are you looking for? Maybe we can help you find him or direct him to you?" Sarah's mother tries her best to negotiate in hopes of getting to a phone.

"I'm afraid he's not trained too well. He's a new pet." The old woman steps away in the falling snow as the light from the lamp reveals a glimpse of her dented veiny legs and wet furry pair of house shoes. "Take care of the doll."

"Doll? Oh . . . I see." Sarah's mother watches in the below-zero temperatures, shivering inside the light gust of wind. "Yeah . . . okay, she's a little crazy." The old woman's cloak-like attire blocks the dull light of the lamp, making her vanish from the parent's view. Thinking of what to do next, a tear rolls down her face as she takes her daughter's icy hand, spotting something in the other. "Is that Teddy?"

"No, Mommy, it's a doll. I was running, and I tripped over her. I found her. Isn't she pretty?" Sarah held up the plastic toy in front of her runny nose and chattering teeth. "I was scared over a doll. I thought it was real. Embarrassing."

"Oh, you were?" Her mother smiles and warms on the inside behind those watering eyes. "Well, yes . . . she is very pretty, but don't you ever do that again." She examines the doll. The moon gleams against the white snow, providing a small form of gentle light. Standing in a deep area, the facial structure and beautiful gleaming crystal brown eyes of the doll catches her attention. "Now, why don't you . . . carry her under your arm and tuck these cold hands inside these nice warm pockets of yours. I was scared to death looking for you. I was all by myself, but now you know what? I'm not even scared anymore." She stoops down and holds and kisses her child on the forehead.

"How come you're not scared anymore? How come?" whispers Sarah.

"Because now . . . I've found you."

Within the hour with her daughter, the mother tries her best to remember the directions given. As they stomp through the deep snow, the wretched, sweet old woman who went looking for her pet watches them from the shadows. Snow blew and collected across their bodies as deep footprints fill and vanish behind them. A wide section of what felt like impassible trees and thickets clear, as Sarah's mother beheld a familiar sight.

Pointing directly at them, a large tree leans. Once mighty and strong, the oak, missing its top, singed far beyond its bark by lightning; the oak, as if on one knee, bends far beyond its capacity, bearing the phrase Joanne, John, and Sarah forever inside a heart carved deeply into its side.

"The cabin's close!" Joanne, Sarah's mother, mutters, pulling Sarah by her bluish-colored hand.

"My feet are cold, and my hands hurt, Mommy!" Sarah complains, holding on to her doll.

"It's going to be okay. Hold on just a little longer, baby. We're almost there. Hold on to me and don't let go!" Joanne releases an expanding cloud of fog from her mouth.

Running noses numbed and gave up on sniffing high above their two legs that buckled and stiffened. Sarah's face decorated in flakes complements her mother, Joanne's, quivering, overchapped lips and white snow-draped eyebrows. Extremely tired and windburned, Joanne's hands begin to lock up, and feelings fade with her spirits. Knowing deep inside they were close, she refuses to tell her child that they were lost.

"Loo-look, Mommy!" Sarah slows and points to the large shack that sit's secluded from the general population.

Inside the depths of the woods, the updated, remolded cabin awaited their occupancy. Complete with a wooden deck and front storm windows, the cabin appear as a peacefully, slightly modernized sanctuary.

Checking for her keys, Joanne sighs in relief, touching the clinging bulge inside of her pocket. Thankful that she did not lose her house key ring in the crash, she rushes to the porch, carrying Sarah on her back. Nearly collapsing, she hurries to the large wooden front door and jiggles the keys inside its lock with her frostbitten fingers. Unlocking the door and hurrying inside, she quickly searches for lighting and heat. Switching on all the light switches, none comes on; she determines something was wrong with the generator. From off the refurbished wooden shelves, Joanne finds a small collection of candles that she bought the last time she was there. Flicking her lighter, one by one, she lights them along the walls around the cabin. Given light, she spots a few kerosene lamps in the corner next to the fireplace.

Deciding to wait to use them, she goes and brings out some blankets from the bedrooms and places them upon her shivering daughter. "Now let's get warmed up and go to bed." Laying her down upon the couch inside the back room, Joanne retrieves the precut firewood and tosses the instant lighting logs into the slowly catching fireplace.

The sounds of burning, crackling wood settles the room as the mother doze out of submission. With one eye closed and one partially open, Sarah peeks into the beautiful eyes of the doll one last time. Kissing the toy's temple, the small child closes her last tired eye and falls to sleep across from her mother who lies on a separate couch. Flakes of snow gently brush and lightly pile around the windows, continuing to cover the cabin, blanketing the sloping land and forest around it.

DAY 1

As the intensity of the sunlight turn the inside of her eyelids bright orange, Sarah's mother, Joanne, awakes to the chills from the cold breeze that flowed fluidly through the back patio doors. Sitting upright on the couch, her blanket falls from her lap onto the floor as a single snowflake lands on her nose. Hearing Sarah's laughter from one of the back rooms, Joanne was assured that her child was still safe inside the cabin. Puzzled, she gets up and locks the door. Following Sarah's voice to the farthest back room, Joanne listens to what sounds like almost a full-fledged conversation. "Sarah, did you open the patio, sweetie?" She fully opens the cracked door and walks into the room.

"No, I didn't, Mommy. Dolly went outside!" Sarah answers, sitting on the floor across from the doll she found. "Mommy . . . you should've seen her! She was really moving and . . ."

"Sarah! You know that it's not good to tell a lie. Now why did you open those doors? Sarah, there's all sorts of wild animals and dangers out there that could get in here. You can't open the doors without me knowing, baby, and you can't leave them open."

"But I didn't, Mommy. I didn't open any doors." Sarah glances over at the doll.

"Sarah . . ." Joanne shakes her head, thinking about this new additional problem she didn't need. "You just found the doll, and already . . ." Her eyes began to water as her daughter's acts top off her rising frustration. "The car's gone, the phone's not working, we're out in the middle of nowhere, Sarah! I don't need this!" She begins to weep. "We almost died yesterday, baby . . . If you leave the doors and windows open, something could come in and eat us, baby . . ."

"Okay, Mommy." Sarah catches a glimpse of her mother's sadness as she exits and closes the door. "I won't do it again." Watching her mother fully shut the door, she hears her mother lean against the wall for a moment, then walk away silently. "See, you got me in trouble! Why didn't you talk? You made Mommy sad. Why didn't you say anything?" Sarah asks as the inanimate plastic doll slowly and stiffly turns its creaking head directly at her.

Listening to her daughter laugh out loud, Joanne sits in the back room on the couch, staring at the bearskin rug. Its soft, fluffy brown fur soothes her nonstop aching feet. The rug's realistic marble eyes peer into its sad past as Joanne herself peer into vast thoughts, pondering on a way to get home. Then it hit her; she remembers they kept an emergency phone in one of the kitchen cabinets. She jumps up excitedly, hoping that it still worked and that she would finally get in touch with her husband. Inches away from the wooden cabinet that had collected dirt from over the years, she touches a small handle and wishes for luck. Squeaking open, cobwebs and small carcasses of insect's string and dangle from the door to the inner shelves. Freeing the phone from a collection of webs, she blows away dust and inhales a dusty cloud, then sneezes. Holding the receiver close to her ear, she listens for a dial tone. Hearing nothing, Joanne presses the disconnect button and checks the chord. Curious, she follows the chord with her eyes, away from the cabinets, along the ceiling, and down the wall beside the cabinets. Nearing the very bottom, pieces of wire, chips of paint, and threads of wire became visibly scattered out across the floor. Squatting down to get a closer look, she can see that the wire had been freshly cut by something and someone. "It couldn't have been . . . a mouse?" Joanne leans over and picks up a tiny tooth. *Too small for a child of its size,* Joanne examines in disbelief and amazement. With nowhere to go for help and no way to call out, the young mother sat gazing at the wire, clueless.

Pulling herself together, Joanne thinks of the next important thing on the agenda: to search for food. Rechecking the cabinets, she finds a container of salt, pepper, a few packs of instant noodles and some canned goods. Rediscovering their storage of food and snacks in the cellar, her spirits lift with so much joy and thankfulness. She felt that if she were to blink, her energy could black out and power up an entire city. Finding a pot, Joanne brings it to a boil on top of the gas stove. Placing three packs of noodles into the heated water, she tears open two packets of seasonings and pours them in. The aroma of spices makes her stomach growl and cramp with hunger.

Soon, the two were smacking over the medium-sized hand-carved table in the front room. Eating, Sarah's mother stares at the cellar door that she left open, thinking about how long it would take her husband to come looking for them.

"I'm hungry. Feed me, Mommy!" A tiny voice disrupts the table as Sarah sits the doll on her lap.

"Look, Mommy, I found a pull string!" Sarah pulls the string, making the doll speak another phrase.

"I love you, Mommy." The doll's voice reaches out. Joanne touches her curly tangled hair.

"Awww, she's too cute. She's a real special doll. Takes a very special person to take care of her." Joanne smiles at her daughter and walks over to the cellar door, slamming it shut with her foot.

DAY 2

The sun attempts to melt the thick blanket of snow that covers the entire woodland area. Small birds talk and peck on branches as flurries of light snow fell from beneath them into the breeze that gently spread and mix them along the ground marked with trails of the live frontier of nature. Standing in the doorway of the patio, Sarah's mother, Joanne, prepares to find the site of their crashed car and maybe find her cell, remains of food, and clothes they packed. Getting old spare clothes from winters ago from inside her closet, Joanne doubles and triples Sarah's clothing while also packing a small sack of food, just in case they get lost.

"Do you think that we're going to find your phone, Mommy?" Sarah looks at all the snow doubtingly.

"Well, Sarah . . . I dunno, but it's a chance I'm willing to take. We need to let someone know we're stuck out here." Joanne explains. "You don't want to be stuck out her until you're the age of that old woman we met, do you?"

"No, I don't want to be stranded, but Dolly says she likes it here, and it's not so bad," Sarah responds as her mother gives her a look of seriousness.

Accumulating a growing dislike for the doll, Joanne takes her child's feelings into consideration and stops herself from throwing the doll to the other side of the globe. "Well . . . you make sure that dolly knows that right now . . . and as of this minute, this is a horrible place for us to be. Right now . . . no one even knows we're here. And what about your father, don't you miss him? He's probably worried sick about us. Don't you think?"

"Yes, Mommy."

"Okay then, so how about you put the doll away for now and help Mommy find the car?"

"But, Mommy, please, can she come along? She can keep me company," Sarah pleads.

"Sarah . . ."

"Please, Mommy, I promise that I won't listen to her anymore, Mommy! Please? Pretty please with sugar on top, Mommy?"

"Sarah . . . honey, okay, but I don't want to hear any more out of her. Do I make myself clear? No more games." Joanne tilted her head, pointing a thin finger down at Sarah's adorable, innocent eyes. Shaking her head, she zips up Sarah's snowsuit.

"Yes, Mommy." With an unclear expression, Sarah tucks the doll tightly up under her arm and takes her mother's hand. Glancing beyond the forest at more trees and snow, she looks up at her mother who wraps a scarf around her face. Stepping out the cabin's entrance, she follows her mother to check the generator. Discovering that it didn't work and was perhaps old and broken, Sarah bravely steps off into the unknown with her mother.

Sunny and bright outside in the open, icicles melt from the splitting and extending branches of trees, dropping off into the wind, down into the tall blades of grass and snow. The cabin disappears far behind the woman and child deep within the forestry. A young deer darts past them, leaping into the thickets as their eyes widened with alertness and fear. Surrounded by nothing but woods, the repetitive sighting of tall trees throw off their sense of direction.

"Are we close, Mommy?" Sarah picks up a small broken branch with two dying leaves on it.

"I don't know for sure, honey, that's why we have to keep our peepers sharp and open. We should be close." Joanna tries to estimate how far they walked after the crash inside her mind. "Let's see . . . the road should be just over there . . . somewhere?"

She slows. Scratching her head, she places her hands on her hips as Sarah walks about.

"Mommy, Dolly says it's this way! Come on, Mommy!" Sarah skips into the woods.

"Sarah? Sarah, wait!" her mother calls out, quickly going after her. Trying to run, her feet burrow deep in the snow, thus slowing her down and tiring out her legs. Staggering to a higher and firmer slope of ground, she determines not to lose sight of her child. "Sarah? Sarah!"

"Mommy, Mommy, look, look!" Sarah shouts, jumping up and down. "Dolly was right! Dolly was right, Mommy! Look . . . I found the car!"

Catching up to her, Joanna regains some hope and faith. "Good job, honey!" The sight of the wreckage instantly makes her forget about Sarah's running off. Approaching the smoldered, melted mass of metal and various materials that nearly severed a tree, a cold chill creeps up her spine as a deep feeling of gratitude and thankfulness to have survived such an event overcomes her. Searching through the burnt rubble, she finds nothing worth salvaging. Not giving up, she continues on searching for her phone with her daughter. Double-checking the parameters around the crash site, Joanne studies the position of the car and determines which way they originally headed off in. "Let's see, think . . . Okay, the car crashed here, and we walked . . . down here. Then you ran off . . . in that direction. I think." She concentrates on remembering where she may have dropped the cellular phone. As new snow began to trickle down, the search becomes slightly more complicated. Still not giving up, unconsciously, she drifts in the opposite direction that she thought they were going, back toward the road.

"Mommy, what's that?" Sarah spots a familiar shiny object half hidden in the snow.

"Is that . . ." Her mother hurries and kneels next to the object. "It is my phone! Great work, Sarah! You found it!" Joanne happily hugs her daughter, whom she was very thankful for. Pressing the power button on the cold and semiwet cell, its greeting screen loads up, viewing the company logo. "It's working."

"Yea! Now we can call Daddy!" cheers Sarah.

"I have messages. He called us! Darn it, now all we need is a signal." Joanne looks down at the absence of bars on her phone. Standing, she begins to move about in different places in the woods, trying to get any reception. "Dang . . . nothing, and it's only got a little notch of power left." She sighs.

"Aw, man." Sarah picks up a handful of snow and tosses it in the air.

And at that precise moment, three signal bars appear in the top corner of the phone. "Thank you, FATHER!" Joanne looks up at the sky and prays to herself as a gust of wind blows gently across her body. Relieved that half of their worries were about to be over, she dials her husband's number as the battery completely dies out. "What? Nooooo! Don't die on me!" She shakes the phone and hits it against the palm of her hand.

"What's wrong, Mommy? Isn't Daddy coming to get us?" Sarah, seeing her mother act out her aggravation, walks over to her, clutching the doll securely under her arm.

"The phone died, Sarah. I didn't have a chance to call him. And the charger was in my bag in the car." Her mother looks down at her, once again shaking her head and once again out of ideas.

"Mommy, are we going to die now?"

"Sarah . . ." Joanne refuses to answer. Giving her a warm hug, she kisses Sarah on the top of her head and gazed absently into the snow as flurries continued to fall down upon them.

THE NIGHT OF DAY 2

Up traveling in a complete circle, the mother and daughter wind up in front of the same old oak that they previously passed numerous times throughout the hours.

"How did we get lost? I can't believe this." Joanne crouched down to catch her breath. "There should be a lake and everything around here."

"Mommy, I'm getting cold," Sarah sputters, shivering in her tracks.

"I know, sweetheart, so am I, but we have to keep moving. Let's try to get back to the cabin before it gets even colder." She starts a new route between the trees. The skies change to a light evening blue as heavy clouds begin to swirl and lower in an obscure manner. Snow begins to blow rapidly and fall as the sky fully transforms into night in the middle of the day. "Strange. This doesn't look good." Sarah's mother analyzes, with only thoughts of a grand snowstorm or tornado coming. With the fear of something terrible approaching, Joanne scoops Sarah in both arms and rushes to locate the cabin. Crossing a small clearing of snow, they pass the remains of the family car. Treading desperately through the dormant thickets, they continue in a straight path only to come across what was left of their car again. "What? No, impossible!" Joanne stares in awe, certain that they had left the car and traveled in a straight direction. "Okay, one more time, baby. Let's try this again." She took hold of Sarah's hand and marched off once more toward the cabin. "It has to be this way!" she yells through the windy cyclones of flurries. Highlighted by the casting of the moon, the white ground and covered sloped forest become slightly more visible than it normally does when your eyes adjust to the dark. The sight of the giant full moon terrified them as the actual knowledge of it really being day sent Joanne's heart sinking into her belly, only to return beating a hundred times faster. She runs with her daughter.

"What's happening, Mommy? I'm scared! Why is it nighttime, Mommy? Wh—" Sarah suddenly quiets as a heavy, deep, and full of bass, snarling growl freezes them. "Aaaaaaiiiieeegh!" Sarah hollers at the tops of her lungs, believing she had gotten a glimpse of some sort of wild beast behind some bushes.

"Sarah, no!" Joanne swiftly covers her mouth and continues running. Unable to pinpoint exactly where the sound was coming from, she knew whatever it was, had to be big.

And as the gut-wrenching snarl grows louder and louder, the sounds of twigs and branches snapping behind them get closer and closer. Dashing out upon what looked like a road, they try to stay on it as it gradually disappears beneath the snow. Continuing to swiftly walk and occasionally jog, the tired two find themselves somehow back inside the maze of woods.

"I . . . I don't believe this. Where are we?" Joanne whispers as the horrible sounds of many unidentifiable animals mixed into one noise that stormed through the trees of the forest. "Oh my almighty!" She pulls Sarah off with all her might. Running for dear life, the noise ceases as she stops at a familiar-looking path. Having passed this way at least a dozen times, she falls to Sarah's feet, balling in tears.

"Mommy, what's wrong? What's wrong, Mommy?" Sarah sorrowfully asks, glancing behind her mother's shoulder. Where the path ends, the forest seems to open up into a slight clear, displaying the corpse of the family car. "Don't cry, Mommy. What are we going to do now? I'm so cold, Mommy."

"I don't know, Sarah. GOD, where are we?" Joanne raises her head and peers into the frightened wide eyes of her little girl. A loud, rumbling howl siren throughout the forest, sending them clenching to each other and peering back at the dark unknown.

"Ma-ma-mommy, wh-what was that sound?" Sarah whispers.

Lifting Sarah and the doll over her shoulders like a tackled football player, Joanne cuts diagonally away from the car. With nowhere to hide from the growling terror, tiresomely looking back, she catches a glimpse of something small and black yet of a nice weight barreling through the snow after them. "Oh my gosh! What is that?" she screams past the old wretched woman dressed in the fur coat and dark rags.

"There's my pumpkin!" Joanne heard the woman speak as she slows and turns around.

Watching the woman stoop down and open her arms to the shadow of some sort of hairy creature, stupefied, Joanne faces forward to flee as her body plummets down a hill. Cuffing Sarah tightly, not letting go, the mother tumbles through thickets of bushes and rocks, sliding down into a soft bed of snow and grass.

Opening her eyes, Joanne glances down at Sarah who rest upon her chest. Watching her daughter's eyes find hers, sighing in relief, she notices branches waving at the top of the hill and a shadow leap from behind them.

"Now you come back here this instance!" the old woman's voice crackled from somewhere at the top of the hill.

Scrambling backward to her feet, Joanne pulls Sarah up as the raving beast burrowed down the hillside after them.

"Dolly says go this way, Mommy!" Sarah shouts as the beautifully dressed doll fall and plummets into the deep snow. "Mommy, Dolly!" Sarah reaches for the toy as her mother yanks her away.

"There's no time, baby. We have to find the cabin!" Joanne yells, now practically dragging the crying child through the woods. Away from the hill and away from the crazed woman's pursuing pet, the two run as fast and as hard as they can through the sloppy, plain woodland, finally collapsing into the soft, cold snow. Sweaty, exhausted, and out of their last fighting breaths, the two rest while hopes of escaping and living on begin to appear as illusions within Joanne's mind. Rolling on her back, she looks up at the stars one last time. Before the beast or whatever it was sniffed them out, the proud mother makes peace with herself and the LORD. Glimpsing at Sarah, who lies there on her stomach, she gently rubs her head as she cries, gasping for air. "My Sarah. The snow isn't so bad after all." She whispers into the chilled air, hearing the sound of water beneath them. As tears fill her eyes and leak down her face, she realizes that they were actually lying on the frozen lake.

And as her mother touches the hair beside Sarah's hot, feverish forehead, she realizes that her mother had given up. Stretching her arms around her to hold her, Sarah sadly cries out loud. "Mommy . . ." She lays her head upon her mother's chest as snow falls over them. Lying for a second, still, she listens to her mother's heartbeat. Then opening her tightly shut eyes, she clearly makes out a corner of the cabin sixty feet away, peeking childishly beyond the trees. "Mommy . . . the cabin." She raises her head.

Joanne turns her head to see. "It is the cabin." Patting Sarah on the back, she smiles through the tears. A sudden growl from the opposite direction sent shocks of energy through her spine. "Come on, we ain't come all this way to get eaten!" Joanne sprung to life and races to the cabin with her daughter. In a burst of newfound strength, she slips across the ice, slicing through the remaining woods, caring only for her child. Coming to the side of the logged wooden house, she swings around the porch and eyes the black ball of blasting snow that howled and stormed after them a short distance away. As an eruption of snow scattered and dispersed all around the monster, it instantly imprints into the mother's brain forever. Joanne burst through the door, shoulder first. "Oh my gosh, oh my gosh, oh my gosh, oh my gosh!" she repeats, slamming the door, locking it, and sliding a large slab of wood across three upside-down hooks, latching it. Dashing to the kitchen, she grabs two large butcher knives and returns to the door. Waiting, hearing nothing, she slides to the floor with her back against the door. Hugging and holding her daughter, they console each other's cry. Unable to figure out exactly what was happening, Joanne rocks in place, relieved they had reached the cabin and grateful to finally have a little more time to think.

As the danger appeared to have pass, around the cabin calms as a loud growling force began to beat on the door and claw its way in. Sarah covers her mouth with both hands, muffling her scream, while her mother ran and braced the door with all of her might, dripping tears continuously down her face. The creature sniffs and pushes on the door a few more times before dashing off as the old woman's voice hollers behind it. "You come back here! Wait till I get you home!" Joanne hears the woman's feet crunching through the snow behind whatever had chased them. No longer concerned with leaving the cabin and too weak to move, she decided that it was best to just sleep in that exact spot for the night, and that's just what she did.

Three hours pass as Sarah and her mother lie fast asleep inside the cabin. On the floor in front of the front door, Sarah rests quietly on a pallet under a pile of covers. Her mother, Joanne, neck crooked and bent, snores heavily into the atmosphere. A warm, cooling string of drool stringed from her chin, soaking between the tiny cracks in the wood while her one leg, bent, crisscrossing the other that stretched across the floor. Laughing out loud from dreaming of a time with Sarah and her husband, Joanne awakens to the sound of multiple laughing. The chilling sound of children laughing seems to have come from outside as more suddenly rang out from the middle of the woods. Startled, she sat up quietly to listen.

"Mommy, open the door. Don't leave me outside in the cold, Mommy," a small voice speaks from the other side of the front door.

Looking down at Sarah, who was still asleep, Joanne sneaks off to the windows. Only being able to describe the voice as unreal and more like a recording than a human's voice, she slowly pull the curtain back and peers out of the window. Tiny, itty-bitty circular prints trailed past the window to the porch as three small knocks tap on the door. "Mommy, why did you leave me outside?"

Closing the curtains, Joanne's eyes widens and heart drops as she falls back, shaking nervously. Snatching a nearby envelope opener, she rushes to Sarah, recognizing the voice of the doll her daughter found. "No, no, no . . . this can't be real"

"Mommy, open up. It's time to play! You make me so happy, hip hip hurray!" The doll's cheer break into perky laughter as Joanne positions the letter opener to stab.

Preparing to open the door and slaughter the doll, Joanne unlocks it. Shaking intensely, Joanne's feels her heart pound against her chest. She stands in disbelief, feet away from her daughter. "You want us, Satan? Well, come and get us!" She swings open the door, ready for anything. Pointing the opener outward, nothing but snow and wilderness can be seen around the cabin. Glancing around outside, Joanne notices small footprints trailing from the porch and back to the woods. Exhaling, sounds of the back patio sliding open catches and draws her breath in.

"I love your soul." The tiny voice now emitted from the house along with the brisk pitter-patter of tiny feet across the floor. "Let's play a game?"

Gasping from the touch of the cold snowflakes and cold breeze that suddenly flowed through the cabin, Joanne shuts the patio.

"What's wrong, Mommy? I was dreaming I heard my Dolly!" Sarah stood behind her, rubbing her sleepy eyes.

"It's no dream, honey. Come here!" Joanna calls out. Placing an arm around her, she holds out the envelope opener between them. Following small footprints of water droplets and snow into the darkness of the back rooms that was made into the kitchen, she eyes traces of water along the handle of the oven door.

"Hide go seek, Mommy!" the doll's recorded toned voice speaks from the shadow of the corners.

"Hey, that's Dolly's voice! I told you she could talk!" Sarah mutters from the corner of her mouth, happy that her mother finally experienced the same thing she did.

Standing in a protective stance next to Sarah, Joanne faces the fireplace, ready to defend. Looking down at the letter opener, she tosses it across the room and picks up the butcher knife from the counter and a steak knife from the drawer under the sink. Inching toward the opposite end of the room, she checks under the two chairs that sat against the back wall. "Here, hold this." Joanne lights a candle and gives it to Sarah.

"Where is she, Mommy?" Sarah, scared yet tying to be brave, waves the candle by the stove and sink.

With both knives aimed outward, Joanne buck her eyes even more to make out what may be hidden in the shadows. The flickering candle didn't make focusing in any one area any easier, but it offered much help in allowing them to see what may run upon them. *Nothing here, and I don't see anything in the corners*, she thought to herself. Wondering if the occurrences could be supernatural, she creeps onto the thick bearskin rug that her husband hunted for her. Approaching the right end of the couch that sat parallel to the two chairs, Joanne steps on a soft but firm lump that wiggles from beneath her foot under the rug. She jumps back; Sarah screams as she quickly advance to the leg of the rug. Adrenaline pumping, Joanne, shaking, stabs at the lump with the butcher knife. Stopping the movement of whatever it was, she hacks at it a few more swift times. Making sure of the killing, she flips the bear over, revealing the body of the largest dead rat she had ever seen.

"Did you catch her? Ugh, yuck! What is that, Mommy?" Sarah makes a disgusting face. Stepping back from behind her mother's shoulder, she moves back to the stove, placing a hand on her now-queasy belly.

Calming her nerves, Joanne's instincts guide her to the corner of the couch. Seeing that it was pretty clear, she realize there was quite a bit of open space behind and under the sofa also. Pausing in place, she looks at Sarah from the corner of her eye, pondering on if she should tell her daughter to move the light so she can stick her head under the sofa or rush in and move the couch, exposing Sarah and herself to attacks. And just at that very instance, Joanne hears movement along the floor. Instantly stooping down, she lifts the skirt of the couch, and stares into the darkness under it as something quietly runs across the ceiling above her.

Glancing at a barely noticeable impression of a small body crawling underneath the bearskin rug toward the head, Sarah stands with her back pressing against the stove, scared stiff. Watching it head for her mother, whose rear end was protruding from under the couch, she screams to warn her. No sound comes out. The scene itself horrified her as her knees began to buckle and knock. As the bear's head rises off the waxed floor, a pair of beady reflecting eyes looked up at her. Frozen in cold sweat, Sarah is snapped out of the daze by the tapping of her quivering body against the cabinet door, which sends a loose pot clanging to the floor, freeing her scream.

"You're not my mommy!" the prerecorded-sounding voice of a child spurt from under the rug.

Caught off guard, Joanne jumps up, dropping one of the knives. The head of the bear also rises two feet off the floor as its body draped over the shape of a small person. As Joanne prepares to attack, the rug snaps from under her and on to Sarah's face. Hitting her head on the couch, Joanne falls hard on her back as Sarah, covered by the rug, yells, jumps, and swings about wildly.

"Mommy, Mommy, get it off me, Mommy!" Sarah shouts, receiving blows and cuts to the body and face. Her nose pops; a trickle of blood drips down one nostril. Hearing her clothes and skin rip from her body under the rug, Sarah fought and pushed the grappling figure off her. Every attempt to escape fails as the rug flung about and bounced around her with every punch and kick Sarah threw. Then seeing a flash, a considerable amount of unwanted pain erupted from her eye, forcing out an array of tears and screams. Wrestling by the oven, Sarah's head snaps forward as the bearskin rug is yanked from over her. The beautiful curly haired doll drops and tumbles to the floor. Sarah spits a tooth into her hand and notices her mother standing across from her.

Bravely, Joanne leaps on the doll as its squirms and tries desperately to run. Catching it inside of the bearskin, she twist it around the kicking toy as it tries to force its way out. In a bag shape, Joanne slams the rug on the floor and against the walls repeatedly, looking for a way to dispose of it at the same time. "The cellar. Open the cellar, Sarah! Open the cellar door!" the mother yells, stabbing the rug while quickly following Sarah to the cellar in the front room.

"Hurry, Mommy!" Sarah opens the old heavy wooden hatch along the wall and floor. "Bad Dolly!" The little girl frowns and watches her mother sling the rug down into the deep depths of the cellar with great force. Slamming the door, she moves to the side as her mother locks the wood latches on the outside of the door.

"Now let's see if you get out from down there!" Joanne threatened over sounds of the doll pounding and scratching on the hatch's thick wood.

Screaming and cursing in English at first, the doll ends in a demonic talk before silencing, leaving the two, mother and child, staring at the cellar. "Mommy, I'm sorry. Just let me out. I want to give you a big hug and a kiss!" the doll asked in a cheerful voice of a three-year-old girl.

"Go to hell!" Joanne hits the hatch as her temper rises and nose flares.

Sarah watches. Quietly placing an ear on the door, she listens to the doll walk down the ladder, deeper into the cellar. And there on the cellar floor, among their last remains of food and stored water, cursing, swearing, and pleading continuously, the doll speaks in evil tongues for five more days.

WEEK 2

After being chased by different unspeakable things, getting lost in the forest, and the day magically changing into night at least three more times when they stepped into the woods, the mother and daughter decided the cabin was safest, and it was best to just stay no farther than around it. Finally, they were getting a decent night's sleep and had begun to adapt to life inside the cabin. Days went along with the snow-covered nights around the cabin as while the two took turns guarding the cellar door, not a peep had been heard out of the doll in two days and still, no one had come looking for them. Night fell and dinnertime had once again arisen as the small food supply that Joanne had brought and stored upstairs was beginning to dwindle. Off a pack of instant noodles and crackers, the two fell fast asleep in thoughts of the daily thick waves of blizzard like flurries with the same old high hopes that the local disaster unit—or better, Joanne's husband— would finally break through and come rescue them.

Sarah lay comfortably snugged underneath her blanket inside her bedroom as light snow fell, brush, and broke against the outside walls. Joanne restlessly spread across the firm mattress in a motionless slumber inside the cabin room. Nothing but something out of the ordinary could disturb them. Then suddenly, that something broke their solitude. Hearing a loud banging on the front door, their eyes fully opened.

Graciously praying that it wasn't the creepy old woman and her deranged pet, Joanne leaps out of bed and wipes the coal out her eyes. Off balanced, she steps into the doorway of her bedroom and stares at the door of the cellar.

"I love you, Mommy," the doll warmly greets her, indicating that she was still live and active.

"Oh, shut up!" Joanne looks over at her daughter, who slowly inches out of her room also.

"Is she still talking?" Sarah yawns and stretches. "Was that the doll knocking?" The hard knocking continues, answering Sarah's question at the same time.

Joanne, having learned her lesson about just opening the door without knowing who's on the other side, peeps out of the window first. Seeing an odd-shaped, mini-sized half snowplow and utility vehicle parked in front of the cabin, she excitedly smiles at Sarah. "I think help is here. Open the door, Sarah. Open the door, hurry!" she instructs as a heavyset officer, walks away from the front door. Quickly sliding the large two by four from across the door, Sarah unlocks and opens it as Joanne appears behind her. "Wait! Hey, excuse me! We're here! We were just sleeping!" she yells from the porch as the man turns around.

"Ahh, so someone is here. How are you ladies doing, ma'am? I'm Officer Witmen from the county sheriff department. We were hoping that you two were still alive. The main roads are out; everything's covered in knee-high snow," the red-faced officer informs them. As a ruckus of chatter blasts out of his walkie-talkie, he turns it down.

"Did my husband, John, send you?"

"I believe so ma'am. I just received a call that someone's family was traveling in these parts and might be stranded at the cabin. There's only one cabin that I know of around these parts, so . . . here I am, risking my life again." He shrugs his shoulders and clips his flashlight back onto his belt.

"Well, we really are stuck and really need to get home. My cell is dead, the phone lines out, and food is low. Sir, we really could use some help." Joanne briefly explains, leaving out any weird detail about the events that occurred.

"Well, you're in luck. That's what I'm here for." The full-faced officer grins, sipping off a hot flask of coffee.

"Thank GOD!" Joanne raises both hands to the ceiling, relieved that they were being rescued.

"Is this your little one?" Officer Witmen's eyes connect with Sarah's chapped face. "Do you ladies need to pack anything first? Or . . ."

"Uh . . . no, not really. But we do need to get our coats and shoes fast and get the hell away from this cabin!" Joanne harped, dashing off to grab their things. "How far is the station?"

"Oh, not far. Only a few miles over." Officer Witmen steps onto the porch. "Hey, you ladies might want to put on a few extra layers. It gets pretty cold on the plow!" he yells into the house as Sarah stands, overlooking him from head to toe.

Forgetting all about the doll trapped down stairs, Joanne collects the extra clothing for her and her daughter to put on. "Come here, Sarah! Sarah? Sarah!" Joanne calls out as Sarah remains at the front door, gazing at the police officer. Fascinated by his bright shining badge and concealed gun, Sarah stood in place, unsure if she should ask the policeman to shoot the doll in the cellar.

Checking out her healing cuts, black eye, and missing tooth, Officer Witmen hid his suspicious expression behind a friendly face. "Aren't you a tough one? What happened to you? Did your mom do that to ya?" he asks as Sarah runs to answer her mother. Peeking into the cabin, a bad feeling came over him as he began to look it over for obvious signs of child abuse. Feeling as if the child wanted to tell him something, he steps inside. "So is it just you two inside this three-bedroom cabin?" He pauses on the inside of the door, maintaining distance.

"Yes, it's just us two girls!" Joanne verifies, quickly getting dressed. "My husband originally was coming with us, but he had to stay due to business. He supposed to have been joining us at the end of our first week, but due to this wonderful storm, so much for that, I guess!" She ties a double knot into Sarah's laces.

"Bummer, that's how the old cookie crumbles for some of us sometimes." Officer Witmen glances around the front room, admiring the design of the cabin, as Joanne and Sarah walk out from the back. "This is a really nice cabin. Oh well, let's get you girls back to good old-fashioned civilization." The officer tries to brighten up the situation a little as the mother and child kiss their misfortunes goodbye and exits the cabin. "You know . . . me and my wife . . ." He stiffs his arms at the front door before Joanne can fully close it behind them. "Wait, what is that? What's that noise?"

"Probably the wind, it's been blowing hard around here!" Slightly hearing the demonic doll, Joanne nervously smirks as the policeman boards past her and reenters the cabin. Instantly picking up the sound of a small child crying, he positions his hand over his gun.

"I thought you said you two were the only ones here? Then whose kid is that?" Officer Witmen peers to the back of the front room.

"It's not a kid. I don't know . . . I mean . . . it's a toy, my daughter's toy. You wouldn't believe me if I told you. But we're the only ones here, trust me." Joanne incriminates herself, making herself look even more suspicious.

"Park it, now!" the officer instructs, unsnapping his holster. Drawing his weapon, the crying intensifies.

"It's not a real person. It's just a broken toy!" Joanne tries again as he looks at her like she had looked at the old woman in the woods.

"Lady, it's awful hard to believe you with a banged-up little girl and a baby screaming from your empty cabin. Now where's the baby?" He points his gun at Joanne. "She's telling the truth! It's my doll! You have to believe us! Take us home!" Sarah shouts, pulling the policeman's hand away from the direction of her mother. "Don't shoot my mother!"

"Mommy, don't leave me down here. Help me!" the doll cries out in a desperate tone.

"What the heck?" The voice led Officer Witmen's eyes past the cellar door.

"Why don't you leave us alone and go back where you came from!" Joanne shouts as the policeman heads for the cellar. "Wait, where are you going? We have to get out of here! Come on, you have to believe us!"

"Lady, if there's a child here, you're going away for a long time." He passes the couches and coffee table and peeks into the master bedroom. "It's okay, little one! I'm a police officer, here to save you. Where are you, little angel? It's going to be okay!" He proceeds into the back rooms.

"Mommy!" the voice beacons from out of the cellar.

"Okay . . . you two, don't move! Stay right where you're at and get your hands flat on the floor!" he instructs Joanne and Sarah. "You've got to be a mad woman. The cellar, really? Hold on, sweetie!" he yells at the top of his lungs, running to the locked hatch.

"Wait! Don't you open that! Something evil's down there!" Joanne quickly moves over to him as he unlatches two out of three locks.

"Lady, get back! Get back by the door!" Officer Witmen, not really wanting to shoot her, raises his walkie-talkie to his mouth. Joanne doesn't move from in front of him. "Oh, 49, this is 162, come in. Lady, you stay right there and keep showing me those hands! 162 to 49, do you copy?" He plays with the volume, sharing loud static with every inch of the cabin.

"49, over," a clear, tough-sounding woman's voice briefly interrupts the fuzz from the talkie.

"49, I have a situation. I'm here responding at the cabin, and there's a child's voice coming from a locked cellar. I repeat, I'm responding at the cabin, and there's a child's voice coming from the cellar." He glances at Sarah, then back at Joanne, thinking about her last words. "I have two suspects detained and going in to investigate, over."

"Copy," seeps from Officer Witmen's walkie-talkie. He clips it back onto his belt and looks at the last latch on the door.

"You open it!" Officer Witmen points the gun at Joanne's chest.

"Okay . . . okay, we tried to warn you. You shouldn't do this!"

"Just open it and stop talking, lady! Open it . . . please?" He stands and eases to the side of the hatch.

"If you must see. Get that gun ready." Joanne snickers in disbelief. Her nervously shaking hands slide the last peg out of the lock. Quickly pulling back the door, Joanne moves back as it hits the floor with a thud.

"Who's down here? Where are you? I can't see you. Are you hurt?" Officer Witmen yells down into the now-quiet, dark cellar, now receiving no response. Puzzled, he clicks on his flashlight and aims it down the shaft at the ladder. "It's okay. I'm here to help you! Can you say something else so I can find you?" He waits for the first sign of anything living. "Weird, what the hell's going on?" he mutters to himself. Placing an ear close to the hatch, he raises his head and looks at Joanne. "Well, I guess you ladies were right. I don't see anything down there except a big hole in the wall, looks like a tunnel. Wait a second . . . a hole? Why don't you take me down and show me the doll that's supposedly making all of this racket. And move slowly," he instructs as a small hand grabs him by the collar of his shirt, and the flash of a body of a small person pulls him down into the square entrance. "Human!" a small child's voice speaks, sending Sarah and Joanne screaming for their lives.

Quickly slamming the hatch shut and locking it, Joanne cringes at the sounds of bottles and containers breaking below them. And over the officer's horrible screams, Joanne scrambles for her child as bullets fire through the floor, penetrating the ceiling and various walls around the cabin. A triumphant wicked laughter echoes throughout the cabin, ending in Officer Witmen's body hitting the floor in a loud bump.

Sending her recently once-relieved heart returning to an ill and empty stomach, Joanne leaps, knocking Sarah through the front door as three more shots firing from the officer's gun, ripping through the wood, nearly hitting Sarah in the leg. "You evil wench!" Joanne stares back into the cabin.

"What now, Mommy?" asks Sarah as they both look over at the officer's mini snowplow.

Checking the vehicle for keys, the two sat inside the unlocked vehicle. "Hmm, no keys, they must be still on him. I'm sure not running through those woods again. We're not taking a chance out there. I'm not trying to freeze or die trying." Joanne weighs out her options out loud as Sarah just nods in agreement. Sitting back, she laughs to herself, realizing what must be done. "Well, Sarah . . . I guess it's just us and that damn doll. I have to get those keys off of that policeman!"

"But isn't he dead?" Sarah's face looks of disgust. She roughly tries to swallow the idea.

"I know, sweetie, but it's our only chance to get home. Something evil's going on with the woods, so we can't go back there on foot. This things fullof gas, we could find the road and drive all the way home! The doll's our only option." Joanne places an arm over Sarah's shoulder and hugs her close. "We have to face that doll-baby! We have to beat her."

"But I don't want to face the doll anymore." Sarah thinks about how the doll got her mom to cry, her clothes torn, and the empty space in her mouth where a tooth once sat, in which she can now slide her tongue between. "It's just a stupid old doll, Mommy. Give her hell!" She gives a crooked, sore, snaggletooth smile.

"Ha! That's my girl!" Joanne unlocks the doors and exits the cold vehicle, determined to return home. "But let's try not to use that type of language anymore."

And with their only option being to die or to face the unknown, they reenter the cabin together, locking the door, and preparing for the confrontation.

BATTLE OF THE DOLLS

First making sure that the cellar door was completely locked, Joanne storms to the back of the cabin and into kitchen. Ravaging through the wooden cupboards, she looks down at her daughter, Sarah. "First, we need protection."

"You mean like weapons 'n' stuff, Mommy?" Sarah tries to figure out what her mother was thinking.

"Yes, and I need your help, baby. I need you to be the big girl that I know you are and really use your head, sweetie. Now listen closely . . . I need you to think of anything that you could use as a weapon or shield around this house to defend yourself with. I need you to find anything you can to clobber that doll with, anything you can find, Sarah!" Joanne instructs, sticking two meat cleavers between her tight belt and pants. "I know fighting sounds like boy talk and don't seem to be ladylike, but it looks like we're going to have to fight to get home," she explains.

"Boy, I'm sure glad I've been around a lot of boys!" Sarah proudly states, running off to find the requested necessities.

Been around a lot of boys . . . What? Joanne is left thinking about her child's remark. "Remind Mommy to have a talk with you later!" she yells, stuffing her double-layered pants and socks with as many forks and knives that she can muster.

Entering her parent's room, Sarah brushes across three branches that stood against the wall that she picked and kept for her father to use for carving. Sending two falling over accidently, she steps on one, snapping it in two. Retrieving it from the floor, it reminds her of a wishbone. And inside that wishbone shape, she pictured a slingshot, just like the ones she'd seen her father and older cousins make when they camped and played in the woods. *If you ever find a sturdy stick or piece of metal shaped like the letter Y, you can make the perfect slingshot!* Sarah remembers her dad telling her and showing her how to tie a rubber band to one during one beautiful sunny day in a park. "Perfect!" She dashes off to find rubber bands.

After raiding the pantry and cabinets of the kitchen, Joanne gazes at the fireplace, a reflection of light catches her eye. Asking herself how on earth she could be so blind, she thanks GOD and reaches for her husband's father's old nineteenth-century-constructed, two-barrel shotgun that hung for years over the fireplace. Made of the latest materials, the steel and wood blend of fine craftsmanship gains her highest admiration. Rushing into her bedroom, she passes Sarah, who quickly exits with toilet paper and a container of baby powder.

Squatting down onto the open space behind the couch in the main room, Sarah snatches plies of toilet paper off the roll. Separating them on the floor, carefully, she dumps a small mound of baby powder into each ply. Folding each tissue into wad S-shaped teardrops, she clips berets onto each twisted end of tissue. Gently squeezing their plumpness, Sarah grins and places each carefully into the breast pocket of her coat. "Ammunition." She bites her bottom lip and snaps her homemade slingshot.

Shotgun shells tumble and roll out of the master bedroom as Joanne follows them out on her hands and knees, stuffing her pockets and loading the shotgun. Equipped with a homemade brown leather holster, she shoves the powerful piece down her back. "Are you ready?" In a low tone, she peers up at her daughter, who is also on the floor.

"Ready," Sarah bravely affirms, stranding with her slingshot. "Oh, one minute, Mommy!" She dashes back into her room. Falling in front of the cedar wood toy chest hand made by her father, she flips the lid and hurtles all sorts of baby toys to the floor. Pulling out an eleven-and-a-half-inch action figure that her cousin once left and a jump rope that her mom used to love to work out with, she wraps the toy and a pillow to her back with the rope. Finding nothing else of use inside the chest, she retrieves a mini Louisville slugger bat from inside the couch in the back room. "Oh yeah!" Satisfied with her selection, Sarah heads for the bathroom. "Just one more thing, Mommy, one more thing!" She bursts into the small bathroom and grabs a towel. Drenching it, she spins it tightly around in a clockwise position and whips a box of tissues off the sink. Then holding both ends of the towel, she twirls and stretches it as far as she can. Pulling and releasing, the wet towel emits a loud cracking snap. "Okay, now I'm ready, Mommy!" She hurries to her mother.

"You're ready? Alright, let's see what you got." Joanne stares proudly at her brave armed little girl. "Can you move in all this stuff?" She gives her a quick glance over.

"Yes," Sarah politely answers before briefly explaining her gear to her mother.

"Wow, you're awesome!" Joanne smiles, making sure that Sarah, didn't have anything of any potential self-inflicting harm. A faint screeching oozes from the closed cellar, catching their attention.

That awful cry, very different from any other sound they had heard during their entire time in the cabin, came from that crack in the wall, that hole that Officer Witmen described. It was indeed the wicked work of the doll. Quite busy during its stay, the demonic child's toy dug a five-by-five opening, festering with sick and evil, leading into a foggy nowhere.

The doll, the old woman, the mysterious woods—all were of the weird and unexplainable to Joanne. Out of all the times she and her husband had been there to visit, seeing the beautiful lake and precious wildlife, why—five years after their last visit—was it all now happening to her and Sarah she did not understand. What seemed once as a getaway was now more like a gateway to hell. What was once something to take advantage of now was something Joanne hated and dreaded. Alone, without her husband, whom she loved dearly by her side, and with her daughter's life in danger, Joanne saw the whole situation much clearer—Sarah had to live. Now standing over the cellar door, preparing to open it, Joanne wipes a smudge of dirt and dried blood from her daughters face. Staring into Sarah's brave little, wide, oval eyes with tears of concern, she frowns in determination and anger. "Okay, baby, undo the locks and get back as fast as you can!"

"Okay, Mommy." Sarah squats down and unlocks the first two latches.

Aiming the shotgun at the floor, awaiting for Sarah's clearance, Joanne takes a deep hard swallow, now feeling her heart as if it were beating through the walls.

Giving her mother one last glance, Sarah pushes the wood block through and pulls the thick, wood flap open. Leaping back, she grabs her bat, ready to swing.

Joanne points the Tate Hammer shotgun down into the center of the dark depths of the square. Remembering the fate of the policeman, she proceeds with extreme precaution, focusing on any movement. Guiding the barrel into the silence of the exit, holding on to the floor, she bent down just enough that only her head was peeking into the cellar. "Where is she?" the anxious mother whispers to herself, pointing the shotgun at the shadows. Startled, she feels Sarah touching her side.

"What do you see, Mommy?" Sarah whispers curiously, having never been in a cellar.

"Nothing. I guess we have to go down," Joanne whispers. Lighting a piece of candle, she tosses it down into the cellar, spotting a large mass that appeared big enough to be another entrance. "Wow! That wasn't there before."

"What is that? Looks like a giant . . . hole, Mommy," Sarah points out as her imagination runs wild. "I hope she didn't make that by punching."

"Nevertheless, I have to go down there. We have to get those keys!" Not seeing any sign of the officer's body either, Joanne becomes more irritated. "She's in the goddamn hole!" Sliding the shotgun down the holster on her back, she places a butcher knife into her mouth and descends down the ladder. At first, seeing nothing but the expected barrels, crates, and shelves of food, Joanne reaches the bloody, stained bottom that also consisted of the recently deceased officer's tissue and flesh. Lighting another candle, she walks through the dirt and stone, up to the large abstract hole. Noticing a smear of red that stretched into a streaking trail inside the dug tunnel, it curved into an even deeper darkness, setting the illusion of possibly going on for eternity.

Watching her mother study the room then follow the traces of blood, Sarah continues to quietly observe from the cellar's entrance above.

Tucking the cleaver away, Joanne pulls the shotgun back out, convinced that the doll was close. Again, her hands become unsteady. Having been familiar with the room, she reaches for a cardboard box of miscellaneous tools and supplies upon a shelf and retrieves the flashlight she found and was saving for the next emergency. Shining light ahead of her general direction, Joanne disappears from Sarah's sight.

As the wind began to blow strong outside the cabin, the small and frightened Sarah continues to look from above. Waiting and watching that creepy dark box sent several chills down her spine. Tensely she glares into the shadows on edge, unable to blink. Becoming dry eyed, she flinches; something sped past her eyes. Too small to make out exactly what it was, Sarah peers intensely around the room. "M-Mommy, I think I just saw something! It could just be the dark, but . . . Mom?"

"Well, let's just try to think positive, honey!" Joanne's voice calms Sarah's worries as she comes across Officer Witmen's blood-covered badge. Still searching the cellar for the keys and any sign of the doll, she stares over at that hole, feeling as if something else weird had happened to the policeman. Illuminating the floor, she nearly vomits, seeing that she was standing inside a thick pool of blood, which also smeared and extended behind the shelves ahead on the left.

While feeling something brush across her left ankle upstairs, Sarah catches her balance, nearly falling down into the cellar headfirst. Lifting her head from the cellar to take a look around the front room, everything appeared to be normal. Feeling a sudden cool breeze against the back of her neck, she watches two snowflakes quietly tumble past her face in a melodic dance, disappearing gracefully into the cellar below. Turning to the direction of the back room, she sees snow blowing in from what looks like the now-open patio. Wondering how it got reopened, timidly, she gets up to shut it. Pulling the sliding door closed, Sarah looks down at her feet, thinking of how wet the floor is going to be after the snow melts. Noticing a familiar set of small oval footprints, which lead and vanish between her legs and into the room, Sarah gasps, "Uh-oh!" and hears rustling down the hall. Rechecking the open cellar, she hears a thud coming from her room. "Something's here, Mommy! Mommy, I hear something!" Blurting out to her mother, Sarah clutches the Louisville slugger with both hands. Bravely walking to her bedroom, she leans forward to peep inside as the door closes in her face. Letting out a seep of fright and pain, she steps back in tears. Feeling as though she should run, her slightly faint and flimsy legs stop knocking as Sarah takes a deep breath. Pulling out her missing tooth from a napkin in her pocket, she remembers the return payment she owed the doll. Holding it tightly in her hand against the bat, Sarah turns the doorknob and kicks open the door.

Immediately, Sarah is overtaken by her childhood love as all her current worries and fears turn and hide behind a smiling bright pink. An overwhelming sensation of joy and happiness overcomes her as she spots her long-lost teddy bear now present on her bed. Positioned on its side, back turned to her, Sarah reaches for her unforgotten companion as it savagely twist its head to look at her, biting onto her hand. Slinging the plush around the room, she wrestles it to the floor, crying out for dear life and her mother.

Standing before the head and torso of Officer Witmen, Joanne wearily checks his jacket and one shirt pocket. "Damn!" She holds her head down in disbelief. "Now where's the rest of you?" She then hears commotion from her daughter upstairs and sniggles from behind.

"Well, I guess it's just me and the doll! I have to get those keys off of the policeman. But isn't he dead?" the doll mocks Joanne and Sarah in their own prerecorded-sounding voices. Standing between ales with the vehicle's key in hand, the doll gives a devious smirk under the flickering candle light that rolled on the floor. Kicking it, the doll darts for the large hole it dug in the cellar. "I love you, Mommy!"

"Shut your mouth!" Joanne goes after the doll, screaming, ready to fire at will. The doll runs past two similar dolls with knives and an action figure carrying a sword in one hand and a small gun in the other. Being knocked to her back by the blast from the old cannon, Joanne blows the toys to smithereens, just missing the doll that summersaults into the tunnel.

Back upstairs, managing to free her hand from the sharp jagged flesh-ripping teeth of her once-soft and peaceful plush bear, Sarah dashes out of the room and slams the door behind her. Catching the snarling and ferociously growling bear's head in the door as it attempts to chase, Sarah smashes the face and body of the hellish bear as it bats and swats its claws, trying to eat her. Revealing a skull and skeleton within the stuffed animal, Sarah slams the door with all her might and runs away hollering and screaming.

Joanne, her mother, on the other hand, had given up on running and now stood at the foot of the giant hole, sizing it up. She can only imagine what types of evil lurked inside. Looking around at the remains of the toys she gunned down, she massages her aching shoulder. First hearing squeaking followed by a light shuffling of dirt, Joanne shines the flashlight, spotting four three-inched army men creeping and screeching from under the ladder toward her. "You have got to be kidding me?" She got ready to run, jump, and smash the figures as her daughter came tumbling backward down the ladder, breaking the tiny soldiers into pieces. "Sarah?" Her mother takes her pulse. "Oh my goodness, honey, are you okay? Wh . . . what happened, baby? Sarah."

"T-te-teddy, teddy-te-teddy, teddy bear . . ." Sarah comes to, shaking and trembling. "Mommy, the bear attacked me, Mommy. In my room! It was my teddy bear, Mommy! It tried to eat me!" she cries as her mother hugs her as tight as she can. "I was calling for you, Mommy. I was calling for you!"

"I'm here, honey. I'm here! Your teddy? What? Looks like there's more of those things in this cabin. But you made it, honey. You made it. We're together now." Joanne consoles her child for a moment, looking at her bleeding hand. Then slowly and gently, she stands Sarah up, dusts her off, and wraps her hand with a torn piece of her shirt. "Honey, look at me and listen really good. There's going to be a lot of strange things that we've never seen before trying to hurt us in this cabin. We have to be strong, brave, and no matter what, always have each other's back. Just like we have all the times we went outside. Now we made it this far, let's keep the faith . . . remember that word, 'faith'?"

"Yes, Mommy."

"Okay, let's keep the faith and make it just a little bit further. Even if it means looking that old mean devil right in the eyes close up! Now who's more powerful than the devil?" Joanne asks, nudging Sarah's head up. "Come on now. Who's always with us, and who's way more powerful than the devil? Tell Mommy, you know this one!"

"Ummm . . . GOD?" The reality of the question brightens Sarah's hope and spirits.

"That's right, GOD. And with him on our side, we can do anything, including get home safely. So don't fret or pout just yet, baby, because there's still hope. And as long as we're together, and I have you on my side, then you can always count on me not to ever give up, okay?" Joanne looks Sarah square in the eyes, hugging her once more.

"Okay, Mommy, but my hand really hurts." Sarah bends and picks up her trusty bat from the black floor.

"You're going to have to tough it out a little, Sarah. We're both hurt, but we have to get that key. Now come on, let's find this doll and go home to Daddy!" Joanne places an arm around Sarah and shines the flashlight down the hole.

"Where did all these other toys come from?" Sarah looks around the floor.

"I don't know, baby. Must've all came from inside here. This is where the doll ran off too. But good or bad, scary or not, we have to go in and get her," Joanne states as they enter the curving dark hole.

The green molded, reddish-black cavern sloped downward, swerving as Sarah and Joanne descended farther into its unknown. As the flashlight dies out a few times, Joanne taps it against her hand, dimly lighting the dirt and gravel avalanching roof and walls. Old coffins and broken stone heads begin to litter the tunnel as the long-lost and forgotten remains of decaying corpse let their presence be known within the dirt and rubble that buried them.

"Eeww, Mommy, it smells bad!" Sarah covers her nose with the neck of her sweater.

"I know, sweetie. Looks like we might be under an old cemetery or something? I don't remember there ever being graves around here. Must be centuries old or some sort of lost burial ground," Joanne concludes from the clothes and jewelry worn by the deceased.

"Ooh, Mommy, look, pretty!" Sarah finds a bracelet made out of colorful beads. Stooping down to pick them up, her mother quickly yanks her back by the arm.

"Don't you touch that! That pretty bracelet belongs to someone, one of these people. And they probably were buried with it," Joanne explains as Sarah makes a hideous face and draws back. "We never take from the dead. I'm sure the spirit of the owner would be awfully sad if you took it. But I'll tell you what, since you like that so much . . . when we get home, I'll buy you an even more beautiful bracelet of your very own."

"Okay," Sarah responds, glancing a few feet ahead. "Look, Mommy!" Her thin finger points, identifying a plump object lying in the shadows. And when the small child walks upon the strange object, her mother flashes it with light, revealing the severed hand of Officer Witmen, still clutched on to his nightstick.

As all sorts of small pitter-patters and little voices lively the remaining undiscovered portion of the tunnel, both Joanne and Sarah cover their mouths and noses from the foul stench of rotting bone and flesh. Yet continuing down the passage, they travel and stumble over more limbs and clothing as mysterious, frightening foreign sounds grew louder in the darkness.

"We've got to be nearing the end, so get ready. She has to be around here!" Joanne yells out as a strong gust of wind hit their faces and body. Dropping the flashlight, the sudden breeze catches it, rolling it off into the darkness as dirt and grime blow about fiercely. Struggling to go forward, with their heads down inside the noisy chatter and wind, the two wind up in a large hall. Lowering their arms from their faces, the mother's and daughter's blowing hair suddenly cease in movement, resting motionless against their necks and shoulders.

"Mommy, what happened? We made it!" Sarah stares behind her mother at the now-still and dead silent corridor. "Where are we, Mommy?"

"What this place is? Is a better question. We're here, and exactly where here is? I don't know, baby." Her mother reloads the shotgun, shell shocked by what suddenly viewed before them. "Unbelievable."

The hall, massive and elegant in its own decor, was carved in the finest of wood. Illuminated by high-hung small chandeliers, it broke into a series of other halls to the left and right as a very large door stood tall at the opposite end. Pictures lined the walls along with shelves filled with dolls of all types. Passing them, Sarah and Joanne can see the plastic people whispering and socializing independently. As the doll's stop to stare back quietly in curiosity, they watch the two walk by. Glancing up at the shelves that hung high on the walls, Sarah and Joanne can also see more dolls looking down at them, some even sat with their tiny legs dangling off the shelves while hundreds crept across the high ceilings, magically, upside down. Too late to turn back, Joanne nervously guides Sarah to the large door ahead as more dolls step out from the corners and shadows of the walkways.

"Momma?" Close to the entrance, in the middle of the first hall on the left, a little boy's voice rang out of the mouth of the saddest-looking toy they ever saw. Sarah jumps at the sight of the deranged doll in diapers as it hisses and drooled over the torn body of another doll it had ripped apart.

"Something's terribly wrong with these doll babies, Momma." Sarah loads her slingshot and pulls back its rubber sling.

"These things aren't dolls, Sarah! Dolls don't walk around or run away with your keys! These things are something else!" Joanne explains, becoming more frustrated the more dolls she spots.

Despite the growing gathering of toys, each of the dolls that saw them keep a distance while others follow behind from afar. The halls lined and filled with cowboys, Indians, clowns, and various dolls of all types of occupations. Speaking a variety of tones, grunts, languages, and tongues, each grew quiet and still when first taking notice of Sarah and Joanne.

Making it to the door, Joanne touches it with her badly shaking hands. Turning the supersized knob, she pushes her way into a larger hall. Quite like a cave, a multitude of bats clapped their wings across the darkness of the jagged ceilings that disappeared somewhere within the shadows created by the sheer height of the cavern's torch-lit walls. A small bowlegged cowboy doll that Joanne noticed in one of the first intersecting halls they passed darts between her feet and swiftly climbs upon the shoulders of a tall figure of a man that continued to tower over them the closer it neared. As the slim, broad-shouldered figure enters the light under the torches, he reveals a pale, dark, and dry face of unearthed tones, patches of other skin, and dead flesh that did not originally belong to his body. Stitched together like one of Dr.

Frankenstein's lost creations, the very inhuman-looking individual stares coldly under plots of hair that plugged into empty spaces of overly large pores along its scalp. As one of his dark-yellow eyes turn toward Sarah, the resurrected-looking fellow tilts his head to the chattering Western-dressed doll.

"Well, my friend tells me that we have visitors," the being speaks in a deep, raspy old voice that shook his plantlike head. "Welcome, I . . . am the Animator. How can I help you two lost man souls?"

"Where's the doll, and how do I convince you to leave our quiet little cabin?" Joanne quickly aims the shotgun directly at the man's head.

"Doll? Oh . . . I see, her. Well . . ." the horribly disfigured man begins as a wretched voice bursts from the door behind him.

"Animator! Here, now!" Familiar vocals of a hag bounce against the hall's stone walls.

"Oh dear, she sounds unhappy again. You must leave before . . ." The tall man continues before being choked up by the calling of his name. "It's too late," he finishes his sentence as the door behind him opens up.

"We're not going anywhere without that doll!" Joanne blurts out as the man slowly turns around and proceeds through the door, leaving her and Sarah following cautiously behind into the next chamber.

The hall opens into a strange laboratory of tremendous proportions. Tables of flasks and graduated cylinders were everywhere as if someone were making potions or biological chemicals. A four-foot stonewall connecting in a circle in the center of the room resembles an almost-ancient well. Its unknown purpose and bizarre presence there made the scene abstract and the scene far more bizarre than it already was.

"Well, hello there, sweeties! It took you long enough," a scraggly old voice greets as the graft-skinned man steps aside, unblocking Joanne and Sarah's view.

"What the—?" Joanne's hand gently guides Sarah behind her as she places the voice onto the face of the old woman from the woods. "You! You were doing this the whole time! What the hell's going on?"

Standing beside the tremendous structure that was indeed a well next to a table of scientific instruments dressed in layers of rags, the elderly lady from the woods smiles innocently with one hand behind her back and the other on her plump stomach. "Yes, it's me, the sweet old woman from the forest. Did you find my pet? Or did he find you? Hee, hee, hee!" The crazed-looking woman giggles hysterically at the ceiling. "You know . . . it was the darnedest thing, that bear of yours. Took me a while to catch it! But after my cleansing it of all the reeks of a little girl . . . still, no matter how many times I changed it, heh-heh-heh, it still wouldn't obey. You must've left something awful on that bear, Sarah! Whew, you're a special child!"

"Who are you? What do you want?" Joanne screams.

"And how do you know my name?" Sarah joins her, then whispers, "I think she's the devil, Mommy."

"I have been called many names, child, but I am not the devil. I am Zamaniken, and he is what's left of my deaf and departed husband, the Animator. Come, my love," Zamaniken calls out to the tall man as he slowly lurches to her. "For centuries, we have watched and waited for the betterment of man to rise in the so-called image of its GOD. But all mankind has done is infest the earth with its filth, greed, and murder of its own kind and anything it doesn't understand. For millenniums, we and our kind have been hunted down and flushed out like insects by a species that is no greater than the rodents that overpopulate space with diseases," she articulates. "I once died too by the hands of your kind and was saved by a great power that was bestowed upon me, giving me life and the ability to change things. Now the time has come for us to reclaim what is rightfully ours. The time has come for a new savior of this so-called humanity. It is as I am to be, this world will slowly be made into my image, continuing with you. Slowly, one by one, life as you know it will meet its end." She points at Sarah; Joanne points the shotgun at her chest from below.

"You're a freaking crazy woman! Zamaniken, I get it. Zamaniken, like manikin, duh! The dolls? I get it now. You're a freaking doll too!" Highly agitated, Joanne's unsteady hands tremble on the trigger.

"I promise you, I'm no doll."

"You got that right. Look, you're a freaking woodland witch, and he's a goddamn wizard! So what? I just want to get home with my little girl!" Joanne stares square into the smeared made-up face of the insane woman, hoping that she would perhaps see things her way.

"Why, you are home! You see, the world consist of many dimensions. You just live in one. All we need is a small portion of a human's liver, and you too can become immortal like us! Live forever," the tall grim man speaks as dolls began to come out from everywhere, showing themselves around the room. "Total peace and happiness within a new race of man."

"That's what you call happy?" Joanne looks around at dolls fighting and attacking one another while the rest display acts of cannibalism and illustrations of other odd, insane behavior.

"Souls lay dormant inside the liver. Unrested, I can control them by providing new host. My husband carves and constructs personality and character into their new bodies. During this process, sometimes discrepancies occur. Most spirits are unhappy with the purification, but after long periods of outer body experience, they forget and become lost and misguided, just as they were in their human life, yet, harmless to nature. Some even try to hold on to bits and pieces of their memories as I erase them and make them my people, solely my children! You could be whoever you like! However, to ensure the normality that you refer to, we have learned throughout the ages that there is only one secret to creating the perfect life-form, and that is only by usage of the innocent, like the sweet soul of a child. This is why I have led you here." Zamaniken nod's to her husband, acknowledging the excellent job they had done.

"Like hell! No one is laying a finger on my little girl! We came on our own free will. Now I'm going to ask again, where is that nasty little doll that you gave my daughter?" Joanne inches closer to ensure a clear shot.

"Such forked tongue you have! Is this who you're looking for?" The clownish-looking woman holds up the doll from behind her back, kicking, screaming, while dangling the policeman keys from its hand.

"No! Don't you dare, not that one!" the tall man cries out, madly in love with his creations. Sensing that the doll was about to be destroyed, he attempts to help spare her life. "Zamaniken, no!" The Animator reaches for the doll; his beloved levitates a swordlike instrument off one of the tables below. Sending it flying, it severs him in half. As his legs topple over, the Animator's upper body tumbles down the short staircase to Joanne's feet. "Don't worry, it doesn't hurt much . . . She's killed me thousands of times." His raspy, eerie voice beckons from his head of fallen flesh and bloody cotton. "I have a good liver. Come join us."

"I hate liver, yuck!" Sarah comments, watching her mother splatter the Animator's head and chest into all sorts of spreading muscle and organ matter, then reload.

"Blah! Who needs a husband anyway?" Zamaniken looks down at what's left of her husband. "Out of all these years, you are the first to get one thing correct Joanne. I am a witch!" She laughs hard, raising the doll over the well. "You see . . . I cannot let you have this one. This doll is a runaway. She tried to help me to prove her worth, yet and still, for her crime, she must be punished and reincarnated. This one shall bring forth the end to all living. Destroy them, children!" She harks out orders to the room of toys. Holding the doll by the neck, the old woman suspends it over the well as a tiny voice seeps out from the body of the doll.

"Help me, Mommy! I love you," the voice box repeats from the doll as it appears to be crying.

Still in dire need of those keys the doll continued to latch on to, Joanne, as though the toy was somehow using them as leverage to get what it really wanted out of her, fires the shotgun again. As the powerful blast mule kicks her to the floor of attacking toys, the blast blows the witches hand clean off, with part of her wrist still attached.

The old woman screeches in a tyrant rage as the doll catches hold of the well's edge and climbs out while her hand tumbles down into the dark center of the pit. "No! You imbecilic idiot!" The old lady tries to escape past them.

Taking advantage of the opportunity and slightly sensing her own death, Sarah maneuvers around Joanne, who swings the shotgun like a club, knocking hordes of dolls about and from around them. Pulling out an aerosol can and a green lighter from the inside of her coat, Sarah sprays the bottle and flicks the lighter, igniting the garments of the one-handed woman with a ball of fire.

"No! Look at what you've done! Animator! Mator!" Zamaniken howls in agony, diving across tables and bumping into the walls, trying to dose the growing flames upon her.

Joanne yanks stabbing and biting dolls from her back and face, becoming overwhelmed as Sarah spots the doll with the keys, standing back, watching the whole thing from the rim of the well above. Loading her slingshot with the prewrapped powder balls,

Sarah is dragged off by the legs into a cluster of raving toys. Just as the doll with keys prepare to leap away, Sarah fires two shots from the crowd, hitting it in the eyes and face in an exploding cloud of blinding white powder.

"I got the doll, Mommy! I got the doll!" Gaining great courage, Sarah kicks, swipes, and pulls the heads off dolls, clearing a path to her mother. Grabbing a leg herself off one of the dolls, she beats the others off the body of her tired, fighting mother before slinging it across the room. "Mommy, look!" She helps Joanne up and directs her attention to the top of the well.

With the vehicle's key still tightly held in the grip of her tiny, plump right hand, the doll, dazed and confused, chokes and gags for air. Spitting out dust of powder, it attempts to wipe clean its covered marble eyes. Wobbling about, nearly falling off the well, and landing down unto the steps near the awaiting mother and child, it steps awkwardly and topples down inside instead.

"Oops." Sarah covers her fading smile of success and looks into her mother's stern eyes, realizing that she just contributed to losing the keys forever. "This isn't good, Mommy." She then glances around at hundreds of dolls encircling them.

And if that wasn't the worst of their worries, little did they know that deep down inside the bottom of the well, an even greater evil brewed. The doll tumbles frantically down the well, bumping into each side of the inner stone wall, breaking off its head. It falls toward the awaiting body of Zamaniken and the Animator's greatest creation of all. Into a large open incision of a creature so dark and cursed that the witch and warlock waited until the worlds end to reanimate it, the remains of Zamaniken's hand, partial arm, and the doll fall. Far worse than any of its previous master's before, the creature, cursed and dormant in its cave-like imprisonment, waits to be given life through blood and a soul. Mixing inside its wound, the immortal hand of the witch and a doll that contained a liver and a soul of the once living is crushed and devoured by the thirsty spirit of hell's hunger for man. As the tormented soul and powers from Zamaniken's tainted mystical blood brings forth new life from within belly of an inanimate object, a loud moan rumbles the room as two large bright-red eyes open and shimmer upward from the bottom of the well.

Covered in a variety of biting, clawing, and punching dolls, Joanne and Sarah fight their way toward the door from which they came by any means necessary. Reaching view of the door, a loud growl grumbles from out of the well, stopping and sending Sarah, Joanne, and the dolls looking backward to see what had made the enormous sound.

"Mommy, I . . . love you!" The dark voice shakes the corridor, crumbling dirt, paint, and wood from the ceilings. The floor begins to quake and walls crack as the enormous forehead and set of window-sized glowing red eyes submerges from the well.

"I hate dolls!" Sarah blurts out as Joanne snatches her by the upper arm and dolls, instead of attacking, leap on them to hitch a ride to freedom.

A large, plump hand followed by a second stretches out of the well as it collapses down to the lower level, breaking the floor behind them. A thick cloud of dust expands and rises throughout the room; an ugly, ginormous, beyond-dead doll constructed of unknown rotten, decomposed flesh, animal and human, crawls out from the cavern toward them. Screaming at the ends of their own wind, they throw and sling away the bothersome nuisance from around their necks and bodies. Bursting through the large red doors, the burning singed body of Zamaniken catches the room ablaze behind them as the giant, monstrous baby doll crawl fully out of its rocky prison. Running and thinking at the same time, Joanne quickly pries and pulls the torches from the walls. Tossing the burning stakes around the room and at the dolls, Joanne passes one to Sarah, then slings two at the monstrous toy that followed behind. It screeches in a burning fury, breaking everything in its sight to get to them.

Ramming through the next set of doors, Joanne takes her and Sarah's torches and set the wooden walls of the halls on fire. Bombarded by more attacking toys, she burrows into a swarm of angry dolls, pulling Sarah behind her. Bucking a fearsome hole in front of her, Joanne clears an open path and heads for the tunnel with the enormous evil plowing through dolls and doorways behind them.

"Mommy?" it cries out. An army of hundreds of bloodthirsty, crazed normal-sized dolls of all sorts engulf the ferocious giant. Smacking piles of dolls away in clumps, the awesome creature gorges on their tiny bodies and smashes the fleeing with its room-sized hand.

"Oh my . . . goodness!" The horrific screams of the beast causes Joanne to leap into the powerful winds of the tunnel that now fought against their frail frames. Then taken them off foot at first, the whirlwind spat them out among the now shifting graves of the dead, as they desperately made their way to bricks of the cellar floor.

Screaming, both slid into shelves, breaking barrels and crates, and scrambled for the ladder to the cabin, which was now in sight.

"Sarah?"

"Mommy," she answered as they both ripped clinching dolls from their legs and arms.

"Are you all right?" Joanne checks, hearing a tremendous roar inside the tunnel. "Come on, hurry! Let's go, baby!" she directs and pushes before Sarah can answer. Helping her up the ladder, Joanne quickly climbs with her. Upon reaching the hatch, a flood of dolls pour down onto them, latching on and attacking their already-tired limbs. Swatting and kicking in terror, Joanne gets a glimpse of the fingers and head of the giant doll breaking through the entrance of the tunnel. As that same familiar cowboy doll jumps on to her face, some dolls climb over Sarah and climb past them to escape. Lifting Sarah up, she pushes her through the cellar door and forces her way up behind her. Missing Joanne's foot, the creature crashes into the wall of the cellar, shaking the cabin. Slamming the door shut and locking it, Joanne steps back as the escaped dolls run amuck throughout the cabin. "Outside, head for the door, Sarah!" she yells, running into the kitchen. "Go, Sarah!"

"But, Mommy!"

"Go now, goddamn it!" Joanne gets the notion to turn on the gas stove. Opening the oven door, she turns the gas on high and places the kerosene lamps next to it.

As the cabin began to smoke, quake, and vibrate from below, in the midst of the creature's loud howls, Sarah makes it to the front door. Barely able to stand, she grabs hold of the knob and opens the door, spotting her father with his arm up, just about to knock. "Daddy!" she cries out colliding to his waist as dolls run out around them and disappear into the woods.

"What . . . is going on? Where's your mom?" Patting her back, he looks up at Joanne running toward him at a high rate.

"Daddy, a giant doll's trying to eat us, and it's coming this way! And a witch made a man and . . ." Sarah blurted out in one breath into her father's stomach as the giant doll lifts itself through the floor covered in burning flames.

"I can't believe you got another doll," her father states in shock, unable to grasp the concept that a monster was coming directly at him.

"John?" Joanne leaps and tackles him and Sarah out the door and off the porch.

"No! Don't leave me, Mommy! I love you!" a dark voice bellied out from the doll's nightmarish mouth as the lower levels beneath the cabin explodes. It tears through the floor and ground to get to them.

Rising to their feet, the family runs through the falling snow and toward the four-by-four pickup truck that Joanne's husband, John, left running. Confused and jittery, John takes off with Sarah and, for some reason, glances nervously back at the cabin door. As the melting doll burst through the roof of the cabin in a fiery of fury, the oven and lamps ignite. The cabin explodes in a fury of flames and smoke, sending the parched front door spiraling into the air. John leaps onto Sarah; Joanne ducks as the hot door flies over them and slams into the side of the officer's utility vehicle.

"That was close. Everyone all right? Come on, let's get out of here!" Joanne screams as they scurry to John's truck. Speeding off into the woods, they soon hit the open road home.

Sarah bounces up and down in her seatbelt, safe inside the backseat of her father's truck. Flinging slush from under the truck's big tires, John drives far over the speed limit for miles before decelerating.

"Mommy, we made it. Mommy, we did it, didn't we?" Sarah cheers as Joanne kisses her father, then stretches back to kiss her.

"So what was that back there? What happened, Anne?" placing a gentle hand on his wife's thigh, John questions her with great concern.

"Trust me, you have until we get home to hear this one," Joanne answers with a thankful smile.

"You know what? I was scared, Mommy, but this was the best vacation ever!" Sarah shouts as the truck rolls over a pothole. "I can't wait until school starts back. I'm going to tell all my friends at school! Mommy, can we come back again next year?"

"Not likely, not even the year after that!" Joanne replies as they reach the first highway sign directing home. Driving off into the rest of their lives, Sarah and her mother went on, thankful of being alive and thankful to have each other. With the greatest story ever, they sat back and watched the car pass familiar houses they saw on the way to the cabin.

Bloody, busted, and burnt, something furry climbs from under the truck onto the flat bed and hides between the tool box and the truck's large spare tire. Hungry and thirsty for blood, Sarah's old stuffed animal, the teddy bear, rest and wait to be discovered as it too rides along with the family to their happy home, into a new day, under the winter gray.

"Yep, they were new folks, all right, Junior. It's a crime shame, a crime shame, I tell ya. What a place indeed. City folks are always in a rush with nowhere to go. A crime shame, isn't it, Junior?" A tall, slender extremely old man sits on the snow-covered porch with his son, watching the occasional traffic go by. Holding out an extending false arm, he opens a hand of cold, hard plastic fingers and stretches them around a glass of lemonade handed by his wife as she inches out the creaking front door.

The little boy turns to his father, revealing a round painted and finely detailed sculptured head of a doll that poked out from the hood of a sweat shirt. "Mommy and Daddy, I love you," a prerecorded-sounding voice plays from inside the child as he looks up at his mother with the clearest round marble eyes.

"Aww, we love you too, sweetie. Now let's go retrieve your pet. Ready?" Rubbing her wrinkled hands together as they sprout from under her garment of black rags, the tall man's wife looks over the snow-covered landscape as her husband grabs a large shaggy coat and throws it over her shoulders. "There are many dimensions. He only hides in this one."

LANDING 3

MILTON'S LITTLE DEMON

One damp day after it had rained, in the dews of young Milton's yard, he tripped upon a piece of mirror and gazed upon the shard.

Oh, how dreadful his life had been, eating vegetables and cleaning with a broom. How miserable it was to bathe and being made to clean your room.

Milton was the type of child who never followed the rules; he never liked playing with other kids or learning words at school.

His father was never around, and life seemed always bad.

He sees himself in the object's reflection, and it made him very sad.

Examining the uniqueness of the glass and its authenticity,

he disregards his mother's warning about touching sharp things and picks up the shining beauty.

Never listening to his elders and quite mischievous as can be,

Milton pricks the palm of his hand and raises it to his eye to see.

Hating everyone and everything, he curses the fragment and throws it down; it hits a small hidden stone and shatters along the ground.

Then receiving a rumble in his belly, he looks back at his house, as something that suddenly sickened him slithered from his mouth.

He stares at the gelatin goo that contained a small figure curled up on its side. He tucks it under his shirt and carries it inside.

The idea of a mad scientific discovery cuts a smile of ivory along his unemotional face as he sneaks whatever it was back into his secret place.

Past his dog, Wheaty, past his mother, Milton snuck to the first stair.

Then he inches up into his room as his baby sister, Shelly, awaited there.

Deviously she grins. "Hello, brother. What do you have behind your back? Is it a penny, a ball, some bubblegum, or a new toy perhaps?"

"Neither, none, keep your voice down!" With his heel, Milton kicks shut the bedroom door. "See . . . nothing." He sticks two empty hands out as something disgusting glides down a leg and onto the floor.

"Eww, what is that? I'm telling Mom!" Suddenly, Shelly got closer and touches it with both hands. She picks it up so delicately, becoming amazed and entranced.

"There's a little man inside," she whispered so not a soul could hear. Milton's face fired and boils with anger as he snatches back his findings, screaming, "Give it here!"

"But I'm your sister. Let me see it!" Shelly snatches it back. "Let me see it one more time."

"Give it to me!" Milton takes it back. "I found it, and that means it's mine!"

"Fine!"

"Fine!"

"Fine!"

"Fine."

Shelly reaches out to her brother's hand and squeezes something awful unto Milton's bedtime book. And after the greenish glob popped and shook, Milton yells out, "Look!"

A brilliant array of fluorescent light emits from the blob, yet to their dismay, the shadowy figure opens its red eyes from inside the slime, leaps, and runs away.

And mere seconds before his sister Shelly could unleash a scream, Milton jarred his hand against her mouth, preventing the seeping sounds of anything.

"If I get in trouble, so will you!" Milton threatens his sister's ear as Shelly nods in agreement, holding back every tear.

"Look, the bedroom doors closed tight!" Milton smiles, watching whatever jumped out, jump around. The brother and sister crept closer to get a better view at what they found.

Then in a flash, standing next to an old soda bottle with no label, a tiny pointy-eared green creature with horns pointing out its red hat leaps upon the table.

Smiling an awfully wide and swirling devilish grin with beady eyes that stare from under a red mushroom hat, it stood on teeny hind legs with a tail curling behind its back.

It wore a broken chain around its neck, under jagged teeth that protruded from its mouth, as something dark and dreary about it creates an eeriness in the house.

"It looks disgusting. What is it?" Shelly lowers a piece of candy, and in front of their hungry green pet it hung. The goblin licks their faces, snatching the treat with a long extending tongue.

Then it eats a lamp and a nightstand before the first five minutes of the hour, and from out its mouth, it gives Shelly a beautiful flower.

"Wow! Did you see that?" Milton cheers, quite enthused by the whole event. Then he feeds the monster chips, dip, his mother's slip, and all his football equipment.

"I don't believe it," Shelly frets. "Mother will be very mad."

Then Milton thinks of all the things the creature hasn't had.

"I have an idea. Let's take it to the kitchen! We could even surprise Mom!" Milton suggests. "There are lots of things that it could eat. It'll be so much fun!"

"I don't know about this. It ate Mom's gown!" Shelly mutters, "Well, he is only a foot tall."

"So how much of a problem could it be?" Milton watches the goblin climb and balance on top of a ball.

Suddenly ending the conversation as if taken by a daze, the small children watches the gremlin devour one wall as swiftly as the wind changes its direction during the days.

And throughout the house, the small gremlin dashed as Milton cries, "Catch it, for Pete's sake!" And he ran with his sister after the imp, amazed by everything it ate.

The tiny monster ate all of Milton's learning books and the upstairs toilet bowl. It also swallows all his unloved toys and all the pennies that he stole.

Sucking down their beds, shoes, hats, followed by their clothes, then down the stairs, the creature gulps down the dishware and swallows their mother whole.

And without warning in one large chomp, the family cat disappears along with the mail. The little demon smiles at poor Wheaty the dog, leaving only the remains of his collar and tail.

And it must've started from this point, when Milton realized something was terribly wrong, as he pondered on how such a horrible thing could hold a smile for so long.

"It ate our mom!" Shelly screams, carrying her last, only uneaten doll by her side.

"It'll eat up everything!" Milton chases the green elflike creature back outside.

And something horrible began to happen. Little did the children know, depending on what was eaten determined the size the creature would grow.

And so the house and family boat disappeared into the monster's belly. The little demon, now the size of an elephant, shook like a balloon of jelly.

Drinking all the water out their swimming pool, it eyes something approaching in a hoody. Carrying a ball was Chuck, the meanest kid and local neighborhood bully.

"So what do we have here, my new pet?" Chuck cracks his knuckles, ready to brawl, as the goblin pounces out from behind the trees and munches him down, leaving only his basketball.

"It ate Chuck too!" Shelly panics. "Look at all the things it did!"

The demon scarfs down all the neighbors, houses, cars, and the mail man who had a low tolerance for kids.

And before Milton and Shelly had time to react, the giant goblin continued down the street, eating as many things as it could, acquiring additional arms, legs, and feet.

Down the road, Milton saw the school he dreaded disappear with the gym; and at an intersection, he and his sister come to a halt. He shouts, "I think we've lost him."

And in the middle of nothing, they think of all the terrible things that they once were made to do and things that once seemed horrible suddenly didn't seem so hard to do.

They had no one left to cook them meals and no one around to teach them a single thing. Everyone was gone, and the life they knew was now a dream.

Inside miles and miles of empty space, without all the different people and free of rules, Milton and Shelly sat lost with no direction as the wind blew chilly and cool.

Sadly, on the curb, their faces fell long as they quietly stare at their feet. *How lonely the world had become*, they thought, and both began to weep.

"Goblin, where are you?" Milton shouts, angered by his choice. Just as he thought, *I should have listened to my sister*, something large caught the last words of his voice.

Milton held on to Shelly. The ground rumbles, trembling their hearts and toes. A tremendous green creature appear, puffing fire and smoke from the nose.

"Where have you been?" Milton stutters as scared as he could be.

He stood frightened by the sight of his giant, who burps out a plane from Germany.

Shelly sorrowfully looks over at her brother, who knew he could not keep it. For the monster was too ferocious to keep as any little secret.

Milton bravely sticks out his chest. "You cannot go around eating everything you find! I wanted to keep you, but now you have to go!" Slowly he approaches the large mouth of the demon and hugs it one last time.

"You ate towns and cities. Now what are we to do?" Shelly looks into the goblin's clear baby eyes, and it appeared that the monster she feared had grew on her too.

"I wish you were good and not so bad." Milton remembers the things that he once had.

And it was at that precise moment that Milton's word must've touched a demon's soul. As the ginormous creature turned purplish blue, then red, it blew out a gust of air of icy cold.

It spun around in wiggles and kicks right where there once was a parking lot. It flipped and suddenly broke out in spots, triangles, and polka dots.

The demon was determined not to leave and put up a fight; it vowed to change for the little boy, first making its wrongs right.

And at that exact time, in a deep swallow right then and there, the creature began to spew everything it ate thousands of feet into the air.

The demon spat out rows of houses, trees, and a copy of the evening news, birds, cats, zoo animals, bats, and Chuck the bully into his shoes.

Returning everything along the path it made, along fell Milton's house, cars, trucks, even Wheaty the tailless dog came tumbling out of the demon's mouth.

It even spit out the stars, the moon, and Milton's mom right before their eyes, and then it burped of cows, balloons, and buses before shrinking to its original size.

Scared out of her wits, Milton's mother speaks, "Get rid of that thing! My insurance won't cover this. Now who's to blame?" Milton gazes at the mother he missed but couldn't bring himself to explain.

The smiling little goblin man snarls, snap, and growl as Shelly tries to find a way to explain how everything got out of hand and wild.

"Oh, Milton and Shelly!" their mother cries as they all were happy just to be together. So the clever demon thought of way that they could be this way forever.

The demon smiles
and swallows
Milton,
Shelly,
and their mom quick and without a trace,
and hops into the house, to Milton's room,
falling asleep in his secret place.

LANDING 4

JOE'S EYES

This is my woman, my love,
the very essence of my heart.
All of those tough years dealing with each other, my love,
never shall we separate, never do we part.
Woe unto the man who brings death unto my dear or shame.
Unto his soul I will bring suffering and untold burning
carnage within furies of anguish and pain.

I watched my future wife sleep motionless next to me, both
liquored up heavily inside our bed. The nonfading times we've
spent together dance inside my spinning head.

Soon the dizziness dissipates as I find peace in resting behind
the shadows of my own eyes. Meeting me in my dreams, a dark
figure stood beside my bed and over my wife to my surprise.

Soaked wild hair drip of water as blood sprinkled in dabs
across his lips. Piercing sharp eyes reflect hate; he glances at my
face as blood ran down a machete into his fingertips.

My body reeks with fear. At last, I drown in darkness,
continuing on in slumber. With last thoughts of my love, I let go,
resting my hand upon hers under the night of rain and thunder.

The end to a passionate night slowly passes as I awake for the
routine bathroom stop. Stumbling over a misplaced object to the
kitchen, I stretch, knocking down the counter clock.

I hope I didn't wake my lady with the commotion and the mess. My feet slip across something wet. I fell to my back, then the broom also across my chest.

Sliding to all fours, I maneuvered to my feet.

Clicking on the light switch, I rub my aching back on legs that now felt weak.

The sink overflowed with dishes as water flood onto the floor, a machete drenched in a path of blood that pooled between the sink and the door.

A cold chill shivers my spine; the urgent urge to urinate goes away. Nausea and dizziness overcomes me, but well balanced I continue to stay.

Over the weapon to see my dear, I fear but manage to hold my most recent thoughts: to warn my lady of a potential intruder. My walk ends in an abrupt halt.

Right there before my watery eyes, in the same exact place, my adorable wife lies still, before I caress her, my mind envisions her beautiful face.

Her limbs and joints were ripped apart and separated as I glanced down on the saturated bed. I remember touching her once-perfect body in which now lies absent of a head.

The white sheets that we slept in, now the color red, drip like the melted ice cream we once shared, I thought, standing over the bed.

Breathlessly weakened,

I couldn't understand,

who on GOD's green earth

would want to do this to my woman.

I ran to the closets and checked every room slow.

I notice speckles of red inside the pane of a window.

The fact remains, the alleged escaped. They took the essence of my half; my wrath shall now be their fate.

And as my shook nerves begin to throb and pound, my blood began to boil and singe. To kill a murderer seemed so bitterly sweet, as I hungered for extreme revenge.

Walking over to the machete, I held it to the light, vowing to avenge my honey's death and take a life in exchange for my wife.

Grabbing a coat from out of the closet, through the window, down the fire escape, inside the alley, I stand against the wall and wait.

With nowhere to go and not enough ideas to start, I stumble over a slaughtered victim inside the alley's dark.

Feeling remorse for the victim, I make out the familiar face. The neighborhood drunk who always asked my love for change now parts in a vertical half from the waist.

The man's blood and organs spurt among his shattered bottle and spilled nickels, pennies, and dimes. It appears nothing had been stolen to accommodate the crime.

I picture the poor fellow falling sadly alone inside the dark. *Could this be a connection to my heart's killer?* I thought as suspicions directed me behind him to the park.

I ran,
still thinking about the drunken man
and how his persistent begging unnerved me,
driving me mad.
I ran
at full speed, I thought of him and my dear
and all the new opportunities they could have had.

Two tragedies, I wonder, *Oh, how lives could end so sadly.* I paused to catch my breath and cry on how I was missing her so badly.

I lean upon a garbage can beside a telephone pole and notice a pushover coming by the name of Bob. Once, he attempted to hit my wife and harass her on the job.

As I remember our short history, a sound struck as clear as a crystal. A body fell in front of Bob and his two friends; he looks around and lowers his pistol.

Under the full moon, the devil plays a tune on his orchestra as his fingers snap a string on the fiddle. Bob and his friends see me and my revenge, realizing it was I in the middle.

And I too could recognize the fire that burned inside Bob's eyes as he drew closely closer. It was due to my mistake. I shouldn't have been seen. I couldn't hold back as I become their second candidate.

"Well, what do we have here, a stray?" Bob approaches me, ready to do harm. "How's that pretty little wife of yours?" He held his gun to my chest; I hack off his hand and arm.

And before he could even scream, each man went for their weapon,

I move between their aims as they shoot each other, beheading the both of them.

"Why did you murder my wife?" I ask as the bodies of Bob's friends began to fall. I grab Bob by the handless arm and smeared him down a wall.

He screams and utters curses of how crazy I was as I could freshly see splatters of my baby's blood across that kitchen floor. I dug into his bone with the machete, not caring anymore.

Freeing his soul forever before Bob could speak a sentence, I dash deeper into the park, hearing sirens in the distance.

Rain sprinkles down upon the head before pouring upon the land, saturating my clothes, hair, it rinses clean my dirty hands.

Crossing a small bridge, I pass an old playground, running through the trees so tall. A bright light flashes from behind me followed by an unwanted call.

"Don't move. Put your hands above your head!" A pitch-dark silhouette of a policeman then screams, "Freeze!"

"I don't believe it. We got him." Another verified, moving from behind his partner with great caution and ease.

"You don't understand," I tried to explain before the first officer cut me off.

"Oh, I understand. Silence, now!" he demanded before taking me for a walk.

At least ten feet behind, they followed, guiding me toward Westside St. like a strung doll. I realized that they weren't policemen, just two poor security guards guiding me to the mini mall.

Before I killed them, I went along to see if I could find a smoother getaway. One places a call to another who places a call to the real police not far away.

The mini mall was a strip of stores I hadn't in a while been to. Through a busted window, the guards point to a rack of machetes, where three once sat. There now were two.

Not knowing quite what to say and with the matching, missing machete hidden up my sleeve inside my hand, I run its blade into one of their eyes, then into the name tag of the other man.

Across the throat and into the back, I cut through even the thickest clothes worn. Played right into the webs of tragedy, I walk inflamed and scorned.

Then I felt coldness direct me, and inside the madness of the pain, I could sense my love, my heart giving me directions in which her murderer came.

With no more answers than I had before and no place to think or go, I ease and submit to a corner worker who approaches calm and slow.

"Well, aren't we in a rut?" Her face told of hardships as her slit jeans gave everyone who saw her a peek. Rejecting her offer, I offer cash for a decent night's sleep.

Lucky I must have been under that old street light,

to get away with all the killings still to find a getaway spot for the night.

Close by, inside an alleyway, inside a run-down apartment I lie. On the top floor in a strange home, I relax my nerves where the lady of the evening stay.

"You need to relax." She glides across my chest under the highlighting moon.

"I don't want to do anything. I'm married." I grab her soft hands and lower them on top of the sheets in the odd quietness of her bedroom.

Her hair was soft and fine as silk and her skin quite warm and sleek. "Quite an angel, like my beloved." I think of her before dozing off to sleep.

Oh, how her eyes captivated me nearly every time,
mad, happy, or sad and crying.
Where her flowers have placed a growing seed,
my heart aches, slowly dying.
How could such a monstrosity take such a big sample
of such a fine wine?
I see myself again choking the man,
like I envision him doing other innocent victims by hand.
Taking the final breath of his last life,
was the ultimate price for taking my wife.

In a deep sweat I awoke, touching the madam's still pants. Soaked in blood from head to toe, I gasp out in chokes, "I . . . I don't understand."

"Not again." I come to tears.

The woman lay beaten inside my arms in the same bed she's had for years.

I threw on my jacket and ran out of the apartment as my own tears block my vision, causing me not to see. On top of the pain that reign on my head, the black sky showers rain around me.

Finally, I must've went crazy, I presumed as I found myself sneaking back home. A few police still roam outside while inside their presence, and my wife's body was gone.

"What's happening to me?" I scream in a whisper. "Someone is killing people around me." It had appeared.

Or maybe my rage has made me lose a marble or two, but that's exactly what I had feared.

Scared and confused I stood, nervously shaking quietly without a sound. Suddenly, I peer across the room at the killer finally found.

His hair lies drenched upon his face and neck; his eyes reveal the evils in my dreams. Covered in blood, he stares at me coldly, waiting to murder again it seems.

The police burst through the front door,

I dare not run from the fate of reality.

As I continue to stare into the emptiness of our bedroom mirror, the murderer holding his machete blinks back at me.

LANDING 5

STAIRS

"Seven . . . eight . . . nine . . ." I find myself counting again from inside of my bed. Up under the comfort of my thick quilted blanket that my grandmother once knitted, I count, "Ten" creeks, which sound like footsteps, creaking through the dead silence into the depths of my eardrums. "Eleven!" I whisper out loud, hearing another step. The slow shifting of the one that followed cut through darkness of the night like a knife, jolting my heart into a drumming flutter of frenzy. *It's a shame, a grown man still imagining he's hearing things. How many adults still go through this?* I ask myself as the twelfth step sends a cluster of shivers coasting down my spine. Growing closer than the others, it emitted loudly from almost the top of my stairs. Staring at the same old dingy walls that now displayed holes from ghost of past hung pictures and posters, my mind instantly analyzes the disturbance and receives flashes of when I was first introduced to the profound noise.

"Momma, I keep hearing someone walking up the steps!" I'd cry out loud. Mom would always bust into my room.

"It's okay, William. It's just the stairs creaking," my mother would always say, perched on top of my bed upon that same blanket that Grandma once sewed. Gently she'd rub my back, leaving a single kiss on my forehead.

"But we only have thirteen steps, Momma. I counted myself! I heard fourteen steps," I responded in a panic at the thought of a stranger being inside the house.

"It's nothing but the house settling. William, go see. We can go together. Would you like to take a look around, William? You'll never beat your fears if you don't face them, William," Momma would always say as I, as usual, refused her invitation to investigate what frightened me. After she'd sit down and read to me, I'd always scarf down a small saucer of her famous chocolate chip cookies along with a warm glass of milk and forget about what was bothering me. In those days, knowing that someone was always there to care for me made it easy to stare at the dry stucco ceiling and walls covered in superheroes and sports until I slowly drifted off into a pleasant sleep.

Now the days weren't as good to me as they used to be. My mother is no longer with me now, only living in memories of her wonderful spirit in my now-inherited house. The nights began to grow longer as every day I am continuously haunted by those same old footsteps from my past, which manifest within my home. Startling my inner peace while disturbing my resting mental, I often feel the sensation of breathing along the hairs of my neck. I dare never to look over the covers at whatever maybe walking and thudding its shoes around my bed. Exhausted once more, I fall asleep under my blanket, only to awaken entangled every time within the unforgiving, twisting folds of sheets and a cover.

Every day since a child, I wake up, go to the bathroom, and attempt to find the true me, somewhere from within the stained and speckled, unclean mirror that pasted to the cracked wall above the old white sink. Brushing my teeth, I drag across the wood and partially black and white tiled floor finding the kitchen. I make and sit with my food and, as of every meal, attempt to devour my breakfast. Getting dressed was always a chore. Attempting to raise your arms and keep your eyes open was hard enough without the actual activity of putting on clothes. When you're tired from days in of restless nights, putting on pants isn't always an easy task. Every morning, my car doesn't start, and so I start my day by getting a jump from the grouchy neighbor until one day he needed a jump too. Work had also become an unwanted exercise as I again repeat the routine of logging in, entering passwords, reading e-mails, filing, answering phones, and talking to happy and unhappy consumers. Soon, I too am consumed, entrapped in my world, my life, and my reality, lost in episodes of unreal time. As the days and months advance, they too are easily forgotten and untracked.

Eventually showing up to pick up my check, I appear on the job on days that weren't even paydays; and on the actual paydays, I failed to pick up my pay. Often not realizing how tired I have become, I sleep at work and through life. Today I dozed off and woke up to my supervisor looking at me strangely, then I recall a recent dream of him yelling at me at the top of his lungs, telling me I was fired. Glancing down at the calendar on my desk, a nearby radio station tells the date, time, and forecast. Awakening from dreaming that I was working, it dawned on me I was fired and actually had been unemployed for the last three weeks.

Walking in a daze, a face stains my mind forever. As I sit in a local park in temporary tranquility and confusion, I am disturbed by dark black eyes outlined by ebony noir mascara.

Her sleek, short black hair complemented her black vampire attire that altogether worked devilishly enticingly. "Hello," she simply greeted, posing directly in front of me, between my legs.

"Hi," I answer back, lifting my head and opening my crusted, sealed eyes.

"So heard ya got canned and still showed up for work? What balls. Is that true?" She partially smiles, tilts her head, and awaits an answer.

"Yep, sounds like me." I recognize her from the quiet corner cubical at work.

"You're a bold man. Cool, so . . . what are you on?" She sits down next to me crossing, her long skinny gapped legs.

"What am I on? You mean like drugs, seriously? Please, I wish! If I was on drugs, then maybe I could finally get some sleep!" Slightly offended by the fact that someone I didn't talk to would mistake me for an addict, slightly bothered, I sit up straight, attempting to pull myself together.

"Hey, I'm sorry. Look, I'm not judging. Whatever you're into is your business. I was just making an observation, you know? You were looking kinda bummed out on the bench all by your lonesome, and one of your shoes are missing." She points out as I broke into a bright blossom of blushes. "Just thought I'd see if you needed help."

"My shoe is missing?" I glance down at my right foot, embarrassed by my dirty white sock and exposed big toe. Clueless by where it might be, I drowsily wipe my face and shook my head. "Well, thank you very much. No one has ever taken the time out of their busy life to help me with anything, lent in the hair, something in the nose . . . I must say this is a first."

"Well, other than handing out the occasional spare change, it's a first for me too." Her pale skin, black-painted nails, and hearty friendliness force themselves upon me, slightly brightening my day.

"So tell me . . ." My eyes catch hers. I quickly break contact; she continues to stare. "Do you always stop and talk to potential drug addicts?"

"No, but I thought you might like to have the other shoe?" She pulls out my dirty, slightly smelly shoe from her bag.

"Wow, that's embarrassing. Thank you." I snatch my shoe as my cold, rough hand accidentally touches her soft, warmth-generating hand. "I gotta get some sleep."

"Why are you so tired? Stress, women, trouble, kids?"

"Kids? I wish it was that simple. Nope, none of those. Let's just say . . . I hear footsteps at night. Still want to talk to me?" For some reason, I blurted out my secret jokingly and waited for her to leave.

"Well, that's an easy one." Her smile shines, and her face appears to glisten to me as my heart began to flutter inside in slow motion. "Sounds like you need to . . ."

"Wait, no, let me guess, face my fears? My mother used to tell me that all the time." I cut off the pleasant sound of her optimistic voice.

"Hey, she was right. That's good. But that's not what I was about to say. Similar, though. I was going to say that maybe you need to journey into the belly of the beast. Meaning, maybe you should just go see where the footsteps are coming from. It just might ease your worries. You might find just the courage you need. It's said that some people who take that path become warriors of life and find their lost destinies, but that's just one person's opinion. I'm on the outside looking in." She then jots down her name and number on a torn piece of paper from her purse and gives it to me. "Good luck. The name's Lynn." She kisses two fingers and places them on my cheek. "If that doesn't work, try sleeping pills or tea!" She walks away, disappearing somewhere within morning traffic.

Frozen in time and space, I fight the aftershock of social success and slowly place my hand on my jaw where she placed the kiss. *This is truly a sign*, I thought, confident and feeling like a man. *Must be my lucky day.* Placing the number into my shirt pocket, I held my head back in the sudden cool blowing breeze. I cross one leg real cool-like, sheets of newspaper smack against my foot, wrapping around my calf. As pages flew, two remain attached to the sole of my shoe by a wad of old chewed gum. "Dang it!" I rip it in half and growled at one of the pages in my hand. It was an article about a blonde-haired, blue-eyed little girl who was currently missing. Balling it up, I shot it against the wind past the trash receptacle. "Cruel world." I humor myself by thinking of all the real problems in the world and then of me, a grown man paranoid over sounds at night that my imagination mistaken for footsteps.

An entire week went by, and every day I attempted to find a job. Dozing on buses, missing my stops, and falling asleep in cabs, I began to call Lynn every night that I awoke in cold sweat to the noises. Refusing to get out of my bed every time she asked, never did I once look or check around my house. My new medicine had become sitting on the phone, talking with her until I fell to sleep. Within that short period of time, Lynn had become more than just a good friend. She had become a night coach. Somehow through giving advice and useful tips and somehow calming me down, she became . . . a personal comforter. It amazed me how she never mind me calling so late and frequent. And all our innocent talks, despite her dark appearance, just reminded me of how much of a nice person she really was.

Tonight started unlike any other of the previous before. The evening had ended quite settling and peaceful as I decided to take the opportunity to catch up on some well-needed rest. Going to bed early, I decide not to call Lynn for anything. I brush my teeth and promise myself that I would investigate any action. "Grow up and stop being a wuss," as my father would say. I wonder if an intruder had been in my house any of those times when I was petrified under the covers. I might have been as good as dead and not even have known it. I'm not afraid of any man, but there was just something about the unknown that weakened my courage and spirit. Chills tingle my spine just thinking about it. Maybe it was from all the horror movies I watched as a teen. Whatever the case maybe, I found myself holding the phone, listening to Lynn's ringer as she answers the other end on the third ring.

"Hello?" Her unemotional voice instantly makes me feel better.

"Lynn . . . hey, I just called to say good night and to tell you that I'm going to prove to you that I'm really not a scaredy-cat but a brave handsome knight. And I promise that even if I turn snow white and my skeleton flees from my body, I will not call and trouble you with my troubles." I say anything just to hear her speak and or laugh.

"What? You are so silly! Brave words, young knight. We'll see." She snickers as my brain goes completely blank. "Just remember that if it's a ghost, not all of them are bad. Some are here to help us, others to warn us, and some are just lost souls who have forgotten their purpose or who won't go to the light," she explains as if she had been slaying vampire zombies for years.

"When did you become such an expert on the afterlife?" I question jokingly yet taking heed to every word.

"I'll just say this: I take interest in the unknown. Hey, I can't help that I'm a Treky and twilight zone head!" She brings about laughter in me, indicating that we were a match made in heaven.

"Wow . . . I guess you can always count on those old television shows to help you when you're in a dark alley by yourself," I state sarcastically, praying that she didn't really get all of her information from TV. "Well, I'm going to carry off and on with my wishful thinking. If I hear anything strange, I won't call. I hope it'll be nothing more than a mouse looking for a piece of cheese or a nice stack of blown papers."

"You poor, brave man." Lynn laughs at the thought of me hiding from a rodent. "But seriously, a sound is a sound, a delusion is a just a thought, and a full spectral apparatus is a government agent!"

I defend my cowardly manhood. "I didn't plan on playing out the whole masculine fearless thing, but I got things to prove tonight!"

"Hey, I don't judge, remember? If you want sleep, you're going to have to take it! You can do it. I have faith in you." Lynn boosted up my strength, convincing me that I was ready to for the night.

"Okay, okay, I'm leaving it alone. But watch who will come out triumphant tonight! You're not going to hear from this poor chap until tomorrow. I'm gonna get me some sleep tonight!" I talk trash, reassuring myself. "You're going to be proud of me."

"Let me get this straight, you're going to try not to call me? Aw, I'm going to miss our little late chats. I was sorta getting used to them." Her tone changes, hinting that my brave efforts were also disappointing on other levels. "Okay, well, you can still call me if you're up. You have my permission, noble knight."

"Okay, but I'm not making any promises. I have got to beat this thing. I'm dying for a good night's sleep!" I said, happy to have met such a person as Lynn.

"Don't worry, count sheep and close your eyes, and it will be morning before no time. Watch how refreshed you're going to feel!" She feeds me more encouragement.

"Thanks, Lynn. I'll call you when I wake up or sometime in the morning. Hey, maybe I'll wake you up."

"Maybe, okay, talk to you later. Good luck and sweet dreams."

"Sweet dreams, Lynn, bye." I hung up the phone quite confident that I would make it through the night without her.

Preparing myself mentally before turning in for the night, I head for my room. Passing one of many dingy and dirty walls of scuff marks, food, and handprints, a peculiar stain catches my eye. Examining it closely, I don't notice the bloody body writing the words "Don't look" in blood with his finger on the wall behind me. Rubbing my half sleep face in disgust of seeing the collection of dirt and grime up close, I continue up the stairs until reaching the second floor. At the top, I pause for a moment inside the darkness. Receiving that familiar feeling of it being more than just me and the house, I swiftly flick on the hall lights. Standing beside my linen closet, I check the rooms on the floor one last time for safety measures, ensuring that regardless of what I hear, I will know that it will be just the house settling and nothing more. "I will definitely be getting some peaceful shuteye tonight," I constantly remind myself, deciding to grab a quick cup of water from the bathroom sink. *No need to go all the way back down stairs,* I think to myself, entering into my grandparents' and mother's former huge remodeled bathroom that took nearly a year's worth of pay to fix up.

For a second or two, things appear just as I remember them as a child. Dim and dreary yet normally golden looking during the day, when the sun cascades through the thin tan curtains, the bathroom sat in its design of the golden age. An old blue tub stood against the far wall elegantly, ready to pounce on four catlike limbs. While a large-sized mirror that gave the impression that someone else was in the room when you open the bathroom door hung upright by crooked, hammered-in nails. Still finding humor in the effect, I remember great times growing up in the old house as the old version of memories fade away before my eyes, leaving me standing in the midst of a new toilet, sink, tub, and freshly painted walls. The old tub that my relatives hung onto for so long was replaced by the new tub 4000, which four people could actually sit in at the same time comfortably. The cracked hanging framed mirror, also gone, now was a wall of well spread flat square mirrors. My grandfather spent so many years working on and building this house; I couldn't just let it go that easily. I was quite honored and happy when they left the house to me; it was like having the responsibility of having to take care of the only piece of them left behind.

Thinking of all the good childhood memories I had in that house, my home, I lift my gray transparent plastic mug up from the counter of the bathroom sink. Filling it halfway full with water, I raise it to my lips. Still extremely tired, I clumsily bump my front teeth with the rim of the cup, instantly reminding me of times when I was young, brushing my teeth. In that room, Grandma always kept these large plastic root beer mugs that I loved; I would drink out of them all day and use it for swishing when I brushed my teeth. Early in the morning and at night, while my parents were out on business, Grandma would make me brush seemingly like forever. So I got smart and brushed in the window. Looking out, I would always see the next-door neighbor, Mrs. Betty, out strolling, admiring her yard. She was such a sweet old soul. Her yard was so peaceful and full of flowers during the days and nights of the spring, summer, and fall.

Sitting the empty mug down, I glance into the mirror at myself one last time before I go to bed. Catching a glimpse of what appears to be the reflection of the deceased Mrs. Betty with empty eye sockets, my heart plummets into what can only be described as nothingness. Turning in disbelief, seeing nothing behind me, my legs turn to butter as I see only my reflection standing in the mirror. "Okay, I must be hallucinating again. I need to get to bed. It's all in my head. It's all my imagination! It's all my imagination!" I repeated to myself, trying my hardest to calm my frail nerves. Flicking the light off with my hand, the swing sends my mug tumbling to the floor in a loud echoing sound. I dart out of my own bathroom, around the corner, and up the stairs, not even bothering to check the remaining room at all. Swiftly I dash around corners and into my room. I leap into my bed and turn on the black lamp that stood on my nightstand. Having been moving so fast throughout the house, I had misplaced the cordless and wasn't about to retrieve it.

Under the covers, my jittery nerves made peace among the sheets as I slowly poke my head out from the covers to hear and breathe. The pace of my heart finally slows to a moderate rate. I get the remote from under my pillow and power on the television. Also having the power to make me uncontrollably sleepy, the tube viewed next to absolutely nothing with the exception of an old classic cowboy Western. Those cowboy movies . . . As a kid, at a time when my grandparents had the house to themselves, they would have me over for popcorn, and I'd sit between them for hours, watching Westerns until we all fell asleep. Of course I was always the last to go.

I remember the time well as I began to drift inside my bed. Dreaming of my daily routines, a noise from the idiot box opens my eyes. But as I stare at the screen, at a cowboy and a native Indian drinking, I notice a little girl staring at me in the far corner of my room's doorway. In a gloomy maroon dress, she stood quietly within her near-colorless skin. Unable to speak, I couldn't recall the child's face or ever seeing her. Her features engraves themselves within me, her dark-encircled with black eyes peer endlessly between her frizzed, sandy tangled hair. The longer I gaze, the more unbearable and tattered she became. Small droplets of something liquid and chunky began to drip and pour from her hair followed by a downfall of maggots before me. Her body wrinkles and shrivels until her eyes, mouth, and ears implode in a splatter in blood.

About to faint, I awake from a dream as the wind of a small whisper saying "don't look" touches my ear, echoing inside my brain. I gaze ahead from my bed at an empty open doorway, a mild cold chill raises goose bumps upon my arms and neck. Getting up and closing my balcony door, not bothering to see what time it was, I click off the television and plop back down on the bed, listening to the clashing of faint nighttime sounds. *You can never have enough sleeping pills.* I smile, pulling out one of many bottles of over-the-counter sleep aids from under my mattress. Sliding two slick blue capsules down my throat without the assistance of liquid, I roll over and close my eyes. The clogged enclosed sounds of the house could be heard the most as an occasional vehicle or two was heard passing by. As my house began to shift and settle,

I find myself counting creaks and squeaks into the wee hours just like I did as a boy. I hated not being able to sleep for days and sometimes weeks at a time. It always left me nervously jittery with shaky hands or semi-delusional, just like the effects of too many sleeping pills, but I was used to it. I remember seeing the shadows in the dark most of the time throughout my life, and most of all . . . I remember the faces of people whom I believe I knew and saw from time to time when they were alive.

I close my eyes again and try to relax, the images of people become dreams and dreams become nightmares as I fought to stay asleep. What I see behind those eyelids of mine is pure hell, yet the sensation of my body and muscles being relaxed and resting for even the shortest of periods is pure bliss. Entering scenes while beginning to interact with my thoughts brought the nightmares forth; I try to wake up. Consciously awoke but still dreaming, it feels as though my sleep had a torturing hold on my body, forcing me back into slumber.

Instantly finding myself playing hide-and-seek with my small cousins in a more calm atmosphere, I feel alive and in complete happiness. Finally taken by my dream, I let out laughter of joy as a strange sound in the far distance startles me. Out of nowhere, a strong wind blows through my cut hair. Suffocating in the gust, I turn away looking toward some old looking woods. A bright-red balloon descends down behind some thick bushes and seemed to block me from the forest. Going after it, I separate from my family. Coming to the plot of greenery, I touch its thorns with my hands. Glancing back at my cousins waving and yelling something that I couldn't hear due to the intense winds, I return my focus to the balloon and crawl into the bushes of thickets underneath it. Coming to a small clear, I stand in awe at a spiral staircase that sunk into a humongous hole in the ground forever. My curiosity provokes me; I inch forward toward the creaking stairs. Placing my hand over the large wooden handrail, something whispers in my left ear. Maybe the voice of young child, perhaps a girl, it warns me again, repeating, "Don't look."

Sadly, I awake in my bed yet again, twisted and lost inside my sheets and blanket. "I'm never going to get any sleep!" I harp, hearing the sounds of footsteps creeping up my stairs and walking around my house. Flipping to the foot of the bed, I place my pillow over my head and ears. Tired of being awake and walking around delusional, half dead, I decided that this was it; I was going to nip this problem in the bud. Jolting from the mattress to my feet, still entangled in the sheets, I trip to the door. Groggy, I go back for some more pills to ensure my outage. Walking to the hall, I struggle with trying to forget or block the whispering voice of the small child remembered in my head. Also struggling with the lid of the medicine bottle, I use my teeth, popping the lid into the air. "One of these should do." I turn the corner to a little girl standing before me.

"Don't look," she whispers soft-spoken words that gently seep sharply into my ears; my instantly quaking hands spill the pills, scattering them about the floor. Her blue eyes twinkle, and her once-curly hair fell against her shoulders drenched in dirty water, just like in my dream.

Stooping down, crawling back, I snatch as many pills from the floor and swallow as many as I could, completely missing my mouth at times. The little girl disappears, leaving me wondering if I was still dreaming. I sat there for a moment, heart racing, nerves on end, clinching my chest. "I have to do this!" I smack the floor, stand, and continue walking. Empowering myself by keeping in mind that I've seen things all through life. The little girl is nothing compared to some of the other delusions I've encountered. Figuring I could handle any figment of my imagination, I neared my stairwell seeing nothing. Taking the first step down, the child appears a second time and flies through my body screaming. Down to the second level, silence could only be heard.

With no more sighting of the kid, I tiptoe to the bottom of the stairs, my foot reaches the bare bottom wooden floor. I hear bumping coming from around the corner and down the hall by the next set of stairs. Arming myself with a baseball bat from the far corner, I move toward the next flight of stairs quietly and swiftly; as the closer I got, the louder and weirder the noise grew. I slow until barely moving at all. So close that all I had to do was turn at the corner and pass the linen closet, and I'd be at the staircase. The child and bumping was both scary yet manageable, but now the sound of hissing, moaning, and foot shuffling was a lot bigger than my courage. Getting flashes of all the time, sounds from this stairwell has kept me up at night, I think about the delusions of people, places, creatures, and nightmares. Most of all, I think of Lynn, her smile, her eyes, and my promise. Maybe it was all in my head, or maybe I had been seeing things all along because of the lack of sleep and the effects of years and years of sleeping pills? Whatever the case, I know that I must face my fears at some time and take control of my life like a man.

With all the little courage that I had, I swat and knock against my fear-locked legs to get them moving again. Turning left, I inch past the linen closet and spin left again to face the stairs. Clearing the first four, I creep to the bottom. Walking to the stained glass of the front door, I look out of one of its glass designs. "Nothing outside." I sigh, relieved that I had conquered my fears and excited to call Lynn.

Still nervous, I make me a cup of water and head back to bed. With everything still in place, windows still locked, I head up the steps. Feeling triumphant and proud to see nothing that really causes a sound, I take one last glance back at the dark staircase to bask in glory. Instead of leading downward to the 1st floor, the staircase now, went on for what looked like forever, down into the darkness of vanishing and reappearing spirits. Two materialize before me, their clothes and skin hung from rotten bone of exposed muscle and spoiled organs. They reach out and move toward me as I collapse onto the floor in terror. Swinging my bat at the closet one, it swings completely through the entity. Losing grip of the handle, it flings off into the darkness. Frantically hustling to my tripping feet, I dash into the nearest guest room. Closing myself inside the large walk-in closet, I take the opportunity to gather myself together. Becoming disoriented from the pills I took, I slid my back to the wall among my collection of junk and boxes. My head starts to spin, sending me dizzily slumping to the floor. Confused and afraid of dying from an overdose; I pass out.

"Why did you look?" a small voice opens my eyes.

Blinking twice, I touch my face and pinch my cheek to make sure I was really alive. Now not for sure if the voice came from my head or a dream, I sit up. In total pitch black, my pupils expand to the fullest. I glance around seeing nothing, I hear something, and then . . .

"Why didn't you listen? I told you not to look," the little girl whispers behind me.

Spinning around, I leap backward as my heart drops into my feet at the sight of her. Her body glows, illuminating the closet, her crystal blue eyes sparkle against the shadows. Scuffed and riddled, her dress draped against her soaking wet body as a long sweater twist over her shoulders and arms, wrapping around her hands. Quietly, I watched her watch me. I stare into her eyes that hid behind the shadows of her hair and ask, "Who are you?"

"My name is Amy," she speaks back, rolling her eyes far into the back of her head.

Squirting some sort of liquid onto me from each corner of her eye, I jerk backward, sliding sideways across the wall. "Holy crap! I-I don't believe this, it responds! I have ghost!" I close my eyes tight and run out of the closet screaming as hangers and various hidden objects scratch and clung to my body, dragging along with clothes. Thinking, *Balcony!* I dash to it, deciding that it would probably be best to take my chances jumping off onto the ground to freedom. Reaching the balcony's closed curtains, frantically trying to pull them apart, the entire curtain rod falls to the floor as a strange glow and what I saw next stops me cold.

A man in a drenched suit floats to the balcony, straight through its guardrails, with a barefooted woman in jeans. Behind horrible moans and shrills, the dirty phantom man of at least six feet tall with wet black hair dripping around his face peer at me through one eye. His hands, enormous compared to mine, his nails, long, cracked, caked with grime and ooze. His southern clothes told the tale of a hard and brutal old farmer's life. Displaying anger and frustration toward whatever was bothering them, he and the woman begin to beat their hands against the balcony's door, smearing skin and filth in blood on the glass door in front of me.

The woman pauses beside the ghoul, turns at an angle, and, broken in posture, manages to maintain her balance as she then walks swiftly back and forth into the door face first. Shrill and shrieking, she frowns a barely seen face that hid beneath a head of muddy hair that stringed past her chest to her stomach.

The tired and quite dead man gazes at me hungrily under a deep-pitched moan. Looking down at his attire, I could see a thick clot of green drip over his neck and down his breast buttons as his hideous mouth bubbles a chunky foam. Instantly, my stomach churned in protest as the woman's right arm falls off. Spewing from the socket, it hung by the sleeve of her shirt. As they morph through the door at me, I recede to the place from whence I'd come—the closet.

"Where are you going now? You looked," the little girl speaks from behind the closed closet door as I reached for it.

"Stop talking to me!" I quickly lock the closet from the outside and run back into the hall. Hesitating to cross those stairs, I run and leap past the stairwell. Landing safely on the other side, faint screams of torture come from downstairs and get louder by the now-normal looking stairs. Thinking of another quick place to hide, I sneak into the guestroom on the left and lock the door. With the lights out, I hold my breath for as long as I can, hoping I wouldn't be discovered by the wandering troubled souls or; hopefully I could completely pass out before they kill me.

Something was different and special about this room though; it was the one I left the same as when my grandparents were here. Two firm twin beds perfectly pushed against each corner of the far walls. An old nightstand with two drawers separate the beds as an old black antique cross separate them both from the large and small dresser that sat catty-corner to each other across from them. A still, tasseled dresser and couch cover covered them and some of my family's precious belongings throughout time. Somehow I knew this room was a sanctuary, and in my heart, I felt that it would be safe.

I lean into the door, listening sharply with my hand still placed on the doorknob. As it began to slightly twist and turn in my sweating hand, I begin to quiver. Squeezing the knob with both hands, attempting to prevent it from turning, a moan and slow shuffling of feet stop at the door. A loud pounding sends my back bracing against the wall next to it in fright. Within the furious pounding and moaning, I check the locked door, as other voices join in the background. Repeating the actions, my brain unnerves as a horrendous scream causes me to scream and jump, and then silence fell across every floor of the house. Inside the quiet, I slid to the floor with not a clue of what to do, where to go, and what words to say about it. Like a beacon of hope, my grandmother's black antique cross stood out upon the wall. Debating if I should take it, I move to get up as sounds on the other side of the wall behind me moves also. Sliding back down to my rump, a brilliant light shines from under the bottom of the door. Slowly tilting sideways, I lower my head to see, suddenly hearing the sounds of wet clothes sliding across the floor at the same time. Having a light anxiety attack, I try to control my breathing. Sounding like a panting dog, I align with the crack under the door just as the intense light vanishes. With no sign of anything, I extend my arm to the brass doorknob. Cautiously, I peer into the far corners to see all I could; a head drops and splatters against the floor in front of me. The familiar split and cracked face peers at me with innocence; it was the head of the little girl.

"Why are you hiding?" With her ear to the floor, head half smashed, and eyes still open, she speaks from a puddle of blood and brain tissue. "Isn't this what you wanted? You can't hide from them. They're going to find you." She cleverly grins into my scared, dilated pupil.

Scuffling back up against the wall, it appears even darker inside the room. "This is insane! What do they want?" I think of a way to get away from the strange. "Wait a second, let me think! Okay, in all the rooms they were in, it was pretty dark . . . maybe turning on the lights will change my odds?" I speak to myself, hearing footsteps of a small child run away in laughter. Inside the silence, I turn on the bedroom lights, quickly opened the door, and stretched my long skinny arm from the doorway to the light panel, flicking on the hall lights. Slamming the door, I wipe beads of sweat from my head. Thankful for my new idea and extremely exhausted, I nearly doze off on my feet, opening my eyes to over thirty free roaming souls standing quietly around me, awaiting my next move. Translating their decomposed looks and snarls into the word "run," I smash through the bedroom door and dashed for the steps to upstairs.

"You shouldn't have looked." The little girl pops up as I run through her.

"I didn't mean to!" I yell in my own defense. Kicking the cordless out in front of me, I jump, roll, and pick up the phone. Shaking dirt and dust from my clothes, I make it to the other end of the hall. Cutting the corner, I break up the stairs, stumbling at the very top, and run off at full speed. Jumping as high as I can, I grab hold of the pull string to the attic, pulling its heavy staircase down into my ribs on top of me. "Shit! What am I doing? What am I doing? Losing my freaking mind! Okay . . ." I crawl out in the upmost pain, unable to figure out why these ghosts were haunting me. To me, checking out a strange sound in your house wasn't a suitable reason to kill or haunt someone. And what were their origins? Where did they come from? My mind surely weren't creating these. There was only one person alive who could possibly help me at this time, and it was Lynn. About to eat my words and promise, I crawl up into the small attic space and dial her number in desperation as I notice the front panel didn't light up and the back of the phone was gutted out.

Listening to the sound of small pieces of something crumbling and hitting the floor, the lights turn out; as from somewhere in the house, the tiny voice of the little girl ask, "Is this what you're looking for? I don't know what happened to your little machine."

Loosing air and nearly every ounce of my sanity, I try to escape through the windows to learn that they were sealed tight and impenetrable by some supernatural force. Knocking down boxes, I ramble through the dark, looking for anything useful. Arming myself with a rubber gripped hammer, I break a long wooden leg off the night stand. Strolling around, I pray that Grandma kept a container of holy water, bible, wooden steak or something as the girl appears in front of me.

"What are you going to do now? You looked . . . and now they're going to find you." She stood in a luminous glow, hovering millimeters above the floor.

"What does that even mean? What am I going to do now? I . . . I'm going to live and get out of this mad house! Look, okay . . . I'm not afraid of you anymore. I believe . . . you are a figment of my imagination, with your gory head and . . . and little cute baby eyes, yeah, I said it! You're in my head! You can't touch me. It's the other ones I'm not so sure of!"

"You're so sure of yourself." The small child levitates toward me laughing. "There's only one way to escape. I could help you." She devilishly smiles, dripping thick red clots from her ears and mouth.

"Help me? You broke my phone! Who are you? What's happened to my house?" I whisper as she vanishes. Leaving me confused in silence, I hear the cries of men, women, and children coming. Then from all around me, the sounds transfer into the confined space. A gust of wind and noise wrap around the small room, blowing paper and items into the darkness around me. Seeing manifesting shadows and total blackness, the howls and screams increase as the attic door falls open and the sound of walking emit from them, buckling my knees. As some of the voices upon me became the mere sounds of loud chatter, the moonlight helps to cast a black silhouette of a ghostly figure walking in my direction. The voice of a woman caresses my eardrum from behind as I fell through the ceiling of my third-floor bathroom. Crashing into the tub, I crack my temple on the side of its rim. Taking the pain, I crawl out of the wood, dirt, and debris. Still carrying the table leg and hammer, I hurry to my bedroom. As blood pour from my head, I pay no attention. Tightly gripping the hammer like the Almighty Thor, I twist and launch it wildly from my hands. Smashing into the balcony door, it busts a hole in the glass, cracking the door in hundreds of directions. I slide across the floor and swing the table leg, completely shattering the remains of the glass door. I break through. Running with next to no strength at all, I dive over the railing. Grabbing a secure hold of the rail of the second-floor balcony, I could feel my arm come out its socket and snap back in place. Gripping the old wooden rail firmly with my fingers, sharp, cracked chips of old lead-based paint and splinters stab and fill my hand. I lose grip, believing I have fallen to my death; life flashes before me as my upper body smashes through the rail of the patio. Breaking my fall, I snap into the uncut tall grass of my backyard.

Lifting an arm, the pain in my back suggested that it was broken somewhere. Wiggling my toes and each limb slowly, I roll over and rise to my feet, bent and hunched. In so much hurt and unable to recall who or where I was, I look at the sky and suddenly remember those hellish faces in my house. Looking at the dirt, bloodstains, and grass on my shoulder, I march to the front of my building.

"You can't hide. You need my help. They're coming for you," the little girl's voice bellows from out of the shadows behind me.

"Shut up! And leave me alone!" I shout brainlessly before scouring about the patch of bushes that grew around the front porch. Among the soil and night crawlers, I snatch my extra set of car keys. Standing, I quickly turn to run, colliding into Lynn; we both fall back to the ground from the impact.

"Ouch, I think you broke my nose?" Lynn sat up, covering her tearing face. "Dang, you gotta hard head, oh my gosh!" She maintains a sense of humor and slaps me on the sore shoulder.

"Lynn, what are you doing here? You have to leave!" I roll and stood one more time, hoping it would be the last. "We have to leave, Lynn, now."

"What's going on? I came over because I couldn't sleep! I wanted to see you. Look at your face . . . You're a mess. What happened? You've been fighting? Oh my gosh . . . you . . . you murdered someone? You killed someone?" She slips her purse down from her shoulders and began beating me with it.

"No, wait! Stop! Wait a second! Wait!" I grab both her arms. "Wait, Lynn, no! It's not like that! Look, maybe you need to come stay with me. Lynn, you were right all along. Ghosts are chasing me in my own house. They're deliberately scaring the shit out of me or trying to kill me one or the other! I dunno, maybe they want my soul or something. Lynn, I don't know what to do."

"What? You're crazy. There's nothing after you! Look at you, you're exhausted, and you just need some sleep. We both do. You look like you fell off a bike or something. I was just joking with you all those times, Will, this is serious."

"No, look, I'm serious, there are . . ."

"No, you look. I came all the way over here so we could sleep together! In other words, I'm ready to sleep, see?" As her straight hair blew in the gentle breeze and her eyes sparkle under the stars, she opens a long black leather jacket to the sight of smooth skin and sexy red lingerie.

"Wow . . . that's not even your color." For a brief moment, I forget about all my troubles. "You are so beautiful . . . but . . . entirely . . . wrong this time!" I interrupted myself as she sort of unfroze in place. "Look, let me explain! There's a little girl who keeps popping up all over my house, and right after she vanishes . . . like a horde of screaming evil comes out chasing and scaring me! And when they leave, the little girl comes out and vice versa, versa vice, whatever, you get the picture! Anyway, I did something I don't know, and it's their turn! Do you understand, Lynn? It's . . ." I pause as Lynn just gazes into my eyes in some sort of possessed daze or spell. Throwing my hand back to smack some reality into her, she speaks.

"You really think I look beautiful?" She gives me a weird look as I pull her by the arm and point to the house of spirits morphing through the walls to outside.

"Yes, I think you're very beautiful. Now let's go!" I run to my car and get in on the driver's side, starting it right up for the first time in life. Unable to open the jammed passenger door, I roll down the windows as Lynn hops through the window into the backseat. I sped off with the dead walking behind us.

"What did you do? What's happening?" Lynn leans between the front seats. "You summoned the dead?"

"I don't know, Lynn. I don't get it. This is what I get for facing my fears, I guess." I swerve back and forth across the yellow line of the road, just missing passing cars. "All I did was check the noise around the house and on my stairs, and spirits from beyond have been coming after me ever since! You tell me what's . . ."

"Where are you going now?" The glowing body of the little girl appears in the passenger seat next to me. "You just don't understand, do you?" She asks as I and Lynn both scream. Swerving off the road, the car flips into a large ditch and tumbles just short of the woods. Emerging from the heap of scattered metal and parts, I fall to the ground.

"Are you okay? Come on get up!" I hear Lynn shouting behind me. Turning my head, I could still see Lynn trapped in the backseat. "Forget about me. Look! They're coming!" she yells, breaking out the window so she could escape. Pushing myself up, I hobble over to the brutally slain automobile to her. Hideous screams bellow out from all around as Lynn successfully makes it halfway out the bent, folded frame window. "They're coming!" She kicks and wiggles. "I hate these hips! Damn, their getting closer!"

"Lynn!" I grab her arm and try to pull her free.

"They're here! It's too late! They're too close! Wha-what are they saying?" she whispers and suddenly cease in movement at the overwhelming sight of hundreds of dead people coming toward us from afar.

"Come on, get out! Free yourself!" I yell, climbing on the top of the car, pulling upward on her body. "Swivel your body!"

"I'm stuck. You go. I don't think they're after me, Will. I won't give up. You go!" Lynn smiles with hope as her eyes tell deeply her belief in death.

"No, I won't just leave you here! I'll just have to die!" I cry out for the only friend I have.

"I know, but one of us has to live to stop them! They're coming for you! It might not end with you. You gotta let go! Hurry!" She pushes me off the car. Unbalanced, I fall upside down into the metal. Cut and bruised, I kiss her on the lips. "Go!" She urged me onward one last time as I ran off into the woods, leaving her behind. Hopeless, she cries out above the horrible screams. As a terrible yell follows, the wind whispers "run" behind me.

Far away from the sounds, I ran until stopping so that I too could weep. On a tree stump, I thought about work, my house, and my stupid life; but most of all, I thought about Lynn. *How could I just leave her there alone?* I repeated over and over again, pouring tears and blood onto my arms. *What if this was all a test?* I thought as a familiar glow catches me by surprise.

"You cannot defeat them because you do not choose to. All they want in exchange for you seeing them is your one and only. Yep, they want your soul. They will keep coming and coming until the right time . . . and find you. Oh, look, their coming now. Wonder what they want? You can either take my help or wait to talk to them, your choice." The little girl floats down in front of me and peers around for the approaching dead.

"Who are you? Why are you helping me?" I cried out, scared and out of ideas.

"You're almost out of time. Here they come!" She smiles.

"Okay, quickly, how do I destroy them? What do I need to do?" Fresh out of ideals, I sit up, talking to the ghost who made contact with me all along.

"You need to call on a bigger spirit, but first you must accept him into this world." Her eyes begin to twitch and roll.

"Call on a bigger spirit? Who? What? Will it work? Will it all go away?" I ask as the winds began to blow, and the screaming roaming ghosts come into view.

"We haven't the time. I am an angel. Do you welcome me into this world? You have to believe that I am the only one who can help you, then your troubles will be freed!" The child explains up close as faint screams of Lynn cripple my heart. "Sounds like they have your friend already. Do you believe and welcome me? Do you accept me into your world as your true shepherd? I could be a savior, you choose. Hmmph . . . maybe I could get my wings?" She hinted, slightly turning her head, grinning in an optimistic expression. I pan around at the army of people nearing. About now, in my mind, Lynn was a goner as I swear to still hear traces of her somewhere inside the noisy distance.

"They won't hurt you! Look, I'm still alive. I'm right here! They're trying to warn you! They've been trying to tell you the whole time . . ." Lynn waves and yells to me, running through the ghastly spirits. Having been shown the truth, the ghosts helped her out of the car before it exploded, directing her to her friend, me, to deliver their message. "She's evil! She's the evil one, not them. Run! Don't listen to her! Run!"

So far away, I hear the souls killing her as I took the hand of the small child, realizing that she was the missing little girl I saw in the newspaper that had attached itself to my foot.

"Nooo!" the spirits shriek around us in a twirl of wind, light, smoke, and leaves, disappearing in whirls around the little girl.

Blowing me backward, I watch the child's frail body transform into a gigantic scaly form. Her head swell with horns, and the muscles in her back give birth to a set of claw-tipped wings. "Promise fulfilled and invitation accepted."

"Wait . . . a demon, what are you, angel or demon?" I ask a bit too late for an answer. Scooting away on my back, I peer up at the sheer mass of the creature above. Its massive eyes glow red of intense fire as its muscular body reek of brimstone, ashes and death. Along with a face design of part feline and half gremlin, the length of its teeth and nails frightened me to death, reminding me of the length of my entire living room.

"Who did you ask for help from, your FATHER? Who did you ask to take away your problems, an angel? Isn't a demon just a fallen angel?" The monster laughs and, in a loud thunderous crack, pulls its grungy, scaled wings tight against its body.

Thinking about the question, I should have called on GOD from the start. HE would have fixed everything without the runarounds and complications. "I asked you for your help. Which angel are you?" I rethink my own words, putting everything together inside my mind. Looking upward, I observe up close, every description of Satan that I've ever read about, saw, or heard about. "You lied to me. You tricked me. You liar!"

"Oh ye of little faith." The demon erupts in a demonic laughter, fully expanding its wings to what seem to be miles apart. Blowing me flat to the ground with a mighty flap, it takes flight upward into the air and disappears into the morning sky.

I see Lynn running toward me, calling my name under the falling leaves. I run to her, shouting out her name with every ounce of breath I have. We clearly see each other between the spread of trees. Once again, I am reenergized by her smile; in return, I smile back, laughing. Happy to see her as she is to see me, we hold out our arms to embrace. "I lo . . ." My arms spread to wrap warmly around her as blood splashes against her face. She glances up at me and I down at her; I follow circles of blood down the middle of her breast and drips on her stomach down to her legs. As a feeling of weightlessness overcomes my body; Lynn watches me in terror as I am lifted into the air by the talons of claws wedged deep inside me from behind. Having made a deal for my soul, the demon whisks me away and my spirit, to love life and memories forever. Inside the dark realms of hell I go to burn.

LANDING 6

THE CLIMB

As a small picture of a clean-shaven man and his two sons dangle from the rearview mirror of an old '80s Chevy truck, admiring the photo on his keychain, Jake Lawnmeyer, a proud father of two sons, adjusts his rearview mirror and grins at the vehicle behind him. The car rides his bumper, yet he continues at the same pace. The car blows its horn twice; speeding around him, it continues past. "Nowhere to go in no time fast." He shakes his head at the very thought of impatient people. Yet anxious to see his two sons, the proud father returns his focus on the road and returning home from a hard day's work of building houses.

Lakeside View, the name of the small-knit community in which Jake enters and resides. It was a small working-class neighborhood of mixed races, all struggling together to better the lives of themselves and their youth.

Pulling onto the main road leading to his street, Jake licks three fingers and slicks down his thick brows as he drives past an attractive-looking woman. Sitting up straight, he strokes back his hair and rubs his scruffy face, eyeing the unknown woman in his side mirrors. "Now she's a babe. Wow!" He turns up the jazz on the radio and soaks up the rest of the heavenly sunlight that suddenly high beams across his face and into his eyes, blinding him. "Oh shi—" Unable to finish his curse word, he swerves around a vibrant teenager who tries to zoom out on a ten-speed from in between two parked cars. "Kids," Jake sighs, just missing the young boy by inches. Pulling the sun visor fully down, he continues on to his house. Hitting a pothole, his pop can jumps out of the interior cup holder and spills onto the right side of his blue jeans, drenching his pocket and crotch area. Cursing like a sailor, he grabs a nearby napkin and soaks up some of the soda. Glancing at the small photo of his boys, he smiles over the misfortune and hits another pothole, spilling the entirety of his drink onto himself.

Finally making it home, Jake cruises past his house and slows in the driveway; passing his two bushy-browed sons sitting on the curb, he pulls into the garage. His sons, Jake II and Julius, two of a kind, usually arose to their feet excitedly to see their dad. But today was different; only one stood. Standing up on his silver scooter, the oldest son rolls to the rusted and dirty garage door. His medium-length dark-brown hair fell scraggily around his head and pale face. Wearing an old used pair of blue jeans and a red T-shirt with an emblem of a skull on its chest, Little Jake, thirteen years of age, greets his father as he steps out of the garage. "Dad!"

"Hey, Junior! I couldn't wait to see you guys today!" Jake walks over to his oldest son and rubs the top of his head. "Oh-uh, what's wrong with Julius?" Holding his large lunch box in one hand, he speaks low. Then placing an arm around his son, he glances a few feet away at Julius sitting on the curb, frowning with his arms folded.

"Well, Dad . . . I think he's a little upset today. The kids at school and around the neighborhood have been teasing him all day. Rough times, you know," Little Jake articulates. "I think he wants to ask you something, again."

"Ooh, I see . . ." His father looks at him and grins, always expecting a question. Looking at Julius on the curb in front of the house with his head down, Jake rest his hands on his waist, peers down at the ground, and lifts his head, imagining all the possible things that his seven-year-old son could have to ask him, only coming up with one.

Julius, slightly more colorful in tone than his brother, in blue jean shorts and a white T-shirt, sat motionlessly. Under his short-cut sandy top and light freckles, a drooping sad face holding and overhung bottom lip began to form. Even when attempting to be tricked by being offered a surprise by his father, Julius rests his head on his hands without budging.

"Hey, champ, what's up? What's the problem?" Jake, not getting an answer, squats next to his youngest to comfort him. Putting his arm around his son, Jake squeezes him close and asks again, still receiving no response. Waiting a few seconds, he places his heavy hand on the back of Julius's neck and tries again with a little more authority. "Julius, what happened? If you don't talk, how will I know what's wrong? Now come on, son, tell Dad what's going on." He sits as a nice breeze relaxes his tired body.

"Old Man Mountain, Dad!" A gloomy statement without a lot of details utters from Julius's mouth. "All the kids are climbing it today except for us! Everyone's climbed it but us! You always say no! I've been a good boy, I clean my room and everything, but you still say no!" The little boy pouts, holding a small collection of teardrops layered along the base of his eyes.

"Dad, he's right, half of the whole school's been up there without their parents," Little Jake interrupts before their father could respond.

"Junior, please! Julius, I've explained this hundreds of . . . Look, guys, I know how bad you boys want to go up there on that hill, but it's just too dangerous. Besides . . . I keep telling you, there's nothing even up there? It isn't even a real mountain! My father warned us about going when I was a child. People have had accidents plenty of times up there on that hill, fellas, even before I got here! I don't trust it, and I don't have time for any doctor bills! I think it's just a bad idea. It's just a matter of time before something goes wrong or someone gets seriously hurt. So I'm afraid I have to say no. No! Guys, it's for your best interest and mine." Jake shakes his head and hugs them both.

"But, Dad, your son's been getting teased all day at school. He's only your youngest son." Little Jake overdramatically tries to sway his father. "Your last son."

"Hey, I can always adopt! Junior, I said no. I'm your dad and I love you two. I'm going in the house to change, and when I come out, we're going to go do something together." Jake removes his arms from around them and heads to the front door of the house. Long the way, he eyes a skipping little girl with a bright red bow on her head, heading to the mountain with her friends.

"Even girls are going, Dad!" Julius wines loudly before his father walks out of range.

"No!" Jake smoothly answers before opening and entering the screen door. "Eh, did the bug man come yet?"

"In the basement, Father," Little Jake sarcastically answers, returning to the curb to his brother disappointingly.

"We never get to do anything fun, and he's always at work!" Julius hears the screen door slam behind him.

Pausing in the inside of the front door, Jake laughs off the semi-hurtful comment of his son. Continuing to his bedroom, he grabs the mail off the living room shelf. Shuffling through the small stack of bills, a small explosion shakes the house. The basement door flies open, scaring him half to death.

"Uh, sorry, Jake, didn't mean to scare ya. Just doing my job, doing my job!" A tall, jolly, popped bellied, insect inspection man emerges from an expanding cloud of insecticide. Dressed in a tan company uniform, shin guards, knee and elbow pads, and some sort of double tank strapped to his back, Ernie the bug man, wipes away a thick layer of bug spray from his goggles. "I just laid a couple of 7.1s in that baby, and they just hatched! The death toll of the enemy infestation will be enormous, and as for any survivors? Let's just say . . . that I shouldn't be seeing ya for many years to come, buddy! Ha, ha, ha!" Ernie laughs in a deep, hefty voice, coughing and gagging. Behind a face covered in dirt, he smiles and slaps Jake on the shoulder, nearly bringing him to his knees.

"Ernie, think you used enough? And why aren't you using your mask?" Jake steps back, covering his mouth with his shirt as the cloud of insecticide fill the hall. "Is this hazardous? Should we be breathing this in, Ernie? Jesus Christ, Ernie, my sons have to walk through here!" He fans the fumes away and slams the basement door.

"Normally, it would be deadly, but since you have children, I used a standard fifty-thousand-dielectric-strength fogger with advance hypoallergenic technology. Give it two hours, all right, maybe ten?" Ernie places his goggles upon his hat, revealing a small pair of black framed, thick-lens glasses.

"Ten hours, Ernie? How much, how much is this costing me? If any things broken, I'm not paying you, Ernie! I mean it. I want a full refund."

"Bug men's honor, I swear."

"Bug people don't have honor. Ernie. How much?"

"A million dollars?" Ernie, large in size with a head to match, tugs on his small well-snugged company cap and squints at Jake. "Okay, we'll make it a square bill for you."

"A hundred it is, and it better be worth every penny. And use your mask, Ernie, geesh!" Jake coughs and wheezes back to the front door. "Thanks a lot."

"Anytime. It means a lot when a customer appreciates the civil duties of a professional elimination management science engineer." Ernie wipes what could be a single tear from the side of his scratched glasses. Attached to his tank by a long hose; he slides a nozzle attached to some sort of insecticide spray bottle into a holster on his hip like an old rusty cowboy. "Hey, I'm in the backyard. Mouse didn't want to block your driveway."

"Really, Ernie? Is that what they're really calling you guys these days? An elimination manager . . . whatever? I was wondering why I didn't see the bug mobile. Wait, why didn't you just park on the street or in the driveway?" Jake props open the front door to air out the house, then heads for the back. "There's not even a driveway in the back of my house, and now that I think about it, there's not even a street? You guys just drove across my lawn?"

"No, not just yours. We started from Fifth Street. Hey, I forgot to tell you. We added some modifications to the Bug Mobile too. It's built like a tank now! Hey, why the look, ol' pal?" Ernie pauses for a moment and thinks, "Oh, the yard. It's legal. We had the lights and siren on! It's the best method of attack! It was the perfect hit on the target! You see, in this profession—and as a sworn veteran of the NPCA . . . the uh . . . National Pest Control Association—you never know when you might need to run, flee, or regroup to your vehicle. So it must always be close. We must always be one. Article: 328, Section 13, can't be breaking code number 55.286294,10, ya know." the large exterminator proudly explains, dusting off loose dirt and bug carcasses from his broad shoulders. His walkie-talkie goes off; Ernie turns it down and lifts it to his ear. "2-4 Mouse. Wha . . . the subject was sighted advancing northward? Copy that! See, the plague begins to spread, my friend." He glances sternly at Jake. "Uhhh, yes, target was destroyed. The hen house is clear. I repeat, the chicken coup is clean, Roger!" Ernie places the radio back on his belt. Standing up straight, arching his back, his flabby chest stuck out like a brave brawler. Cracking his neck, he adjusts his goggles that held his small company ball cap even tighter upon his head as a small plastic mask hung securely close to his neck. A large utility belt filled with bombs, pellets, gadgets, traps, and other useful things that trick and poison insects and rodents alike-wraps around his chest and waist. Two large tanks with pictures of a skull and crossbones stuck to his pack, both attached to long hoses that ran into the triggers of the nozzles that sat on the tops of cylinders, which rested in individual holsters on his hips. In scuffed work boots, pads, and bright-yellow-looking dish washing gloves, the insect warrior stands like the last superhero. "It's been a pleasure serving you, Jake. Now unfortunately, I must depart from this site. Got a class 4 activity going on in Delhi. I hear these little buggies are monstrous too." Ernie approaches the back doorway behind Jake.

"Uh, yeah . . . right, that serious humph?" Jake looks up at the odd six-foot-ten-tall man of whom he once attended high school with. Being the only person of a reasonable price that he could get to fix the spider and cricket problem in the basement, Jake writes out a check and hands it to him. "Thanks, Ernie. I appreciate it. Tell Mouse I said hello, and I hope to see him at Al's next poker game. He beats the socks off of me every time, but you tell him the next beating's on me!" Jake holds open the door, letting Ernie out with the fumes.

"Sure thing, Jake." The spray man walks to his van and slides open the side door. Taking off his gloves and tank pack, Ernie rubs his plump fingers through his sweaty, curly dark-brown hair and disappears into the vehicle, slamming the door behind him.

Waving goodbye to his old odd friend, Jake shakes his head and grinds his teeth as he watches his lawn kick up in shreds from behind the large wheels of the van. Watching the vehicle leave, he follows the tire tracks with his eyes, slams the back door, and locks it, still determined to have a good day away from work. Before going to his bedroom, he hears commotion; his sons were fussing with other children outside, in front of the house. Undoing his tie and top buttons of his favorite light-brown work shirt, he rushes to the screen door to make sure there wasn't a serious problem.

"If my dad says that he can't go, then it's cool, Cyntica. Who cares? It's not even a big deal! Who wants to climb that stupid hill anyway? It's not even a big deal!" Little Jake defends his angered little brother as a few of the local kids tease Jake's sons in front of their own house.

"You really want to climb that stupid hill, that bad don't cha?" said Mike, one of the tallest, coolest kids in the twelfth grade, all starring in girls' honor and bullying bullies.

"Ah-ha!" And outweighing most kids his age, Cyntica, a local troublemaker also known for pounding on innocent children, points his chunky finger deep into Little Jake's chest, mugging his little brother with the other hand at the same time. "Kids who don't climb Old Man Mountain are little babies in diapers, and they smell like you!" He makes a mean, frowning face similar to that of a bulldog.

"Leave them alone, Cyntica! Let's go. Let's just climb the stupid thing!" comments Mindy, a freckle-faced, black haired, half Asian girl with ponytails. In a yellow T-shirt and cuffed blue capris, Jake couldn't break eye contact with her, as the two bullies cosigned beside her, interrupting his day dream.

"Babies!" harps Cyntica.

"They're not babies! Leave them alone!" Raheem Jackson, preferably called Rah, a very smart, respectful friendly kid, and also Julius's best friend, picks his small fro and shouts, slowly stepping in front of Mike and Cyntica. Rah, dark skinned, small in size and height and dressed in a basketball t-shirt and jeans, bravely defends his friends.

"And what are you going to do about it? Are you with him or with us, Rah?" Cyntica's face turns red under the backward cap that stretched around his round head.

"It's them or us." Lil Ricky, a very short, spiky, mused-headed miniature version of the bully, steps in as the others began to walk away.

"Hey, I hope your pop changes his mind, fellas! If not, it's okay. He'll come around . . . they all do. Catch ya on the court, Little Jake!" Mike, feeling compassion for the two, tries to make them feel better. "It took some time before my parents let me go up there too. Come on, you two, before I take you back home!" he strokes his hair and yells at Cyntica and Lil Ricky in front of the brothers and winks.

"Lucky!" Cyntica looks back, pops his knuckles, and catches up to the others as Lil Ricky shuffles behind him.

"See you guys later, don't worry about them. Peace." Rah, not really wanting to leave his two close friends for the event of a lifetime, sadly stares back and drops his round, normally happy, baby face, low, before walking away.

"Cyntica and Lil Ricky . . . Losers!" replies Little Jake kicking into the wind, as the group of kids leave. Sitting down on the curb beside his brother after school, they watch small groups and lone children of the neighborhood march past up the street, traveling to the small mountain.

As the bug guy's insect mobile zooms up the street, flashing bright-yellow lights, and sounding a bizarre pre-programmed siren that played a snippet of a famous 1969 song by Creedence Clearwater, still behind the screen door, Jake, the boy's father, witnesses the whole altercation and thinks about the next to none time that he's spent with these great sons and their independent ideals of fun compared to his. Remembering another time and another place when he was a young boy asking his mother and father if he could climb the mountain, Jake stares through the screen until it becomes invisible.

"It's not even a mountain. It's a piece of rock! I'm not taking any son of mine to the hospital for falling off a rock!" Jake's father would always end his speeches about the subject as his mother would always finish in a promising "No!" Jake remembers storming out of the living room and out of the house, spilling his emotions and feelings onto the doorstep. Sadly watching packs of children hike up the street to the mountain, he vividly recalls hearing them laugh and play along. Snapping out of the short remembrance, Jake quickly takes off to his room and puts on his walking sneakers. Rolling up his sleeves, he changes watches and puts on his old camping watch from the good old boy scout days. Since he probably was going to end up dirty and had already spilled pop on his pants, he kept them on. Snatching up a small compact bag and his sons' school bags, he grabs face towels, flashlights, and batteries. Then going to the kitchen, he takes chips, bottled water, and stuffs them into the school bags. Snapping the daily newspaper from the coffee table, Jake exits the house and locks the door behind him. Turning to face the sadness from the unadventured eyes of his beloved children, Jake stands tall, placing both hands upon his belt and belches out a nonchalant, manly voice, "Tough life, huh, boys? Well, since you're all down and out on the curb, guess I'll . . . go climb the Old Man Mountain by myself? Know any brave-hearted explorers who care to join me?"

"Dad? Yes!" the boys cheer and swarm around their father as he catches them in his arms. Beginning to walk in the direction of the small mountain, he hands them their book bags.

Being the last group of people journeying to the mountain that day, the middle-aged father and his two sons slowly strutted up the street, talking, joking, and catching up on lost times.

"Hey, Dad, do you ever miss Mom?" Julius watches an old man helping his wife into a car.

"Sometimes," Jake calmly answers, shaking around three pebbles that he picked from the ground in his hand. He looks down at his son. "Sons . . . you know I would never talk bad about your mother, ever. Your mother once was an awesome woman, but she has decided on living her life the way she feels is right for her, and that doesn't include me anymore," he adds, noticing his eldest, facial expression slightly change.

"She's worse than you. She doesn't even have time to call us. She doesn't care about us anyway. She's way busier and hasn't even come to see us yet! It's almost been two years! She doesn't miss us. I can see why you two hated each other." Little Jake kicks dirt as they walk, leaving his father silent, nonresponsive, and sensitive to the statement.

"Wait . . . now hold on one second here, guys. Look, I know that me and your mom had our differences, but we never hated each other, okay?" Jake stops and kneels down. "That's the first thing, now two. Listen, I know we can both be some lousy parents at times and sometimes for long periods of time but . . . we're humans. We all make mistakes, and it takes time to even see it and to learn from it sometimes. But . . . but most importantly, I love you, and even though it might not seem or feel like it right now, whenever you cross paths, I'm pretty sure your mom will tell you the same. And just think, you could be worse off if I ever told you the truth."

"What truth, Dad?" Julius's eyes widen as he listens closely.

"Well, since we're on this trip and you're of age now, guess it's time that I told you about me and your mom . . . we're really . . . well . . . aliens." Jake ends the conversation, tickling his shocked sons as they began laughing and playing up the broken sidewalk.

A few blocks and strip of housing made the walk even more enjoyable as the scenic view provided life, beauty, and memories during the times they weren't talking. The street crawled up into a crooked hill and then gradually barreled down to a slanted intersection at the base of a small mountain. Two neighboring streets pitchforked in front of the giant hill as the main street continued past it. A few more blocks of hiking along with a little muscle power set the father and sons down the street from their climb as they sip on waters and glance at one another one last time in preparation before proceeding. At the intersection, the three overlooked the architecture from a distance, amazed by the landscaping of man and how their neighborhood was carved into and around a small mountain. As the road ended and split into three different directions, a light flow of traffic pass by around them. Remains of a small crumbling brick wall borders the front of the mountain as housing line its sides and sit on its top like a hat. Bushes, weeds, and tree limbs litter the hillside as trees of all sizes sprout and bloom in all directions off the body of the mountain. Glancing down the street, their eyes follow the contours of the mountain and admire the life it supports as birds soar high above it under the passing sun.

It was a beautiful late afternoon and indeed a nice time to choose to go climbing; the two brothers agreed, crossing the street proudly with their father. Stepping onto the concrete of the dry and cracked sidewalk, they approach the three-foot wall. At the foot of the mountain, sight of large collapsed rocks and sliding shrubbery began to give them some doubts. Small avalanches of loose rock and dirt tumble continuously to the bottom as Jake scans the area for a suitable path of some sort to start upward. Bushes and trees cover the mountain's base as the three stare at the job ahead. Stepping and climbing over the wall, they hear the laughter of children coming from somewhere along the mountain.

"Dad, come on, Dad! We gotta hurry!" Julius quickly picks up a stick. Diving into the thickets, his father and older brother could hear him slashing away stems and leaves.

"Julius, wait, no! Come on, son!" Jake yells as Little Jake follows his brother. "Hey!" Jake burst through the spiny and stinging branches to catch up to his sons. Young rubbery to old and hard branches whips across his body and face, leaving welts and scratches on his skin. "Julius!" Jake calls out, tripping over sliding rocks and staggering through bushes on the slope, hoping to come to a clear.

"Dad, look!" Julius stands, pointing at a path as his dad and brother appear behind him.

"Steps? They look old," Little Jake mutters, pulling twigs and plants from out his hair and clothes.

"Stairs? Julius, I can see they're stairs, but that's no excuse for you to go running off like that! You could have gotten seriously injured out here, Julius . . ." Jake calms, picking leaves and small vines from the inside of his clothes as well. Taking off one shoe, he flips it over, dropping out tiny stones. "We don't do things like that. We have to always stick together, son. It doesn't matter how long it takes. We'll get there eventually, okay?"

"Okay, sorry, Dad," Julius apologizes, looking up at his father, whom he knew was trying so hard to make them happy.

"And no second or third times either? The thought of one of you missing scares the crap outta me!" Jake holds his chest, smiles, and rubs Julius's sandy blond head. "Deal?"

"Deal, Dad!" Julius agrees as Little Jake's mouth drops open.

"What? Come on! He got a deal . . . and that's all? There is no way you would have let me off that easily, Dad! You would have clobbered me!" Little Jake groans to his father.

"No, I would have rung your neck, then I would have clobbered ya!" Jake corrects him as they began to walk up the stairs. "You're the oldest?"

"You're getting soft, Dad." Little Jake snickers, strolling behind them.

The stairs, wide and deteriorating, sunk into the ground before them. The vanishing path constructed of concrete and bricks of old fossil led farther up into the sloping wilderness. Various types of birds and insects could be heard from unseen places all around the party of three as they turn to the far sound of cars, spotting the street and wall at the bottom of the mountain below them. Parting through the woods with their hands and Julius's stick, Little Jake spots some things that might prove to be useful on their exploit. Picking up some sort of steel rod for himself, Jake finds a nice stick for Little Jake to swing. Slowly traveling up the old remains of stone, the steps soon vanishes completely as the ground becomes steep and more slanted.

"What happened to the stairs? They just disappeared?" Little Jake places his hands on his head, frustrated.

"That sucks," gripes Julius, searching for traces of something to grab hold too.

"There were probably stairs here a long time ago. Over the years, the path must have crumbled off or something," Jake explains, walking into the bushes ahead. "Let's just climb."

As the incline increase, the trees and shrubs begin to lean more horizontally, placing the three into a crawling position. Holding on to the snapping roots of plants, the three pull themselves up to keep from sliding down the hillside. Hoping that it didn't get too physical than it presently was, Jake, their father, enjoyed the overall time with his sons as they ventured up the mountainside. The more they laughed and talked, the higher they went, seeing and discovering new things. Looking at plants, rocks, and tiny lizards basking in the sun, Jake occasionally stops to show them a fossil or two. Explaining that the entire area was once underwater millions of years ago during dinosaur times, Jake captivated his sons with common history.

"Can we climb just a little higher before we go home, Dad? I want to see what's on the top." Julius sat upon a stone, looking at the beautiful view of nearly the entire city.

"Okay, to the top! We'll climb to the top, then head home," Jake agrees as his sons cheer him on. And so the father heads to the top with his two sons, knowing that they might have to turn back if it got too dangerous. Onward they went, happy to say they did something together as a family and proud to just be able to say they climbed a mountain together, father and sons. Lifting themselves up from a giant platform of rock in a single file line, Jake and his sons climb the last small portion of mountain. Dangling at times by the sheer strength of their muscles, they slowly ascend to the top. Grabbing onto the natural grooves along the smooth surface of the rock, Jake admires a wider expanded view of the city. Two pigeons soar across the top layer of the sunset as Jake's hand loses its grip. Catching hold to a small clump of branches, he shoves his right hand into a deep grove along the rocks.

As Julius's finger grab what feels like the edge of a cliff, he pulls himself up to safety. Standing before more bushes, he offers a hand to his brother and Dad, helping them up as well. Getting an even fuller glimpse of the town under the lowering sun and odd reddish full moon that sat clearly behind the darkening sky, the three stepped into the bushes that grew on the edge of the mountaintop. Out of the woods and into an opening of grass fenced by trees and wild greenery, they hiked into an oval-shaped opening that led to a very old and dark house.

"Hey, a house!" Julius shouts excitedly, cleaning dirt from the top of his baseball cap.

Made of wood and brick, the house sat alone between a few tall trees that stood off to its sides as if making way for the building. Shingles and boards of wood were missing from sections of the house, providing a fine home for squirrels, birds, and bats who used the holes during the different times of the day.

"The main road back down should be somewhere behind this house," Jake guesses, feeling somewhat good inside to have conquered the mountain with his two children. Taking the lead, he steps in front of them, noticing a bright-red bow sticking slightly out of the grass. Stooping down to take a closer look, he remembers seeing a little girl walking with a group of kids, wearing that same type of bow around two of her pony tails.

"What is it, Dad?" Little Jake ask as the sound of a door slamming catches their attention.

"Whoa! It's Old Man Winters!" exclaimed Julius, pointing to the man stepping off the porch of the house. Remembering all the hideous tales of horror told to him by other kids about the man on top of the mountain who ate two children, he moves behind his father.

"Winters? No, it's Old Man Meyers," Jake whispers from the corner of his lips.

"Meyers? I thought it was Old Man Eyeballs?" Little Jake stood with a dumb look on his face.

The man approaches, hobbling menacingly. From a large hump connected to a broad slanted collarbone, long slinky arms hung by his sides. With the face of a catcher's mitt, a frown of fatty, bulging skin hung over two deeply sunken yellow eyes as an old hunting rifle trembled inside one shaking hand. "Get away from my property and take the grown up with you! Troublesome kids!" He squeezes a loud cracking voice between the gaps of his missing teeth.

"Now hold on, Mister!" Jake calmly holds up both hands. "Me and my two boys here just decided to go mountain climbing today, that's all. We don't mean to trespass or to bother you!"

"Well, you are bothering me!" snaps the old man, waving his fist and pointing his rifle at Jake's head. "All day long, you stupid mountain climbers been walking on my lawn, littering all over the place, and sneaking into my house! So I think you and your sticky-fingered little ones best be climbing your tails on back down where you came from. What are you climbing for anyway? Don't you know this ain't even a real mountain, sand brains?"

"We can't go back down that way. It's too dangerous, and they're just children." Jake positions himself in front of his sons. "We're just taking the street way back, sir. Sorry to have disturbed you!" He slowly steps in the direction of the street with his sons.

"Oh no you don't! You hold it right . . . there!" The old man blocks their path as a terrifying scream of a little girl shrieks from his house. "Dang it! Damn sneak'n kids! Get out of there. Get out of my house, goddamn it!" He fires a warning shot into the air and limps speedily back to the house. Hurrying inside, he rants and raves at the top of his lungs.

Mind blown by the last three seconds of his life, Jake looks at his sons. Ducking and shielding them under the sounds of two more gunshots that bellowed out of the house, he hugs his sons close. "Come on, let's . . ." Covering his sons, he glances at the red bow blowing in the grass. Remembering the little girl he saw hopping along, he imagines her being his child, a daughter, or a friend's child inside that house. Kissing Little Jake and Julius on the tops of their heads, he knew he was the only one around at the time who could help the little girl and possibly save her. "Jake, Julius, listen, I need you to do me a favor. Listen, I'm going to try to save whoever's in that house screaming. I need you to promise me that you'll make it off this mountain and call for help."

"Dad, no!" cries Julius.

"Dad, come on, no! He has a gun, Dad, and you have nothing! Let's just go and . . ." Little Jake tries to talk some sense into his father.

"Silence! Now look, we're the only ones right now who can help those kids inside there. Only us!" Jake shouts as they begin to listen and think about his words. "Jake, I need you to take your brother, find the street behind the house, and head for home back down the hill. Look for Dillard Street. It'll take you straight to the intersection. If I'm not behind you in an hour, call the police and tell them everything!" Jake directs, hugging them once more.

"Help them, Dad." Julius smiles with eyes full of tears.

"I love you, Pops." Little Jake looks up at his father and hugs him as tightly as he can.

"Love you too," Jake replies as more shots and screams were heard. "Now hurry, go that way!" He points to the trees along one side of the house. Pushing them along, he keeps down low, watching his sons reenter the woods. To the house, Jake quietly sneaks up the porch, quietly opens the door, and creeps inside.

Meeting a long hall dividing numerous rooms, Jake foots softly across the carpeted floor. Inside no breeze and little ventilation, the smell of mothballs and moldy walls flooded the house. In sudden total silence, Jake pushes doors open, glancing inside each room he walks past. Sliding his hands across an old fireplace poker, he arms himself with the slender weapon. Shelves filled with paper and a collection of miscellaneous miniatures line the walls as a small amount of trash litters and sprinkles the walkways. Hearing a medium-toned scream and another rifle blast, Jake races to the back room, which happened to be the kitchen. Turning off the faucet that ran nonstop, overflowing the sink, a light creak from a slightly unnoticeable door catches his eye, numbing his body. Inching over, he holds the door open and peers downward into the dark coolness before descending into what appears to be the basement. Wrappers and empty containers of food scatter the wet floor as Jake reaches the bottom. Following a trail of woodchips and a light cloud of dust, his eyes lead him to a man-sized hole in the floor. Listening to movement, he stares down into the pitch-black hole. "Is anyone down there? Are you okay? Hello!" Not hearing anything or able to see or make out the bottom, he decides to get help. Slowly turning around, he glances at all the empty food containers, crumbs, and litter, drawing the conclusion that somebody had been living down there. Taking a step back to head for the exit and his sons, part of the old corroded floor collapses, sending Jake plummeting to what he believed to be his end.

With nothing on their minds but their brave father, Little Jake and Julius carefully move through the mountaintop in the direction Jake told them to go. Walking as quickly as they can and as safely as possible, Julius steps off a ledge as his big brother, Little Jake, grabs him by the inside of his shorts, pulling him back to safety.

"I think we'd better slow down," Julius suggest, wiping the sweat from the sides of his face.

"Right," agreed Julius, hearing low sounds of people yelling. "Do you hear that?"

"Hear what, the wind or my scared chicken heart beating?" Julius answers, quite jumpy from the ledge.

"No, listen!" Little Jake whispers, creeping up to a large flatbed of rock that forms a small portion of the cliff. Staring at each other and then at the ground, more sounds shot from the woods behind them. Looking around, seeing nothing, Julius signals him to take a look at a small burrow in the ground. "Julius, what are you doing?" He laughs, shrugging his shoulders, watching his little brother put his ear to the dirt and against the four finger-sized hole. "Dude, like those sounds came from behind us, they cannot be coming from that little hole. Bro, it's impossible!" Little Jake shakes his head and goes to help pull his little brother up as a tortured scream and a ferocious noise belches out of the hole.

"Did you hear that? Did you hear it?" Julius turns toward his brother, convincing him to drop down and place his own ear up to the hole.

Then among quietness again, fearlessly, Little Jake reaches into the hole and pulls out the root of a plant. "Ooookay?" He looks back at his brother, Julius, as the large flat rock that sat on the edge of the cliff suddenly shifts. The edge of the rock tilts upward and is swallowed instantly into sunken ground, sucking surrounding earth and the two boys inside with it.

And as the piece of rock disappeared into a thick cloud of dust, elsewhere beneath Old Man Meyers's house, Jake, the boy's father, emerges from a cloud of dirt and debris. Covered in grime and gravel, he dusts himself off, picks up his sunglasses, and locates his newspaper. Shaking his hair like a mangy mutt, Jake straightens his posture and pops his sore back. Noticing a flashing light in front of him, he realizes that he was actually in some sort of stone room and heads for the visible entrance that linger in the clearing dust. Cracking his aching neck and back again, he places both hands on his sides and steps to the center of a doorway. Jake's mouth drops open at the view of an enormous cockroach, quadruple the size of a full-grown Doberman, swinging around to face him.

The monstrosity stood twelve feet tall with spiderlike appendages made onto its face and around a pincher like mouth. With dark-brown and black spots, the huge insect displays a single large egg, transparent and throbbing with life. It appeared also ready to hatch thousands at any moment. Within seconds upon the sight of Jake, it advances hungrily to devour him as part of its body and head explodes before Jake's eyes. The headless giant scurries off down a black tunnel, leaving Jake speechless, shaken, and covered in insect body fluids, matching the walls of the entrance.

Horrified and disgusted the same, Jake wipes his face and lifts his head. Looking down into the complete remains of another prehistoric-looking carcass of most likely the same species, he sees an old man slowly step from behind the dead insect. A middle-aged man of Indian descent follows him, holding a kicking little girl. "Put down the girl!" not in shape and not in any position to play hero, Jake speaks loudly, pointing the long black poker stick directly at them.

"You again?" Old Man Meyers snaps, aiming the rifle with an attached flashlight directly at Jake. "That's no little girl."

"Wait! This man is correct! This is no ordinary girl. We've been trying to save her and all she's done is run away into these beasts and drawing them to us with her intolerable continuous screaming!" the yellowish-brown man screams, pouring sweat from his slick black head of hair. As the little girl slips from his hold, she runs and hides behind Jake.

"Guess I'll be taking her from here then?" barks Jake as the girl hugs his waist and quickly backs away, wiping insect juices from her face and hands.

"Good, she's your responsibility now. Let's go." Old Man Meyers wrinkles his face even more as his companion pauses.

"Wait, are you the only ones down here? You two didn't kill anyone, did you?" Jake raises the rod higher and looks back at the little girl who was sneaking off toward the entrance.

"No!" The old man looks at him dumbfounded.

"I'm Taj. I'm looking for my son . . . David. He is still down here somewhere with his friends. There are other children and other people stuck down here. What are we going to do? We can't just leave!" The Indian man unzips the neck of his jacket and rolls up his sleeves. "I believe there are other ways that people are getting trapped down here. We all didn't come this way."

"Nothing is all we can do and go for help! Darn kids and the neighborhood. Always gotta go see something!" Old Man Meyers frowns a prune face and spits on the ground. "On top of it, the damn floor went in on me! I found these two idiots and now one more!"

"Look, my two sons have gone to alert the authorities, and it looks like the little girl has found a way to climb back upstairs. So . . . I guess I'm in to help you find your son," Jake chooses, looking back at the body of the humongous dead insect. "Okay, it's the three of us. We have a rifle and a poker stick between us. We need to . . ."

"Three of us? Ha!" Mr. Meyers interrupts, quickly shoving Jake out of the way.

"Yes, three of us."

"I'm climbing back up and letting the fumigators handle this. I should have done it a long time ago. Besides anyone dumb enough to fool around down here underground ought to be stuck down here! I'm not creeping around in this mineshaft! I didn't even know this was down here!" The old man firmly stands his ground; a loud scream echoes from behind him.

Running back into what looks like the main tunnel under the house, they stood in amazement and fear at the sight of swarms of giant cockroaches migrating in and out of the foundation of the Meyers's house. At the foot of the mound of dirt beneath the exit of bugs, the little girl screams as one of the giants slowly tugs and drags her up the wall by the leg. "How do you live in that house?" Jake quickly grabs the long hot nose of the old man's rifle, snatches it away, and fires it into the body of the insect. Dropping headfirst, the little girl hits the dirt and rock floor. As the wounded insect lands beside her, another comes after her. Screaming in a scared panic, a strong arm and hand reaches around her as Jake pulls her away from the entrance.

As Jake falls back, the Indian man guides them back into the corridor as the old man knocks off any bug that tries to pursue them. "Oh my, there goes our escape route! What are we to do now? I have to find my son!"

"We're going to have to go deeper inside and find another way out!" Jake suggest as Mr. Meyers slowly approaches them from behind.

"There is no way that I'm going into that cotton-pick'n death trap!" he snarls a toothless set of gums that come out of hiding in his mouth.

"Well, there's no way that you can get back into your house the way we came. It's infested with those things!" Jake comforts the little girl as she held on to him, shaking in fear.

"So we have no choice, Mr. Meyers, our hands are forced. We must travel deeper inside," the Indian man agrees, turning toward the dead insect in which already had babies, and medium-sized roaches starting to feed on it.

"Weren't you guys coming from that direction?" Jake thinks deeply on the situation.

"Yep, we're doomed." The old man places his hand upon his head in disbelief. The sound of dirt sifting and falling rubble breaks their conversation.

And while Jake thinks of how to get to his boys, Little Jake and Julius catch their breath and adjust their eyes in the darkness of another part of the mountain. Wedged in the midsection between rock and earth, Little Jake's upper body and legs dangle out what looks like a wall of rubble. With the sensation of being moderately pinned between two buses, the oldest stares at the nonmoving body of his baby brother, feeling as though it was the last time he would see him.

"Jake?" Julius faintly calls out, hanging upside down in a twist of vines and tree roots just opposite his brother. As one hand touches the ball cap that was still secure on his head, the other reaches out for his brother. "Are we dying? Don't die, Jake." Beginning to cry, he becomes faint, blacking in and out. As Julius closes his eyes and stretches out his arms as far as he can, Little Jake tightly clutches onto his hands.

"Ouch, this hurts like crap!" Little Jake coughs among the flying dirt as the branches that held Julius snaps him to freedom. Julius free-falls, and his weight pries the still-holding-on Little Jake, completely off the wall behind him. Rolling and tumbling down a slant into a maze of unseen tunnels, the two slide deep into the mountain's belly. Breaking through the earth, their rolling bodies knock the heads and limbs from enormous insects as they tumble and slide uncontrollably. The two catch hold of some sort of rocky ledge. "I think this is it, Dad!" Little Jake starts to lose his grip.

"Me too, I love you!" Julius hands slip away as they both fall at the same time.

Landing on the back of a giant roach, its head and back end explodes as its belly splits open in a splatter of juices and insect matter, breaking their fall. In a sitting position, the brothers look around emotionless, covered in insect insides, as the twelfth-grade senior Mike cowers in bug intestines in front of his eleventh-grade sweetheart Tracy. Cyntica and Lil Ricky the neighborhood bullies tremble behind Rah as another ninth grader by the name of Mindy, stood behind them all, covering her mouth in shock. Thankful to see each other, Little Jake and Julius smile in thanks for being alive. Sliding off the giant creature, they jump to the ground in a cloud of dust. Standing up, one of the fallen missing-limbed insects snaps its huge pinching jaws and crawls toward Little Jake. As he steps and falls backward, unable to defend himself, something large snatches the dying insect into the darkness of a large crack in the corner of the cavern's roof. Nearly wetting his pants, Little Jake quiver's inside his shoes. Still clinching on to his ball cap, he spins it backward upon his head. "Julius?" His brother's name was the first word to come out his mouth. Running to him, he hugs him tightly. Then taking the red ball cap from his brother's hand, he gently places it on Julius's head.

"Look, Jake, people! How did they get down here?" Julius asks.

"I dunno, must've fell down a hole too, bro?" Little Jake removes his hand from his brothers shoulder. "It's cool. I think we're safe, for now. What are those things? And how are you guys down here? Is there another way out or something? Tell me there's another way out." He gazes at the small audience of school kids for any possible relieving answer.

"I can't believe the two turd faces here killed the giant bug," remarks Cyntica, intrigued and ready to nitpick since the coast was clear.

"Let's trash 'em before those things come back!" Lil Ricky pounds one fist into the palm of the other.

"Leave 'em alone, Pla-cyntica and Egor boy!" Mike defends them, still managing to crack a joke at the same time despite their disparity. "That was great work, little bros! You two are awesome!

I thought we were goners for sure." He stands up, wiping his temples; he helps his girlfriend, Tracy, up from the ground. "We found a cave, but it caved in on us, and those giant bugs started coming out from all over the place! We're still looking for a way out."

"There are other people running around lost and trapped too." Rah walks up them, exchanging hardy handshakes.

"It's freaking horrible in here!" Tracy tucks the hanging strains of hair behind her ear.

"Yeah . . . and those things, those bugs you just squashed . . . they eat off dead bodies too. We saw a man get his head bitten off by a giant cockroach!" Cyntica tries to frighten them as Lil Ricky adds to the tale.

"His blood and guts squirted out everywhere. You could even hear the bug crunching on his bones!"

"You're a fool if you listen to these idiots." A low unemotional voice crept from Mindy's mouth. "We heard screams and that was it. We we're too busy running to see anything. They're just trying to scare you." She steps out from behind Mike and Tracy. With dark raccoon eyes and long dark hair that covered most of her face, in black jeans and T-shirt, she stood with her arms folded in front of Little Jake.

"Look, kiddies, party time's over. We have to keep moving. You can get to know one another along the way!" Tracy stomps off ahead.

"She's right, guys. Let's go before more of those things come out and eat us!" Mike suggest, following his high school sweetheart. "Let's go you two. We can talk along the way."

"What was that thing that ate that bug? It flew into one of those big holes in the wall," Julius, while walking, speaks in a low voice, staring at all the cracks and tunnels around them.

"I don't know, little guy," replies Mike. "All I know is that it didn't have wings."

"Bro, there are some things you just don't want to know about." Little Jake glances around for any more surprises. Placing a hand on his brother's back, he moves him along as Mindy and the two bullies slowly walk behind them. Two loud yells are heard ahead. Tracy panics as Mike points to another large hole in the corner of the cavern's wall.

"I'm not going in that thing!" Julius gripes as Mike goes in first, then Little Jake, Rah and Mindy. Hearing the sound of movement and scurrying, he dashes for the unknown hole.

"Hold on a minute. Isn't this what one of those things came out of?" Lil Ricky asked before following.

"Great, we're all going to die." Cyntica thinks he sees a shadow moving and runs into the large crevice like a ground hog who's seen its shadow.

Totally unable to see, the group fumbles deeper into the tunnel. Flickering on a handy black mini flashlight that hung onto an orange string around his neck, Julius flashes it ahead, happy his father packed it.

"It's cold." Rah describes as Mindy felt the walls and the ground beneath them with her hands.

"Watch your step, guys. It's getting slippery down here," Mike announced, holding on to the waist of Tracy's jeans.

"It feels like water's leaking from somewhere," Tracy states, beginning to lose her footing. The tunnel slants downward, becoming slick.

"Uh, guys, I don't think this is water." Little Jake looks down at his hands and smells them under Julius's light. Rubbing his hands, he notices a thick white residue of a slimy matter all over the place. "Uh, guys, I don't think this is a . . ."

"Shhh!" Mindy quiets the group as they all froze incredibly still.

"What?" Cyntica groans hungrily, ready to go home. As everyone's eyes grew wide, he asks one more time, "What?" He belches at them, then turns around. Crawling directly for them was half the body of one of the enormous giants that Little Jake and Julius slaughtered. Screaming, he shoves and pushes his way through the group as they all began to slip backward into the suddenly slanting tunnel toward the insect. Gradually, one by one, the eight fall. Holding on to one another for dear sweet life, they accelerate downward, breaking through a rocky maze of tunnels and bends, disappearing farther into the unknown mountain.

The brothers' father, Jake, worries indeed about the well-being of his sons and if they found their way back home okay. They stayed on his mind the whole time he climbed and squeezed between rocks with the two men and the little girl he was with. "I can't believe you knew these things were down here, and you didn't notify anyone." He cuts his eyes at Mr. Meyers and looks back at Taj.

"You didn't notify anyone? It's totally absurd and irresponsible of you!" The brown-skinned man scratches the top of his long nose and gaze at the little girl holding Jake's hand and strokes his handsomely fine beard.

"They were pets. I was only feeding them from my basement." Mr. Meyers rolled his head and eyes, wanting to hear no more of the conversation. "It was only one or two of them. I thought they were a special breed."

"You we're feeding them? No wonder you had all the food containers in the basement. You must've been feeding them for years? And guess what? From years and years of your spilling foods and liquids, it's no wonder the floor caved in! Don't you know one or two bugs lead to many? How do you know which one is male or female? How do you know the one that you were feeding wasn't pregnant? Roaches, and I'm sure especially the ones that are as big as baby elephants make millions of babies. Meyers, what were you thinking? You know what . . . my kids were right. You're one crazy old man, Meyers."

"Well, hell, how was I to know exactly what they were and how many it was? They never got into my house! Hell . . . looking through that vent, it's so dark! I couldn't make heads or tails of what I was growing! I didn't know they were bugs! All the sounds they were making, why heck, I was wishing for a huge raccoon or a baby bear or something? I just wanted a pet. Just goes to show best be careful what you wish for." The old man's sad face recedes back into its mean and frowned composition.

Reaching inside his camping bag, Jake pulls out a forgotten-about flashlight and points it around the area. Formations of strange dripping rock hung from the ceilings, stretching to the floor that more formations grew from. The mountain itself, so far, had many tunnels, corridors, and caves inside it. Jake was amazed at how well the mountain maintained these abundant empty pockets and crevices for all these years. Walking down what only could be described as natural-made steps of minerals, Jake and the three enter a damp and narrow tunnel. Its spiky, spiny, low ceiling ready to fall at any time teasingly jab at them as it gradually raises and disappears into the darkness above. An odd smell whiffs into their noses, too faint to identify with.

"I'm thirsty." The red-headed, freckled, and dirty-faced little girl glances up at Jake as her stomach noticeably growls. "I'm hungry too. I'm going to die of starvation."

"Wait, what's your name?" Jake takes advantage of the little girl speaking and tries to communicate with her. Taking off his book bag, he squats down and searches for something.

"Liz . . . well, Elizabeth," she speaks and stoops down next to him.

Feeling around the bottom of the bag, Jake retrieves a small bag of chips. "Look, Elizabeth, it's not much, and it's probably all you're going to have for a while, so make them last, okay?" She nods in agreement as he gives her the small bag of chips. "Now we don't know exactly where we're headed, but we're looking for his son and a way out. Those crawling things are all around us, so we have to stay close together at all times, and we can't stay here. No matter what, Elizabeth, we have to keep moving to stay alive all right?" he explains, carefully reading her reactions and body language. Noticing how surprisingly comprehensive and willing she was, he feels more confident about her and continues walking.

"It's getting a little nippy down here. How's that? It's a full breeze!" Mr. Meyers looks around puzzled as the hairs on his arms and the back of his neck stand on ends.

Blowing a visible cloud of warm air from his mouth, Taj slightly quivers, rubs his hands together, and follows behind them.

"I can't believe this mountain has all these caves. Who knew?" Jake feels his way through the sedimentary stone and crystallized caverns, astonished by the sheer beauty of nature's naturally designed walls and ceilings. "Reminds me of caveman times."

"Some things are better off left inside the past, preserved in its own time." Taj steps past him, looking for any signs of movement.

"Let's just hope no dinosaurs will come popping out of the walls on us anytime soon, okay?" Jake sniggers as a loud scream bounces of the stone walls into their ears.

"Who was that?" Taj looks at Jake, thinking of his son.

"It came from in front of us!" Old Meyers raises his rifle to eye level inside the darkness.

"David!" Taj calls out his son's name. And above all his fears and worries, he gallops off bravely toward the sound of what could be his endangered child.

"Taj, no, wait! What is wrong with you people today?" Jake eyes Elizabeth closing the bag of chips. "Liz, stay with him!" Jake hurries off behind him, leaving the little girl with Mr. Meyers.

"That old fool, he's gonna be the death of us yet!" grumbles Mr. Meyers, feeling the little girl clasp onto his waist.

Armed with the fireplace poker in hand, Jake points the flashlight in front of him. Entering an opening just big enough for a large man, he sees a woman dressed in light clothing cowering to the ground before a man holding a video camera in the batting position behind her. Hurrying to them, Jake spots Taj hold a large stone above the beaten remains of one of the insects near the feet of the woman. Taj steps away; the creepy sounds of scouring and crunching immediately come from the pile as many smaller insects of at least a foot long, devour and rip apart the new finding right before their eyes.

"Good goobly goo!" blurts Old Man Meyers coming through the entrance, eyeing the mound. Firing a round into the frenzy of feeding insects, he explodes the target into a mist of limbs and various body parts that sprayed over everyone. "Pesky Bu . . ."

Jake look's at the man and woman and back at Meyers. "Mr. Meyers! Would you please quit doing that? Would you watch how you shoot that thing? I-I don't know how much bug blood I can drink! Geesh!"

"Ew, disgusting!" Elizabeth spits clunks of meat from her mouth and wipes the foreign liquid from her face.

"Thanks a lot, I think." The woman pushes herself up next to the man and cleans her face with the inside of her shirt. "Thank you."

"I'm glad that we could assist you. Hi, I'm Jake, and these are my band of merry men. Are you guys okay?" The tired father holds out a hearty dripping hand to shake. "Sorry." He pulls back his hand as the woman holds up hers that was just as nasty. "That's Taj, Mr. Meyers, the bug detonator, and she's Elizabeth. Wait, Jane?" Under the gunk, he recognizes the woman as being his ex-girlfriend in the days before marriage.

"Jake? It is you! Wow." The woman looks away oddly. "It's Dr. Jane Wallace now, preferably, and this is my assistant and handy cameraman, Reeves," she introduces, plucking bits of organs from her curly brown hair.

"Howdy." Waves Reeves, securing his camera safety upon the strap draped over his shoulder. Carrying another medical bag of some sort upon the other, he adjusts a long hunter's knife cleverly tucked behind a wide Mexican belt. "So you two know each other?"

"We used to be a couple a while back. You still look better than ever. So what's your story? How did you guys end up down here, know a way out?" Not really caring about what professions they had, Jake asks on behalf of getting to his sons, whom he thought were at home.

"Funny you ask. You know . . . me and Reeves here were just asking ourselves the same thing before you stumbled into us." Dr. Wallace eyes connect with Jakes as he observes her long eyelashes and small, yet wide luscious lips. Under the light of Reeves camera, they both join Jake's party. "A bizarre thing, we were inside the office late one night, walking the halls, and all of a sudden, my friend Barry was snatched by this . . . this thing! We tried to save him but fell with it. We were carried by it or something. We don't know. It was pitch dark. But we ended down here, and whatever it was that swept our friend Barry up and away forever, it wasn't one of those things." She pointed to the dead bug.

"That thing you speak of, if it isn't an insect, what is it then? What else could possibly be down here? How long have you been down here? Have you seen a little boy, a small child who looks like me?" Taj touches her shoulder and looks the woman in the eye under Jake's light.

"No, no little boys. The people we have encountered, unfortunately . . . didn't make it," Reeves answers for them, placing his jacket around his partner.

"We've been here for days, maybe weeks. I've seen horrible things, people being eaten alive." The doctor finds a small bag sticking up out from the dirt.

"Sounds like we're in the same heap of trouble we were already in. We're never getting out of this mess! It stinks down here," Mr. Meyers grumbles, smacking his mouth. "Now what are we going to do, smarty pants?"

"He's right. Those bugs are coming from all directions in which we are traveling. What must we do? They're everywhere! It appears as though we're trapped in this forsaken mountain for good. We'll suffer the same fate as the others!" Taj begins to panic, thinking about his life and options. Thinking of all the actions he was capable of making, he glances at the cave of survivors and realizes they didn't have a chance in hell of living. "We're never leaving this place!" he screams in frustration, lowering his head to the sight of Elizabeth slurping from water that streamed into her hands from the walls.

Spitting some out, her face shrivels up as she sticks her tongue out and gasp. "Yuck, it must have minerals or something in it."

Following the origin of the streaming liquid to the tops of the walls with his flashlight, Jake peers into the darkness of the almost-endless-looking ceiling above them as a pinch of movement catches his eye. "Liz . . . I don't think that's water, and, guys . . . let's try not yelling from now on, okay?" Before he could know for sure, hundreds of brown bats pour down through the cave in a river of screeches and loud winged claps.

Jake grabs the little girl as they let loose gut-wrenching screams, running frantically through hundreds of awaken brown bats. Some landed, hopping about, scrounging for food while others pick off various parts of the dead insect. Looping and zigzagging in the darkness around the fleeing party, the swarm flew back and forth through the corridor. A large bat, half the size of Meyers's body, blindly collides into his chest, instantly breaking its wing and sending the old man down to the floor of the cave.

"Meyers?" Shining his light in Meyers's direction, Jake wedges the poker inside the body of the bat and grabs it by the right wing as Taj assist him by grabbing the other. As the winged rodent displays a great wingspan, it tries to go for the elderly man as Jake and Taj together toss the creature into an oncoming swarm of hungry bats. Taj picks up Meyers's gun and shoots down a bat the size of a small child.

"Did you see it? We are cursed! I'll take my chances!" Taj stutters and mindlessly dives through a crack that he hoped was the way out. As the others follow, so do the bats as the tight space filled with screams and gunfire.

Elsewhere at the moment, deep inside the cramped confinements of a pit, Jake's sons, Little Jake, Julius, and the other six lie squished between loose rocks. As the oldest male of the group, Mike kicks loose a stone, breaking a small hole that opens into a larger entrance. They dump out into a larger space. Coughing and wheezing, the adolescences emerge from rubble and dirt.

"Where the heck are we?" Cyntica balls his hand and dabs his eyes, leaving two clean circles in their place.

"We're still inside this stinking mountain, that's for sure!" Mike dusts his clothes and scans the area for trouble. "Everyone okay?" he asks before calling each by name.

Waving his hand and in some kind of gesture, Julius responds to Mike. Also standing, he notices that he was covered in grime and slime. "That was some slide. I think parts of the floor are alive."

"I think we took a wrong turn." Little Jake arose, coughing, dusting his hat again.

"We finally got away from those things." Mindy cleans her shirt and spat mud onto the ground.

"I've got to get out of here!" Tracy ties her unlaced shoe tightly in a double knot inside the dark, unsure of which direction to go.

"Dang, how deep is this place? We're on . . . another cliff," Rah observes that they were actually on the tip of a large boulder.

Delicate deposits minerals and iron, which took millions of years to form, grow coned and orange-brown-colored, sprouting in every which way. So fragile that most could break off and shatter from the mere vibration of sound.

"Look, dweebs. There's a bottom, I think." Cyntica points to another level just below them.

"Cool," blurts Lil Ricky with wondrous amazement. Despite the fact that they were lost and bugs were trying to eat them, he stood inside the beauties of a naturally brightly lit cave that stretched at least a mile, filled with holes of many other naturally glowing caverns and caves.

"This is like historical, even the giant bugs! Think about how long this place has been here undetected and well preserved right up under our noses." Mindy treasures the natural wonders of the caves.

"It's probably like over thousands of years old." Little Jake crawls between two enormous spikes of minerals beside her on the ledge. "It's so hollow. There are so many ways we could go. I see why it's so easy to get lost."

"Let's go that way. It looks like it's the best way to get to the bottom." Mike points to a fallen pillar of settlement that naturally formed into a bridge of crystal and stone that led to a less slippery and dangerous path.

"But how do you know which way doesn't lead to those bugs?" Tracy nervously follows the group through the odd shapes of rock and crystals.

"We don't." Mike takes the lead and steps upon the giant slab of crystal.

"Look, I found an old coin from the early 1900s. Someone's been down here before us!" Julius shouts excitedly, drifting along behind them.

"So what, pipsqueak? Give it to me! Now!" Cyntica demands, holding up a balled fist to Julius chin.

"Let 'em go, Cyn. Look, real dinosaur teeth . . . and claws! We could get money for those!" Lil Ricky smiles, picks up the ancient bones of some creature that once walked the earth, and hands them to his running buddy.

"No way. Cool findings, you little creep!" Cyntica snatches a large claw from his hand and examines it next to Little Jake as Mindy trips and falls over something.

"Hey, guys, I think I found something. Look, more dinosaur foss—" Mindy instantly turns pale; her heart drops into a cold emptiness inside her body as she screams, face-to-face with the bony arm of a human in her hands. Gasping, she quickly drops it and runs between Mike and Tracy, who made it under the naturally formed archway on the other side of the collapsed pillar.

"Hey, look, y'all!" Rah cries out. "No, really, look!" He yanks and pulls Little Jake and Julius until they too saw what he was hollering about. Creating such a commotion, everyone in the group stopped and mouths dropped in their tracks. Raheem and the others bear witness to the sight of historical people, tools, and events all trapped and frozen in time within the rock, crystals, and natural workings of the mountain.

Skeletal remains of hermits, native Americans, and creatures of long ago fill the lower darker shades of rock as the imprints of later life and civilizations decorate the ceilings and higher levels of stone. Items and objects from various periods of time litter the base of the open corridor; small avalanches of dirt and rocks fall and tumble from around the tops of dripping-looking stone. The humungous corridor was of a glowing array of colors as Little Jake and his brother shine their flashlights back and forth across the stones, switching them from their true colors to their glowing essence. As the group continues on, they can see that the inside of the mountain had preserved mainly the prehistoric era; but during the course of the years, other things from the time of man were also left, trapped, and preserved.

"I think some of these crystals and bones absorb and make light." Little Jake leads the way with his flashlight as Mike walks, covering his wide open mouth. "It's still a little dark, but who knew it was possible?"

"This is amazing," states Mike, pulling Julius to the front to help lead with his brother.

"We're going to be millionaires if we make it out of here!" Julius smiles deviously. "No one even knows this place even exist." His mind begins to ramble off into all the discovery shows he's watched and all of the stories of great exploits he's read or heard about.

"All of this history, this is awesome stuff." Mike looks around, full of wonder and surprise.

"Ugh! I never liked history or geology!" Tracy pops her gum as Cyntica and Lil Ricky nod in agreement.

Crossing a small incline, they head down a delicate thorn slope; Tracy loses her footing and slides to the bottom, breaking age-old formations. "Ow, stupid mountain," Tracy complains, dusting and rubbing her aching rear. As Cyntica hurries to help clean off her body, Mike smacks his hands away and gives him the evil eye.

"Don't even try it, meatball!" Mike threatens as the group holds back their laughter. "Tracy, are you all right?"

"Look, guys, an old miner's kart and . . ." Julius flinches, startled by the skeletons of three miners dressed in torn clothing. "What are miners doing here? There aren't any tracks."

"They must've got trapped here a long time ago." Mike walks upon the bodies.

"Gross, they all look scared of something." Mindy notices that all the deceased miners had their faces covered or hands out as if blocking something. Two of the bodies' clothes were torn to shreds, and one was missing the lower portion of its body.

"Where do you suppose his legs went?" asked Little Jake, starting not to like the area as much.

"Probably bugs," Julius answers as he stood next to Rah, stuffing his newfound coin deep inside his pocket.

"Let's go, bro." Little Jake nudges his brother along as they all step away from the site.

"We'll keep going this way, everybody. We can't stay here for long," Mike directs, looking in every which way for an easy exit.

"This place gives me the creeps," gripes Tracy; Mike puts his arm around her like a true gentlemen.

Julius pretends to do the same to Mindy from behind as Little Jake clips his foot, tripping him to the floor. "Wow, here's a foot and some more pieces of clothes from the dead guy." Little Jake opens his eyes to the bony leg lying under his nose.

"How did it get way down here?" Rah glances back at the pile of human remains they left behind.

"Hey, there's a tooth wedged inside the pants leg. Looks like he was eaten by something." Little Jake raises up a long rigid tooth that belonged to some type of animal.

"Well, at least we know what happened to them," Cyntica replies, comparing the tooth that Lil Ricky gave him to the one that Little Jake was holding.

"They match. Wait, that doesn't make sense. Those look like prehistoric teeth, and those miner guys are from a later time," Mindy analyzes the facts in the back of her mind.

"Jake, was that thing lying under or next to that foot?" Mike asks.

"It was wedged into the bone, see? It fits perfectly back into the hole." Little Jake inserts the tooth back into a small hole along the leg, fitting it back in like a missing puzzle piece.

"So what does this mean?" Tracy rubs her cold hands against her arms as a low growl from somewhere unknown silence them.

"Oh my gosh . . . What was that?" Mindy whispers as they try to focus on any sign of movement in the dark.

"Let's get moving, now!" Mike instructs, trying to avoid contact with whatever made the sound.

Below the low ceilings of the caves and down what felt like almost endless tunnels leading to very different patterns and unique sequences of fossilized rock, the group steps quickly. They begin to come to dead ends and impossible passages. In an area where they all had to crouch down, they soon find themselves crawling through a damp, dark, and quite narrow space. Feeling through a small puddle of water, Mindy feels something alive glide through her fingers. Having strung the flashlight around his neck, Julius clicks on his flashlight and carries it in his mouth, freeing his hands. Feeling through the cool waters with his fingers, Julius shines the light inside the small pools, revealing scouring, wiggling, blind shrimp. As he screams, Lil Ricky quickly covers his mouth as Julius calms and snatches away his hand, unsure where it's been.

"Do you see that? It's some kind of baby lobster in here with us, a whole bunch of them!" Julius whispers.

"Watch your voices. We don't want this thing caving in on us!" Mike reminds everyone.

"I don't think lobsters are the only things in here with us." Rah shushes them with his finger, convincing them to listen.

The sound of shifting and sliding dirt from afar alarms them of something else being present. A rumbling and deep bass snarl moves their souls, sending the girls screaming and the boys joining them in hollers. They race to the dead end of the tunnel.

"Hey, I think the floor is loose," Tracy states before the floor gives, sinking her swiftly into the depths of dark murky water.

"Tracy!" Mike shouts. Feeling the floor for the hole that she fell through, he dives in after her, followed by Rah. As Mindy turns around and grabs Little Jake and his brother, she pulls them unwillingly into the water. Holding on to each other for dear life, Cyntica and Lil Ricky quake in place at the shadow and sounds of something ferocious sloshing and creeping down toward them, halting their breath and swallows.

"Forget this, I'm outta here!" Lil Ricky unlatches from his companion and leaps in the water after the group.

Alone in fear and splashing noises, Cyntica whips out his trusty black lighter that he had stolen from his uncle's dresser. "I . . . I . . . I gotta take a crap!" Nervously shaking, he flicks the lighter a few times, wetting it more with the water from his hands. Not able to get it to work, he wipes it on the shoulder of his T-shirt and blows on it. Attempting again, a small flicker stabilizes as he holds it down to the hole in the limestone floor where his friends exited. Not able to swim, he licks his dry lips and turns around to face whatever was coming in their direction. Starting to pour sweat, he begins to sniffle and cry, accidently blowing the fire out. Hitting panic mood, the fear overrides the sadness as he struggles to produce another flame from the lighter. Suddenly hearing sets of tapping approach, Cyntica flicks the Bic again as a small dim light dances upon the head of the lighter. "Yes!" he cheers as a horrible warm stench slowly engulfs his head. The small fire tilts in his direction as two incredibly huge reflecting eyes pierce through his. Screaming at the top of his lungs, Cyntica falls sideways into the water, paddling as hard as he can. Invisible and indescribable matter and life brush across Cyntica's face and body inside the cold waters. Kicking and swinging his arms desperately, it felt as though he was getting nowhere. As though death was upon him, his body slows as he blows out his last remaining air. Lost and out of hope, he listens to his heart beat against his chest. About to take in water, he sees a bright light grow bigger and bigger. Time slows and stops as he thinks about his life and all the bad things he's done. Accepting his fate and wishing things could have been different, he reaches out to what he believed to be the hand of the CREATOR. As if he could capture the light inside his hand, he closes it over the brightness. Still blinded by the great light, everything around him becomes visible as the divine ball of energy becomes actually Julius's flashlight. His heart pounds loudly inside his head as he swam. Under the light, he can visibly see different species of fish and freshwater species around him. Stepping on mussels, he scrapes the floor and walls clear of cave shrimp and vegetation, swiveling by the spiny bodies of angler fish that cut and poke at his clothes. Drowning, Cyntica races through the strange variety of fish. Finally, gasping for air, Mike pulls him from the murky water.

"What took you so long, meathead?" Mike smiles down upon him like an angel.

"I . . . that thing," Cyntica tries to explain as liquid gushed from his mouth followed by hard swallows and chokes and gags.

"That was close. I thought you had left us!" Lil Ricky tries to help him up as Cyntica swats him away. "What?"

Stepping out a muddy tunnel, the group continues on their journey home. Climbing over and under an avalanche of limestone and minerals, they crawl up and downward into another clearing. The grand cavern illuminates with their lights, reflecting through millions of clusters of crystals. Realizing that they were standing in some sort of old camp or hide out, Tracy and Mindy cover their mouths and point to the remains of old deceased soldiers.

"Oh my gosh, where are we? It looks like they lived here." Tracy steps away from the bones and accidentally touches some decomposed poop with the toe of her shoes. "Yuck, that can't be what I think it is."

"Looks like they were lost too and never got out. Guess they made this place their final home." Mindy moves in close to Little Jake.

"Cool, some ancient crap!" Lil Ricky squats next to Cyntica, who was already kneeling, examining the find.

"If it's ancient, how come it's still a little fresh? Look how mushy it is." Cyntica touches it with a slender piece of crystal as Lil Ricky takes the back of his head and presses the tip of his nose into the awful goo and dashes about, laughing hysterically. "You little worm!"

"Knock it off you two! We'll have plenty of time to play after we get out of here. I need you guys to concentrate and help us find a way out of here." Mike polices the situation; Cyntica still manages to whack Lil Ricky on the back of his neck as he runs by.

"Shush, guys, listen!" Julius silences them, very weary of something that he sensed was following them.

"What do you hear? All I hear is water," Little Jake whispers and is shushed again. Carefully listening, he and the entire group pick up the raspy and heavy sounds of something breathing. "Where is it coming from?" Little Jake whispers in Mindy's left ear.

"There's a bear in here!" Tracy grabs hold to Mike, pushes away, and begins to walk among them, scanning around the cave for anything large and furry.

"This isn't the place for a brother, that's for sure." Rah also peeks around with extreme caution.

"It's not coming from near here. I think the cave's just picking up sounds from all over and bouncing them off the walls," Mike says in a low voice, poking inside a small opening of mummified looking bodies. "Hey guys, stay over there, you definitely don't want to see this." Shoving his hand inside, he squeezes through the crammed space and pries an old torch from the stiff hands of the deceased and swiftly rejoins the group.

"Up there." Julius shows them a set of large, oddly misshapen stones that led to another dark tunnel.

"Wait, I don't have time to explore. I want to go home as quickly as possible. Look, there are hundreds of tunnels. How do we know which one is the right way?" Tracy moves her aching neck from side to side.

"We don't. Right now, anyone's guess is a good guess, right?" Little Jake attempts to bring logic to his brother's suggestion.

"Why can't we just stick to the lowest levels and stay away from those things, Mike? I have bug guts in my hair! And what was that noise behind us? We're hearing it more and more. We're lower now, and nothings trying to eat us. I want to be safe, Mike, not lost and following these . . . these brats!" Tracy huffs, storming off in her own direction, knowing Mike would follow.

"Tracy, Tracy!" Mike calls for her. Amazed by the uncanny outburst, he stood next to the other appalled children. "I don't believe this!" He rubs his forehead, lights the torch, and runs after her.

"I'm starting not to like that girl." Mindy folds her arms and squints her already slanted eyes devilishly.

"What's her problem?" Julius looks over the flashlight at his brother.

"I'll tell you what her problem is. She needs a real man to slap her, then kiss her in the mouth." Cyntica then goes into his eighteen-and-older joke as their brief moment of awkwardness is interrupted by a heart-jumping scream that came from the tunnels above. The lone group of adolescences react without fully thinking of the safety of their own lives, and began to climb.

Mike gets a glimpse of the kids climbing up the cave wall; catching up to Tracy, he grabs her by the arm and turn to run with her as she snatches away from him. "Tracy, I know you're upset right now, but they're just little kids, they're innocent! We can't just let them die. And you know what else? They're all pretty smart and decent kids too, and I like them! We have to stick together to live, Tracy, to survive. You know I love you, and no one comes before that. But we used to be just like them, we're the only adults they have right now." He can see the whites of her eyes gently cut the darkness of the glowing cave.

"Well, who do you love most? If you love me so much, Mike, then you'll make those brats come this way because there is no way that I'm following them anymore! Bad things have continuously been happening to me since you've brought them in my presence. I'm not going back in that direction, Mike!" Tracy stomps her foot and turns her back to him as a screaming young man plunges to death in front of her having fallen from somewhere in the connection of caves, one hundred feet above them. Covered in small hand-sized cockroaches, the bloody, twitching person raises his hand at Tracy, sending her screaming in the direction of the children. "Mike!" Hurrying up the large stones of jagged rock, Mike and Tracy come across the children and two more survivors.

"Hey, Mike, this is Corky and Temmis. They go to South East Middle," Julius greets as Mike and Tracy came closer.

"What happened? Are we in danger? You guys find a way out?" Mike asks, placing his arm around Tracy's shivering body.

"Great, more freaking kids." Tracy rolls her eyes and blows in her hands.

"I was trying to pull Temmis out this wall when this huge spider attacked me!" Corky a tall and brittle looking little girl rambles on, wiping off her beret and girl scouts uniform.

"Only they weren't huge." Julius held up Corky's shoe, revealing a smashed spider the size of a hand as she snatches it and places it on her foot.

"They were all over me," ends Corky.

"How'd you two wind up down here?" asks Mike.

"We met in a tunnel with two others, but they didn't make it. We ran from these giant bugs, fell down this hole, and crashed through, like three floors, and crawled our way out this tiny hole," Temmis, a smart fifth grader, quite chubby for his age, and in glasses with a head full of black straight hair, explains. "The roof caved in on me, but your friends pulled me out!"

"Okay, Corky and Temmis, looks like you're stuck with the eight of us." Mike shrugs his shoulders.

"Oh, trust me, we could use the company." Corky's scuffed face begins to cheer up.

"Well, since we can't go the way that you guys came, looks like we're going to have to try this way." Mike directs them to a new series of caves as from somewhere, the strange sounds of clumping and heavy breathing continued to follow them through the cavern walls.

The breathing becomes excessively louder as the group's journey met another dead end. Sharp icicle-like deposits of crystallized minerals grew abundantly also in this section of the mountain. Evidence of fallen icicles lay everywhere inside as the tallest ones stretch from the ceiling to the floor and vice versa.

"Listen, there it goes again." Julius can hear the sound very clearly at this point. "What if it's an alligator?"

"I think Tracy's right. There has to be bears in here. They do live in caves, little bro," Little Jake states as a few strings of his hair began to sway back and forth.

"Guys, do you feel that?" Mike holds his hands against a section of the wall. Sliding his fingers along the cracks above the protruding section, he felt a small breeze flowing along it. "Wherever there's blowing air, there's outside!" Mike smiles a great set of teeth, touching and trying to find a way through the boulder-looking portion of the wall. "I think whatever's breathing is on the other side. Remember when we crashed through that wall? Maybe we can somehow break through here and scare away whatever that is on the other side and make our way home."

"Break through? We've done enough damage to this place already, don't you think? Do you know how long it took these rocks to form? Decades, no, maybe even centuries?" Corky protests as Little Jake interrupts.

"What if it is a bear and we don't scare it, Mike? We could get shredded to pieces." Little Jake waves his ball cap as he speaks. Julius had never seen his brother speak or look so serious in his life. He knew his brother was worried when he watched him slap his cap on his head any old kind of way.

"Oh, the blood, the gore!" shouted Cyntica as Lil Ricky sprung up enthusiastically. "Scare a bear? That's nothing, I can do that. Besides, if we stick together, it's all of us, against them. We all can't be eaten at the same time. Forget this place, I'm outta here!"

"Sweet horror . . . cool!" The two bump knuckles and dash off in lightning speed. Using stone, powerful kicks, and hand blows, Cyntica and Lil Ricky plow through the collapsing soft and brittle portion of the wall, screaming and yelling, both, falling to their faces in a thick cloud of rubble and dust.

"Aw, man! There's nothing in here." Cyntica raises his head from the mounds of dirt and rock and rises to his feet slowly in disappointment.

"There's nothing here, guys!" Lil Ricky verifies under Julius's light shining behind them. Signaling them to follow, he peers down the shaft of large broken rock.

The pack follows a cool breeze that clears the air as one of the flashlights goes out. Finding themselves in another hollow passage of strange and alien-looking rock, Mike relights the torch he found. A few remains of past civilizations of man remain undisturbed and intact around them. Old ancient and modern tools scatter about cave drawings of mammals and events along the smooth surface of certain sections of the wall.

"Wow, how cool is this," Rah utters. Captivated by all the old uncovered tools that could be seen with the naked eye, he finds a small Indian spear.

"Quiet!" Mike silenced the group again.

Familiar with the drill, everyone stops in place. Listening, a loud unusual bellow scares them all as Mike signals them to stay and creeps ahead. Coming to a corner, he peers left and right. "Guys . . . oh my goodness, you really, really need to come see this! You are not going to believe this!" he said before disappearing around the corner.

Imagining anything and everything up under the sun, the children race to his location under Little Jake's flashlight.

Suddenly lagging behind, Cyntica, Lil Ricky, and Temmis slow to a walking pace.

"This is stupid. I, I just want to go home," Temmis grumbles.

"Wait up, guys, I gotta breathe!" Cyntica tries to jog in spurts.

As the kids gather next to Mike, quietly, they stood in wonder. On a ledge of stone, looking down, they gaze in astonishment at what appear to be a wounded and crying furry elephant the size of a full-grown polar bear. The large mammal extends out its long hairy trunk, its huge brown eye filling with tears, and pain that connected with the children. Corky and Mindy become the first to carefully climb down, walk up to it, and touch its soft, coarse hair.

"I don't believe it. This is totally amazing!" Julius walks around it. "I think it's a wooly mammoth, a live wooly mammoth, right here, alive in our mountain, in front of us! This is so cool! Just like in the dinosaur books."

"Julius, if we make it out if here alive, we'll be famous. We'll make history!" Little Jake gives his brother a high five and a pat on the back.

"Yeah, we'll be millionaires, no, billionaires!" Cyntica bear hugs Lil Ricky. "We're rich!"

"But . . . how did it survive? They're all extinct." Rah stands behind them as Mindy draws back her hand and thinks. "Why is it so small, I thought they were way bigger than that? And look guys, look at this part of the cave we're in, it's an enormous canyon. It looks like Swiss cheese! This is starting to get a little crazy."

"They haven't existed for over thousands of years," Mindy mutters. "I think this thing is a baby, but where did it come from?"

"Hey, look at all the scars on it. Ouch, its leg is broken," Julius observes. Covering his ear's from the loud wails of the animal.

"Must've fallen from one of the cliffs up there." Little Jake looks closely at the animal's injuries. "But it doesn't explain all those gashes. I dunno, maybe it hurt itself getting here. I mean, elephants supposed to travel in packs right? Where's its pack? It can't be the only one left."

"I don't know, guys, I agree with Raheem. This is getting weirder and weirder by the second, don't you think? I'm sorry, there's nothing we can do for it. We have to keep going." Mike starts to receive bad feelings in cold chills upon his the back of his neck. "Let's go, we have to find a way out.

"Ew, that's disgusting anyway, and it smells like butt!" Tracy pinches her nose and covers her mouth. "I can't believe you even touched it! What if it has fleas or an ancient cave disease or something? I can't believe I'm in this Ninja Turtle cave with freaking mutants! I mean the giant bugs were enough, then the indoor mountain river. I don't need this shit, Mike. What else is in here with us? We have to go, now!" Tracy uncontrollably yells, sending Corky and Mindy scooting backward, thinking about how unclean the creature might have been.

Continuing onward, the group of youth travel deeper inside the mountain, staying only on the most passable passageways. Coming to a steep cliff, they peer down into a rocky pit of extinct animals, vegetation, and human remains. Descending down, they creep through the unbelievably tall plants and shrubbery.

Seeing something inside the green growth, Cyntica feels an odd furry texture and softness of a beaver that stood the size and height of a large boar standing on its two hind hooves. A snap and a terrible screeching roar sends them climbing for dear life into the network of tunnels above on the far sides of the pit. The large rodent beast flees into an unseen dark yet humungous burrow.

"What . . . what the heck was that?" cries Julius as Little Jake helps him into one of the caves along the wall. "Where's Rah? Raheem! Raheem?"

"I don't know, bro. I just don't know." Little Jake looks at him sorrowfully as Mindy leans up against him.

"Wait, where's Temmis?" Corky looks through her dirt-filled glasses.

"Over there!" Julius points out Mike and Temmis running through a shaft on the other side of the pit to different levels. "Temmis!" he calls out as the others join in. "What's the matter? Why are they running?"

"I don't think my cave is connected to yours!" Temmis shouts out. "There is no way, nope, can't do the beaver! Little me, no way!" he mutters before taking a hard breath of his inhaler. Having climbed up to a tunnel of dead ends and only caverns that went deeper into the mountain, he stares across the pit at his friends inside the cave walls across from him. Barely escaping the large insects before he encountered the children, Temmis was not willing to go back down near the man-sized beaver just to climb up to the others. "Impossible, this is unreal!" His nerves flutter rapidly around his tired lungs that drastically pump for air. He debates on staying behind or taking chances in the pit.

"Wait there! I'm coming to get you!" Mike yells after finding a connecting tunnel to the others. Going for the ledge, Tracy yanks him by the collar.

"Do you know what's down there or in here, really? You're going to get killed, Mike. Don't do it. We have to leave him." Trickling tears, Tracy looks into his eyes.

"Mike, I know you care about us and all, and you are a brave guy, but, I think the babe's right." Little Jake touches his arm, looking at him with a concerned face. "There's a giant baby bear-beaver-raccoon thing down there. Don't be an idiot, dude. We're pretty high, so if you fall . . . you see the bones down there. Yeah, I think that's what happened. And that moose rats gonna eat you."

"Don't go, Mike. We need you here with the rest of us. Maybe there's another way." Julius looks down at them from the ledge of the tunnel just above.

Temmis, who was on the other side, unfortunately couldn't hear what they were saying and was focused on staying put. Squatting down, he hollers out, "Don't worry about me. I'm staying. Go ahead!" His fear is overwhelmed by thoughts of his desire to go home. Sobbing, he pulls out his inhaler and squirts it into his mouth. As the container hisses out the dosage of medicine, something hisses and growls behind him, sending his legs and body spinning around in terror. Two large marble eyes make contact with his soul from the blackness of the cave just behind him. "Guys, uh, Corky? I think we're in trouble!" His loud words join his own screams as the set of large pupils sink and slant back as if getting in a pouncing position. "Corky!" Temmis leaps off the ledge as a huge paw knocks him into the wall and down to the rocky pit. Flipping over on his back, Temmis can faintly hear the others shouting something. Two saber-toothed cats viscously descend upon him, only teasing their very crave for meat.

As they began to scream, Mike covers Tracy's mouth and Tracy covers Corky's, urging them both to climb. Mike watches the deadly feast of the child helplessly from afar as the giant beaver appear just in time to be next upon the menu. Figuring it could possibly buy them some time, Mike ascends with the others into a series of more mazelike caverns. Pausing to rest, the group can't help but to hear the awesome sound of helpless life being devoured alive, echoing throughout the cavern walls.

"Saber-toothed tigers, saber-toothed tigers, saber-sa-sa," Cyntica repeats, trembling in place next to Lil Ricky, who was silently shaking in his boots and scared out of his wits.

Usually, Lil Ricky's eyes were beady and small, but at this precise second, Julius noticed under Mike's light that they were gapped wide open with fear. "Try not to be scared, guys. You know animals can smell fear," he reminded everyone in a low tone.

"Don't be scared?" Corky's voice cracks into a whisper. "That's the same as telling me not to panic after seeing my friend being eaten by saber-tooths!" Her voice crackles into a dramatic echo of noise, alarming everyone.

"Corky, keep it down. You're too loud! You're going to attract those things!" Mike scolds her as a sudden familiar sound startles them. "Okay, where is that coming from?"

"What is that?" Little Jake shines his flashlight on everyone.

"Oh my gosh! Something's coming through the walls to get us!" Tracy steps behind Mike and holds on to him tightly.

"I'm sorry, you all." Corky sits upon the cavern floor and weeps, mentally preparing herself for death.

Gravel and stone break away from the ceiling above them; a large and heavy body falls into Mindy's arms. Under Mike's torch, the dust settles and Mindy opens her eyes. Nearly face-to-face, she watches the creature, covered in dirt and mud, lick its lips like a lizard and open its humanlike eyes. Mindy screams as the others joined her. Flipping over and leaping back inside the settling cloud, the monster pulls back its shedding mud-covered skin. With the form of a small man, the creature reveals itself to be not a creature at all; but in fact, it was Raheem, Julius's best friend and a missing person from the group.

"Nice catch. Wassup, fellas? I thought I was lost, but you guys make an awful lot of noise. I thought you all were dead." He gives Julius a handshake and cleans his face with the inside of his t-shirt.

"We're far from dead, but we're sure going to be history if we don't get moving and find a way out of here soon. We just lost Temmis." Mike remarks.

"I didn't see anything. What's the problem, more roaches? Dang, I barely survived that fall!" Rah complains.

"No, Rah, saber-toothed tigers! Let's go!" Julius stops and warns him.

"Well, I guess that's better than . . . Hold on, did you say saber-toothed tigers? Wha—" A wild snarl from afar turns him around. As Little Jake aims his flashlight, the silhouette of a fanged-mouth creature causes Raheem to instantly disappear from the group, into the depths of one of the nearby cavern tunnels.

Behind the children, the second saber-tooth, magnificently colorful, struts behind the other, cleverly sniffing with large wet noses and tasting with open mouths of purple panting tongues. A more scrawny one, dirtier and darker in its oranges and blacks, appears last. Perhaps weakest yet hungrier than the rest, drooling, it smacks its bony jaws, slings its head, and takes off after the children first, provoking the other two. At first starting off slow, the saber-tooth picks up speed behind the children and dashes into the caves and caverns that split and connect with elaborate tunnels and shafts. One saber-tooth got so close to Lil Ricky that a swipe of the very tip of a single claw snatched a patch completely off the rear of his pants.

"Hurry!" yells Tracy as the floor gives away beneath her, swallowing her, Mike, and Corky.

Cyntica and Lil Ricky slid inside a small crack as the saber squeezes in behind them. They crawl and climb out into an open space; the passage caves in on the bloodthirsty cat that hunted them. Sprinting into a cave, Little Jake, Julius, and Mindy are followed inside by the two sabers. Running fast, Mindy reaches out for Little Jake's hand as Julius breaks between them and runs ahead as a saber-tooth crashes into the walls and claws the floor, trying to get to him. Little Jake spots an old stick of wood protruding from the floor. Wanting to use it as a torch, he remembers he didn't have a lighter or match. Dashing to an intersection of tunnels, Cyntica runs out from the tunnels on the left as Lil Ricky runs out from the right.

"Cyntica, toss me a light!" Little Jake shouts as the two spin around each other.

"What?" Cyntica, sweating and out of breath, yells back before seeing the felines running down the tunnel behind him.

"Toss me your lighter!" Little Jake runs toward him, yelling. Cyntica quickly shoves his hand into his tight small pockets and throws him the lighter. Almost dropping the small butane lighter, Little Jake ignites the dry, corroding stick of wood. As one of the sabers gain on him, opening its mouth of jagged teeth wide open, Little Jake tosses the burning wood directly between the cats opened mouth as its head engulfs in flames. It runs around dizzily, howling into the other as Little Jake dashes off behind his friends.

Running for their lives, Cyntica, Lil Ricky, and Julius hightail through the tunnels as Mindy and Little Jake cut through separate caves, both appearing behind them. Barely able to see, Raheem dashes out of a crack and crashes into Little Jake, knocking him five feet backward. Blacking out for a second, Little Jake opens his eyes to a growl quite equivalent to the sound of thunder. Raising his head, the remaining saber-tooth, singed on the leg by the other, slyly creeps near him. Remembering there was a broken ledge just above a reachable cavern behind him, he decides whether to run for it or use the lighter to try to scare the saber-tooth. Digging in his pocket, the saber-tooth leaps for him as Cyntica and Lil Ricky pulls him by both arms, dragging him backward down the tunnel. "A cliff, there's a cliff, you guys!" Little Jake screams as the large cat pursued them. Kicking wildly, he strikes the beast, knocking it away several times. As the saber grew on them, Jake spins around to his feet, not missing a step. Shining his flashlight, he sees his brother, friends, and the cliff he was referring to ahead. The saber goes in for the kill, swinging its muscular arm and long sharp claws. The six children leap off the tunnels edge. Leaving the cat behind, misjudging the ground, they fall inside a crater that drops them stories down onto a slide of rocks that avalanches them down a hillside into the largest cavern they had ever seen.

Breaking their fall on enormous leaves and the trunks of large healthy vines and plants, they tumble into a warm and vast marsh. Bumping his head on what felt like the bark of a tree, Little Jake sits up and quickly makes sure his waterproof flashlight wasn't broken. He turns it on as the children discover that they were suddenly inside an ancient-looking forest. The sound of great elephants trumpeting scarily veer across the walls of other canyon caves as herds of small pygmy mammoths, thought long ago extinct, stampede from the bushes. Hearing screams, Jake points the flashlight at Mindy being carried off on the back of one of the mammoths; then Julius and Raheem appear on the back of another, followed by Cyntica and Lil Ricky, who were hanging off the long straw-like brown hair on the back end of a round and plump mammoth trying to stay on. Within their yells, laughter, and the pygmy mammoth's squeals, grunts, and blows, the children found fun in an unlikely ride as Little Jake follows them into a clear, amazed. As if he was in a dream, he sees Mike and Tracy riding on two mammoths ahead as corky hung onto one sideways screaming.

"I think these things are blind or something. Where are they going?" Tracy lifts her legs as the surviving mammals bump into one another, plowing through the marshes.

"I'm not sure, but this is the safest route for now. Hey, guys, over here! Look, they made it, and they had the same idea? See, I told you they were smart!" Mike holds up his torch high so the others can see him. Crossing his fingers and toes, he hopes they make it out. And now with a new sense of hope inside his heart, he looks back thankfully as a saber-toothed cat tackles a line of mammoths behind him.

The cow-sized beasts sound their trunks to alarm the others as Little Jake jumps on to the back of the fleeing mammoth Julius was riding. "Where's Dad when you need him?" he shouts as they ride on the back of a pygmy wooly mammoth running into the unknown darkness of the cave.

Little did they know, their father, Jake, had problems of his own. Nauseated and about to pass out from asphyxiation, the brave dad covers his mouth along with the others as they push forward through a long tunnel of bat urine and guano.

"It smells really bad in here!" Liz complains as Reeves covers the upper portion of her body with his jacket.

"Save your breath," suggests Jake, noticing one of the smaller monster roaches searching for a way out just as they were. As if unable to bear any more, the insect spreads its wings, crawls, and glides over the wall to freedom. "This way, hurry!" Jake had the idea to copy the insect.

"I won't make it!" Old Meyers sunk down to one knee as Taj allows him to use his body as support.

"Yes, you will, just a bit farther, wise one," Taj encourages him as he and Jake watches one of the bugs climb up the cave wall on their right and crawl into large dark crevice.

"The air's gotten better. It's a little normal here." Dr. Jane Wallace uncovers her defined cheek bones and thin face. Slowing, she is flabbergasted by the intertwining shafts of rock under Jake's flashlight. "You know, this place looks awful different when you add a bright light to it."

Jake, believing that the insects would lead them to outside, watches more plump, hand-sized insects disappear into the long crack that sat between the flat portion of the wall and a giant boulder-looking piece. Under low, flat, hanging rocks and holed ceiling, Jake's group cross over the tops of gigantic cracks of rock.

Feeling as though his strength and energy was returning the farther away from the bats they got, Mr. Meyers pauses to rest a bit. "Not . . . not as young as I used to be, eh, fellas?" He shakes his peanut shaped head as the others slowly walk ahead. Slightly worried about the old man's health, Taj pauses and waits for him just a few feet away. Mr. Meyers rubs his forehead and holds his rifle in hand; Taj spots a gathering of antennas behind the hanging formation of limestone just above him. And like a collection of black marbles defying gravity, hundreds of black roaches, six inches to one feet long, spew out from the opening and over the old man's shoulder. Before he can utter a sound or warning, Taj, without thinking, ran for Meyers's hand. As the group look to see what was causing the sudden outburst from the old man, Liz lets loose a fearsome scream; Taj snatches Meyers out of the glob of man-eating insects.

"Gosh, darn it!" Meyers yells, smacking clumps of bugs from his head and body as Taj stomps around him. The more they kill, the more seem to come as they began to run toward the others. Jake shines his light steady as Mr. Meyers falls behind Taj. Flipping over on his back, he reaches for the fallen rifle just a few feet away, instantly engulfed by the murderous insects. Ripping into his soft, thin skin, they tear into his tender muscles. He screams for the Lord and Savior.

In disbelief and not wanting to leave him, Taj dashes off behind the others, followed by a growing black blanket of creeping insects. Picking up speed, Reeves stumbles by Jake as he waits for the others. Jane, pulling Liz tightly by the wrist, pushes by him next as Taj falls victim to a flood of vicious insects ahead. Unable to help him up, Jake watches a small army carry away his head. Looking back one last time where the old man once stood, a brilliant flash of light and a loud bang trembles his body. Bringing about a joyous grin, the sight of Old Man Meyers breaking out of the riverbed of insects, cursing and swinging about wildly, jolts his spirit. Running to help him, Jake steps into the swarm. Grabbing his hand, Jake pulls him away as Meyers fire into the floor and ceiling. Crashing and breaking sounds of falling rubble rumble from behind them as more giant cockroaches, young and adult, pour out of the floor, walls, and ceilings, changing the background into a scene from the darkest nightmare. "We have to get out of here!" Jake yells without looking back. Passing the first crack that also began to seep bugs, they climb inside a large split along the wall. Squeezing between large rocky plates, they squash a few bugs before climbing and tunneling down into another large cave. Holding back their screams, they gasp at a mass grave and mound of dead bodies and skeletons that covered a thirty-foot-wide space. Along with the bones, weapons, and torn clothes from different ages, the remains of ancient tool makers, the Civil War, and World War II memorabilia sprinkle around them.

"This has got to be some kind of feeding ground! We're too heavy to stay on top!" Jane screams out as Liz slips from the grip of her hand and sinks into the pool of bones.

Reeves fought to keep his head above the quicksand of skeletons as Jake and Old Man Meyers sink into the madness with them. In bones stacked and smashed compactly together, the five swim across the decayed oasis. What they witnessed and saw with their own eyes in the short period inside the cave underneath Jake's flashlight and the light on Reeves camera, was only equally comparable to the Vietnam War times ten. As the floor gradually slant upward, the group breaks through the bones to the other side. Crawling inside a huge archway, they scramble across a bridge of stone. Feeling safe for a minute, they slow after passing the half margin; but because of their weight, the crossing began to crumble and break. Jake leaps and grabs hold of a metal pipe that protruded from the ceiling as Mr. Meyers catches his leg. Jane grabs the old man's waist, and Reeves catches hold of her legs while Liz sees it all from below, hanging onto of him.

Everything below them vanishes into the darkness as that pipe Jake hung onto became their sole surviving force. If he could only follow it, he would know that just on the other end were the likes of two very unlikely rescuers.

"Mouse, you got those bombers ready?" Ernie the Exterminator speaks loudly into his walkie-talkie. Inspecting a small infestation inside the backyard of one of the old neighborhood apartments in his fieldwork, he eyes some odd activity coming from a small burrow in the ground.

"Umm, no, almost. Gimme a second. I'm pulling up!" Mouse, Ernie's scrawny, loyal, and trusting assistant, pulls their van close to a fence. As a small cloud of dust emits from the small hole, it collapses into the size of both of Ernie's large hands. Roaches of four to five inches long suddenly scurry in and spring out of the hole. As a gently breeze clears the fog of dirt, it reveals a long vibrating water pipe poking out from the ground.

Ernie's eyes widen at the sight of all the insects running around the hole of the pipe. Jogging to the van, he takes a rope already connected to the tow reel and ties the other end around his waist. "Mouse, this looks unsteady, I'm going to need you to hold on to me, just in case this hole falls in. I found an incredible infestation! We're going to get paid by the city for this one! Whoa, like look at the size of those things!" He smashes one crawling near his boot as it explodes in juice. "This is going to take everything we've got." Ernie pops open the back double doors and steps inside his van, loading up all kinds of extermination equipment. Mouse turns around and watches him load his body with extra things. Ernie holds up the walkie-talkie. "This is it, Mouse. This is the big one!"

"Yeah, yeah." Chewing on a straw from a broom, Mouse swivels back around and sighs to himself. Digging in his nose, he flicks something greenish yellow out of the window. Scratching a prickly face, his large blue popped eyes watches Ernie gallop back to his current position in the rearview mirror. Taking off his exterminator hat, he frizzles his short cut, sweating blonde hair with his hand.

Quickly returning to the pipe, Ernie takes out his special equipment and listens to the ground. Checking the readings on the instrument, he places a small rod connected to the machine by wires into the ground one more time and lifts his head with excitement. "Listen to those weird sounds. This is incredible. There's an enormous talking civilization of insects right here underground! Right in this mountain! This is unbelievable." The hefty, pudgy-faced man wipes his forehead of sweat and glances at the trembling pipe in front of him. Pulling out his map of the city's plumbing, he unfolds the duct-taped blueprints and sits it down, making no sense of it at all. "This pipe leads to the monster's nest. I bet it isn't even supposed to be here. I'm doing them a favor. I'm pulling it." Licking his lips at the view of more roaches gathering around the base of the pipe, he reaches for it. As it began to vibrate rapidly, the tips of Ernie's fingertips touch it. The ground caves in beneath him as he catches hold on to the only thing around him, the pipe. "Uh, Mouse! I might need a hand here, buddy. Pull me up. I'm in the hole!" Ernie releases the talk button and clips the radio back onto his belt as the left hand held on to the pipe and the weight on its opposite end pulled him deeper into the hole.

"Copy that. Assistance is on the way, assistance is on the way!" Mouse replies, not even looking in Ernie's direction. Trusty, yet lazy and stubborn, he waits a few minutes before actually getting up and activating the motorized towing spindle.

Feeling as though the pipe was connected to something important, a nest or the world that he heard through his equipment, for whatever his own personal reasons, Ernie, held on to the pipe with every ounce of strength he could muster. Now staring into a sunken pit, it sinks again below him as the shaking, vibrating pipe starts to shake and whip Ernie's body around like a wobbly car antenna. Then as the foundation of the house that once stood there nearly over a decade ago began to plummet into the earth, the pipe quickly pulls Ernie and the van he was attached to into the growing swimming-pool-width hole. The van slowly reels Ernie in by the rope that squeezes and cuts around his large belly the longer he refuses to let go of the pipe. "Okay, let me go, Mouse. Drop me! Lower me down, Mouse! Reverse the line, Mouse. Mouse? Uh-oh, okay, Mouse, I think I'm going to be sick." Unable to hold on any longer, Ernie lets go of the pipe and is slung up into the air by the tight rope. The bug mobile flies by his head; Ernie back flips, catching hold to the roof as it free-falls through the earth wailing a siren of the Creedence Clearwater Revival, Bad Moon Rising.

And not far below, Jake hangs suspended from the other end of the pipe as it starts to swiftly drop feet at a time among falling rocks. Watching Jane and the others fall hundreds of feet into black below him, the entire cavern ceiling splits and breaks above him, sending him tumbling down like a ragdoll. Smacking into a surprisingly soft surface, Jake lands on his back as rock and huge boulders fall and collide around him. Covered from head to toe in dirt and crystals, he rolls over, dodges, and weaves around three falling stones of extreme proportions and dives before the remains of an old bathroom and kitchen sink that nearly smashes him to death. With a weird sense of a small earthquake happening, Jake's shaky hands flick on his flashlight. Looking down at the strange colors on some patches of the floor of what appeared to be yet another enormous cavern, he peers afar, up at Mr. Meyers and Jane, grappled and suspended in midair by two giant tentacles. Thousands more stretch and extend from all around them as miles beneath the earth, the main body of a creature towered throughout the unknown upper crevices of our planet's crust.

"What is it?" Liz cries out hiding behind Reeves's tall pair of legs.

"I don't know. GOD help us." Reeves looks down at the thick globby matter under his feet and eases into a large opening of rock.

Firing his rifle, the bloody and tired Mr. Meyers frees himself yet again. Falling to the ground, he lands on an extending limb with a mouth on the end of it. "What the hell are they? What in tarnation? Dang varmints!" Swiftly unbuttoning his shirt pocket, he reloads his rifle and blows the snapping mouth into smithereens.

"Meyers, beside you, help Jane!" Jake hollers out. Running toward them, he leaps over and slides through the snaillike limbs. A blast is heard as Jane falls into his arms, sending him back to the ground. Grabbing one of the long tentacles still attached to her leg, he twists and snaps the jagged-tooth mouth from her flesh, preventing it from being completely devoured by many more on the arm. Helping the woman up, she looks at Jake and Mr. Meyers with high gratitude.

"Thanks." Jane looks down at her bleeding leg. Before she can say another word, they're forced back to the dirt as the ground shifts slanted, sliding them into precious historic formations of rock and crystals that shatter around them upon contact.

"You're welcome." Feeling blood trickle from his busted lip, Jake pulls himself up from the cave floor as it levels. "Where the hell are we? And why is the floor soft and moving?" Helping the drained Mr. Meyers up, he eyes Jane rising to her feet.

"This is no floor." Meyers shoots downward as a bubbling moan rubbles the cave.

"Look . . . at . . . that." Jake shines his dimming flashlight ahead; many mouths of various sizes attached to the tips of hundreds of limbs and tentacles that sprout from pore-like openings in the floor all around them. Following the floor miles ahead with his eyes, Jake realized then that they weren't standing on a floor at all as the floor stretched into an enormous morphing body that towered thousands of feet underneath the body of the mountain. "Incredible. I bet that's what's making all these giant tunnels. So what do ya think, Meyers? Meyers?" Jake and Jane turn around to the head of Mr. Meyers choking on his own blood and saliva as an arm of the monster silently devours him whole. "Meyers!"

"Oh my gosh!" Jane shouts and screams as Jake snatches the rifle from below the suspended body of the old man being eaten; his constricting body gives off a snapping and crunching sound. "It's killing him!"

Taking her by the hand, Jake sprints through the creature's hellish arms and extra limbs that sprout and attacked upon movement, trying to escape. Tentacles reach for them as other grow mouths and antenna-like feelers that forces them onto one side of the cavern. Ducking into a cave, they kneel against a wall as the rock break open around them, leaving them exposed upon a small flexing muscle of the giant. "Okay, what now?" Jake glances at Jane clueless. With no way out, a tremendous portion of pointy and jagged-sized rock collapse on top of the main body of the creature. Hurt by the fallen rock, it emits some type of earth quaking roar, loosening a long strip of crumbling stone that smashes into it, carrying the speeding bug mobile and Ernie the Exterminator on its roof.

"Goodness gracious!" Ernie, stunned by the awesome sight and the survival of his fall, draws a cross with his fingers across his chest and says a quick prayer. Using his tired arm strength to pull upward, he crawls to the front of the roof to make sure someone was still driving the van. Peeping down through the top corner of the windshield, he taps on the glass and signals Mouse to go faster as inner structures of the cave, sections of streets, and buildings come crashing down around them. Spotting Jake and Jane ahead of the van's bright automatic headlights, Ernie reaches for his walkie-talkie. "Mouse, I'm okay. Keep doing what you're doing! How are we holding up?"

"I'm alive, Ernie. What the fuck, man? How the heck did we get down here? Where are we? We're in hell, dude. What in hell did you do?" He drives over, fleeing abnormally sized roaches and smashes through a crisscross of hungry extending appendages. "Is that . . . is that Jake? What the hell is he doing under . . . underneath the ground? See 'em?" As his skinny body tremble with fear, he grips the receiver of the CB radio nervously in the palm of his sweaty hand.

"I see them. No way! We have to get them! Go for it, Mouse, ten o'clock sharp!" Ernie directs as they shoot off in Jake's position. Driving straight for a moment, the body of the enormous monster swells, Ernie locks his feet into the rail on the roof of the van as it suddenly barrels down a slope of dozens of frolicking and retracting tentacles sliding to a halt in front of Jane. "Get in the back. It's open, hurry!" Ernie shouts from the roof as the pair, without questions, open the doors and climbs into the back of the van as Mouse drives off.

"Howdy! How you folks doing? Jake, what the heck you doing way down here, and who's the lady? She's a beaut, and you better not say Satan's helper 'cause I ain't on no witchcraft stuff, all right?" Mouse takes his eyes completely off driving and turns around to look at them.

"Mouse, drive!" Jake yells as Mouse retakes the wheel. "We fell and got stuck like everyone else, Mouse. This is Jane, my ex-girlfriend," he briefly introduces. "Now . . . I don't mean to rush you, but in case you haven't seen it, we're on a giant squid-looking thing, and there are thousands of man-sized roaches down here trying to eat us! How the heck are we getting out of here?" Jake looks out the back window at the body of the creature growing even taller in the distance.

"Do I look like I have a plan, Jake? How the hell do I know how to get out of here?" Mouse hits the dashboard, shakes his head and scratches his thin unshaved stubby neck.

"Why is Ernie on the roof? Is he okay out there?"

"Yeah, he's good." Mouse stares through the window at the spreading tentacles growing around them. "Well, since the good Lord dropped me here for some GOD-awful reason, guess I'll kick in the front door like he asked me. Hold on, we're going in," he announces and steps on the gas.

"Going in? Now you wait just a sec—" Jane is thrown to the floor on top of Jake as the vehicle hits a bump at a fast speed, automatically triggering on the bug mobiles siren.

Along the body of the creature, the vehicle cuts into a shattered section of tunnels, plowing through more insects and giant frail crystals of minerals. Popping a wheely through a gapped opening, the van climbs onto an enormous moving arm of the creature.

"Wait, Mouse, where are you . . . Damn, Liz!" Jake yells as the back doors fly open and slam close.

"Shit, Reeves!" Jane suddenly remembers her coworker as numerous spray cans of insecticide tumble down on her; something tumbles into her jacket pocket.

"I think I saw him bail out." Jake crawls to the fence that separated the front of the van from the equipment area.

"Whoa, did you see that?" Mouse's big eyes widen even more as he turns completely around again to look at Jake.

"Mouse, no, look where you're going!" Jake watches firsthand the vehicle veer directly into a mouth the size of a small house.

Swallowed by the arm or leg of the prehistoric monster, the portion of the unknown limb of the giant serpulid where Ernie's van was being digested expands and bubbles into a veining brownish purple. Receiving an internal negative reaction, the sluggish appendage falls against the body, splitting open in a melting mesh of disintegrating mush. With his feet planted and the rope wrapped securely around his waist and the plastic bug on the roof of the van, Ernie rides out from inside of the giant feeding arm on the roof of the van, squirting streams of his special toxic insecticide from the sprayers in both his hands. Tossing a couple of bug bombs behind him, the potent spray and mist eats enormous holes along the giant. Upon feeling the reaction to his chemicals, the creature shifts and contracts, slinging the van into the air like a toy car and away from its aching limb. The tubeworm roars a horrible sound as the van flips into a tunnel landing on all four wheels, ending quietly, slap dead at the end of the first verse of Bad Moon Rising. Skidding at least ten feet, Mouse turns on the high beams as Ernie spits out a small tentacle and finishes another prayer on the roof. Having both received slight cuts and bruises on their body and face, both Jake and Jane sit up inside piles of exterminating gear.

"That was some fancy driving, Mouse. Now do you think you can give me a hand down from here?" Ernie crawls to the window's edge as a sudden noise lifts his head. "Wait, Mouse, don't get out just yet. I hear something. 1, 2, over and out."

"Roger that, buddy, 3, 4." Mouse holds the receiver close to his lips and places one hand on the wheel. Glancing back at his two passengers, everything goes black as another limb swallows the vehicle.

Reeves and Liz continue to run inside the darkness of the collapsing caves as the sound of falling rock and giant insects follow them, haunting their every direction. Fitting inside a small crawl space, the two tunnel down between tight slabs of granite, and limestone before breaking through a wall and taking a slide down a long spiraling tunnel of sharp-edged stones. Bursting through a wall of loose rock, the two land on a flat bed of dirt. Switching his camera to night vision mode, Reeves looks over Liz and at himself for injuries. Scoping out their surroundings, he also recognizes an old primitive torch covered in dirt next to him. Putting down the camera, he picks it up, finds his lighter, and lights the stick of wood, noticing someone else's hand still attached to it. Still on the ground in disbelief, Liz lifts her head to see the body of a dead person lying next to her in the same position she was in. Rising to her feet, she scoots next to Reeves as they stand in a colony of bugs, in the middle of a nest of giant roach eggs that lay among the dead bodies of their parents. Huddling in fear, Reeves holds his camera like a batting weapon. Gripping the gold cross around his neck, he prays. Foreseeing their doom and the end of their lives, Reeves stands up straight and bold, prepared to die fighting the swarm of now approaching insects; an enormous tentacle bursts through the wall and extends miles away in front of him. And like hot wax, a large hole melts along the side of the large limb as Ernie's van rolls out its center at high speed sounding its siren.

Gaining the attention of the giant insects, the bug mobile heads straight for Reeves and the little girl, demolishing a path of insects along the way. Ernie sprays away and throws out his bombs as the giant bugs' bodies explode and fall. The van swerves and skids, braking yards away from the man and child.

"Reeves, get in, hurry!" Jane calls out as Jake opens the double doors.

Shoving Liz ahead, Reeves races behind her to the van. Holding off the approaching insects behind them, he fights for their lives, wrestling one off his back. As Liz makes it to Ernie's utility vehicle, Jake yanks her inside. Almost at the van, Reeve's hears his longtime friend, Jane, shouting for him as loud as she can. Wishing to never see that expression of fear, concern, and panic for him on her face again, he vows to make it alive. Tossing her the equipment bag, he reaches for Jane's hand and is snatched by dozens of the octopus-like creature's smaller arms that branch out from three larger tentacles.

"Move it, Mouse. Let's go. We can't stay here." Ernie smacks the roof of the van disappointingly as Jake closes the back doors. Mouse continues driving.

"Reeves, no!" Jane cries out. "My good friend, Reeves. Oh my . . . no." She sobs into Jake's arms. "What the hell is that thing?" She cries out.

"I don't know," Jake mutters, only able to think about his sons at the time.

"Ernie, what the heck do you think that thing is?" Mouse turns up the CB and packs a pinch of snuff behind his bottom lip, thinking to himself about the noise coming from the roof. "You okay, good buddy?"

"Mouse, I'm a little busy right now!" Ernie, fighting the giant bugs on the roof with the leg of an insect, kicks two off the sides and sends the last insect's head flying into the distance. As the body falls off the rear of the vehicle, Ernie tosses the leg off to the side as puss-colored insect blood splatters onto his face.

"Wait, stop the car!" Jane screams as they reach a clearing.

"Lady, you have got to be out of your cotton-pick'n mind if you think that I'm going to stop this vehicle! I don't mean to be rude, but didn't you just wave goodbye to your little pal back there?" Mouse glances at her strangely in the rearview mirror.

"Easy, Mouse." Jake slows the sensitive subject. "Lady, you have got to be joking. You were just out there. You know how dangerous it is. We could all get killed, any one of us," replies Jake, dumbfounded by Jane's suggestion.

"Now's our chance to analyze this thing. If I could get a sample of that thing's tissue, maybe we can stop it. I have a portable DNA sequencer in my bag. Maybe we could find out what this thing is and stop it. Reeves and the others don't have to die in vain. Now's our chance . . ." Jane looks at Jake sincerely before something outside the vehicle draws her attention to the window. "Look!" She points to a piling, twitching mass of wormlike limbs being attacked by massive insects. As they feed off the body and fallen soft fleshy tissue of the giant eel-looking monster, Jane observed the creature also feasting off the cockroaches.

"It's like we're in the middle of a freaking war!" Mouse began to apparently slow down the vehicle. "Hey, lady, do you think you can really stop this thing?"

"I don't know, but I can at least take the first step and identify what it is. If we can't stop it and if I do or don't make it, at least someone will have the information on what's happening beneath us every day," Jane explains, opening her bag that was actually a computerized case.

"What is that? Looks like something a secret agent would use. Wait, who are you, really?" Jake asked as Jane takes off her jacket and rolls up her shirt sleeves.

"Uh, Mouse, why are we slowing? We're stopping, Mouse. What's happening?" On his belly trembling, Ernie smears away purplish goo from his goggles, viewing the ongoing frenzy of feeding around him clearer. "Mouse?"

Placing the fastened strapped case around her neck, Jane prepares to capture a sample. "To keep it simple, I'm many things now, Jake. I work in a crime lab and study to be a famous scientist on the side. And this little darling around my neck here just may be the ticket that gives us superpowers over this thing." Jane opens the sliding side door to the van and hops out.

"Bet that dame's some type of CIA specialist. Bet she knows lots of secret things and stuff." Mouse tunes out Ernie as Jake and Liz go to the window.

"Mouse, why on earth did we stop? Mouse?" Ernie then sees Jane run away from the section of tunnel remains they were in, toward the remains of the gargantuous creature. "Wow . . . now that is one crazy woman. Oh well, I better reload!" He eases down off the van. "Hi there!" Ernie opens the double doors.

Running at top speed, Jane falls to her knees and slides to the base of the nearest specimen. Feeling for the locks along the sides of the case, it opens like a laptop. A bright header fills its screen as Jane ejects a small petri dish and scalpel. Pricking the meat, she rubs a dab on a small electronic petri dish and slides it into the machine. Taking another sample, Jane saves it in a small vile. Oozing from behind her, a dresser-shaped slab of meat begins to move and wiggle. Extensions of mouths and tentacles sprout from the severed tissue. Blossoming like a rose, its skin peel and rip as a much longer and wider feeler stretches from the body and crashes to the ground, lifeless beside Jane.

"Time to go!" The side of the van door opens as Jake yells out, "Come on, Dr. Wallace! Jane, lets hurry!"

Seeing herself facing the same fate as her friend Reeves, Jane races back to the van. Climbing onto the unstable piece of tunnel, she reaches for Jake and leaps in the vehicle as it sped off, screeching its tires inside the cave.

Jake's sons and the other children had evaded the grave danger of the saber-tooth's on the backs of the long-thought, extinct pygmy mammoths. Separating from the other herds, a few groups of the fastest and strongest mammoths cross a bridge of melted stone that stretched across a deep valley of igneous rock.

"This is scary," Julius states as Little Jake pats him on the shoulder with Mindy holding on tightly to his waist.

"This is so high." Tracy shares a mammoth with Mike. "Why is it suddenly so hot?"

"It'll be okay," Mike comforts her. "I think we're actually inside an old volcano or something? I think that's how mountains are formed. Maybe we're getting close to its center."

"This is cool!" Lil Ricky smiles behind Rah as Cyntica whacks him on the head.

"Of course it is you, idiot! Whoa!" Cyntica almost falls off the mammal as they rode ahead of the majority of the herd. As the natural bridge of old cooled lava residue narrows, the mammoths move into a single line. At first holding tails, the mammals began to spread farther apart, creating more and more distance between them.

Thankful that they we're alive, in front, Mike worries about the sabers that he heard not that long ago. "I don't mean to sound negative or anything, but I hope that if those big cats come back, they munch on all those mammoths in the back first!"

"Me too!" Rah replies as Julius agrees.

"We need somebody to watch the rear at all times. Who's it gonna be, any volunteers?" Mike scans the area for trouble.

"We could walk faster than these dumb things!" harped Cyntica as his mammoth continuously released a potent foul smelling gas from its rear. "Phew!"

"I can't believe we're still inside the mountain. I mean, how big is it really?" Little Jake questions. Mindy leans into his ear.

"I don't think we're still in the mountain. We're actually miles and miles underground. Probably in the earth's mantle. The caves are starting to look different. Did you know the earth is primarily water? Which means that every piece of land humans live on is really the tip of a mountaintop that's poking out of the ocean. Caves have the best collection of rocks, and this one was right beneath us," Mindy informs them.

"Cool, you're pretty smart." Julius listens, intrigued by Mindy. And for the first time, he slightly began to like her as a friend. "How do you know all those things?"

"I read," Mindy answers as the strangest howl of death causes them all to look back. Watching a cluster of mammoths pitfall in a cloud of dust and rocks, she eyes packs of the descendants of the ancient mammals plummet off the sides of the bridge into the darkness as dozens of savage saber-tooths wipe them out from the rear.

"They're coming this way!" Tracy gasps. "It's a whole bunch of them!"

"Get down and run for it!" Mike instructs as the others slide down from the sides and backs of the panicing mammoths.

Being the last one, Cyntica slips off the back of the mammoth, breaking his fall by catching hold of the mammal's thick wool hair. Accidently pulling out two painfully large plugs of hair, he sends the animal colliding into the others, creating another stampede. Running alongside the lead mammoths in the back, the saber-tooth's cut in between the humble, frightened creatures, swiping and chomping at them like chew toys until spotting the children. As a small group of the large cats take chase to them, the natural bridge gives under the weight of the action; it begins to crumble underneath the feet of the ancient beast. Fleeing across, the children glance back at the creatures who unfortunately become extinct again. Almost on the other side, a wild saber climbs up from the side of the rocks and charges after them aggressively.

At the bottom of the cavern, Jake and the survivors inside the bug mobile witness the animals tumbling off the long crashing bridge. "What the hell is going on over there?" Jake stares out the window at the carcasses of what appear to be tigers and baby elephants. "Are those animals down here too? Geesh, guess those bugs aren't our only worries. So what are you doing? What is that thing, what exactly does it do?" He turns toward Jane, who was analyzing tissue samples inside her mechanical box.

"This is my friend, the IQ. It does many things. One of its many functions is reading any sample of a living or deceased organisms in real time and break down its genetic code." Jane focuses on the reading of the screen and types on the keyboards touch screen of the panel.

"That's nifty," Ernie states, strengthening his pesticides and mixing chemicals into containers.

"So what does it say?" asks Liz curiously with faith in the woman.

"Oh my gosh, it's totally amazing. So far, according to the data, it appears that we're dealing with some type of slug or worm. This is the first ever! By the length of its DNA strain, it's a descendant right out of the prehistoric era. Its genetic code is as old as a dinosaur," Jane informs them excitedly. "We have no record of some species because their makeup was so soft and tissue-like, that when they died, their bodies pretty much totally disintegrated. This is . . . this is big!" She tugs on her collar, beginning to get hot.

"Prehistoric dinosaur?" Jake replies.

"I can't yet tell how old it is, but it is indeed a surviving relative. This is truly a remarkable discovery." Jane's face lights up over the screen.

"A slug humph, anyone got salt?" Jake look's over at Mouse.

"Okay got it, I think. Yea, okay, it's a . . . a giant tubeworm." Jane looks at the readings on the machine closely and slides back on her jacket. "It makes since. All these years, we've studied and talked about dinosaurs and rocks. We forgot about the micro world back then. What if the smaller things flourished and blossomed right beneath us, unexposed to climate change and the ice age? And tubeworms that survived, may have had the power to evolve into a whole new species. We know little about them. Humph, a prehistoric tubeworm, incredible."

"Well, I don't know about you ladies and gents, but the bug man's not going out without a bang. That thing ain't eaten ol' iron heart Ernie that easily. Looks like I'm going in the belly of the beast with my children." Ernie the Exterminator draws attention to the straps of deadly strength insecticide gas grenades that crisscross the middle of his chest. "Now who's ready to go home?" He stood heroically padded with all sorts of super-potent concoctions and equipment. "I got a little something, something that I think will melt down that sucker."

"Save it, Ernie. We need to find a way out of this mountain first. The military can deal with that thing! How far do you think we can get in the bug mobile?" Jake's only concern was returning to his boys.

"Well, gas is getting mighty low, and it feels like we're going up, maybe in a big spiral. A few buildings came crashing down a little ways back there, so that meant that we had to be close to the surface at one point. But we can get back off this thing and cut through one of them holes in the walls at any time." Mouse scratches his scruffy face.

"Yeah, right, it's where the holes lead that bothers me! It could lead to a deadly drop or another cave of bug filled tunnels." Jake thinks of all possible options.

"Why don't we just keep going whichever way is up since it's where we started?" Liz stunned them all with the great simple suggestion as they all agreed.

"She's going to grow up to be the president someday." Ernie smiles down upon the little girl and opens the side door. "I got to get back on the roof and devise a strike. I think it's the best position! Giant bugs and monster tubeworms, here I come. This is Armageddon." He taps on the full insecticide tanks on his back. "Prehistoric tubeworm-slug thingy with multiple mouths, check!" He secures his bomb sprays and decides to use the back doors since a small ladder was connected to it. Sliding the side door of the van open, a plane-sized tentacle thrashes through the ground in front of them. As Mouse hits the gas and makes a hard turn, he throws Jake, Jane, and Ernie out of the side door of the vehicle. Mouse cuts the wheel again with all his might, speeding off into a dark tunnel, with Liz screaming in the back and Ernie dragging behind by the tow rope hollering.

The sound of breaking and an erupting rock was heard all around the stranded two as they stood, just missing a hillside of sharp rocks. Jake peer into the pit below filled with water and more tubeworm. He takes Jane's hand and runs into a large crack along the wall; a hand-shaped limb snaps its jaws behind their paths. Making their way through the sharp painful stone and minerals, Jane cries as Jake moans in agony over their sore, bruised, and cut tired limbs. Inside the bottom of a small pit, Jake shines his light upward as it becomes clear that they would have to use the rock climbing skills that they didn't have to make it out of there. After climbing and crawling through narrow spaces several more times, the two wind up inside of a nearly perfect tubular structure. Feeling a slight breeze, the two decide that it was very likely that the direction they had chosen led to outside, and so they followed it. For what seemed like hours of miles traveled, through his final observation, Jake began to firmly believe in their theory that the tubeworm and the insects had constructed the tunnels within the mountain's caves.

"We seriously have got to find a way out of here. This doesn't look good," Jake staggers next to Jane, whispering in the dark. Hearing all types of movement and feeling all sorts of vibrations in the floor causes them to pause, stop, and listen cautiously. Resting for a second or two, Jake switches out the batteries in his flashlight with some good ones he found in the bottom of his bag. Flicking it on, it gleams brightly, revealing another active nest of giant insect eggs. Among the large mazelike space, hundreds of transparent eggs and giant roaches mix into a collection of garbage, human remains, and items from the dead throughout the last millions of years. Not able to turn back, carefully, they step between the clusters of unhatched eggs, coming to a hideously fat and repulsing enormous cockroach. Having to be the queen, nearly completely still, except for its bottom, in an unconscious state, the insect automatically produces multiple eggs as large as the insects that carried them away and placed them. Some of the bugs stored food around the frisky larvae as others added fresh food to the mounds of trash.

"Unbelievable," Jake blurts out as Jane screams behind him. He turns around to the sight of a busted egg and miniature versions of the giant insects covering her body. Taking his breath away, Jake stumbles backward, falling onto a bed of eggs as a brown gel-like substance explodes under and over him in undeveloped swimming and crawling cockroaches. Attracting all the giants at once, the two become encircled by bugs.

Finding one of Ernie's bombs labeled "Atomic Jack" in her jacket pocket, Jane pops its cap, steps on the insects she knocks off her body, and throws the small canister, releasing poisonous gas into the open. As she covers her face, Jake thinks about life, death, his sons, and all the killings he's seen. Squatting down into the garbage, Jane sees him come up with a machine gun, clearing the wave of bugs in front of them. "Whoa, where did you get that?" asked Jane, hardly able to hear.

"Look around, baby, there's more where this came from!" Jake replies. Picking up an old flip lighter, he scopes out a treasure of weapons within centuries-old garbage. "Come on!" He guides Jane, crawling up a mound toward a box labeled "TNT." Using a scrap of metal to pry the lid open, he marveled at dozens of old sticks of dynamite. Taking one out of the crate, within seconds, an intense glare is captured on the wall from a ball of fire that explodes in front of him.

"Nice, still works!" Jane smiles, carrying a flamethrower.

"So cool . . . and they're highly flammable." Jake picks up a long sword. Swiping the air, he holds it outward in the light in front of him, seeing other unopened crates of explosives and large packs of black crawling bodies of insects coming for them. Grabbing handfuls of dynamite, he stuffs his bag and shirt while tossing dozens around the queen and on the tops of nearby eggs.

Quickly moving, Jake discovers more clips among the dead body of a soldier and fires into the giant cockroach army, running down the tunnel at the same time. Jake yells to Jane, "Now light 'em up!" as she sets the closest bugs on fire and aim for the eggs, she causes the area to ignite in a spectacle of explosions. Knocking them off their feet, they crawl to the sound of each other's voice in the dark, finding the other in the scatter of fire. "Jane, get up! Jane, move your ass now!" Jake's voice becomes quite clear as Jane pushes herself up beside him, running three steps into a large pinching head. "Grab onto me!" he yells as Jane places her arms around his neck. Using great timing as the large pinchers snap, the queen's head veers to the left at them, allowing Jake to dodge and leap onto the long, thick antenna of the monster. Climbing onto the hairs upon its head with Jane, Jake's flashlight rubs against the creature and clicks on. Glancing at the passing ground, they catch a glimpse of the most surreal scene.

Hurt by the explosion, the queen is unable to remove the pests from her crown. With half of its body missing, insides and fluids drag behind the queen as it searches for a new nest and hive. Hundreds of her hungry children thirstily sprawl out from the shadows, following her blood and cry.

Jane sets them on fire from long range, holding on to the flamethrower and flashlight as Jake kept them secure, clutching on to the large highly evolved Blattidae with all his might. The action slows; a few insects drop from the ceiling as Jane sprays them with fire. Genuinely bursting into an upside-down sizzling frame, one left covered in fire, springs out for a taste of the queen. Dying hungry before the mouthful, its burning fire catches hold of the queen's leaking fluids, igniting her remaining inner workings. And like a launching starship, Jake and Jane rockets miles ahead through the tunnel, clearing everything in their path, including insects and stone alike. The queen's body explodes as the head breaks off like a deployed space capsule. Crashing down into earth and rock, it rolls and vanishes silently.

"So what's the plan now, hero?" Jane sits up in the dirt, bruised and sore. "And where did that thing's head go? I sure as hell didn't hear a bang."

"I dunno." Jake gathers the fallen TNT from around him and staggers to a cliff. "Damn, I found it. Looks like our only way is down." He stares down a slide of fallen rock that poured into a larger natural shaft of darkness and unknown dangers. Hundreds of feet in the air with giant insects somewhere behind them, Jake and Jane slide, tumble, and swiftly fall down the rocky hill somewhere inside the earth.

Close by, Little Jake, Julius, Raheem, Mike, Tracy, Cyntica, Lil Ricky, Mindy, and Corky stand huddle flat against the wall in terror. In an open cavern of caves, a single mammoth stands between buying them more time to live and the last sabertooth chasing them. The saber growls ferociously at the pygmy mammoth as the wooly sways back and forth closer to the kids.

"We're going to be pancakes or diced liver!" cries Cyntica, squeezing behind them all.

"Get 'em, mammoth! Don't be afraid!" Julius whispers to himself, balling up his fist, watching.

The descendant of the great elephant turns and blows his mighty trunk and bows his long cracked tusk up and down. As the saber charges at the mammoth's faces with curled claws, the final blow snatches the mini mammal off to the side and slings it down into the pit. Snarling a moment, the proud female saber slowly licks her paws and inches forward gracefully.

"We're about to be eaten! I don't want to be eaten!" Rah pours out crying, looking every which way for a place to run. Seeing nothing but the direction they came, he thinks of his mother and hardworking father. Oh, how he would never see them again. "I'm too young to die."

"It's been nice knowing you, Lil bro. You're the best little brother a guy could ever ask for." Little Jake hugs his little brother one last time.

"You were always my favorite big brother." Julius smiles back in tears. "I wish Dad was here!" he screams out before the saber. And as if his wish was answered by the heavens above, suddenly, they hear a loud crackling sound as Jake burst through the wall and ceiling in a rain of rock and material.

From the clearing fog of dirt, the boys' father rises from the gravel and small boulders along with his ex-girlfriend as Little Jake's and Julius's faces light up with joy and hope. "Dad!" they cheer, running to their father, hugging him.

"Where did you come from? How did you know where we were?" Julius jumps up and down.

"That was cool, Pops!" Little Jake compliments his father's entry. "What are you doing here?"

"It's a long story. I'm just happy that you two boys are in one piece . . . Hey, don't you two supposed to be safe at home? How did you get way down here, and who are all these kids?" Jake glances around curiously.

"Wait, guys. What happened to the tiger?" Mike whispers to Tracy as they both stare into the dissipating dust. Creeping past the small reunion, they crept to the ledges around them. "I don't see it. It's like it disappeared."

"It probably got clobbered by their dad. Cool!" Overhearing the conversation, Cyntica moves in between them and looks back at the pile of rubble surrounding Jake.

"You think it's really buried under there?" Lil Ricky stares beside him.

"What's with your friends? What's under where?" Jake interrupts the conversation with his sons and responds to the chattering children.

"What are you guys looking for?" Jane blurts outs.

"You might not believe this, sir, but giant bugs and wild saber-toothed tigers have been chasing us!" Mike briefly explains. "One was right here, but it apparently got buried or . . . vanished or something. We don't see it."

"Saber-toothed tiger?" Jake and Jane repeat at the same time.

"Yeah, we were about to get sliced to shreds and eaten right before you like . . . crashed through the roof of the cave!" Tracy looks over at Mike.

"It's a good thing I found you." Jake places an arm around Julius and peers down at Little Jake as a tattered saber-tooth suddenly leaps from the pit and attacks Mike and Tracy from behind.

Knocking Tracy, gasping to her knees for air, the lone saber crunches down upon her shoulder and thrashes her about. Weighing down a leg with a mighty muscular arm, in one great swipe of the left paw, the cat, not knowing its own strength, claws Tracy from the leg and slides her body over the cliff to join the mammoth. Mike shouts behind his love; instantly, the saber pounces on him, slicing his face in three as Jake unloads a round of bullets into the saber-tooth. Mike falls helplessly at Julius's feet as the saber crouches down in injuries. Then in an upright position, it leaps into the air for one last attempt at a kill as a large tentacle stretches from a tube-like entrance and smashes the saber into the floor between them. As the enormous appendage retracts, it snatches the deceased cat along with it, replacing the open cave with silence.

"What . . . was that?" Little Jake shouts as Mindy screams horrifically.

"You really don't want to know. Run! Through the hole behind it!" Jake instructs the group as they begin to flee into the dark hole. As Jake led them in from the rear, a faint crackling voice catches his ear. Over Mike's brutally thrashed, broken, and bloodied shivering body, he sadly watches the dying boy's quaking hand touch his ankle as if to speak. Startled and remorseful, the kindhearted father stoops down to hear the teenager's last words.

"In . . . the . . . pit." Mike soul leaves his body.

And like a giant eggplant of various colors, the tubeworm's tough wide outer tube of whitish chitin erupts with thousands of snakelike plumes from the upper portion of its body; sessile anchored roots dig deep into the lithosphere, stretching out in numerous tentacles and various mouths that intertwine into dozens of double—and triple-twisted sets of arms down in the canyon just below them.

"Dad?" Julius calls out from the tunnel.

Jake catches a glimpse of the full multi-octopus, plantlike creature before following his sons and the others. "Those things are its roots."

"It must have evolved over the years. Usually, tubeworms absorb chemicals and microbes to use as food. With this one, apparently . . . to survive, it's anything goes!" Jane hollers out.

As the insides of the mountain starts to break apart, a large tentacle pounds into the ancient wall of sediment behind them. Climbing to a higher level, the group found themselves in another series of mazelike passages. The caves crumble, and floors collapse as the nine race into a longer and more widened cave. As the hungry mouths fill the spaces behind them, they fumble with their flashlights, entering a cold, wet area.

"I think we're going to make it!" Julius yells, walking into the darkness that was filled with baby giant cockroaches. "Uh-oh!"

"We have to run through them. Come on, they're just bugs!" The brave father takes the lead. Firing his weapon, he bursts through the insect's head first, followed by his sons as they all disappear into the crawling black mass. Holding hands, they exit fighting before running a short distance and climbing another wall. Hearing the coming arm of the tubeworm breaking through the stone, they feel the weight of uncertain doom loom upon them. Jake gathers the group and peers into darkness from which they came.

As the hungry limbs come into contact with the bothered insects, the scurrying are picked off and randomly devoured by the masses. The tubeworm launches its powerful arms forward, just missing Jane's head, smashing into the wall behind them. As the limb retracts, wiping out the swarm of small giants, the group stares at the newly made tunnel behind it. Dashing for their lives into the blackness, Jake aims his flashlight down the large shaft. Pulling Little Jake, the scared and tired father carries Julius on his back, with Raheem and Jane beside him. Another terrible limb smashes down, ripping the entire darkness away behind them, leaving an open canyon-like pit. As seawater quickly rises inside the canyon from underneath the earth, the tubeworm destroys everything in its path before retracting again. Then sending in a sentinel arm, the creature whales into them as Jake and Jane push it back in pain, blazing shots from the machine gun and flamethrower.

With no way out and nowhere to go, the children peer up at a humongous limb flying toward them faster than they can escape. As it smashes to the floor in a slushy, bubbling manner, it explodes onto them like a popped pimple. Then the arm and body of the tubeworm start to fill with holes and disintegrate as the worm's insides foam out from within its body. The infected arm near Jake and the others fall as if suddenly dying as the creature itself erupts in venting, squirting gasses and its own blood. Two bright lights flicker from inside a large approaching swell in the twitching melting arm as the group stares oddly into the open wound.

"What is that coming, gas? Get ready, guys! It's something big!" Lil Ricky runs off to the side with the others. As Jake stood in front, shielding them, small holes open into a large wound upon the slowly drawn back limb of the tubeworm. As the mouths and extra extensions retreated into the large muscle, the swelling and glowing circles grew closer and closer, moving at a fast pace. Then as gallons of tissue and blood gush out of the opening, a lone siren loudly plays a verse of Creedence Clearwater from its speakers as Mouse drives out the tubeworm's arm with Ernie strapped to the roof in a gust of insecticides. Skidding onto the surface of the cave, the vehicle stops before them.

"Anyone need a lift?" Ernie pulls down his face mask and smiles down upon them like a knight in gruesome armor. The children cheer as Liz opens the side doors.

"It's the Bug Guy! Way cool. I know what I want to be when I grow up!" Cyntica looks up at the monster warrior.

"Me too!" Julius stares amazed as Jake pushes them into the van.

"This is going to take lots of undoing Ernie," Jake grumbles to his friend upon entering the van.

As portions of the mountain began to split and crack, letting forth great beams of sunlight, Mouse takes off and speeds into what resembles an open man-made looking cave. In a gushing roar, the ocean pours in after them. Rolling over cliffs like demolition experts, the rough bumps messes with the vehicles electronics, making the headlights flicker. Both the siren and radio simultaneously malfunction, sticking to playing a Bad Moon rising in its entirety, as the automobile barrel horizontally down steep rocks, streaking sparks from under its exhaust and bumper. Meeting the powerful water head on, they break through layers of age-old stone, shooting down a maze of man-made dividers and familiar things, the Bug mobile streams through a tunnel of displays and old inhabited caves of shrimps and bats, in a whirlpool of ocean. Bursting through the floor in a geyser of water and rocks, the van is spat across an exit and entrance. Ernie, lifting his head from the side of the roof, coughs out water and taps the van, giving his speechless friend the okay to continue. As Mouse rolls off onto what appeared to be a road, Julius crawls to the window of the bug mobile and reads a large freshly painted sign.

"Welcome to Mammoth Cave, home of hundreds of miles of unexplored caves." Julius looks back at his brother and father quietly as seawater shower from the sky like rain under the end solo guitar strings of Creedence Clearwater Revival's Bad Moon rising.

LANDING 7

EATEN ALIVE

"Finally, a chance to relax and see the stars! No teachers or parents reminding us to do our homework!" Peter, a slinky, wiry, brown-haired fellow, exhales. Young, book smart, and a freshmen of college, he looks over at his older brother, who was hunched over the steering wheel of their Ford Explorer.

"Bro, I think taking this camping trip was a freak'n cool idea! Who'd ever think that you, wanting to play with your stupid telescope, would attract girls? That's crazy awesome." Raising his head in a huge smile, Paul, his brother, quite tall, slightly more handsome, and a graduate of Yale, continues to drive upon the flash of a green light, chauffeuring his brother and his best friend, Turk, to an unknown campsite. "I still don't understand why the stupid surprise. Why can't you just tell us where this spot is, bro? I mean, we're like miles and miles away from civilization. We all had to rent cars. This had better be one heck of a campsite, turd face!"

"Hey, don't worry. I got this, bro. I got us plugged into the GPS on the phone and laptop," Peter reassures him. "And as for the spot, my contacts said it's like you have the whole world to yourself."

"Don't worry, Pete, we trust you. I mean really, Paul, this is my last time asking you dude how tall you are, seriously. The steering wheel looks like it's in your pelvis, dude!" Turk, a very youthful twenty-year-old, playful and energetic, teases his best friend's brother as usual. Jumping back and forth between seats like a little kid, he leaps into the back row and continues his portable video game. Dressed in a vest, T-shirt, and old faded blue jeans, Turk laughs and jokes throughout the ride, only ceasing at times to stuff his short dark-rooted, blonde, spiked hair into a backward blue ball cap. And as they drove on, their friends Yakoo, Chip, and Miles drive steadily behind them, doing sixty on the scenic November cold road.

"Where the hell are we going?" Yakoo, the driver of a deep-red minivan, gripes. Tall and also well educated, he touches a small drip of sweat from his dark African skin, wipes his bald head, and glances in the passenger seat at his good friend Chip, who just throws his head back, tossing caramel popcorn into his mouth. "Maybe we shouldn't have trusted Peter with planning this trip. I don't understand why we have to follow him. Why couldn't he just tell us where we're going? I don't like this."

"It's cool. Have faith in him. He's like a genius! He's been begging us to let him plan a trip for at least three years." Chip, oily faced with sandy hair, muscular with the cockiness to match, pulls out his rocker sunglasses and turns the volume up on the already-loud, rock 'n' roll music that blasted out the stereo.

Covering up his ears, their two-hundred-plus-sized pal, Miles Ruben, shakes his head, stretches between them, and presses the power button on the radio off. In an army fatigue bubble vest, pants, and red long-sleeve shirt, he bends over, struggling to tie his boot. "Yo . . . yo! Yo, Yakoo! How you going to let a white boy touch a black man's radio and play that mess? That's unheard of!" His plump brown hands twist his fitted ball cap backward. He stares into the back of Yakoo's shining head. "And you should know better. You a real African! You from where we originate from!"

"Miles, how is it a black man's radio when we all put our money together to get this minivan in the first place?" Chip tilts his head and calmly awaits a response. Yakoo snickers beside him.

"He's absolutely right, Miles. We're sharing it. And just so you know, my origin of birth has nothing to do with your ignorance. Besides, I like all music. Rap comes from rock 'n' roll anyway, doesn't it?" Yakoo grins at Miles's response in the rearview mirror.

"What? Where rap comes from? Are you crazy? Listen to this! Oh my goodness, I don't believe this. They got you programmed man!" Miles changes the radio to a hip-hop station and turns it up loudly. "You telling me that this comes from that? Un-uh, you bug'n. You cannot believe that! You can't do this to that, Chip!" Miles begins to dance and move to the beat in his seat. Turning to the side, he sees their friends Christina, Rebecca, Valerie, Samantha, and Glenda passing them in another vehicle. "I wonder where they're going." He takes off his cap and quickly picks out his small fro.

Rebecca pulls their full-sized '94 blue Chevy van next to Paul's black truck; Samantha flashes them in the side window. "Roll down the window, roll down the . . ." she blurts out loud and illustrates with her hand. "They don't get it. Men are so stupid!" Rebecca, a long-haired, blue-tipped brunette and most serious of the young women, swerves out of the opposite lane along the narrow two-lane road.

"I don't think they know where we're going at all." In the backseat, Christina, the smartest of the bunch, tightens her bun and tucks a strand of bright blonde hair behind her ear. Adjusting her thin-framed glasses on her slightly acne-broken-out nose, she looks over two maps of different sizes, tracking their direction with a marker. "Maybe we should stop somewhere."

"What? That's off the hook! I mean . . . I trust little Peter and all, but a sister ain't tryna be lost, ya'll! And as a matter of fact, I don't even supposed to be camping, okay?" From the middle row, Glenda, a vibrant, nicely thick-built, strong-headed, brown-skinned woman in her early twenties looks at her close friends inside the van with concern. "Come on, guys, we can't be lost. Pass Yakoo and catch up with Paul!"

"They are so hot." In Paul's car, Turk leans over the driver's seat to talk as Paul mugs him into the back and rolls down the window.

"Wassup, Val?" Paul looks over into the passenger seat of Rebecca's van. Turk leans forward to see also; Paul shoves his face behind him.

"Pull into the next rest stop!" Valerie's light reddish brown hair pulled back into a ponytail brought out her bright, freckled face and beautifully dark arched brown brows. Her dark eyes and small plump lips tended easily to the boys' likings as they found themselves entranced, not hearing a single word she said.

"Wait, what?" Paul snaps out of the gaze as Peter touches his shoulder.

"Paul, that's not how you talk to women! Now watch me," Peter whispers. "Sorry about that. He couldn't hear you. Our music was too loud." Peter raises a brow as if to give her the look. As his thin, slightly open shirt blows in the breeze, their eyes make contact. He sits back and turns to his brother in blushes of red.

"I said pull in the next rest stop!" Valerie yells at the tops of her lungs as Glenda cracks open the side window.

"Don't act like you can't hear, punk. We'll kick your ass!" Glenda shouts, laughing, as Samantha, short-haired and wild child of the bunch, flashes them again. "Girl, quit being nasty!"

"Uhh, Val, Valerie sweetie, did you know that you gals are on the wrong side of the road?" Paul smiles sarcastically as the road began to swerve back and forth.

"Shut up, Paul, just do it! Ahh, Becky, look out!" Valerie screams as an extra-large semi heads directly for them, blowing its horn erratically.

The Chevy fills with more screams as Rebecca cuts the wheel with all her might. Their vehicle steers off road as the truck still manages to catch the back end of the van. Sending them in the direction of the woods, Rebecca somehow maneuvers back onto the road. Gravity and speed then takes the truck, sending it diving down the hillside in the opposite direction. A large explosion is heard; the vehicles slow at the sight of a thick cloud of black smoke that shot into the air just beyond the trees in the distance. Parking, the group watched in amazement.

"Oh my . . . I . . . I don't believe this is happening." Valerie shakes her head and steps out of the van. Glenda gets out also as Samantha and Christina join her, both with small abrasions on their upper bodies. "Did you see that guy? Why didn't he slow down? Oh my goodness!" She looks up at the giant ball of smoke in the sky in disbelief. Yakoo, Chip, and Miles quickly walk up next to her.

"Are you girls all right?" Yakoo looks over them for injuries as Chip looks at the cut on Samantha's rosy cheek. "You two are a little banged up, but it doesn't look too bad. Are you dizzy or anything?" He examines Christina's head with his large hands as she nods no. "I think something was wrong with the driver. I saw green paint or something all over that truck, and people . . . hanging off the driver's door."

"Man, people? I don't know about all that, brotha. I definitely didn't see any people hanging on the truck. You seeing things, my African friend. We thought it was over for you ladies! Look at the back of your van. The whole bumper's gone, down the street. Boy, y'all lucky!" Miles takes his hat off and steps into the grass.

"That was some incredible driving, Rebecca. I'm so happy that you all made it. We're all lucky to have survived that one."

Paul approaches with his brother and Turk following close behind. "Let's get out of here and let the police handle it. After all, we didn't kill anyone."

"Are you kidding me? The entire truck just blew up behind us! This is bad, very bad. We need to do something. What if there's a forest fire, or worse, that guy is dead? We shouldn't just leave, guys. We have to do something." Peter panics as Valerie agrees.

"He's right you guys. I mean, look at that. There has to be a dead body down there somewhere. We should at least report it. We could be anonymous," Chip suggest as four loud bangs fire from the woods where the truck crashed.

"Damn, those were loud. Okay . . . right, let's be responsible. Who has a cell phone on them?" Yakoo asks as Turk steps between them.

"Wait a sec, guys. I don't know about this. Let's think. They're going to trace this back to us! What if they need a story? We gotta have our story straight," Turk intervenes as Miles joins in.

"Right, right, hold up. We need to talk about this before we go down there or talk to anybody. Black people usually don't have good luck in situations like these. Our van didn't hit nobody! We didn't touch nothing!"

"That's bullshit! Now you wait a second. You nearly crashed too!" Samantha snaps as they begin to argue among everyone.

"Wait, guys, guys . . . hold on! Okay . . . guys . . . shut up!" Rebecca quietly steps from behind them and breaks them up. "Look, you all have good points, but the matter of fuck'n fact is that each one of our vehicles played a part in this, and we are all in this together! Now what are we going to do? Going at one another's throats isn't working too well, so let's do what's best for all of us, okay?" Her large black watery eyes, peer into theirs deeply as a loud, unusual, lingering cry interrupts the moment.

As they all freeze listening, Yakoo gazes at the bright flickering light coming from the growing fire somewhere beyond the trees at the bottom of the hill. "Miles, get me a phone, now! Something's not right about this." He places a large hand on his chin. "Okay, first, we're going to report an accident, and then we're going to search for survivors. Someone needs our help."

"Search for survivors? I got news for ya, buddy. They ain't surviving! They're dying and probably burning to death, and I don't want to see it. I don't want no part of that, dude," Turk smirks, refusing to go as Christina tries to shed a little light.

"Regardless, it's not wise to flee the scene, Turk."

"Flee the scene? We're not even there yet, and nobody even knows we're here! I can't believe you people!" Miles complains, passing his cell phone to Yakoo. He walks a few steps away, aggravated. "I say we go get her bumper and go."

"Well, we all don't have to go down there, but someone should go. You could just stay in the parameters of the accident." Chip takes into consideration that women were with them.

"Paul, let me use your phone. I'm not getting a signal." Yakoo gives Miles back his phone. Watching him place the phone in his pocket, Yakoo takes Paul's cell. "It's not allowing me to dial out or even call 911."

Valerie retrieves hers and returns to the group. "Mine isn't working either."

"No bars or signal? Great, we are in the middle of nowhere," groans Rebecca, wiping tears from her eyes.

"Hey, try Chip's phone. His is top of the line!" Miles remembers and retrieves the phone from the van. "This is crazy, y'all. He isn't getting any reception either!" Miles yells, exiting the side door of their van.

"Okay . . . this is starting to get a little crazy. Guess that settles it. Come on, guys, let's just make sure that no one's like . . . alive." Valerie slowly begins to walk in the direction of the crash. "I'm going. Whoever wants to stay, stay."

"Let's get one thing straight. I ain't touching no bloody people. It's AIDS and all types of diseases out here big time nowadays! I am not playing!" Glenda firmly states as Yakoo, Paul, and Rebecca go to their rides and pull their vehicles farther off the road so cars could pass with ease.

Since they couldn't drive down the side of the sloping road, the group of young adults decides to hike to the crash site. The walk became a tough one as the party soon come to realize that the truck had drove farther than they had expected. Through the cold dying grass and crunching fallen leaves, the terrain becomes wooded and rugged. Miles away from the road, the group follows the large path of split trees, broken limbs, and damaged bushes. Going so far, it had become very apparent to them that the truck must have burrowed deep into the woods at a tremendously fast speed, leaving next to nothing behind it. In a wide clear, the pathway mysteriously splits in two.

"Okay . . . there's two giant skid trails. What did it do, split in half?" Rebecca oddly looks over at Valerie. "It goes clear over the side of that hill."

"Hmm, wonder what's with all the snares? Most of them are in the direction of the hill." Yakoo glances at many animal traps spread about loosely.

"Maybe they we're set to catch something or someone?" Turk grins devilishly.

"We'd better go this way. I hate to see any of us accidentally step on one of those things." Yakoo tries his best to ensure his friends' safety.

Farther down the path of fallen trees, on a flatter plain, the truck rest in a twisted bed of mangled metal and miscellaneous materials inside the center of remains of smoldered trees. Small flames and waves of heat dance around and throughout the massive length of the wreckage, bringing an eerie feeling to the clearing.

Turk, scared yet itching to be mischievous, enters the cooled steamy darkness of the open trailer that was smashed and ripped opened like the exposed rib cage of an old undiscovered dinosaur. Bent and folded with holes, along the black ash-covered ground, the trailer emits a thick, burnt stench, and only the sounds of Turk's footsteps could be heard, as the group waits quietly, peering around for any sign of life. Suddenly, in a loud horrible utterance as if being burned, Turk leaps out of the trailer, holding up a piece of wood and some type of cotton material on fire.

The group jumps back in horror and curse words until noticing that he was okay. Miles drops his chips and burst into an uncontrollable laughter. "He scared the crap outta y'all. You should have seen your faces! I'm sorry, but that was good. That was a good one that time, bro. He got y'all, ah-ha-ha-haa!" He veers off to the side.

"You asshole!" Samantha harps, wiping a trickle of her own blood from her face.

"Knock it off, Turk! Look how far this thing slid. And who screamed? I don't see anyone." Peter scans around the area.

"Is anyone alive? Make a noise if you can't speak so we can hear you!" Paul yells out in one breath.

"Nothing." Chip looks up at the clouds in the evening sky.

"Listen." Yakoo directs their attention to a faint moan and sound of movement coming from the front of the truck.

"I hope nobody jumps out," Christina mutters, stomping her feet on the charred ground as they inched toward the front of the singed truck.

Crates and buckets of deceased and diseased specimens along with body parts littered the ground ahead. Animal parts and clumps of a goo-looking substance seep from the once-contained canisters and sides of the open belly of the trailer. Upside down, the actual truck simmered in smoke and burned along some trees as hot oil and green antifreeze pour from around it.

"I hope this stuff isn't contagious. This must've been on the way to a lab or something. This stuff looks toxic!" Using quick thinking, Chip wraps his thin jacket around his hand and pulls on the hot door handle. A faint moan comes from behind, causing Chip and the others to look.

"Is that a person?" Christina spots a figure crawling farther down the hill, deeper into the woods.

As Chip turns back to the truck, he opens the door to reveal what must have been the driver, burnt and smoldered with his back to them, still in the fetal position. "Gross." Observing smoke and some of the person's skin still bubbling with heat, Chip backs away from the truck, leaving the door wide open. "He's gone." A sorrowful expression overcomes him.

"Come on . . . let's go." Rebecca, beginning to feel like it was all her fault, looks down at the ground sadly as they all drift toward the direction of the crawling body that was seen. *It can't be all my fault. I got out of the way*, she thinks to herself. Preparing for the worse, Rebecca lifts her head and tugs on her sports jacket, mentally accepting any punishment the law might enforce upon her.

"Where'd they go?" asks Paul as Peter squats by the foot of the tree where the body was spotted.

"There, look!" Peter points at a trail of blood that extended beyond the trees and bushes nearby. "How can they still be alive losing all that blood?"

"I don't want to see this, guys," Valerie blurts out as Glenda and Samantha stand with her.

"Go on, Miles, you're the bravest." Glenda slaps him on the back, causing him to choke on his own saliva.

"I'm the what? Shit, I don't want to see it either! What if he don't got no eyeballs? Nah . . . man, y'all go ahead. I'll be back here with the driver. At least I know he's dead." Miles shuffles back near the truck to wait as Paul and Chip follow the blood into the woods.

"I don't see him," Paul blurts out as Rebecca slowly follows close while Chip checks the opposite side.

"I don't either. Wait, what the . . . I found him. Guys, guys?" Chip acknowledges as Paul, Yakoo, and Peter rush to take a look. Chip's hands spread apart the bushes; the upper half of a man's bloody body digs into the cold ground as the head takes full bites out of the earth. "Hey, you need some help? We're here to help you. Excuse me? What the hell, he's nonresponsive."

"What's he doing?" Peter nearly turns pale watching the dying man devour dirt and gravel. "And where's the rest of his body?"

"The girls have got to see this!" Turk pops up beside them. Before getting a laugh off the girl's reactions, he spreads open a section of thickets even more to get a better view for himself. Finding some sort of sick amusement from the injured man eating rocks and roots, he smiles horrendously. As stems snap and break beneath Turk's hands, the feeding man stops and takes notice to the sound. The victim's busted, swollen head twist 360 degrees to view the boy until a popping of bone is loudly heard. The dark curly head of wet hair and rolled eyes goes limp and falls, as the man's last breath wheezes from his hanging mouth. Slowly moving toward Turk, the nervously now-jittering arms begin to slowly drag the empty torso and head, loudly chattering teeth underneath it. "Whoa!" Turk involuntarily jumps a few feet away.

"You see that?" Peter leaps back with the others.

"That's humanly impossible!" Rebecca draws back.

"Let's get out of here now, Paul!" Peter demands his brother as they run to the others.

"What happened? What did you see?" Valerie asks as Samantha is snatched away.

"He's dead, Val! Ladies, we have to go!" Chip takes hold of Valerie's arm and pulls her away quickly.

"Nothing, we saw . . . it was nothing! The guy was chopped in half and dead! Now let's go before the authorities come, and we have to explain something we can't explain. Where's Miles?" Yakoo pushes everyone forward.

"He was right there by the truck. I dunno. Maybe he went back to the van. Hey, didn't Chip leave the door open on that truck? It's closed?" Christina asks as they high stepped past the truck. "Hmm, maybe Miles didn't want to look at the body."

"Let's just keep moving. I don't want to see any more bodies. I'm going to have nightmares for months about today. This is too much!" Samantha passes the door with the others as Turk lags behind them and takes one last look for his curiosity.

Opening the heavy truck door, Turk's face forms a frown of confusion. Not only was the body of the driver of the rig in a totally different position, but also the crisp, burned, disfigured head of the victim seemed to be looking directly at him. *Odd. Why did Miles move him? Probably to scare us. Geesh, he's weirder than me!* Turk thinks, turning to join the others. Within the first step away from the immobilized vehicle, a ripping sound was heard as a cool red liquid begin to saturate and pour from his left pants leg. Feeling a sudden electric sensation of pain, he looks down behind at his leg and spots the severely burned corpse that was in the truck, sinking it's bent, broken teeth, deep into his buttocks. "Ouch!" Turk snaps away as he turns and watches a piece of his jeans and rear end get chewed and swallowed in the black bloodied, singed, lipless, remaining mouth of the dead trucker. It leaps to attack him.

"What is that? Shit, man, what the fuck is that?" Chip runs and kicks the corpse off his friend as Turk runs for the van, screaming and howling in pain.

"I . . . I don't understand this!" Yakoo beats the once-thought dead man with a large fallen branch and rushes to his friends.

"This is . . . crazy! What is going on here?" He rubs his head and debates on going back home altogether.

"Come on, let's just go! This is getting way too outta hand!" Rebecca rubs both sides of her small chilly arms. "Creepy." The risen corpse of the truck driver could be seen staggering by the remains of the truck as she rushed beside her friends to their vehicles. "Wha . . . what about Miles? Did anyone find him? Where is he?" Rebecca makes it to the van and yells out the window at Yakoo, who stops in front of their door and peers into the woods.

And as they begin to worry and think about what to do about their missing friend, little did they know that just a little less than a mile away, Miles, after encountering and seeing the truck driver move with his own eyes, ran off in fright, leaving the cars, his friends, and even his possessions behind. *Fuck that, fuck that, fuck that!* he repeats to himself. As the skies began to turn dark, with no light, anxiety starts to eat away at the fear of being alone and lost. Oddly hearing no birds and no crickets, out of breath and tired, Miles hears a slight movement in the woods. Spooked, he hurls forward in a great trust of weight, yelling in panic until his vocal chords stretch into the strumming sound of almost a woman's scream. With images of the burned trucker moving in the truck, the heavyset young man snaps through stems and shrubbery, burrowing through the thickets like a wild man. As wiry vines and dying weeds entangle his feet, he flips into a barrel roll and slides on his back into the large stump of a tree. Sitting up slowly, he listens. Hearing no sound, he rubs his aching head. Slightly dizzy, he realizes how far away from the others he had actually ran. "Where is the road and the cars? Damn, I messed up. Must've ran the wrong way! Miles, you're an idiot. How stupid," he speaks out loudly to himself, trying to figure which direction he should go next. "Okay, Miles . . . think. What to do now? Damn it, I have to find the van!" Pushing to his feet, Miles's eyes begin to adjust as he peeps around the dense depths of the forest. More movement breaks the quaint silence, catching his attention. "Who's that? Is somebody out there? Speak now! Or . . . are you an animal?" His loud voice breaks into whispers. "Chip? Yakoo?" Pausing to listen, more snapping twigs slightly morph into what sounds like large animal footsteps. "That ain't no damn Chip!" His mind plays tricks as he concentrates and tune into the sounds of outside, mistaking a low noise for a growl. Scared to death by the signs of what he envisioned to be a predator, he takes off in the opposite direction of the noise again. "Black people don't belong in no woods!" He boulders through the thickets at top speed, clotheslined in the end by a low-hanging tree branch. Both feet whisk into midair. Miles's large and massive round body crashes to the grassy ground, landing the back of his head upon a large stone. He blacks out into a dark void of nothingness.

And then in a brilliant light, Miles Ruben relives his life as a child. Visualizing hours on end in his room with his toys and beautiful sunny days outside, playing with friends, Miles sees his mother cleaning his face. He revisits a time when he was sad and she brought him cookies and milk in bed. Flashes of when he first met his little brother enters Miles's mind as he drifts to the time they spent, and the fatal moment in which he saw his little brother get taken from them. He returns to the exact time of his brother's death, when a bus drives by him, striking his brother off his new bicycle. Receiving the remorseful feeling of sorrow and regret for the loss of his loved one, Miles's beautiful mother appears before him. Her strong-featured round chocolate-colored face gleams pure and clean yet bares no smile. Slapping him hard with her hand, she blames him for the careless watching of his sibling. Miles falls back and began to cry, noticing his mother already streaming tears. Her bodacious frame glides close, and her face leans in as if to say sorry or to kiss him. She slaps him to the floor instead. Miles awakens to a very skinny and actual red-necked, rugged-faced hillbilly, lightly slapping at his plump, chipmunk cheeks.

"Come on, fella, attaboy. Are you all right? You look, uhhh . . . sorta injured there. You aren't hurt, are ya?" The stubble-jawed man asked, chewing the small butt of a cigar. His large eyes and big teeth illustrates a look of concern and half-sane goofiness. Observing Miles come to, the old grime-covered man slides his hand over something in the grass beside him. Raising up a shotgun, he shoves it directly into Miles's nose. "Brother, you need to talk or say something awful fast. Are you one of those things? What's your name?"

"M . . . Miles Ruben," he stutters, trembling in place. "Whu-what thing, a burnt-up guy?" Miles starts to remember, also becoming very alert.

"Now I know what done happened, and I know what you're talk'n 'bout. But those weren't no regular burnt people! Those are dead men walking, and that ain't natural. Two of those things tried to attack me!" The medium-height graying man slowly moves away his weapon before standing and zipping up his orange workmen's suit to his collar bone.

"Wait, dude . . . I . . . I don't think we're talking about the same thing." Miles, relieved that he wasn't murdered in the woods and body abandoned, tries to slowly move. Glimpsing into the eyes of the peculiar man, he debates in his mind if the man was insane or not.

"Well, maybe so." The old man cocked an old worn gas station hat to the side of his head. "Did you see the truck with them things hanging all off of it?" he asked as Miles arose to his feet.

Not really wanting to tell the man anything to incriminate himself or his friends, Miles holds his scarred neck and responds, "Yes, it almost ran me and my friends off the road, but I didn't see anything on it. You know, my friend described the same thing, but what are you talking about, things like what?"

"It's hard to say . . . it all happened so fast." The countryman spat out a wad of chewing tobacco to the ground along with the stout bit of cigar. "Well, there I was, following deer and bear tracks, when that gigantic truck covered in green stuff and people barreled right over me. It knocked my truck, Betsy, and all my traps, clear down the hill, then it exploded."

"Green stuff? People? Man, what's up with you and Yakoo's eyes?"

"Yakoo?"

"Never mind." Miles gives the old man a weird look. *This guy's a nutcase. He's lost it,* he thinks to himself.

"Well, yep, there was some sort of green stuff all over it, sorta like mud. It was just wiggly and jiggly, falling all over the place. The truck flew straight over my head. I had to leap and run for it! And when that fire had just about simmered out a little, just enough for me to go down and see if anyone was still alive, that's when two of 'em who were still hanging on to the truck, attacked me, and chased me through the woods," the old man rekindles the event while looking around, full of paranoia.

"Yeah, we definitely aren't talking about quite the same thing. But what happened? Where'd the people go? Who were chasing you?"

"You don't see any of them around, do you?" The old man laughs jokingly. Miles thinks about the oddness of the once-thought dead trucker whom he saw move at the same time.

"Well, they chased me up until the point that I finally found my truck, and that's where I laid 'em down. I pulled out trusty ol' Sarah here and whammo!" The old man firmly grips his shotgun in both hands.

"Oooo . . . kay." Miles grows quiet. "You killed them . . . people?" were the only words he could think to say. "Wha-what's your name? Then again, I don't want to know. I gotta go!" Miles began to walk off.

"Wait! Where ya going, big fella? The name's Gus, by the way. It's about to get dark. Don't think you should be head'n that a ways." Gus follows. "Hey, you, wait!"

"Can't talk no more, old man. Like you said, it's getting late. I have to—"

"Hey, well, wait, if that's the case, then you really shouldn't be going that way! The only thing in that direction . . . are wolves. They'll be heading in this direction soon."

"Um, Gus, is it . . . did you say wolves?" Miles freezes in his tracks and reevaluates the situation. "How do you know?"

"Oh, me and my hounds been tracking deer here ever since I was a tadpole. Can't see things changing too much on account of you tourist." Gus winks and wipes his face and neck with a dingy handkerchief from his back pocket. "I saw some vehicles parked off road a bit down yonder there at the top of the hill. Is that the friends you're looking for?"

"Yes, what direction is that?" Miles's spirits lift. "Just point, I'll find them! I don't think I was out that long. They shouldn't have left just yet." He squeezes the light on his watch and looks at the time.

"The roads just up that way. You just traveled in a circle. Just climb the hill. You betta be extra careful, though. I wouldn't want to see any of them things getting to ya!" Gus points to the hill and watches Miles disappear into the woods.

"Thanks, Gus. I owe you one!" Miles shouts into the wind as he hurries. "You be safe too, and quit eating tobacco! It'll kill you!" Skeptical about the old man's information, he wonders how wise it really was to have listened. If the Southern-speaking man was lying, Miles knew that he was indeed in trouble. Miles looks behind; the image of Gus disappears behind the tall, slender trees and woods. Tearing through the forest to the hillside, he struggles through the thick dichotomous bushels, gaining leverage by help of nearby branches and shrubbery, until finally he found himself having to nearly claw up the steep hillside. Covered in dirt and grass, Miles rises to his knees and feet before spitting out small pieces of crushed leaves and gravel. Dusting off his red hat, army fatigue jeans, and bubble vest, he glances down at the front of his T-shirt, which was covered in outside. "At least my hat didn't get dirty." He grins as the cap tips off his head, facing the same fate as the rest of his clothing. "Shit." He snatches his hat up from the dirt and hears a familiar chanting in the distance. Standing on the same road he took to get there, he glances down the narrow street, recognizing his friends' three vehicles rolling slowly, kilometers up the street from him. Glenda, Chip, and Joanne walks behind them, calling out his name. "Wait! Hey! Chip!" Miles shout out, running desperately to catch up with them. "Hey, guys! Wait up! I'm here! I'm here!" Frustrated and extremely exhausted, he stumbles, collapsing over the edge of the street, as his friends spot him.

Finally able to leave the initial area of the truck crash, the team of friends hit the open road yet far away from the nearest hospital. Paul and Peter lead the way in their Explorer as Turk yells in agony from the backseat. Cristina and Glenda rides with them, tending to the wound on his buttocks with bottled water, gauges, and cleansing pads.

"We have to find a hospital or clinic, like now, guys! He's gonna need stitches," states Glenda, with only a few actual nursing hours up under her belt.

"So much for the camping trip. This has been one weird day," Paul mutters while trying his best to drive and spot any street signs at the same time.

"No! It'll heal. Just bandage me up. It'll heal," Turk utters as a drip of saliva slung from his bottom lip. "I'm not gonna let this spoil the trip. I'll live. It's only a bite."

"Just a bite? Wow, big words from a guy with a hole in his butt." Christina giggles at Glenda, who breaks a smile above Turk's rear, slightly impressed by his brave stupidity.

"Dude, what if it's infected, or worse, what if that thing had a disease, like rabies, or a flesh-eating disease, or something?" Paul adjusts and tilts the cracked rearview mirror at Christina and Glenda as they enter a moment of unspeakable worries for their friend.

"Well, don't you guys got something that disinfects, Lysol spray or something? You two are always prepared, man!" Turk exclaims as a sharp pain shot down his leg, followed by his body breaking out in hives and a feverish sweat.

Unbuckling his seatbelt, Peter reaches down under his seat and pulls out their trusty medic kit that always came in handy. Opening the small square container, Peter lifts up his head and turns to his brother, driving. "All we have is a bottle of 91 percent rubbing alcohol." Peter looks back at the two young women as their face twist up as if witnessing an execution of a loved one.

"What? Rubbing . . . oh shit. Well, pass it to Glenda and pour it on, now! I don't wanna take any chances. Go on, do it. I can take it!" Turk insists and braces himself on the legs of the two females.

"Turk, think about this. Really? Are you sure you want to do that, Turk?" Christina catches the bottle of solution. Twisting off the lid, she holds it over him.

"It's all we got, and I'm not blowing this trip. We've came all this way, driving for days, and you know there isn't a hospital for infinite miles! Go ahead, I can take it! Do it, just do it!"

"Turk, you positively, absolutely sure you want to go through with this? I think you should really rethink this. Turk . . . it's alcohol on your butt," Glenda interrupts with the upper portion of his body lying across her laps.

"Come on, Turk, it'll probably work, but if that stuff burns little cuts, imagine what it's going to feel like on that missing chunk back there," Paul explains, searching for the next street sign.

"Do it, man, get it over with! I don't want no kinda infection, dude! Now do it, come on! I can take it. Just don't let me know it's coming."

"All righty, you heard the man." Christina eases the bristly gauge from Turk's damaged skin as Glenda takes the bottle and pours the isopropyl antiseptic onto his open wound.

Glass and thunder was an understatement compared to the actual electrical striking sensation felt inside Turk's exposed flesh. His friends cover their mouths and scream also as Turk emits a mournful plaintive sound before the shock causes him to black out.

"Where the heck are we going now? I guess we're not going back." Rebecca throws her hand up out the window, steering the bumperless Chevy van behind Paul.

Valerie, whose face was jumbled and squinted up, drastically attempts to find their location on the map. "She was way better than me at this, I can't believe Christina rode with them. I don't know how the heck she could even read this thing. I hope Little Turk's okay. I can't believe that man bit him like that. That was wild."

"No, I'll tell you what's starting to be bizarre. How come every so often, when we pass a house, it looks empty or like no one's been living in it for years? Have you noticed it?" Samantha stares out the side window as Valerie rubs her strained eyes.

"You saw houses? I haven't seen one yet. I haven't seen a house, a street sign, or another car for miles now. I hope we're not lost," states Rebecca, always expecting the worst out of life.

"I dunno, Sam. I'm looking, but all I see is woods and more woods on both sides of the road." Valerie squints out the passenger window.

"Try to look behind the woods. There's more over there, see? Right there!" Samantha points, smacking and chewing her gum loudly.

"Wow . . . I think she's right, Rebe. But I don't think those are woods. I think everyone's yard is wild."

"I see them now. Doesn't anyone cut their grass around here?" Rebecca refocuses on the open road as a sign reading Rest Stop, 2 Miles catches her eye as they drive by.

And close behind the full-size van, Yakoo's minivan brings up the rear as Chip occupies the time by playing a private game of basketball, consisting of tossing cheese puffs from a sandwich bag in the front seat, into Miles's open, drooling and snoring mouth in the middle row. Occasionally waking up chewing or swallowing, he finally opens up his eyes to Chip smirking in his face before falling back into a comfortable slumber.

"You know what's so funny about this? It's like he never gets full!" Chip laughs to himself before a piece of corn chip goes down the wrong wind pipe, choking him.

"Now that's hilarious." Yakoo grins, concentrating on the road. "It doesn't look like we're turning around. Where are we going? There are no hospitals in these parts, and Turk needs a doctor. I think we need to go back the way we came. What are those guys doing?" Analyzing their location, his expression through the windshield looked as if he was struggling to find a word on a crossword puzzle.

"Maybe Turk's feeling better, dude. I mean, he just got bit, right?" Chip tightens his cap, pops a few more popcorn kernels into his mouth, and a few cheese puffs into Miles.

"Did you see all the blood and the hole in his pants? He was bleeding all over the place. His skin was turning pale when he got in the truck, looked like he was getting sick. I would hate for anything bad to happen to him." Oldest of the group, Yakoo tries to make sense out the situation so far. "He's a young kid and a good guy. How'd that guy get out that truck and move around? That man was dead. We all saw him."

"Dunno, maybe it was some natural reaction to that toxic stuff that was all around? Hey . . . they say some dead people are known to get up and walk around during the embalmment process. Now that's some freaky stuff!"

"Where did you hear that at, on MAD tv? I've never heard of such tales. Sounds ridiculous. I don't know. Maybe it is possible." Yakoo relaxes his thick frowning eyebrows.

"Well, that's what they say. I don't make the rules. Hey look, a sign. Welcome to Townesville." Chip reads, sitting upright in his seat. "So that's where we are!"

"But where is that?"

"Never heard of it."

"Google it. Are our phones working yet?" Yakoo feels his pockets for his cell and glances at Chip.

"Nope, still no signal. Guess we've finally made it to the middle of nowhere." Chip turns his cap around correctly and pulls the bill down over his eyes. Tilting a black lever on the side of his chair, he descends down to the floor. "Wake me up when we're . . . somewhere."

Looking in the rearview mirror at Miles's bobbling head, Yakoo glances at his own tired yellow eyes. Returning his full attention to the road, he stretches his long right arm to the glove compartment and retrieves his silver cell phone. Automatically dialing Paul, he gets a busy signal, and then another when calling Glenda, followed by a no-service flash across the phone's small screen. "No service, humph? Well, there goes the GPS. This truly is no-man's-land," he groans and strokes his clean-shaven head. "Where are we going, Paul?"

Taken notice to the sign first, Paul leads them into the small city in hopes of finding a doctor or aid. The road running into town soon became cracked, dry, and covered with plants and weeds that sprouted out of the tar. The vehicles quickly enter into what appeared to be an abandoned city of wilderness. Tall wild grass broke from the ground between the cement sidewalk squares like a green fire as full leaves and vines climb the surrounding buildings like giant extending fingers, stretching onward and out to the trees. A few old automobiles sat broken and rusted underneath the settled dust and grime scattered about them. Two deer surprisingly were seen frolicking in front and between the cars before disappearing through a gas station that stood perfectly still, peaceful yet cold and frozen away in time. Each house, every building also seemed quite the same. Although different in color, size, and shape, most were designed of the same model. Absent so far of any other sign of life, the three vehicles continue to drive. Rolling through some sort of overgrown garden of trees and luscious flowers, the friends found themselves in the middle of what looked like the town's square. Engulfed in plant life and fungus, a tall bronze statue of a broad-shouldered man holding up an oil lamp stood triumphantly upon a platform in the center of the square. Coming to a slow, the group crosses another broken road that nearly hid a sign that read "Grave Street." And from that intersection, the view of a huge eerie house that almost looked like an old mansion sat overlooking them from way upon a hill in the far distance. Down a barren road, now of dirt, they went, going into a larger area of woods and untouched, old modeled housing.

"You guys see a store, the town's doctor, or anything?" Paul tries to be easy on the bumpy terrain.

"We're never going to find anything cooped up in here. We need to get out and explore if we're going to get Turk meds!" Peter points out the window excitedly. "Hey, look, a path! Probably takes you directly onto the main street. Let's check it out."

"What about Turk? Think he'll be okay?" Paul stops the Explorer and glances back at Christina and Glenda.

"Well . . . he would answer you, but he's knocked out back here, and I don't want to wake him. He was like in real . . . pain. So . . . he did say that he didn't want to go to the hospital, which is highly dumb, but maybe we could find some help or supplies that could help him out until we get to a hospital. What do you think, Glenda?" Christina gently peeps under the bloodstained gauze pressed against Turk's rump.

"Umm, I think that's a good idea. We should lock the doors and leave him here. We need to find him some painkillers, quick, and get back to him. He's a big boy. He should be okay in here by himself. But first, let's change his pad and put some more alcohol on it before he wakes up. You don't want him to be bleeding all over the place again. Why'd you stop right here, Paul? There's way more friendlier looking houses where we just were. You shouldn't listen to Peter. This place looks haunted!" Glenda pulls the bloodied cotton square from Turk's sticky skin. "What the hell are we doing way out here anyway? I thought we were going camping, not to the other side of the United States."

"Yeah, piss pot, that's a good question. Peter, ol' boy, where exactly are we going because it seems like we're miles off in the wrong place anyway? Are we at least in the same state of the campsite?" Paul cosigns for Glenda.

"Miles off, pift!" Peter shrugs his shoulders calmly. "You people should know me better than that. Why, I'm glad you asked. You see, didn't want to say anything. I know you guys never fully trust me as much as you say, so to cover our asses—that's our asses might I add—instead of relying on man's flawed technological support, secretly, I've been monitoring our position on my pocket map right here, see." Peter holds up a small blue portable map book. "When I looked this place up online, there were comments of how friendly the locals were and everything. Believe it or not, but this is the place, only fewer people." He jokes, "It's not quite what was described. But we're really close. There should be a camping area right over there in that direction, somewhere. We should find the medicine store or ask where the local doctor is, then go take a look. Maybe Turk could recover, and we could still camp. I know you guys would love it. It's the perfect spot." Peter tries to motivate them. "He did just get bitten on the butt. It's a nice-sized bite, but it's just a bite. He'll live," he states as they all just look at one another, speechless.

Flagging their friends behind them, the four exit the explorer, leaving Turk behind asleep.

"What the hell are they doing? Where are they going?" Rebecca groans angrily, trying to roll down her jammed window. "Is this where we're stopping, right here?"

"Maybe they're taking a piss or something," Valerie answers.

Samantha stops putting on her lipstick and yells out the passenger window, "Hey, where are you guys going? What's going on? We're all together, you know."

"The campsite is this way! We're going to look for medicine and a doctor! Come on!" Glenda shrugs, then flags them to join in both vans. "We're leaving Turk!"

"Did she say, the campsite and . . . leaving Turk? We're still going camping? Wow." Rebecca gathers her small bag together and puts on her jacket. "Guess Christy was wrong. They did know where they were going."

"Leaving Turk? Guess it's probably for the best. It's not like he can walk. Well, I'm staying too until they come back and tell us something. I didn't drive way out here to go hiking this time. I was going to let you guys do that. And what if you don't find anything? There's no need for all of us to go on a wild goose chase." Valerie smacks her mouth.

"Right," Rebecca agrees.

As if gazing at a wondrous event, Yakoo and Chip gaze out the front window of the minivan at their friends.

"What's going on now? Oh boy, here we go, another one of Peter's expeditions." Yakoo unbuckles his seatbelt, grabs the green vest he was sitting on, and throws it over his tan sweater.

"Come on, lazy ass! Damn, did you work out or something while you were in the woods? Get up!" Chip slaps Miles across the chest with his hat, waking Miles from his vibrant dream.

"Where is every . . . Gus . . . what, man?" Miles sits up, sleep talking. Rubbing his eyes, Miles glances down to a variety of snacks and crumbs rolling and tumbling from his chest and belly. "What is it now? This doesn't look like home to me!"

"We're going out. Everyone's parked. We're going to see what's going on. Paul and Peter are on the prowl again."

"Look, man, I ain't going nowhere, finding no more dead people. I thought you said Turk got bit in the booty or something? You two come back for me when you've found home, a restaurant, or the camp, all right?" Miles insisted. Falling back in his seat, he takes off his fatigue vest and tosses it over his head to stop the any light from interrupting his sleep. "I'm not fooling with y'all. I already walked a country mile on the last stop."

"Okay, Miles, we understand. We'll be back after the exploit. This time, don't run off where we can't find you." Yakoo opens his door and steps out.

"We'll be back for your soul in a second, scaredy-cat." Chip throws a handful of popcorn over his chair at Miles.

"Man, Chip!" Miles gets agitated as both his friend's exit, slamming the doors behind them. Thinking about the last words that he heard, he quickly locks the doors. Sitting back in his seat with his eyes wide open, he is unable to easily drift back to sleep.

"Hey, guys, wait up! We're going too, hold on!" Chip shouts out as he and Yakoo catches up to the others.

Taking the path Peter pointed out, they journey into the woodlands talking about Turk's condition. As the brown rocky line of ground extend and disappear ahead, the six march in zigzags between the bushes. The sight and sound of not one bird nor insect still sets off an aura of overwhelming creepiness that surrounded them all. And before they could get to questioning Peter about his great idea, the crew found themselves in a clear within a parklike area. As they stood before a once-lit campfire smack in the center of a small barren circumference, a small cabin sitting right in front of the trees just a few yards away catches their interest.

"We found it. This is the campsite I told you about guys! It was closer than I thought," Peter announced. "And there's the cabin. I wonder if anyone's there."

"You wonder if anyone's inside what? Little bro, you're usually good with these things. You don't even know if it belongs to someone? What a crock. I knew I should have picked out a spot. Sheesh, Peter!" Paul shook his head as the others groaned.

"No sea biscuit, it's a free-for-all cabin. The ad said whoever uses the grounds can use the cabin. And you don't see any other campers, do you?" Peter explains.

"Peter, that's the most ridiculous thing that I've ever heard," Chip adds as Christina agrees.

"Look, guys, no one is here." Peter looks around. "That would make a great place to put Turk."

"Wait," interrupts Yakoo, "let's check out the cabin since we're here. We came this far. Let's see if anyone's home. Come on, Chip." Yakoo takes his car pal and struts up to the cabin's front door. "Hello, is anyone here?" Yakoo knocks on the cabin door.

"Hello?" Chip knocks a few swift times before kicking the door completely open. "Well, there you have it. I guess that makes it ours." He turns to the others as a wild deer leaps directly for him.

"Whoa!" Yakoo tackles his friend to the ground as the deer leaps over them, galloping into the woods.

As the others break into an awful burst of laughter and cheer, Paul and Glenda go and tell the others. Examining the cabin, it was discovered to consist of four bedrooms. Two of which sat upon the left of the front door and the others on the right. A small shabby kitchen occupied the far corner of the cabin as a fireplace stuck out against the center of the far wall. Chipped of paint and scratched about, a small tattered wooden table stood on four skillfully carved cat legs and paws that wobbled when touched between a worn-out love seat and an old rusting metal chair. In front of the old used furniture, lying flat across the floor was a scruffy, shedding bearskin rug that once complemented the wood interior. Happy with their findings of the empty cabin and campsite, the group of young people decided to search the town in the morning and celebrated the night in jubilee, pitching tents and settling in. Blasting a battery-operated boom box, the ladies, along with Chip and Yakoo, prepared the food and snacks. Sustained by painkillers found inside the cabin, Turk points out the drinks and pulls out his hidden illegal substance. As the night dawns over the heads of the party members, they soon settle themselves under the moon and around a blazing campfire.

"This is a great spot, Peter. I can't believe you found it." Christina munched on a box of trail mix.

"Yeah, this is tight for a first-time camper like myself!" Miles held onto a partially burnt hotdog on a stick in one hand and a stem of roasted marshmallows in the other.

"Well, I was star searching in my telescope, and all of a sudden, a huge falling star caught my attention. It was the biggest I'd ever seen! I followed it on my computer and tracked it around this location. It appeared to have fallen here somewhere. I was hoping to be able to locate it. Thought it might be fun to recover a piece of another planet with you guys and show you how cool these things really are up close." Peter looks down at the screen of his malfunctioning laptop, feeling sort of silly.

"Wishful thinking, brain boy," Samantha comments, sharing some spicy jerky with Chip and Valerie.

"Pete, you really don't believe that you're going to find a piece of that star do you? I don't want to crush your dreams, but do you know the odds of that?" states Chip as Miles flings a hot marshmallow down the front of his T-shirt. "Oooh-oww, ooh hot, hot!" He dives and rolls in the dirt, hollering as they all laugh.

"I know how far-fetched and childish it sounds, but hey, I felt the idea over all was neat. Plus, it did fall around a great spot." Peter looks up at the stars that glittered above them.

"Keep searching, little bro. It is a great idea, and you know what, this is an awesome spot! I'm digging it. We got a week to stay here, and tomorrow we find the town's doctor for Turk." Paul always encouraged his brother more when others seemed to bring him down. "Hey . . . where's Yakoo and . . ."

"Glenda?" Samantha finishes the sentence. "I think they're in the cabin, doing who knows what to each other. You know those two haven't seen each other since our last outing. It's tough living in different cities."

"Well, where's Rebecca?" Turk joins in, lying on a pallet. Christina smacks him on his injury. "Ahhhhhhh!"

"She went to take a whiz, but she has been gone a few minutes too long." Christina begins to ponder to herself. "Maybe she had to do number 2."

"Announce her business to everybody, why don't you?" Samantha rolls her head and stands; a loud scream bellows from the woods.

And as the group all turn toward the cry, Rebecca bursts from the darkness of the trees, screaming frantically. Waving her hands, she swats away at her body as if fanning away swarms of bees. Running at her friends, they brace themselves for impact, watching in high profile for whatever she was running from. Tripping, she catches her balance and slows as something small, fury, and unseen to the others dashes out through the grass behind her and jumps on her back.

"What is going on?" Yakoo comes and opens the front door of the cabin in his boxers. "Who is that?" He tries to make out the person as Glenda pokes her head out from behind him.

Rebecca hits the dirt, rolling, yelling, and flipping in front of the others who watched in confusion and shock. Paul and Peter slowly snap out their daze as Yakoo becomes the first to take the initiative to help. He runs out to assist her at top speed. Freeing the creature from her legs, it jumps at her chest as she catches it with her hands. Quickly prying the attacking beast from her face, Yakoo slams it into the dirt and smashes it with the heel of his foot. An unforgettable squeal pierces their eardrums, creating memories as Paul and Chip step around him to examine.

"What was that?" Peter questions, shivering among the women in the camp. "A mouse?"

"Nah, probably a bat carrying food or something? I think it dropped it down her shirt and was trying to get it back, right?" added Miles, watching Yakoo wipe and smear some sort of fluid off his foot on the grass.

"Nope," answers Chip, walking into the campsite.

"Well, what was it then, a lizard?" Valerie's curiosity overwhelms her fear.

"Believe it or not, people, but it was some type of squirrel." Yakoo returns with Rebecca, examining the top of his foot. "A very mad attacking squirrel too. Who'd ever guess?"

"This trip is getting better by the minute." Turk rolls flat on his back slowly. Placing both hands over his face, he thinks about how on top of everything happening, he now had to defend himself from killer squirrels. As the night went on, Turk and the others got little sleep.

The next morning, the sunlight brightly beams through the old largely spaced holes in the walls and roof of the cabin. A thud hits a window, and the smell of burning eggs opens Yakoo's eyes. In one of the smaller bedrooms, he slowly bends his muscular frame into a stretch, feeling the soft body of a woman. Remembering everything that took place the day before, he touches Glenda, who lies silently asleep against his soft, firm chest. He eases from under her and slides out of the bed naked. Finding his underwear at the foot of the bed, he inches out of the middle room, pricking his baby toe on a protruding nail. Holding back his yell, water instantly form in his eyes. Cursing into a balled fist, he looks down at the old rusty nail as Samantha catches his attention.

"You okay? Breakfast?" Samantha asks. In a muscle shirt, panties, and a pot holder mitt, she wields a spatula and a sizzling hot skillet.

"Uuuuhh . . ." he began as the bedroom door cracks open behind him.

"Where is everybody?" Glenda peeps halfway out the door. "And uhh . . . where are your clothes, Sam? Yakoo, you need something on too!" She utters as Yakoo, not wanted to disrespect her, runs in the room and retrieves his pants.

"They're in Chip's tent. Hey, I just came to make breakfast. Eggs?" Samantha offers as they follow her to the dining table. She scoops a few eggs and dumps them into a few plastic bowls that sat between them. "Everybody was outside huddled around Peter. I think they were planning to go hiking or something."

"Hiking, like where?" Yakoo runs out, fixing the belt on his pants. "Why aren't you going?"

"After last night? Whew! I've got to catch up on some sleep. Your boy Chip is a dynamo!" Samantha plops down loosely as Glenda giggles off to the side. "I see how you two are friends. They say birds of the same feather flock together! Ha, isn't that right, Glenda?" Samantha gestures at Yakoo; Glenda's face blushes reddish brown.

"You too . . . I'm going out! I'll be back, Glenda. Why don't you two catch up on some girl talk?" Yakoo kisses her and finds his shirt and shoes.

"Oh, I intend to. We've got a lot of girl talking to catch up on now." Samantha smiles as Yakoo too blushes into a more purplish tone and goes out the door.

Outside, a frigid, misty chill waves across the landscape as Yakoo appeared to be the only one outdoors. Nearing the cooling black fire pit, he steps on the crackling, smoking remains of the black timber that surrounded the outside of the pit. Trash, pallets, and a few sleeping bags were left scattered about for someone to clean up, but Yakoo just shook his head at his careless peers. Scanning around, he takes notice to the entrances of the tents used by him and his friends. Seeing that they were all left open, he listens as the sound of foraging disturbs his train of thought. From nowhere, something grabs his leg from behind. Muttering out the first syllables of a yelp, he exhales and covers his rapidly beating heart at the sight of Turk crawling from out of his blue bubbled sleeping bag.

Looking very weak and pale, which was the total opposite of his normal self, Turk flips on his back and laughs. "What's the matter, dude? Did I scare you?"

"The living crap outta me." Yakoo places his hands on his hips and calms his nerves.

"You should have seen your face, dude. What . . . did you think I was, a bear or something?" Turk tries to laugh as an uncontrollable cough forces him to grasp at his stomach in pain. Triggered by the word "bear," Yakoo returns his attention to the tent as Miles stumbles out, munching on cookies.

"I should've known." Yakoo sighs in relief, then turns back to Turk's sunken raccoon eyes. "You're not looking too well, buddy. How are you feeling?"

"Like I got a fever or something. The good news is my butt doesn't hurt anymore. I think I can get up and walk, but I haven't tried it. But other than Miles breaking wind freely all over the place and this mild headache, I'd say I feel . . . pretty good." Turk wipes away the beads of sweat pouring from his forehead.

"Really? That's good because you look like crap." Yakoo felt the center of his forehead with the palm of his hand. "You're ice cold! As soon as the others get back, we've got to get you to a clinic or something. Where'd they head off too anyway?"

"They claimed they were off to explore, and you know what happens when Paul and Peter go exploring? They'll probably be hiking for miles and miles. Shoot, my feet hurt. I ain't having it! I told them I would stay back and guard the food. Besides, someone has to look after this, fool." Miles eyes Turk on the ground.

"Fool? Man suck my . . . Give me a cookie, idiot! I'm starving!" Turk holds out his hand as Miles tosses cookies on his body. "Quit wasting them! I'm going back to the car."

"I ain't no idiot! You's the idiot, booty bite!" Miles sniggles off to the side.

"Well, I guess I shouldn't go look for them. As soon as they return, we should leave and find you some help," Yakoo suggests as they both peer down at their injured friend who is quietly fast asleep before them, suddenly stretched out on the ground. "That's weird."

"He just passed completely out in less than a second. Man . . . he must be sick!" Miles looks at Yakoo in awe.

Separating to let Peter search for his falling star on his own, Paul, Chip, Valerie, Rebecca, and Christina enter the grounds of the city. Agreeing to meet back at a certain time at the town's square, the girls scour the grounds for stores while Paul and Chip run amuck throughout the streets, searching for a clinic and goofing off.

"This is like, so strange and really cool at the same time!" Chip repositions his ball cap on his short-haired head.

"This is pretty insane. Hello!" Paul shouts out. "I've never seen an empty city before except for in the movies. I wonder how it happened. It's sort of spooky. I mean, why is it empty? This could be an awesome thing." He bumps knuckles with Chip, who now holds an uneasy expression on his face. "Wassup?"

"Shhh!" Chip silences him. "Bro, tell me you saw that."

"Saw what?"

"A guy ran past us." Chip illustrates the walk with his body. "He just ran across the street."

Even though Paul wanted to believe him, Chip was also a practical joker and sometimes hard to take serious. "You're joking, right? Now's not the time, Chip. I didn't see or hear anything."

"I'm dead serious! Dude, an old guy was just right there, and he looked right at me. I was in shock! Before I could even spit it out, he jolted right through the intersection right there! I dunno, maybe he speed walked, but he was right there. It happened!" Chip tries his best to explain.

"Well, if he's old and a real person, then he shouldn't be able to outrun the both of us, right?" Paul eyes Chip confidently.

"So . . . what are you saying, you want to go after him? Let's do it."

"Let's go. Maybe he can tell us where a doctor is and where's everyone at." Paul jogs off with Chip in a sprint through the intersection. "I . . . I don't see a thing." Paul stops and hunches over to catch his breath.

"Dude, you're out of shape. Look, I know what I saw! There's a whole bunch of little side streets. Maybe he turned down one. Come on, let's check down here." Chip suggests as they look for the man, ending up covering more blocks instead.

Although winter was coming and hadn't yet quite placed its chilly mark upon the landscape, plant life had indeed flourished it seems for years inside this surreal place. Very few cars sat still in place, covered in dirt and leaves from the years that must've passed. The absence of humans and little to no movement of wildlife brought a feeling of emptiness and danger to the vacant neighborhood. Insects also had yet to be seen as Paul began to connect all the observations with something bad. Stepping between two buildings, Paul stops at the foot of an alley. Spotting a bit of movement in the far darkness, he tries to focus on what he made out to be a human figure. "Uhh . . . Chip, Chip!" he whispers.

"What, dude? Do you see something?"

"I think. Look down the alleyway." Paul points with a nervously shaking finger.

"What? Where the heck are you looking?" Chip looks all around the building.

"There, there in the alley, pea brain!" Paul takes the back of Chip's head and aims him at the alley.

"Aw, man, it's just a shadow. It's nothing. It's not even moving." Chip snatches away, barely able to make out the image behind a group garbage cans and large metal dumpster.

"It moved! I'm telling you!" Paul loosens the neck of his shirt and pulls out the tucked part of his shirt from under his sweater with clinching teeth.

"Dude, it hasn't budged. It's just a shadow. Don't get all bent up about it. It doesn't even look like a real person," Chip argues as they slowly crept down the alley.

"Okay, we'll both take a look. I bet you any amount of money it's a person. It's probably that old hermit I saw, seriously!" Paul, determined to find out what it was, takes lead in the investigation. "Hey, hey, excuse me, sir?" he speaks out in a pleasant voice. Receiving no answer at all, he glances back at Chip and continues walking toward the shadows of the back of the alley.

"See, it's a dead end and a bunch of garbage." Chip kicks a can and gasps at something large and black swaying behind the large garbage bin. "Uh, Paul. I don't think that is . . . a . . . dude. I think it's an animal, Paul!" Chip warns him in a low voice. If it was a wild animal, he didn't want to draw its attention.

"Animal? You're insane!" Paul whispers and waves him off, suddenly freezing in his tracks.

"Careful, bro." Chip slows behind him, trying to make out exactly what they were seeing behind the dumpster in front of them. "Eww, what's that stuff all over it?"

Paul's eyes widen with fear at a swollen, puffed, dark-haired mass around the face of two large solid white eyes. Lost in thoughts of death, he cringes at two large sets of hoofs that walk out from under a massive body of exposed ribs and stringy bloody hair. Plugs of bleeding and infected bites and wounds cover an extremely large frame of flies and mosquitoes.

"Ugh, it's bleeding and gashed up, Chip. You were right. It is an animal. I still can't tell what it is. It's too dark, and the sun's in my eye. I think it's some sort of calf or something? Look, there's some kind of dress or cloth on its head?"

"What?" Chip slowly follows behind his friend.

"Yeah, I think its head is stuck. It needs our help! Maybe I can snatch it off. If it can't see, it's going to have a hard time eating and defending itself." Very cautiously, Paul moves in a tad bit closer.

A full-grown moose leaps out of the shadows before them. Huffing and snorting out snot and mighty sounds. It slings a large black curtain onto the ground, unveiling its large expanse of thick, cracked and chipped bony antlers. The curtain and its broken rod rattle to the street as Paul and Chip fall back in terror.

"I think you made it mad, Paul!" Chip hollers. As he goes to run, the animal charges at them at full speed.

"Haul ass!" shouts Paul. The crazed animal suddenly rams him from behind, snatching a circular patch off Paul's sweater vest. At the same time, it tries to gnaw at him, heavily bleeding from the mouth. From a powerful head buck from the moose, Paul flies off to the side. Crashing through garbage cans, Paul braces himself along the wall of a building and manages to quickly return on his feet. Stunned and now feeling pain from the impact, he is seized by the shoulder as Chip yanks him away just before the injured moose crashes into the building madly.

"I . . . I don't believe this. It must have rabies or something?" Chip flees with his friend at full speed as the raging moose shakes off the collision and a window screen from its right antler.

"We've got to find the girls and get out of here!" Paul yells as they are chased throughout the quiet city.

Not too far away, inside of an empty, used clothing store, Christina, Valerie, and Rebecca, having forgotten about Turk, catch up on their clothing collection.

"Wow, now this is cute. This place has some awesome skirts and jeans. It's a shame that nobody's here. They'd probably attract a lot of business." Holding a pair of pants up to her legs for Valerie to see, Christina admires a pair of fitting stonewashed jeans.

"Those are hot. I wonder if it's still considered stealing if no one's even here." Valerie blows a thick layer of cobwebs and dust from off a glass counter, revealing old jewelry, gadgets, and small shelves of electronics. She looks around for keys to the unlock them.

"Well . . . I don't know exactly what the rules are to stealing, but we did like just throw a brick through the window just to get in. It's totally breaking and entering." Christina slings a few shirts over her shoulder, getting dust in her eyes. "Hey, Rebe, find anything you like yet?" She wipes her face and the dirt from her glasses.

"Nope, not at all," Rebecca answers, walking toward the back of the store. "I hate vintage stores! It smells awful in here!" She touches the sore, bandaged squirrel bite on the back of her neck and grumbles as the roll of a small ball bearing down a small flight of steps catches her attention. Looking over her shoulder, she notices wooden stairs leading to another level of the store. "Hello? Is anyone there?" she calls out before bravely checking for life. Hearing a low thumping of what sounds like feet, she quietly crept up the stairs and into a small hallway with doors occupying both ends. Standing directly in the middle of the hall, in front of a large picture of a mountain scene, Rebecca takes a deep breath and checks the far rooms. Finding a very filthy bathroom in one, she checks the far rooms and another door at its far end. Inside the room's doorway, she places one foot inside as a large picture fall to the floor behind her. Startling to the heart, Rebecca remains calm and walks toward the bent framed picture. "How the hell?" She ponders on how it fell on its own. Picking up the nail from which the artwork hung, she rubs her thumb and index finger together, feeling the thick chalky drywall that was caked around the small nail. Thinking she heard the low cry of a small baby, Rebecca glances at the wall, a large hole roughly faced her directly where the picture was located. Looking into it, she could see the green numbers on what appeared to be a thousand dollar bill. It was somehow wedged into the deep grapefruit-sized crevice. "Jackpot!" A smile came across her grumpy face as she thought of all the things she could do with the money once they made it home. Thinking of all the spiders and insects that possibly resided inside the hole, she slowly reaches inside, deciding that the grand was worth the risk. Stretching in her already bitten arm, it became obvious that the hole was a lot deeper and open than she imagined. With the bill in her grasp, she reaches even farther, feeling the cool paper along her fingertips. Gripping the money, she began to pull it out as an unknown force clamps down on her arm. Jammed inside, she attempts to free herself as all efforts fail. "Humph, hey, guys, guys? I think I'm stuck . . . Something's got me, guys!" she calls out as something squeezes tightly down on her arm that was seriously trapped. "Great, just great!" She hits the wall with her left hand, relieving frustration. Placing her head against the old chipped lead paint, she continues to call out for her friends as loud as she possibly could. And while no degree of movement seemed to pry her arm free, she counts to ten, trying not to panic.

And in trying to control the state of panic within man, most of the time, it is quite obtainable; however when panic is induced by an unknown force or entity, it becomes inevitable as Paul, not far away, finds himself pinned at the foot of an establishment outside by the animal that one would believe to be resurrected from the darkest pits of hell.

"Chip! Chip!" Paul cries out in fear for his life as he distances himself from the chomping jaws of the deranged-acting moose by grabbing hold of the antlers and pushing it away. "It's trying to eat me!" he describes as the giant crushes Paul's left leg within a single step of a bone-exposed hoof and drags him away down the street by the neck in one bite of his mighty jaws. Bucking about wildly, Paul is jerked and flung about frantically as he flips onto the moose's back. Paul still manages to hold on as the large animal smashes into a fire hydrant, splitting open its head and sending Paul flying into the ground a few feet away.

Having picked up an iron pole from the nearby trash to use as a weapon, Chip rushes to help his friend. The moose plows into Paul from behind again, sending him twisting and sliding face first across the pavement. Then going in for the final kill, the moose charges once more as Chip comes from the side; stabbing deep into the animal's face, he pokes out one of its eyes. The moose roars off in a frenzy of loud noises, allowing the two young men to narrowly escape once more. The ghastly beast, wailing in a considerable amount of pain, stumbles and staggers in a daze. Dripping, oozing, and salivating in a thick maroon from its mouth, head, and body, the half-dead moose appears to slowly follow them, then walks into a building.

"Now's our chance, buddy. Come on!" directs Chip as Paul leans and hops against him for support. "We have to move fast. How's the leg?"

"Broken, like the rest of my insides," Paul jokes sarcastically as the flow of pure adrenaline numbs the sensations of pain. Ducking alongside a building, the two hide as the moose charges past them. Paul glances down at his wet red hands and soaked clothes.

"Does that thing ever give up?" Chip peeps around the edge of the building at the moose as screams of Rebecca echo throughout the inner city around them. "The girls!"

"It came from . . . that way." Paul holds his ribs and rests against the building, standing fully on the good leg. He tries desperately to disregard the pain.

Those cries, those awful sounds spun from Rebecca's small quivering mouth as Valerie, with one foot on the wall, and Christina, with both arms around Rebecca's waist, try drastically to free her arm from the hole in the wall. Kicking and screaming as if something was pulsating through her body, Rebecca, throws and knocks her friends about as they fought to pull and hold on to her.

"Rebe, what's wrong? We're trying to help you!" Christina tries to calm her to find out exactly what the problem was.

"Something's in there! It's hurting my arm!" Rebecca screams as tears stream down her face and chin.

"Why would you put your arm in there?" Valerie becomes upset. "We're trying to help, Rebecca, but you have to calm down! On the count of three, we're going to pull as hard as we can, okay? Okay?" Valerie forewarns her as Rebecca begins to shake and tremble.

"I can't! It hurts! Ahhhhhhhhh!" Rebecca yells.

"Come on, Christina, you ready?" Valerie glances at Christina in desperation as she nods in agreement. "Three!" Valerie skips the first two numbers. Pulling as hard as they could, the three go tumbling backward down the stairs.

Opening her eyes and still breathing, Christina peers down at her body, which was drenched in someone else's blood. "Rebe?" She sits up as Rebecca draws back in cries and curse words.

"My hand, look at what they did to my hand! Fucking bastards!" Rebecca yells out, rocking back and forth, holding her arm.

"Let's see, Rebe. Let me take a look at your arm!" Valerie tries to get her to straighten out her arm. "Let me see, Rebe." She puts an arm over Rebecca's shoulders.

"I can't, my arm . . . my arm!" Rebecca kicks and trembles as she hunches over her arm and hand. "I'll kill you, sorry fucks!" She howls at the tops of her lungs.

"Rebecca, you're bleeding badly. You have to let us take a look, Rebe. It's the only way we can help you!" Christina instructs as Rebecca covers her face and holds out her aching arm. "Oh my GOD!" she utters in a breathless manner as Valerie takes a look and vomits beside them.

Gushing with blood, Rebecca's arm extends with extensive teeth, bite marks, and plugs of flesh ripped and eaten from her forearm. Viewing her bare, exposed bones in various places, Christina tenses up at sight of her hand, which was partially missing along with three of her fingers.

"Come on, we've got to get you to a hospital!" Christina, staring up the stairs at the wall, helps up Rebecca as Valerie joins them.

"Someone or something is in this house with us . . . and in this city! We've all got to leave, now!" Valerie shouts, moving them along.

Paranoid and unaware of what was actually going on around them, the three head to the front room of the store. Carefully looking around, Valerie rips down one of the curtains that hung openly along one of the windows and tears it in half. Wrapping her friend's hand, Chip and Paul rushes in through the front door, bloodied and bruised also.

"There you are! I . . . I told you they were in here! What . . . what happened to you guys? We heard screams." Paul, moving in pain, looks down at Valerie and Rebecca.

"We have to get out of here. There's an insane moose outside with a disease or something. It was trying to kill and eat us! It broke Paul's leg! What . . . what's going on here? What the heck happened to her?" Chip chokes on his swallow when seeing the mess among the women.

"Some . . . something inside the walls tried to freak'n devour her arm. I don't know what's going on around here, but we have to go and get her to a hospital before she bleeds to death!" Valerie shouts in a slight hysteria.

"We need to get her to Glenda. Quick! She's a registered nurse!" Christina helps to escort Rebecca between them as she moans and cry.

"I . . . I don't want to die! Owww . . . my arm!" Rebecca went on as they head to the front door.

"Wait, you said something's outside." Valerie, more concerned about Rebecca than what Chip had to say when they entered the store, finally slightly analyzes what he said when she looks at Paul limping against Chris. "What happened to you two?"

"We were attacked," Paul replies, now in an unbelievable amount of pain.

"Attacked? By who? Your shoulder's bleeding . . . and what's wrong with your leg? You're limping." Christina also looks over Paul. "Can you move out of the way?"

"A moose bit me and broke my leg, but I'll live. I'm sure it's nothing a tetanus shot and a cast can't cure," Paul tells as they walk past the counter of cobwebs and all sorts of dust.

"Wait! Let me go first and check for that moose. It was right behind us," Chip insists. Stepping in front of the group, he opens the front door. As he peeks out, a clicking, double-barrel shotgun touches his nose and walks him backward as an officer follow them back inside.

Behind a pair of deep black-tinted shades, the two officers, a white male and a black man, both stood oddly inside the doorway with their guns drawn. The Caucasian officer stood intensely still next to Chip's ongoing babbling. While the black cop, with pistol ready, stiffly pans his head like a nervous cat at the sound of every little movement.

"Wait . . . wait! We didn't know that anyone lived here! The whole town looked empty! My friend is hurt. Please help us!" Chip pleads as the sound of a small child running through the walls causes him to look at his friends, just before one of the policemen clunks him on the back of the head with his gun, striking Chip to the floor unconscious.

Unaware of his brother and friends in danger, Peter, alone in the mist of the woods, sits down his laptop, flips open his cell phone, and looks at the time that was still wrong. "I haven't found a thing. Where are they?" He looks around at the sky, determining how late in the day it had gotten and how he hadn't seen a sign of anyone. Reading no service on his phone, he puts it away and glances down at his feet in thought. Eyeing something silvery by his computer, he squats down to study the object. Lifting it into his hand, he examines the metallic object and its rocklike properties. Peering around sharply, he picks up the laptop and finds himself in a thin trail of the weird, unidentifiable debris. "This is the crash site . . . I' I found it! I found the meteor! Yes!" he cheers to himself, dropping the laptop on the ground, shattering it to pieces. "Dang it!" He thinks of nothing but the falling star he believes fell there. Following the newly grown grassy dirt path of metal and iron-like pieces, Peter stumbles across a shocking discovery. Traveling uphill, around where he was walking, he sees bits and pieces of automobile parts scattered across the ground in every direction, as if automobiles had been dragged there. Bits of bumpers, glass, tires, and materials from the interior of old cars become as luminous as the moon. A mirror crackled up under his feet as small sheets of a window reflect the sky in front of him. In a bed of plastic, aluminum and rubber, Peter spots two lone figures cutting through the woods in the distance. "Hi . . . Hey, guys, wait! Over here, guys!" he calls out as the silhouettes disappear among the trees. Dropping the scrap metal, he runs behind them farther up the hillside. "I'm down here!" he shouts at whom he thought were his comrades. "Paul? Chip? Dang it, they can't even hear me." Peter gives up yelling and decides to just follow them in hopes they would stop or slow. *Where are they going? They must be lost.* He ponders on which direction they went. Beginning to see a slew of tires and steering wheels too, he remembers how there were barely any cars seen in town. Clearing a section of trees and thick bushes, he abruptly comes to a tremendous gate. Peering past it, he sees that extremely large mansion that sat by itself on top of a large hill. And between the mansion and the gate where Peter stood, along the hill lay a massive, twisting graveyard covered in all kinds of flipped, wrong-side-up automobiles and motorbikes and appliances of all types belonging to the town. Dropping his mouth in amassment and confusion, he spots the two figures pick up some large items then climb and hike through the towers of cars and trucks toward the mansion. Seeing that the build of the people was not that of his friends, he was still happy that he had found life and maybe help and some insight on what happened to the town. Squeezing his bony body through the large bars, he halts at a headstone. Looking at the obstacles of vehicles and furniture ahead that faced him, he glances down at the harsh, cracked earth that allow him to nearly see four feet beneath the land. Large in some places, deep in others, splits ran everywhere along the unbalanced incline. Peter knew that it was going to be rough climbing over the trucks and vehicles that lay in every which way, but he was quite up to the challenge.

Stepping on headstones to avoid twisting his ankles in any of the large cracks that rippled through the ground, Peter grabs hold to the frame of a large jeep and climbs upon its side. Jumping down, he wonders how so many cars ended up in this grim place. Glancing up at the top of the hill, which grew nearer, he maneuvers around the toppled old mobiles and forgotten Fords. Hearing the sounds of mass movement and the squeaking of old bicycle wheels appearing to be coming from below, he eyes the moving ground around him. Feeling a painful sting of a pinch on his calf, Peter kicks his right leg like a stubborn mule looking behind him. Seeing large bleeding white eyed rats seeping out of the ground, racing in his direction, he is startled with terror, and quickly darts up the hill as thousands of rats spew out from the open graves, engulfing the lower half of his body. "Yaaaah, rats! Get off, get off of me!" he screams, dusting the rodents from his clothes. Stepping on them, one crawls up his pants leg, causing him to squirm and hop around ballistically as he slings it out of the other pants leg. Closing in on the mansion, Peter dashes with all his might to the top, crashing through a tall stone head of an angel along the way. Leaping over a motorcycle, one of his feet steps between dry crumbling cracks as more rats attack, cling and cover his entire body by their jagged mouths of sharp teeth. Kicking and hollering, he frees his wedged foot from the ditch and tosses his trusty hunting vest of creatures far down the hillside as other rats rip it to pieces. As small necks and frail bones make the sound of crackling twigs up under his feet, he breaks through the loud squealing bodies. While some skeletal remains of past citizens partially protrude from the ground, Paul steps on an unseen skull and high jumps onto the top of a tall and wide rectangular gravestone. Leaping onto it, he hops down to the ground and dashes to the entrance of the mansion. Smacking the remaining rodents away, he hears a loud shattering noise that causes him to cover his ears and glance behind. Now in silence, he observes that all the rats have completely retreated and vanished.

"That was weird, what the hell?" Peter whispers into the wind, preparing to knock as the door creaks open back and forth. Sneaking a peek through its opening, he chooses to press the doorbell, not wanting to be rude. Apparently not working, he pushes the door open and eases inside. "Whoa!" is all he could utter when viewing the large main room in its cluttered enormity. Greeted only by a floor of spare parts, mechanical pieces and garbage, a slamming door echoing around the room causes Peter and his heart to jump as he stands alone. Slowly, he heads toward the direction of the strange sounds coming from the floor below. Sounding like people in great hurt and need of help, he bravely balls up his fist and walks through an open doorway. Entering a small messy hall of doors and connecting halls, timidly, he opens a door to a room that an old lady occupies. "Ex-excuse me . . ." he speaks in a low tone in which only an animal with superior hearing could make out. As if meditating in the middle of the old antique room upon a carpet, the woman squats and sways her wrinkled body in all directions. As he inches up to her, the tiled floor creeks underneath him. Peter reaches out to touch the back of her shoulder; the woman turns around, revealing a set of wide round eyes rolled into the back of her head. Her pupils change solid black as she gnashes on a human leg stuffed into her torn and stretched open mouth. Thick muscles and sprouting veins contract and expand throughout her neck and face as she shrills then hums in a calm vibrating monotone. Peter, covering his mouth in fright, quickly creeps out and shuts the door without a peep of a sound.

Very ready to leave, Peter dashes out to the door from which the cry came. Hurrying down a long hall of garbage and recyclable materials, he turns a corner into another door that led to a winding staircase of almost pitch blackness. Also covered in aluminum paper and unknown trash, Peter gazes down into the darkness of the stairs, hearing more moaning and shuffling coming from somewhere at the bottom. *What was that*, he thought, enthusiastically wanting to help the person heard. Not able to shake thoughts of the man-eating woman he just encountered, he bravely eases down the stairs with caution as stiff uneasiness fill the air around him. The awful smell and sounds of suffering get stronger and louder as he descends down two bends of stairs. The faint light from upstairs disappears, causing him to slide his hands across the slick, nasty walls. As his feet began to crunch and slosh through soft places, he thought he made out the body of a dead bird as he maintains his composure and pay his imagination no mind. Coming to the faint shadow of a woman in a crawling position up from the bend, Peter pauses on the steps. "Are you okay? What's happening here?" he softly speaks, hoping that a serial killer wasn't around, or worse, another man-eating person. Receiving no response, he leans down to assist the tired yet perhaps sickly woman. "Don't worry, I'll help you." Bending, Peter feels wet lacerations and holes along her arm and face. Pulling her up to walk, he notices the lightness in her dead weight as he struggles to hold her up. "Can you walk? Who are you running from? Who's hurting you?" He throws his arm around her waist and attempts to walk backward with her as she flops about limply in the shadows. Fighting to carry her up the steps, Peter gets a decent lighting from the hall's curtainless windows at the top of the stairs. Halfway up, he feels wetness along his legs, dripping into his shoes. "Great, you're urinating." He glimpse down into the dark globs of guts and tissue oozing down his clothing. As her spinal column dangles on his stomach, he drops the upper half of woman like a hot potato in a horrific yell. The corpse tumbles back down the staircase, skidding and ricocheting off the walls into the black of awful wails.

Having seen enough gore for the rest of his life, Peter scampers to the exit as an old man startles him. "Who, who are you? What are you doing with those people down there?" he questions as the crease-faced old man tilts his head, pops his neck, and smiles a set of long, rotting and foul missing teeth.

"The town," he responds, partly closing a pair of watery solid black eyes. He lunges the tip of a keen-edge piece of broken metal beam into Peters neck. Yanking it away, he strikes the young boy with the thick end of the bar, sending Peter hurtling down the steps, clanging across the mounds of junk and body parts.

Helplessly gasping for air, Peter reaches out for leverage. Flipping, he rolls into a pit of scrap metal and hellish despair. The head and shoulder region of the dying woman he tried to help passes by his face as he too is overtaken by his own screams of agony and pain. Crying and slowly dying, Peter is pulled and ripped apart, devoured in a pit of starving, raging beings.

And as overwhelmed and overtaken was he, so was his loyal brother and friends as they remained inside the city. Somewhere in the town, in an old small cobweb-infested police station, Paul, Chip, and the slowly dying Rebecca await inside a small barred cell. While out in the open, their sobbing friends, Christina and Valerie, sit cuffed at a table, whispering and crying among one another inside the brick building.

"What are we doing here? You haven't told us anything? Why are we here?" Christina shouts out, fixing the slipping glasses upon her face as best she could.

"You can't do this. My uncle is a lawyer! You can't just arrest us and not tell us why. This is illegal, you assholes!" yells Valerie as the two officers who arrested them stand blank and absent together in the middle of the floor.

The tallest officer, the Caucasian man, slowly steps near them. He stoops down and shocks them with a gesture of blowing across one finger. He leans in and opens his mouth, showing something green moving at the back of his tongue. Giving a lingering, ear-puncturing squeal, his sunglasses slightly slide down his nose, revealing his animal-like solid black liquid—filled eyes. Closing his mouth, he silently stands as Christina watches, confounded with fear, cursing him in the back of her mind.

"Wait a second. Excuse me, sir." Chip tries to get the policeman's attention off the girls. "Our friends are injured. Can you at least take them to a doctor?" He points out Rebecca, who was passed out on the floor of the small holding cell, still receiving no answer. "I . . . I don't think you guys are police at all. Where are all the people? Where's all the other policemen? I want to see the sheriff! Where's the sheriff if you guys are for real?"

"It . . . it doesn't look like anyone's been in this place for years," Paul mumbles, gathering his strength, frustrated and irritable. "This isn't a real prison. This cell is . . . fake. Just . . . for show I bet. It's some kinda two-bit police office."

"Look . . . guys, this is kidnap! You can't do this! Let us go so we can get our friends some help! We haven't done anything! This entire city is abandoned." Chip stands with his head pressed against the bars.

As the other officer of African American descent slowly lifts his walkie-talkie to the side of his head, a strange range of static noises emits from it. In full attention, he appeared to be listening as his mouth began to move as if he was talking. "Trespassing." He gurgles as something bangs loudly against the thick steel door behind him. At that very moment, that same something or someone, begins to beat on the steel structure over and over again. Its sound is muffled due to the thickness of the steel door. The officers approach the door as one gives it a few hard whips with his hand, quieting the noise.

"What the hell is behind that door?" Valerie's eyes widen with dread as she leans in closer to Christina.

"I don't know . . . Val, but did you hear the sound that guy made? I don't think that's foreign they're talking. I don't think they're even human," Christina whispers nervously, beginning to form her own thoughts about the strange cops.

Chip and Paul also notices the nonhuman behavior and began to plan their escape. "This is unreal!" whispers Paul. "Look at that thing sticking out from that guys neck." He points out some type of vein that began to move like a limb as the officers appear to be somehow communicating.

"Dude, we've got to get the heck out of here. This is mad." Chip starts to worry about their lives instead of going to jail.

Deciding not to make any sudden moves or distractions, Christina tests her flexibility; and quickly and discreetly, she loops her arms, easing her legs and body between them. As her chair slides back, making a small screeching sound across the floor, one of the officers notices the abnormal movement. Releasing a loud high-pitched, strident, alarming sound from his mouth, the large white man hurries to restrain her as the other cop follows. Kicking the officer back with every ounce of woman strength from her legs, he flies backward into the other. Going around his stunned partner, the black officer leaps onto her and begins to bite through Christina's clothing. Pulling away skin and muscle from her small body, he weighs her down with powerful arms and eats away at her back. The room fills with terrible screams as Christina knocks the officer's keys to the floor and kicks them to the cell of her friends. Breaking the table, the powerful man lifts Christina into the air with two hands of ox-strong strength as she rips herself away from his clutches, catching Valerie's high-pitched cry. Falling to the floor on her side, Christina spots the tip of the officer's shotgun on a nearby table.

Moving in toward Valerie, the stunned, clay-faced bluish pink officer snarls, showing all his bloodstained teeth. With eyes reflecting nothing, he licks his lips with a strange muscle that extends from his throat. Illustrating hunger, long whimsy, snail-like feelers stretch from his bubbling neck and pulsating muscles in his face. A skin fold of wrinkles melt over his forehead as he begins to eat into the shoulder of the cuffed college student. And in the mist of the gruesome act, the room lights up against the sounds of a small cannon. Hearing his companion scream in great pain, the morphing officer turns to see as his head, lower portion of neck and mid-section explodes over Valerie's severely bitten body that is also knocked back by Christina's shooting. Still standing, the partial-headed body of the policeman falls onto Valerie as some sort of green goo wiggles from the man's open wound. As if trying to escape, it oozes along with blood and brain tissue across the floor. And as if seeing her, a tiny node forms on the top of the unknown form of matter and swells in her direction. Shrinking into an irregular-motioned gelatin ball, it squirts into Valerie's open mouth.

Chip and Paul hurry to Valerie, knocking the kneeled and slumping body of the first officer to the floor. Chip uncuffs her as she uncontrollably chews on the disgust and swallows. Gagging, she sits upright, shaking and choking up blood. Paul stares at Chip through a large hole in her abdomen, created by the shotgun blast.

"Oh no . . . Val?" Chip touches her leg as her body falls forward lifelessly. Laying her back, he cushions her neck and kisses her on the lightly tanned forehead, weeping. Christina falls to her knees behind them as Valerie dies in Chip's arms. "Gone." Tears for his friend pour from his face.

"Valerie." Christina, still handcuffed, drops the shotgun and burst into a crying frenzy as a loud banging emerges from the steel door along with more muffled noises. Paul frees her hands and helps her to stand. Christina stares down over the body of the dead officer that attacked her, watching him twitch and gurgle blood and slime. "What the hell? What the hell are they?" she mutters as Paul helps her to sit upon one of the tables. "I . . . I . . . I killed her."

"It wasn't your fault, Chris," Paul consoles her, looking down at the monstrosity, then across at the steel door. "We have to leave, Chip! What are these things? What is this place?"

"I don't know," Chip answers in a low tone, staring at the pounding door, questioning what was on the other side, wanting to be let out.

"Don't do it, Chip. It could be more of them!" Paul points his trembling hand.

"If it's bad, those things would have opened it. But they didn't, they didn't want to open the door for a reason, just like it wouldn't let us out! There have to be people behind that door." Chip, despite the trauma, tries to rationalize.

"What if it's another animal? Don't do it, Chip." Paul looks him in the eye.

"It can't be."

"Chip!" Paul attempts to stop him but is grounded by internal pain; Chip walks to the door.

The swollen gruesome body of the Caucasian policeman lies flat on its back with a crater formed in its chest. Looking closely, Christina could make out small slits opening and closing around its neck, resembling what she knew to be a pair of gills.

"Stay back, you two. Paul, please?" Chip glances at Christina, who looked as though she was deeply concentrating and entranced with something she was seeing. "What's it doing?"

"I . . . I don't know. Fighting to live or something?" Christina wipes her face and answers, still not altogether.

"That's what you get for killing our friend!" Paul spits on the fallen officer. Stooping down, he slaps the cop's face as a growth of tentacles push out from the skin and fall to the floor jittering, sending Paul jumping back into the table. "You see that?" He looks at Christina and returns over the body. Watching the man's mouth shutter, Paul notices a lump moving inside the officer's throat and behind his nostrils. "Ugh . . ." Paul's face twists in disgust as the officer suddenly seems to mumble something. "What the fuck? You have got to be shit'n me. It's talking."

"What . . . what is it saying?" Chip unlocks the latch on the door as the loud knocking commences. "Hey, it sounds like a man's voice behind here!"

"I hope you're right." Paul glances down at Christina and the officer as the soft sounds of English catches his ear.

"Host . . . feed . . . host . . . trespassers fee . . ." the policeman slurs off as red and green mucus-like fluids drain from the corners of his mouth.

"I think he said host and . . . and . . ." Paul lifts his head as Chip swings the solid door open, slamming it against the wall.

Knocking a hovering cloud of dust around the room, from out of the darkness of the room emerges a tough-looking, graying, elderly man with many furrows. Perhaps a hunter, he dust off an earth-covered camouflage vest and fitting jeans. Clumping small clouds of dust onto the floor from his worn, sewed brown mountain boots, he tightens a bandana around his balding scalp of wild white hair and sits a hunting lodge cap, tilted upon his head. "Whew, I thought I was a goner! It's good to see normal people!" He thanks them, rubbing his stubby white facial hairs that poked out like a lion's mane around his dirt-smeared face. "Look out, boy!" The old man's voice crackles as he points over Chip's shoulder.

Mesmerized by the discovery of another normal human being and too slow to react, Paul snaps out his daze as two long slimy, unsegmented extensions stretched beside his head from the middle of the fallen officer's face. With a single eye attached to each end of both extended limbs, they retract past Paul's face, receding back into the policeman's nose. Jumping back once more, Paul quickly dodges something green that spurts out the head of the man, past his face, and onto Christina's head. She hollers, frantically kicking away at the chairs and office furniture in fright. As it forcefully squeezes in between her lips, Christina snatches off the gel and fling the squirming body directly into the chest of the newly found old man.

"Dang, nab it, it's got a hold of me! The goblins done got me!" The energetic elderly fellow rolls along the wall. Square dancing around, he drops to the tiled floor, fighting the jellified creature. Stuck to his body, the scrawny old man pushes it away as one end divides into a branch of limbs that desperately tries to enter his ear. "What in tarnation, goodness gracious!" he yells as the others move out of the way, not knowing what to do. As the thing separates in different ways and directions, it covers the man's mouth and slithers into his nose. Slamming the small, liquified substance on the floor, the more slender end shoots a quite wiry and lengthy string of drip out at his face. With a small mouth and tongue on its tip, it chatters inches away from his eyelid. Rolling and slamming against the floor and tables, the weary fellow cries for help as Chip finds a small torch lighter inside his pocket. The old man holds the squalling creature out directly in front of him, and at that instance, Chip runs and flicks the lighter underneath the green glob.

The hot Jell-O goo pelts into the air, landing on the back of Christina's shirt. As she tries to catch hold of it, the slippery fiend glides down into her pants, causing her to jump and run around frantically. Wiggling up and down, it slides around her legs as she squeezes her knees together. Lumping in the crotch of her pants, the three men watch in awe as Christina moans and falls to the floor. The imprint of the creature disappears in a bubbling sound deep into the opening of her womb. Shaking and jerking in place, Christina's head and arms began to twitch and gyrate. Groaning and gurgling, she slobbers out unnatural sounds as her pupils roll to the tops of her eyelids. A small slit opens and releases a cloud of blackness around her eyes' sclera. "You will all become our host . . . You will feed the vessel," she growls an unnerving sound in front of them. Leaping at them, Christina relinquishes a low, guttural sound, cuts to the side, and jumps, breaking through the nearest window headfirst.

"Well, I'll be a rabbit's ass. That was not a zombie." The old man stood stupefied, trembling at the same time. "They're making monsters or something out of us! Did you hear what that . . . thing said? It wants to make us a vessel!"

"Christina! No! A vessel for what?" Paul looks over at Chip, heart pounding against his chest.

"Probably for more of them little green things to invade us! I bet ya! And I'll say one thing. That's the fastest I've seen one change, that's a record for sure!" The elder takes off his filthy cap and scratches his bristly, unshaven face.

"What do you mean by that? You know something? What else have you seen?" Chip leans against the wall to catch his breath, also shaken by the whole ordeal.

"Well, a few days ago, I had come across a few more of them things and a trucker stranded inside a rig in the woods. He was burned to hell terribly and had bites all over. I mean, nearly bitten to death! I asked him what happened and tried to help him, but he refused to accept and whispered to me what had happened to him. He said he and his partner were attacked by these demonic people. Hell, I didn't believe a word he said, thought he was out of his mind. But I listen good. He explains how his friend turns into a zombie and tries to eat him. Said he set them on fire to escape. He wanted me to lay him down as well, said he was changing or something." The old man sits the bent and battered cap on his head and cocks it to the side, pausing for a long moment. Rubbing the corner of his balding, freckled head, he smacks his dry, thirsty lips as if to say something but second thought it.

"Well, what happened?" Chip blurts out.

"Well, I'm here, ain't I, and he's not. Anyway, I had to eventually. I did think he was pulling my leg until he too quickly changed, your friend and just like those policemen right there." He rubs his neck and gives Paul the evil eye. "Have you been bitten? Cause you look like hell!"

Nodding yes, Paul begins to sob at the very thought of changing into one of the things they encountered. "I'm . . . I'm going to turn into one of those? Chip?"

"And what about you, fella? You kinda banged up too." The wise man peers cautiously and kindly scoots away.

"No, no one's bitten me," Chip answers, now quite worried about Paul. "So what . . . what do we do now? What . . ."

"Is it just you two? Where's the rest of your buddies? I know you young'ns run in packs. Was there anyone else with you who were bit?"

"Just . . . just our friend at camp and . . ." Having forgotten about Rebecca, Chip looks at Paul as they both turn around to the cell.

Looking at them, the black pupils of their friend Rebecca jolt into the back of her head as she leans forward. Her head slants as if she was eavesdropping on the wind. Slobbering foam onto her feet, she licks her mouth hungrily like an animal. Rushing forward, she shoots her intestines through the bars from her stomach and grabs hold of her friend. Snatching him to her, Rebecca bites into Chip's arm as he knocks her away with a chair. As she flies back awkwardly into the cell, Paul slams the automatic locking barred door. Rebecca kicks and howls violently. Crunching down on the iron bars with her bony teeth, she began to crack and shatter them. Desperately trying to get to her old friends, Rebecca falls back and charges at the bars, splitting her head and mouth. Showing no indications of her former self, Rebecca runs around savagely in the small brick space as Paul, Chip, and the old man watch, just a few feet away.

"She chewed a plug right out my damn arm!" Chip tries to put pressure on the bleeding as Paul rips away a piece of his shirt and helps to wrap Chip's arm. "Guess I'm a goner now too, dude."

"How long do you think we have, old man?" Paul, already cold and trembling, glances at him, quietly shaking his head, mind boggled.

"Look, I don't know how fast it spreads, but from what I've seen in this so far, it's different for everybody. It's like a virus. I think you change faster when you've been bitten a bunch of times," the elderly fellow explains, peering out the busted window. "Whatever the case maybe, we've got to get out of this town! Maybe they'll have cure for you guys in the city, in the hospital."

"Where's that?" A gleam of hope twinkles in Chip's eye. "We were trying to find it."

"Uhhh . . . about sixty miles south of here." The old guy slowly bends down like a rusty lever and ties his boots. Making a painful expression, he rises and checks his pockets as if he was about to leave.

"Can you take us? If you're near, you could ride us back to camp to get our friends. Come on, man, you owe us. Chip freed you." Paul also feels a small amount of chance and stares at the experienced man sincerely.

"Sure . . . I can take ya, but the moment you start acting loopy, I'm taking ya out back quick." The old man strolls over and picks up the shotgun from the floor.

Back through the tall gate of fencing, past the graveyard littered of metal and rubber, upon that eerie slope of a hill, that dreary and unclean, old and cracked with age mansion lurched. Inside, the murderous one who victimized Paul's brother, Peter, receives a low and sad feeling of two close deaths. Equipped with extra-enhanced senses, he mourns the loss of his blood that was embedded in the shell of the two human officers. With his head down and arms behind his back, he paces back and forth inside the large hall of scattered metals and garbage. Stepping into several overlapping skid marks of blood and meat, he glides into the elegant bedroom of splattered animal and human carcasses and the old twisted woman.

"The others have been destroyed . . . children severely wounded." The wrinkled faced man then grunts a series of unidentifiable languages unknown to man.

Glancing around the blood-infested room of antique bookshelves and furniture, upon a beautiful king-sized bed, the old woman looks up at a large sparkling chandelier, then spins her head 360 degrees to the man. "The humanoid host are too insubordinate. Need more food for vessel, more . . . host for children." She shrieks back a deep tone.

"Agreed, but . . . knowledge of existence . . . to species . . . is detrimental to survival. Must be done." The man chokes in a flange of sounds and moving tentacles

"Release host. We . . . have suffered, al-al-already. Must be done." The old woman's head snaps back in place as she returns to a meditative stature. "No more host. Let them feed on . . . trespassers. Must begin . . . transportation of vessel."

"Thy will be done." The old man exited the room. Carrying out his orders accordingly, ten of the savaged are released from the basement pit as he controls them all by sound from his body. Guiding them outside, he shook angrily in fear that if man got knowledge of their existence, there was a chance that the probability of survival for his kind, his species, would drastically lower.

Paul, Chip, and the man who was locked in the room make their way through the doomed town, hearing the mindless people dispersing through the woods from afar.

"Chip, sounds like they're coming right for us! What to do now?" Paul talks low, pressed alongside a building.

"I dunno, bud. Maybe this is it. Hey, old dude, any ideas?" Chip nervously tries to think of options. "Do you know your way around town?"

"A little familiar, everything's changed since my day. Our best bet is to hide in one of them old houses somewhere." He begins to worry about his life and when the time comes for the two boys to change. Of a very big heart and full of compassion, even though he didn't say it and since they saved him, the sparky old man was determined to help them for as long as he could carry on. "This way." He takes them behind a section of homes and small yards.

"Hey, by the way, what's your name? I know that this is an odd time to get to know one another, but I think it's a better time than any right now. I'm Paul . . . and he's Chip." Paul hobbles against Chip, ripping his jeans as they took turns clearing a fence.

"Gus, the name's Gus. Nice to meet ya." He gives a rugged smile of filthy teeth, peering through the clearest true blue eyes surrounded by the corners of the deepest crow's feet.

"In there!" Chip points to a black back door that was already open. "What if someone's already in there?"

"We'll just have to kill 'em. It's them or us, and we got everything to lose and nowhere to hide. So pretty much this is it," Gus whispers as they crept into the house.

Gently shutting the door behind him, Paul checks his undamaged cell once again. Getting no service, he places the phone back into his back pocket as suddenly, he begins to feel quite ill. Tightening in the stomach and across the chest, he tries not to think about it. With one hand against the wall, he begins to sweat while quietly listening to Chip and Gus checking the house.

"Paul?" Chip calls out in a loud whisper as Paul finds them entering a basement door. "Down here."

Tiptoeing down the steps, Gus scans the dark and cold compact area, claiming it to be clear. Stuffed with used furniture, boxes, and junk of all sorts, they chose an area in one of the corners to hide. Behind an old bookshelf, they took refuge to discuss what their next plan of action was.

"So what now? What now?" Paul rubs his hands against his arms to stay warm. "What if it's just us, Chip? What if it got so bad the others left us behind?"

"You really think Peter would ditch his one and only bro? Come on, dude. And you know how Yakoo is. He's probably worried to death and mad." Chip crouches down next to Paul. "I sure hope we make it to a hospital. I don't want to eat anyone, dude. Hey, feel my hands, they're super cold. I think I'm dying." Chip blows across his hands and fingers.

"Sounds like you fellas got some hell of a friends, if they're worth going back for. You've got to be strong if you want to live to see them again. Right now, even in you two's condition, the best thing to do is wait till morning." Gus finds some hockey sticks and squats down in the corner across from them.

"Morning? You want us to spend the night in this god-awful town? It's suicide." He rolls the bottom of his pants up and examines his broken blue and purplish veiny leg.

"You can't see what's coming after ya at night. At least in the day, you can see where you're run'n." Gus rest his head against the wall as the full moon and stars shined slightly through the basement window.

"What if I turn, Gus? I don't want to kill you or Paul." Chip touches his numbing face.

"I know you don't, kid, but don't you worry. I can take care of myself." Sitting back, Gus's face disappears inside the darkness of the corner. Between an opening of crates and boxes fanned out, only his legs could be seen.

"I hope the others are okay. What do you think is going to happen to us, Paul?" Chip sticks his arms into his shirt, feeling the blood run from his arm and down his stomach.

"There's no telling, Chip. Let's just keep our fingers crossed and hope for the best." Paul answers, quickly drifting into an uncontrollable needed sleep. "I think we're going to change before the morning." His head bobs as he tries his best to keep his eyes open.

"Hope not. Tomorrow, maybe we should just head to camp as fast as we can." Chip, also extremely tired, stands to avoid going to sleep. "Maybe we should sleep in shifts just in case those things sneak up on us. How does that sound, old man? Gus?" Chip whispers as a faint snoring emits from the direction of Gus's legs. "Guess it's me and you, Paul. Who should go first? Paul?" Chip stares at the sleeping silhouette of his crippled friend. Deciding that he was going to be the responsible one, he shakes his head and sways in place.

Waiting till morning, Paul drifts into what feels like an endless sleep. Dreaming of his brother, Peter, he finds himself inside the bathroom of the cabin. Washing his face, he pauses at the sight of the cool dripping water that slowly poured from his face and transform into peeling muscle and skin drenched of bright yellow and red blood. Waking up soaking wet and gasping for air, his eyes adjust to the morning light. Peering through the bookshelf, through the quietness of the basement, he sees Chip peering out of one of the small closed windows. Before Paul could clear his throat or utter a mere syllable of Chip's name, in the blink of an eye, he shutters at the loud shatter of glass and splitting wood, as his friend Chip is snatched headfirst out of the small rectangular window. Leaving only his two legs held together by the crotch of his jeans, Chip's torso and part of his arm tumbles from the window and splatters onto the floor. And as his soul journeys into the unknown, his remaining living nerves signal his dying limbs to twitch one last time.

"Snap out of it, fella! Catch!" A familiar country voice awakes him from the shock as Gus tosses a set of steel golf clubs into his chest. "They're onto us! We've got to fend for ourselves! We're up next for dinner! Now point me out to that cabin!" he yells, stuffing a few clubs down the back of his tightly tucked shirt. Nearly stumbling over a fallen tilted tool shelf, Paul finds an old dull axe. Strapping the clubs into the loops of his pants, he tightens his belt and grips the axe firmly while Gus arms himself with two hockey sticks taped together.

"You ready, son? It's now or never, and I ain't planning on giving in just yet!" Gus bravely stands next to him as Paul looks down at the remains of his pal. "He ain't coming back, and we're gonna end up just like 'em if we don't get out of this house and get some running room."

"I'm ready! This is for Chip." Paul holds up the axe, prepared to swing at anything.

"For your friends!" Gus touches his axe with the hockey sticks as a wild looking man with multiple mouths bursting from his face, lands inside the basement in front of the busted window, letting loose a loud war cry.

Immediately, Gus and Paul beat down the creature intensively with clubs and hockey sticks. Paul hacks off its arms and breaks off its legs. Making their way to the stairs leading to the first floor, another unwanted body greets them.

Covered in bruises, bites, and dying rotten flesh, a little baby still in soiled dirty diapers cries hungrily at the top of its lungs, slobbering blood. Running for them, its solid black eyes catches movement as Gus mercilessly bats him through the next room and out the window.

"FATHER, forgive me." Gus draws a cross upon his heart with his hand and hockey stick as he helps Paul out the front door. Stirring up so much commotion, they draw the attention of two more hungry people. Frightened to death, the brave Paul and courageous Gus manage to slip past them, reaching the outskirts of the town. "We made it to the woods. Where in tarnation is that camp of yours?" groans Gus, tired and beyond exhausted.

"It's through the woods, along a path. It's a campsite for groups. It's pretty big." Paul wearily slices his way into the thickets. About thirty paces from where they entered, Paul notices a familiar tree. "I . . . I think we're going the right way! I . . . I remember this."

"Dang it, son, you better know this tree! The way I see it, we're running out of running places!" states Gus as the sound of smacking gets their adrenaline pumping.

Hearing a crunching, slurping sound near them, they pass a tree and spot Paul's friend Christina hunched down on the ground. Slowly lifting her bloody, beady-eyed face, she stands and looks at them blankly, securely holding on to the rest of Chip's eaten head with her mouth.

"LORD gracious . . ." Gus mutters, sensing his end nearing.

"Christina . . . no. Shit, get ready, Gus." Paul slowly backs away as they prepare to run for their lives. Quickly raising his axe, the blade flies off into the unknown, leaving him with just a stick. "Shoot." He throws it down and pulls out the clubs, which were now bent and curled. Glancing at Gus who was down to just one hockey stick, Paul looks into the eyes of his wicked friend who drops her stringy blonde head and smacks her small-slit mouth at the sight of him. Holding out her viciously chewed arms, she releases a frightening screech that rumbles over the nippy morning dew of the chilled damp wilderness. Preparing to feed within seconds, she vaults forth as the giant, half-eaten, one-eyed moose appears charging from behind them. The two leap off to the side in opposite directions as the moose collides with Christina, ramming her into a huge tree, knocking it down. With shattered limbs, chest, and crushed rib cage, Christina shivers inside the branches of the tree, paralyzed, spilling her intestines and other bodily fluids below her. Hearing the galloping and bristling of leaves in the woods, Paul and Gus spring to their feet and run in the direction of the cabin with the moose behind them.

"I can't believe it's that same moose!" Paul shouts, hopping and falling over shrubs and bushes.

"Moose? I can't believe them dang animals turn too!" Gus barrels over him, tumbling through the sharp, spiny thickets. "Look, there's some tents!" Gus shouts as Paul points out the campgrounds.

"Head for the cabin! The cabin!" Paul yells as they both clear the woods, not looking back. "Look out!" he warns as the elderly man trips over a small stump, missing impact with the moose's bucking antlers.

Over Gus's body, the large beast rams into Paul, forcing him to the ground. Getting mulled from behind, Paul flips over to face the wilding animal. "Gus, you have to make it to the cabin!" he yells. "Warn the . . . the others! Please!" He sees Gus sprinting away. His voice fades out as he begins to accept his own demise. Keeping away from large chomping pendulous muzzle, his body is dragged, scooped, and tossed about. A large hairy arm swings above him as Gus gouges out the other eye of the beast with a hand full of kitchen knives. Releasing the sound of a large bullhorn, the moose staggers back. Snapping blindly at them, Gus wedges his last hockey stick into its mouth. Paul and Gus hold him back by the hockey stick and antlers as the moose drag them from the woods and slings them to the cabin door.

"At least we made it to the cabin." Gus lifts his head to the view of the half-dead creature running off and charging at them from the distance. "Nice knowing ya."

Paul suddenly observes all the human corpse spread around the cabin and thinks of his friends. Grabbing hold of Gus, the two scream in certain doom as the moose approaches at full speed. Upon nearing them, the moose lowers its head for impact as the long nose of a rifle shadows above them, firing directly into the brains of the beast. Its two front legs collapse from under as its broad head crashes lifelessly in the dirt and rocks. At over twenty miles per hour, the moose's body crashes and slides into Paul and Gus, pushing them fully into the cabin, still screaming for their lives.

"Where are those things coming from?" The tall, well-built frame of Yakoo stood over them. Placing his foot on the moose's head, he shoves it back through the door. Using all his muscles to shut it, he locks it with a two by four. "Paul, where's your brother and the others? Tell me you just got separated and they're on the way?"

Gathering themselves, Paul sits up as Gus helps him slowly rise to his feet. "Yakoo! Peters not here? My brother . . . no, the others didn't make it." Paul's eyes water as he turns away, covering up his face with his bloody, bluing hand. "My little brother."

"Damn, that's nearly all of us!" Yakoo peeps Paul's injuries and eyes the old man up and down.

"Your friend's been bitten. And the names Gus, by the way." Gus looks over Yakoo also. "No bites I see."

"No, but I know the effects of getting bit. It hasn't been all peaches and cream here either. Come take a look." Through the cabin of bullet holes, Yakoo guides them to one of the bedrooms. "How long ago were you bitten, Paul?"

"A day ago, and just now by that damn moose." Paul limps next to Gus. "Same thing with Christina, Chip, and Valerie. Only none of them made it."

"That's bad news all the way round." Yakoo pushes open the door with his large dark hands. "We were overrun by crazed people, waiting for you guys. The cabin was our last resort when we got attacked. But we killed them off . . . well." He glances around the room. "Miles and Turk, who was really sick, ran to the vehicles, and Samantha went to retrieve them. This is how she returned to us."

They all stood silently in front of the bed with Samantha strapped to it with belts. Glenda attends to her as best she could, unable to do anything about the unknown condition. Samantha's lips of smeared red lipstick curl and bawl in a chatter of speechlike sounds as she tries her best to bite off Glenda's succulent hands.

"She's strapped down now, but certain ones can morph and do things with their bodies. You two better lock her in this room tight, she may change even more." Gus warns them.

"It's hard to put down your friends." Eyes tearing up, Glenda speaks in a low tone. "It's good to see you, Paul, but not necessarily in that state. Where's the others, Chip, Val, Christina, your brother?" She pauses to hear a statement like "in the other room" or "waiting in the car." Instead, she watches Paul shake his head sadly. She stands up and quietly leaves the room sobbing.

"Yakoo, you and Glenda have to get out of here with Gus. From the looks of it, I'm . . . I'm not going to be with you for long. Gus knows how to get to the hospital." Paul shivers more than ever as a thick red seeps from a variety of openings in his body.

"Hang in there, Paul. We were waiting for morning to go out to the vehicles. And . . . it's morning. We at least can see what's coming. This may be our only chance." Yakoo loads his rifle with the last of his ammo.

"Nice, mind if I ask where'd you get it?" Squinting one eye, Gus admires Yakoo's piece.

"Here, I found it in one of those rooms." Yakoo walks to the bathroom to get Glenda as Samantha start to wail of hunger. "Hey, Glenda, you ready? It's time." He taps on the wooden door.

"Yeah," Glenda mumbles. Wiping her face, she opens the door, gives Yakoo a warm hug, and kisses him before walking away. "Wait!" she states on the way to the kitchen. Arming herself with kitchen knives and a large frying pan, she meets with the others. "Let's get the hell out of here."

Leaving the cabin of hideous belches and cries, they stop and look back at the structure of wood. Silently, Yakoo, struts away from the group and reenters the cabin. Closing the front door quietly behind him, two loud booms are heard throughout the campsite. Returning to the three, Yakoo walks to the vehicles without saying a word as Gus munches on an apple.

"R-rest . . . in peace, Samantha," Paul mutters in the wind as they all repeat his words.

And past the bodies, cautiously down the trail of blood and dirt, Paul, Gus, and Glenda follow Yakoo to the cars.

"Before Sam turned, she told us that when she got attacked, Miles started up the truck and drove off, trying to save his own hide. Isn't that something? Coward," Glenda shares with Paul and Gus, making a strangling gesture with her hands. "Hopefully, the other vehicles are still intact. Maybe we could rig one."

"Hopefully. Rigging them's not the problem." Yakoo glances at Paul, who was becoming very heavy and beyond white in the face and barely able to keep his eyes open. "There's still a chance of getting you to that hospital, bro. But you've got to stay with us, Paul. Just a little longer."

"I . . . I'm fine." Paul coughs into his arm uncontrollably like a smoker. "Okay I'm . . . I'm not fine, but I think I'm going to make it." He makes them all laugh as the tightness in his chest causes him to breathe in small spurts as his heart felt as though it was pounding in his head.

"The rides should be up this way, I think," Yakoo directs, picking up the pace quite enthusiastically. "We parked a bit off road and up a little from this path." He guides them to the edge of the woods.

"Oh my . . . look!" Glenda spots the vans flipped upside down and turned on their sides, beaten and dented. Following tire tracks with their eyes in the opposite direction, they noticed the truck that Miles driven. It had crashed off the road somewhere farther down in the woods, and it was still smoking. "Stupid, stupid, why did he do that? Now what?" Glenda begins to panic, drowning in thoughts of never being able to see her family again.

"So much for the bright ideas," Gus utters.

"Miles did what he had to do, I suppose. Who knows what any of us would have done in the same situation. We're out here, alone, with no help." Yakoo thinks on the brighter side of things as he always did. Sounds of glass shattering draw their attention from behind.

"Look!" Paul points to the passenger window of one of the vehicles.

In a tint of total bluish green, Turk crawls over the body of the van to the ground. "Eh, guys, I'm starving. I can't take this hiding anymore. Got any grub? I'm so hungry. Feels like my stomach's eating itself." He stood and staggered in their direction. "Did you see all those people last night? I think it was a riot or something. I must've slept through the whole thing."

"Your friend's turning. There's no food on earth that can satisfy him now. That fella wants something more human!" Gus moves behind the party, paying close attention to Turk.

"Quiet, old timer. He's still our friend and himself. By the looks of it, he's still human." Yakoo defends Turk as Glenda walks up and hugs him from the side.

"Yakoo, maybe he's right. What if he's right on the verge of changing?" Glenda eyes Gus as Yakoo reaches in his pocket and pulls out a candy bar.

"That wasn't a riot last night. It was a band of undead, inhuman-like people who attacked us. Can't believe you don't remember. You slept through all of that? Figures." Yakoo peers at the flipped van behind him. "Here, Turk. We can't waste food on you if you're about to change! This will have to do for right now." Yakoo tosses Turk the candy bar as he quickly unwraps it and shoves it in his mouth.

"What are you guys talking about, Yakoo? Band of what? Whatever! I'm fine. My butt don't hurt or nothing. And change into what? I'm not changing clothes. I'm a man. I could wear these things for a week without stinking! I'm just a little tired." Turk, with his mouth covered in chocolate, looks down at his filthy bloodstained clothes and begins licking on his fingers and biting his nails erratically. "Maybe I am . . . a little dirty. Hey, what's up with Paul, and where's Peter?"

"Guys . . ." Paul begins to throw up and dry heave in front of them. "I don't think I'm going to make it." He grabs his stomach and holds his pounding head. "Yakoo, the moment I change, do it. Please." The pain takes Paul back to his knees.

"Paul? Okay, okay, Paul, whatever you say. You just hang in there, buddy, until we can get you to that hospital." Yakoo tries to calm him. Hating the entire idea of shooting another friend, he knew what must be done.

"Promise me that you will find my brother after I go." Paul spits up blood and breaks down in a loud cry. "I really hate camping! Come on, guys, promise me!" he shouts as they all agree to his request.

"Paul? What the hell's wrong with Paul?" Turk walks to him. Yakoo holds him back with one arm.

"Turk," Yakoo speaks loud and clear from the chest. "I . . . I love you to death, buddy, but I can't let you get to close to him. Paul, well . . . he could change at any minute, just like you. The funny thing is, you look way further gone than he does." Tears of sorrow for his friends began to fall from Yakoo's face.

"What? What are you saying? Change into what?" Turk stops and think for a second. "You mean change into one of those rioters from last night? You mean there was something wrong with them?" Turk discreetly nibbles off the side of his finger and stares at them curiously, still feverishly pouring sweat. "Look, there's nothing wrong with me! I'm just a little hungry, that's all.

You guys locked me in the car with no food. I haven't eaten since yesterday."

"No, Turk, listen to them. They're . . . they're telling the truth!" Paul interrupts, feeling slightly better. "Slowly we're turning into some type of monster, Turk. Something's making people attack people here. They even got Rebecca, Chris, and Chip."

"And Samantha this morning," adds Glenda as Turk steps away from them.

Too sick to cry and too confused to analyze, Turk glances at his discoloring arms and hands. "Peter, Rebe, Sam, they're gone? How . . . by what? We're going to turn into some crazy person, and you're supposed to kill us? Is that what I'm believing? Is that what's going on here?" He begins to cry and curse, squeezing not one drop of liquid from his eyes. "Fuuuck you!" he screams at the top of his lungs. "Just kill me then, just kill me now! This is what you guys brought us here for? To read us a fairy tale and kill me? Bastards!"

"Turk! I know, I know how it all sounds. But it's true. You have to believe us. These things are more zombielike than people, bro. Now nobody's killing anyone unless they have to. Unless you fully turn, you're still human to me. We're trying to get out of here and reach a hospital, Turk, so you have to calm down. I don't know how this works, but you were bit first, and you're not one of them. Others were bit later, and they changed and tried to attack us right away! Only a doctor can get us answers now. I want to help you, Turk, but you have to pull it together and come with us." Yakoo attempts to console him, still keeping a distance.

"Turk, Paul, I know you're the victims, but you're our friends, and that makes us victims too. We're all in this together. Now let's just try to stay together and keep moving. We have up until that exact moment you turn to make those stupid decisions. We're behind you 100 percent." Glenda also talks some sense into them as they pass the first battered and summersaulted vehicle. "All we can do now is put everything in GOD's hand and pray that we all make it out of here in one piece. I think first we need to focus on getting out of this hellhole. Whether it's by foot or boat. Maybe if we hike it and stay on the main road, someone will eventually see us and pick us up. It's better than staying around this place. Whatever the case may be, I think it's worth going for. You never know, you two just might make it after all." Glenda gives them heart-filled words of encouragement as their spirits lift and strengthen them to carry on.

Journeying past the overturned van to the next, an enormously large woman emerges from the open, busted back door. Rotting and swollen from trapped gasses in her organs and veins, the reanimated woman reeks of a trailing scent of rigor mortis and fungus. Gruesomely attacking Paul from behind, she yanks his six feet body like a rag doll. Sinking her crusted teeth into his soft flesh, the woman swings and dangles him about as he calls for help. Yakoo tries to free him. Rushing in, Yakoo hits her with the gun and tries to pry Paul loose with the rifle.

"Hit her in the head, fella!" Gus coaches before jumping in with the remains if his hockey stick.

"Yakoo!" Glenda grabs Turk and hides behind him as she is also snatched by the hair and dragged into the woods by something fast, hollering for life.

"Glenda!" Yakoo witness Glenda's feet disappearing just beyond the grass line as Turk leaps to grab her but falls short on his face. "No . . . not her!" Yakoo fires into the back of the tall woman's head. Then firing into the dense forest, he dashes behind his lover and friend. Remembering her face, their past times shared and new experiences together, he falls to his knees weeping, then slowly stands.

"Let her go. She's gone now. Gone." Gus grabs hold to him by the back of the shirt. "Save your ammo. Save the bullets if you want to live." He reminds them as they stand once again in another awkward silence.

"Glenda!" Yakoo calls for her, hearing no screams or sounds of struggle. "Glenda!" He falls to the ground again. Releasing a flood of more tears, he punches a hole in the dirt in anger. Turk and Gus help him to his feet as a faint growl and a sound of movement catches their attention like a light catches fireflies.

Full of energy and breathing new resurrected life, Paul rises to his feet inside his own pool of blood. Inside the grass, heavily breathing, his lips curl and bluish pupils vanish, and are replaced by an upside down dripping of solid black and infinite darkness, that seem to pour over his eyeballs. Paul snarls in anger and fury as a single bullet opens his skull from front to back; Yakoo stands with his back him, resting the rifle over his shoulder. Wiping the last tear from his eye, he listens to two bodies drop as Paul's body flops over, followed by the large elderly woman who mindlessly arose to her feet behind him.

"Rest in heaven, Paul." Yakoo stares furiously at the woods between Turk and Gus, ready to avenge his friends and especially Glenda's life.

"Now that's what I'm talk'n about. That's what I call some mighty fine shoot'n! I'm just sorry that it had to be your friend." Gus tips the bill of his dusty hat. "He was a good person, I think, from the short time I knew him. That's why I chose to help him and to stand by his side until the end, ya know? I saw the good in him." Gus pats him on the back and steps in the direction of the city. "Sorry for your losses, but I helped your friend just as I promised. Now I need to get to my truck quick and in a hurry and get the hell out of here! Unfortunately, it's that a way back into town. You're welcome to join me."

"That was my last bullet, and I had to use it on my friend." Yakoo looks down at the earth.

"It was him or us, remember that." Turk suddenly pops up beside Yakoo. "Hey, you got any more of those candy bars? That one didn't do nothing. It feels like I'm starving!" He suddenly talks with a constant hand up to his mouth, nervously biting at his fingertips. And denied of more food, for the next fifteen to twenty minutes, Turk complained of how hungry he felt. Not able to take any more, Gus stops them in the middle of two intersecting streets somewhere in the city.

"Will you quit talking about how hungry you are? We're not giving you no food. And guess what? We're hungry too, numb nuts! We're all hungry, and as a matter of fact, you make me more hungry by talk'n about how hungry you are! Now shut it up, dang it! Just shut it!" Gus slung his hat with every word, ending in a shaking finger pointed into Turk's chest.

"But you don't understand. I could eat you, but I just can't bring myself to do it. I was joking earlier. I really do think my body is eating itself." Turk looks at them with a worried expression as they continue on walking. "I'm so hungry I could eat a wild rabbit raw! Come on, Yakoo, toss me something, dude! Yak? Yakoo?"

"Turk!" Yakoo also grows tired of his complaining. "We're trying not to think of how hungry we are. Please, shut up! We don't need to hear that right now, please!"

"But . . ."

"No!"

"Yak?"

"Turk!"

"Oh my stomach," Turk continues to grumble. "This stupid conversation is making me hungry. Hey, the back of your head looks like an apple."

"Son, what's your name?" Gus leans into Yakoo. "I mean, run it by me again. How'd ya say it again?"

"Yakoo."

"Yak, Yakoo, that fella there is gonna end up eating us alive." Gus whispers, pulling him to the side just far enough for Turk not to hear them talking. "The boy's get'n real bad, son. He's becoming worse and worse by the minute. Now it's all a matter of time. When he changes, he's gonna be a monster. He will eat us."

"He hasn't changed yet. He's still my friend, and I think we could still use his help. I think we need all the help we can get, don't you?" Yakoo places his hand on his forehead to think. "He hasn't changed yet. We'll just have to keep a close eye on him. I guess."

"Keep an eye on him? Really? You're out of ammo, and I don't have any reliable weapons. How do you think . . ." Gus is interrupted by loud sound of obnoxious crunching and smacking. "What the?"

They both turn around to the sight of Turk standing behind them, biting the remaining fingers on his left hand clean off. Gazing at them in a dreamy bliss, his eyes roll, viewing nothing but the whites of his eyes. Mouth and neck covered and dripping of his own blood, Turk roughly swallows and looks at them. "Why are both of you looking at me like that? What's the matter? Uh-oh, don't tell me I'm one of them. No . . . One of them is behind me, aren't they?" He tries to read their expressions as Gus covers his mouth and points to his hand. "What? I still don't see it?" Turk looks in all directions for the attacker.

"Loo-look! The boy done plum ate off all his fingers! Your hand, son, you . . . you ate it!" Gus whispers loudly.

"No, no, I didn't." Turk looks at the missing fingers on his hand and hides it behind his back.

"Turk, you just chewed off your fingers. Man, you're one of them!" Yakoo yells. Stepping back next to Gus, they glanced at each other with no answers or explanation. Turning their attention back to Turk, they watch him swallow the remains of the rest of his hand in its entirety. Realizing that he was unconsciously munching off himself, Turk pulls his blood-squirting arm out of his mouth and belches out a demonic wail that sends Gus and Yakoo running in the opposite direction.

"Guys, you don't understand. Hey, I didn't know. I'm just so, so hungry!" Turk runs after them trying to explain. "Yakoo, hey, bro, I'm fine. It was just one hand." He corners them behind a parked car and a house. "It's okay. I'm fine now, see?" He pleads as they carefully look him up and down and appear to verify with each other through eye contact. "See, I'm fine."

"This is some weird shit, Turk! You're one of them, Turk. Look at your eyes and what you just did. Gus, you were right!" Yakoo shouts, bracing himself against the wall with the rifle in hand now used as a bat.

"I know, but it doesn't hurt at all, look!" Turk whips his arm around in front of them, smiling a bloody face. "I just taste like the most delicious piece of chicken to me. Pretty cool, humph? I'm still me, see, for some reason."

"Well, I'll be a monkey's uncle. I think . . . I think he's immune to them things or whatever virus is in them that spreads! You said he was bit days ago. Hell, everybody else we've encounter has changed in less than a quarter length of that time. Hell, I'd say he sure is one lucky son of a bitch! How's about that? You've still got one of your friends. GOD is truly amazing." Gus pats Yakoo on the back and walks around Turk in amazement.

A loud unidentifiable animalistic sound echoes in the wind, falling throughout the city. As Turk picks it up, clearly understanding it, he listens and tunes in. Covering his ears as if hearing extremely loud concert music, Turk looks at Yakoo and Gus. "You guys hear that?"

"Hear what, Turk? That howling sound? Yeah, we all heard it. It doesn't sound friendly." Yakoo frowns, thinking of what it could be.

"Sounds like it's coming from something big." Gus also ponders on the origin.

"Noise? No, guys, it's more than noise! Listen . . . you hear that? It's an announcement!" Turk describes. Yakoo and Gus look at him curiously. "It said, 'Return to the colony that's located on the hill.' It gave the location! It was a voice as clear as day. Like a new language or something, but I understood it." Turk laughs, placing his arms by his waist.

"You could understand that crap?" Yakoo twist his face, trying to comprehend what was happening.

"Yep, he's definitely one of them now. Why is he still himself, I dunno. Must be the grace of the ALMIGHTY. Sure is good to have one on our side." Gus smiles.

"It's a weird thing. I can feel some strange pull or force coming from the hill up there." Turk points past a sign that read "Grave Street." "It's like I got voices in my head."

"That must be the source of our problem. Bet the whole town's probably in that God-forsaken place." Gus spits on the ground.

"What we need are weapons. Looks like we might be the only ones around alive who knows about these things. We have to do something in the name of our friends." Yakoo hits his fist into the palm of his left hand. "But what?" He peers around at all the litter-covered ground.

"I don't want to see more of those things, but maybe you're right. If we don't try to stop them, this thing could secretly spread around the earth, if it hasn't begun already. And I don't want to help contribute to that one. We have to try and stop this, fellas! There was an old army and sports surplus store on the other end of town, a little ways down yonder. It's near the station where me and your friends were held hostage. We sure could use what's in there." Gus comes up with the first part of the plan.

"Wait, you guys plan on marching into that building where it could be hundreds of those things? Whoa . . . hold up, bad idea. Whatever that thing was talking, it felt powerful. What if they have some type of ray gun or something? Lasers would disintegrate us for sure!" Nibbling on his wrist, Turk continues to think of reasons not to go.

"Turk! Please, that's disgusting. Could you please stop eating your arm?" Yakoo gripes.

"Sorry, I never knew how good my body tasted."

"Let's just get to that army surplus store. We could gear up and make a surprise attack tonight." Yakoo thinks about preventing a global takeover.

"Sounds good to me." Gus sticks a toothpick in the corner of his dry mouth. "Let's get going."

"Ashes to ashes . . ." Yakoo holds out one hand as Gus places his over top of Yakoo's.

"Dust to dust," Gus finishes the statement as Turk places his meat-hanging, blood-dripping arm over Gus's hand.

"Till death do us part." Turk chuckles at his own ironic statement, remembering that he was already pretty much dead.

Smashing the side window of the Army Surplus Store, Yakoo, Gus, and Turk, climb through the illegal entrance on high alert. With nothing to lose, ready for anything, the three search the one-floor establishment for any useful items or weapons. Finding a lawn mower, sheets of metal, torches, various batteries, and knives, Gus helps Yakoo, who was in the field of robotics, wield an adjustable chair into a motorized chest plate of spinning blades. Positioning the seat over his chest, he lays the backrest over his shoulder and chains the chair around his back and body. Finding a double-barrel shotgun and shells, he loads the shells for it into his pocket. Still carrying a golf bag around his shoulder, Gus equips himself with a sawed-off shotgun, swords, more golf clubs, and hockey sticks. Inserting blades around a few of the sports gears, he turns to Turk and watches him cram the blade of a broken medium-sized sword deeply into the center of his forearm where the hand was missing. Burning the remains of flesh and muscle around it, Turk wraps his arm with gray electrical tape.

"At least I won't be biting it anymore," jokes Turk. Turning his old ball cap backward, he lifts a spiked bat of nails that he made off the table. Putting on a jockstrap, elbow and knee pads, Gus shoves a butter knife into his boot. Taping a variety of knives beneath his vest, Gus glances at Yakoo, then back over at Turk as they signal one another's readiness. Prepared to strike, they sit and wait for nightfall so they couldn't be seen.

After darkness fell across the land and only the moonlight helped to illuminate the small ghost town, the three ran through the city like a clan of storm troopers. As monstrous screams and war cries were heard in the shadows, bright flashes from their loud smoking guns delivered them from evil along the way. The group comes to the huge gate of the graveyard and peer over the tombs buried in automobiles and scrap.

"I'll handle this." Gus pulls out a pair of long wire cutters from his bag and cuts an opening through the wired fence that lined the sides of the tall barred gate of locked doors. "There's that, sucker. There's the mansion!"

Focused on the enormity of the building that sat on the hill in the distance like a plump scarecrow scaring away all life and light, before they could reach it, the trio, had to get past the obstacles of cars and furniture. "Look at this place. We got to find a way to get around these things."

"I can see where all the cars went to now," Turk sarcastically comments.

"Wonder how they all got here. Looks like a giant just tossed them around." Gus falls into an open grave as Yakoo helps him out.

"This place is wicked!" Turk thinks of the climb and hike ahead. "What's that sound?" It causes them to pause on the side of a school bus.

"Sounds like an old rusty Ferris wheel." Gus scans around but sees nothing.

"Let's just get to the top, quickly," Yakoo orders, hopping down onto more exposed graves. "This place smells." They travel a few feet on as one of Turk's leg steps into an obscure hole in the ground.

"Yeow!" Turk tries to free his jammed leg from the hole. "I have got to be more careful. Look at my jeans." Pulling his leg completely out, he touches his now-shredded pants and touches the ferocious bleeding scratches on his leg. "What the heck?" He fiddles with the shreds of cloth.

"All right, let's go, move it!" Yakoo gets a bad feeling as dozens of large turned rats flood from the graves in the ground.

"Rats!" Gus gasp.

"What?" Turk freezes at the sight of hungry rodents gathering all around them.

"It looks like they're thirst'n for us!" Gus blasts a temporary pathway through the rodents and stabs away at the remaining with knives.

"Where are they coming from?" Turk bats away the limbs and bodies of rats as some stick to his spiked bat.

"It doesn't matter, just run!" Yakoo directs, stomping through the plump bony bodies of rodents that squirmed under his feet and snapped at his legs. One of the larger-sized rodents, perhaps a sewer rat, leaps at his face; he catches it by the tail. Curling the raccoon-sized varmint's tail around his hand, he swings and snaps it into his fist like a punchball balloon. Knocking away a few of its kin, Yakoo spins and slings it into the air behind him.

Leaping, climbing, running, and kicking, the three men finally reach the mansion's doorsteps. Another strange sound bellows over them. Except for Turk, out of breath and weak, they look behind at a peaceful trashed graveyard with no rodents in sight.

"Well, I'll be, how do you like them apples? They're gone." Gus stands in complete wonder, holding a dead rat on the end of a butter knife. "This is one freaky place." He wipes his face as Yakoo kicks in the front door. "Look at all this mess. Someone needs to clean their room."

Two dead, mind-controlled men, slowly shuffle around the trashed corners of the large room they entered. Smelling fresh food, they explode on sight by the barrels of Gus and Yakoo's guns. Fully entering the building, the trio cautiously steps down a vast hall of litter. In a doorway ahead, a grim figure appears in the shadows, walking toward them. Bleeding and corroding, the grave person falls to one knee as an old man stands behind him connected to his head by tentacles that pump green fluids from his fingers and hands.

"You must not interfere with the survival. You will join the vessel and become . . . the host." The mouth of the victim bled out bodily fluids among the twisted sounds of the words. "Mammal kind . . . must be harvested. Your bodies shall be a feed of nutrients . . . and . . . a great transportation for our . . . race." He drools out as an army of people fill the room to annihilate them.

"They're freak'n aliens. I should have known." In bursting rounds, Gus and Yakoo fire into the great overwhelming numbers.

"Get out of here!" Yakoo leaps in front of his two comrades. Preventing them from being directly attacked, he uses his body as a shield, firing away into the direction of the octopus hand man. The old floor collapses under the extreme weight of its occupants, dropping Yakoo into a black pit of screams and howls, still firing his gun.

"This is our chance!" Gus, holding on to the base of the wall, takes advantage of the situation as he yells at Turk, who also hung on for dear life along the wall on the other side of the room. As they race around to the middle wall of flying paper and trash, a giant limb knocks Gus lower on the wall; he catches hold of a protruding piece of metal. As he and Turk climb higher and close to the level they were on, impelled upon a long, broken wooden frame of the floor, they see the tall old man shaking and jerking about, twisting parts of his body and limbs into indescribable shapes. As his muscles stretch and contract, his head stretches five feet and swings around his sporadically jolting body.

"Now that's gross," Turk comments as the alien leader seizes them in the coldest clutch of branching tactile organs. Slicing himself loose with the sword on his arm, Turk plummets back to the edge of the hole, still managing to catch hold of a large crack in the wall. "Yakoo?" His night vision eyes peer into the darkness at lower walls made of spare earthy metals. He makes out what appear to be components on portions of its design. Starting to realize that he might be inside more than just a building, he spots a fearsome battle that raged on below his dangling feet.

Enclosed in a cluster of dead people, Yakoo rises from a mound of bodies with his face partially eaten away. Knocking off heads and tossing the corpse of the remaining attackers over his shoulders, Yakoo screams in tremendous pain and anguish as his motorized bladed chair slashed and carved anything it touched. "You want to eat me? You want to eat me? I'll eat you first!" he shouts loudly from the remaining muscles of attached lips, swarmed by a flood of human bodies, invaded by man-eaters. Snapping necks and ripping arms out of the sockets of the undead, Yakoo fearlessly becomes the predator and starts biting into the bodies and soft rotten flesh of the abducted, like a mad lion. Swallowing and drinking the sour and spoiled, he grabs hold of what feels like a man. Pulling him close with all his might, Yakoo chews into his head, as the chair chews into the victim who suddenly hollers in terror. And among the cloud of dirt and piles of dead and undead, Yakoo crouches at the view of people crawling and backing away from him in fear. No longer casting the smell or carrying the sweet taste of man, belonging not to them but to a new breed of the species, Yakoo's eyes disappear into the back of his head. As his senses are enhanced and memories and thought fuse with another, he drains the last juices from his victim and tosses the body clean into the air just past Turk. Feeling powerful and plenty, a greenish glob burrows into the opening in his head. He touches the place where his nose used to be; he makes small fingerlike limbs extend and retract from his jaws. Ripping away a shred of fabric from his shirt, he wraps it around the lower portion of his face as a loud roar catches his attention from above.

Loud shots are heard and Gus falls, grabbing hold to the edge of a remaining piece of floor as hungry people huddle below him, ready to feed. "This is it, young'n!" Gus blurts as his shotgun tumbles from his clutches and slides into the dark pit.

"Yakoo?" Turk yells. "Say it's still you down there, please? Is that you? Yakoo, come on, bro! Yak, is that you?" Turk's voice fades out as the large head of the creature extends over him.

Of flesh attached to a long serpentlike neck was the head of the most horrific face. Its stretched and split, wide-opening mouth viewed a set of a small human jawbone of teeth that merged into a hideous rubbery body of wiggling antennas, tentacles, and arms. The alien being whips its head in a slashing motion, attempting to take out Turk. Its head separates from the neck as Yakoo fires another round into the chest of the beast from below.

"Yak . . . you're back!" Turk cheers as the creature's head rolls through the door, along a slender attached section of the first floor.

Killing all of the remaining reanimated by the fire of Gus's sawed off, Yakoo runs up the wall like an insect and helps his two friends. Thanking Yakoo for saving them, they push the large body of the alien into the pit and set it on fire.

"Looks like that's the end of it," states Turk as a light fluttering from across the other room catches his attention.

"What in tarnation is it now?" Gus spots the alien head bouncing and rolling across the floor in front of them. And as the three follow it, the head stops and splits in half as a green gelatin entity surfaces and sprouts legs. "It's one of them green things. It likes to jump in your mouth! Cover your mouths!" Gus yells as the creature grows a small set of eyes and runs for the front door. "Shoot it!"

Yakoo squeezes the trigger of the sawed off. "Empty."

Going for the open exit, the front door, the green ball of jell is slowed down by the rapid fire of two automatic pistols belonging to the dead officers at the police station. Filling with holes of smoke, the creature splatters of green bits and bubbles. Exactly as it tries to piece itself back together, Valerie steps in front of the glop, picks it up, and devours it whole.

"Mmmm, delicious. You guys miss me?" She smiles with solid black eyes and a green purplish tint. Covered in blood with an enormous hole in the center of her body, Valerie sexily switches toward them.

"You guys sure got some bad eating habits." Gus stands mesmerized once again. "That's . . . she's one of your friends from the police station. Your friend who was with her accidentally shot her trying to escape. She should be dead, just like you . . . rock head." Gus points at Turk.

"Val?" Yakoo mutters in pain and saliva. Blood fill and soak into the fabric of his face and ran down his neck as he hugged her.

"Yakoo, Turk." Valerie then gives Turk a joyous hug and steps back. "I've been everywhere looking for you guys. This was the last stop. What happened to you two? You look like crap."

"Look who's talking, the green people eater," Turk speaks under his breath, taking small bite-sized nibbles from his normal arm.

"A lot of things happened, Val. We're the only ones left. What happened to you?" Yakoo stares at her dead-looking appearance and she at his as well.

"I don't know for sure but . . . we were attacked by those things and . . . one got in me. I came back. And . . . I know things now."

"Me too, but it's still coming to me. You don't by chance have any clue as to what exactly is going on here do you? Why . . . we're still alive?" Yakoo looks into her black missing eyes.

"Yeah, anyone figure out how come we're still us, only dead-like?" Turk asks.

"I don't know for sure. Maybe it's what we eat after we've been bitten." Valerie places her guns into the holsters underneath her chest. "I think they're some kind of highly advanced protoplasm, a bacteria of some kind. It's old and holds ancient intelligence. I think it's parasitic and spreads like a virus, reproducing through a host."

"It's an overgrown germ we're fighting? I think it needs new bodies to interact and to build." Yakoo begins to acquire pieces of unknown logic and knowledge absorbed through the genetics of the life-form he digested.

"Wait a second! That ol' gal just might be on to something." Gus points at Yakoo. "You just changed after eating a mouth full of those zombie people who were chasing us. You had to eat one of those blob things in the process 'cause I can see it through the openings in your head. The idiot box here turned, and we know for a fact that the first thing he sunk his teeth into was well . . . candy and himself. Maybe he's a zombie slave of himself, or something of that nature. And you"—he holds his hairy hand up at Valerie—"looks like you got a hanker'n for the slime balls themselves that come out of some of those things. Those little bastards go in any hole they can to get inside your body, and you likes 'em for breakfast!" Gus glances down into the fiery hole. Rubbing his chin, he searches his pockets and places another toothpick in the corner of his mouth. "Apparently, if you take a chunk outta a person, they become a mindless wanderer, a slave, like some of the ones that came after us. Maybe it makes it easier for those things to invade the body." Gus smacks the pocket of his jeans. "You know, I don't think those things calculated the outcome of you three. I think we're looking at maybe the ultimate weapon to combat against these things. Their own kind, maybe a new, undiscovered, even more evolved breed of 'em. Two actual alien spawns and a zombie fool. GOD has to be on our side now." He winks at Valerie as the ground begins to rumble.

"Uh-oh, I feel sorta weird," Turk states as Yakoo and Valerie appear to feel the same sensations, the presence of something even bigger than before.

"This way!" Yakoo takes them deeper into the mansion. Giving Gus his gun back, he reloads the weapon as Valerie replaces the clips of hers. Down a long hall, a boisterous shrill bounces off the walls over them.

"What in blazes was that?" Gus follows behind the three.

"Wow. Did you hear that bitching? It's the queen." Valerie holds her hands over her ears.

Yakoo's gut feeling guides him to another door that he kindly kicks open as well. Revealing a bubbling body of an old woman slowly descending from a flight of stairs, she jumps and sticks to the high ceiling. Crawling on her back to the door, the team fires above their heads at her. "You have destroyed our host!" the alien woman squeals and roars in a language that only Yakoo, Turk, and Valerie could understand. Bullets miss her skin, and she flips and rolls across the ceiling, defying all known principles of gravity and laws of physics. Treeing arms shoot out from her body as her mighty bellows rattle the entire house. Taking more fire from Valerie's guns, the queen splits her riddled skin and splatters five feet in length. In a dark green mass of wiggling arms and tentacles, two huge black eyes lower down between Gus and

Yakoo as a small mouth pan around the room. The trio fire across the ceiling fixtures as the creature falls, bursting through the wall behind them. Squirming down the hall, the alien queen escapes into the walls of the house.

"Where'd she go?" questions Turk as Valerie walks by following the trail of scattered slime. "She sounded teed off."

"Mad." Yakoo nods his head in agreement.

"Incredible. That perfume is lovely." Gus covers his nose to filter out the stench that exploded from the erupting skin that hung and dripped from the ceiling above them.

"This way. I can feel her, can't you?" Yakoo runs slightly ahead as the others follow. Down a hall of rooms, they come to a bare wall with a bus-sized hole smashed through its center and the floor.

Through the enormous crevice, they find themselves exiting out into some kind of floorless metallic compartment. Lowering themselves down pipes from the foundation of the mansion, they drop into a narrow shaft of pitch black, pushing through a tubular structure of wires and exoskeleton-like materials.

"Where . . . I . . . I think we're inside a real live spaceship. This is unnatural." He stands in the center of vast walls, circuit boards, and flashing lights. The hairs on the back of Gus's neck stood on ends; he nervously raises his gun with shaking hands, ready to shoot anything that moved.

"I feel like I know this place." Valerie touches her temple, suddenly realizing that she has obtained more knowledge of the alien species somehow. Everything begins to vibrate around them. "It's like I know exactly what they know now."

"I ain't no genius, but it feels like we're moving. Feels like we're about to take off, just like a plane." Gus begins to seriously worry for the first time. "I ain't ready to go to no red planet."

"Mars? Cool." Turk bites a chunk out of his right arm.

"Turk! Stop eating yourself! We've got to stop this thing!" Yakoo slaps Turk's arm down from his mouth, seeing all the panels around him. "Val, do you know how this ship works? Is there a self-destruct mechanism somewhere?"

"I don't . . ." Valerie stops and ponders to herself. "Yes, this way." Valerie leads them.

Traveling deeper into the ship, they are attacked a few times by more alien-abducted people, sending each one back from whence they came. Down into a very large corridor of the unknown craft, Valerie leads them to a giant egg and slime-covered nest inside a chamber of machines, more panels, and highly advance equipment. Sliding her hand inside one of the five-foot, large jell bubbles, Valerie retrieves and eats the slippery, jiggling larva. "Just like mother used to make."

"I don't know whose worse, you or Turk." Yakoo gives Valerie an odd look. Facing Gus, he places his hand on his shoulder. "You've helped me and my friends a great deal, Gus, and we owe a lot to you. If we don't make it, I just wanted to say . . . thanks. You will always be remembered and considered a friend."

"Wait, what are you talking about, Yakoo? We have to—"

"Gus, I need you to get out of here and warn the world about these things. There may still be some out there! We'll take it from here, old buddy." Yakoo grabs him by the collar and waist of his pants, and tosses him high into the air into a ventilation hatch.

Breaking through its panel, stunned for a moment, Gus rolls over to his stomach. "Take care, young'ns," he utters, crawling off past jellylike pods that stuck to nearly every wall on the ship, he stabs them each with dining utensils.

Sloshing through clumps of eggs and swimming matter, Yakoo secures the entrances. "Any chance you know how to shut this thing off too?" He flags Valerie. Pulling the string from a lawn mower, he clears their path of eggs with the spinning blades of the chair.

"Uh . . . I don't have a clue. Nothing seems to be working," Valerie replies, pressing different buttons, switches, and gears displayed on large complex panels on the floor-modeled machines around her. "I don't think this is the control room!"

"Where are the weapons and explosives on this thing?" Yakoo tries to make sense of the screens as some type of foreign countdown begins on all the screens around him. "Uh-oh, that's not good. We're launching."

"Let me see. Yep, it's a launch." Turk jumps in front of him, dining on more of his arm.

"Move it, Turk, and stop eating yourself! You're going to be nothing but bones left in a couple of minutes." Valerie shoves him out of the way. "This ship is taking off, but I think . . . this is a countdown of something else." She stares at a specific screen as if having seen it before. "No?" She straightens her posture and cuts her eyes to the clusters of now rapidly growing eggs around them. "This definitely doesn't look good. It's not a launch, it's a hatching. It's a countdown for these things to hatch. The babies are going to be released and invade earth!"

"It must be hundreds in here! They'll invade the whole population!" harps Turk as Yakoo aims his gun at the computers.

"We have to stop this thing!" Yakoo cocks the shotgun. The queen, having felt the pain of her own bloodline being spilled, oozes from the shadows above them.

Landing in a loud thud of organic matter, the queen unleashes a gut-wrenching cry as Turk runs and leaps into her midsection. She catches him in with a squid-like limb and slams him into the floor several times.

"Turk!" Yakoo separates a few arms from her body with a blast of buckshots. Valerie counterattacks from the sides, shooting into the queen's body and face; she is knocked flying into the corners, into some open emergency hatch packed of eggs, as a large heavy door closes automatically, locking her inside. Destroying parts of the corridor's wall, the alien queen smirks as her seedlings began to move and hatch around them. Sending a bone-chilling cry throughout the room, aliens began to fall and burst like raindrops around them as Turk slits the queen's belly with his bladed arm.

Near the entranceway to the outside, Gus runs for his life to a doorway of light as two pair of green legs dart past him and out of the exit. "What the hell?" He dashes behind them with his gun drawn as fast as he could. Seeing nothing but clouds ahead, he collapses. Grabbing hold to the frame of the doorway, breath taken. Trying not to fall out of the basement of the mansion, he rested hundreds of feet in the air upon a flat, open, undetermined section of a giant craft. The mutilated bodies of people, some still moving, slid off into the atmosphere as green globs of life-forms leap from the ship, some splattering and landing in empty bodies, reanimating them in midair.

"This can't be happening." Gus finds a way back into the inner workings of the ship. Blasting a hole in anything that looked flammable or important, he heads to find his friends.

Knocking steel beams flying across and into other corridors of giant pods and hatching transparent eggs, the alien queen snatches up and pounds Turk and Yakoo into the metallic floor. Her biggest limb grows spines out of bones as she drops it on Yakoo, who catches it, preventing them from being smashed. As the queen and mother of many let loose a dark and ominous laugh of threatening evil, hundreds of gelatinous aliens invade every hole in Turk's and Yakoo's bodies. Grinning deviously at her winning achievement, the queen admires her new offspring and welcomes an era of new life and the end to the world of mammals. Looking down at her hatching multicellular followers, her huge head explodes in a rain of green slime and fluids. Her semisolid body falls over as Gus peers down from an open vent along the ceiling, firing round after round into what he thought was the computerized network of the ship. Hitting a fuel line, fire erupts through the bowls of the alien ship, triggering a rift of tremendous explosions. Throwing the giant craft off course, the ship flies off at an angle like a fallen Frisbee. Returning to the ground from which it came, the ship blows up in a thunderous cloud of fire, metal, and rock as a small unidentifiable object exits earth's atmosphere.

Twelve years later:

Light-years away in an old solar system, just neighboring the Milky Way on a lone celestial body of cold and eukaryotic organisms, a highly evolved, multicellular, metamorphic green germ of ancient intelligence thrives. With depleting resources and failing technology, the advance race of enlarged pathogens remotely flies in a single escape pod of decades old into their gassy atmosphere. Landing the ship on the small inhabited, dying planet of towering earthy mounds of mold and cities, lakes of unified prokaryotic organisms stream and part toward the return of the vessel. Gathering anxiously inside the plain of free-floating organisms of energy and light, hundreds of complex cellular life-forms, along with their great elders, spew out from the glowing oceans of conscious parasitic beings awaiting the return of the queen and the new findings for the life and salvation of their ever-increasing population. Every few hundreds of years, their kind must become parasitic to any surrounding and dominant life in order to flourish and survive. Questioning what new tasty forms of life the queen and her seekers have discovered and chosen, the malevolent beings of millenniums before sadly watch the pod, curious of the history and travels of their missing starship. The door of the giant pod opens as hundreds of small purplish green, newer jell-like beings of their own image slither and walk upright on limbs from the craft. As the eldest of the civilization slither and roll forward to welcome the great travelers, the alien visitors begin to savagely attack and eat at their life-forms. Infecting and transforming the population into mindless host of their own, the invading globs proceed to devour and spread throughout the surviving race. The alien attacker's empress, Queen Valerie, slowly emerges from the craft and marvels at the jellied green life-forms that coward at her feet. Lifting the eldest and mightiest of leaders from the ground inside her hand, she chews off pieces of them as the wisest and strongest shiver and turn purple inside her palm. Placing them back onto the ground, she commands them to join the others through a single internal sound. Strutting a medium-built, hour-glass frame, Valerie slowly and seductively sways toward the chaotic city at war. Annihilating all life on the planet, she takes a seat upon a mound of cities, reigning over the gelatinous world for the next four billion years.